Zines are self-published booklets favored by some creatives and thinkers as a way to disseminate their art or points of view in an inexpensive physical form. Often zines are photocopied and personal, but vary infinitely in style, materials, and subject matter. As few as a single copy may be manufactured by hand or thousands by machine. The term is derived, ultimately, from the word 'magazine,' and is pronounced the same: 'zeen.' Practitioners of the art form are referred to as zinesters or zine makers.

–jd

ALSO BY JOHN DISHWASHER

The Gods of Our Fathers
The Would-Be President: An American Farce

Previous Acclaim for John Dishwasher

"Finalist, Best Political Zine of 2021"
   –Broken Pencil Magazine

"[Here's the Story...] leaves you a little awestruck...The inscrutable danger in the message, the idiosyncratic prose, the seemingly atonal references. This piece is weird. But you derive such joy reading it aloud--the feeling of these word combinations in your mouth, the cadence as they leave it--that you read again and again until it decodes itself and you're left in another, small awe. It communes with you profanely."
   --Axolotl Magazine

"...[Papyrus] perfectly captures the 'voice' and wisdom of Ancient Egyptian fables. That's no easy task."
   --Spank the Carp

"Nominee, Best of the Net 2018"
   --Cererouve Magazine

"[A] lament on the inexorable erosion of the human spirit, "Robots in Underwear" [is] a deceptively simple tale that begs for several readings."
   --The World is a Text

"Longlisted among the best very short stories of 2012"
   --Wigleaf

"...[Zugzwang] uses a distinctively erudite style...and employs a device seldom seen in modern fiction, but one familiar to traditional storytelling: deliberately revealing the outcome of the tale at its opening, then engaging the reader with how it gets there. I was strangely moved by this work; that is, by what transpires within it, inevitability be damned."
   --TQR

"prize-winning"
   --The Helen Jean Play Contest, 2017

"...[Cartoon-Girl] explores deep, contemporary, relevant questions.."
   --The Medulla Review

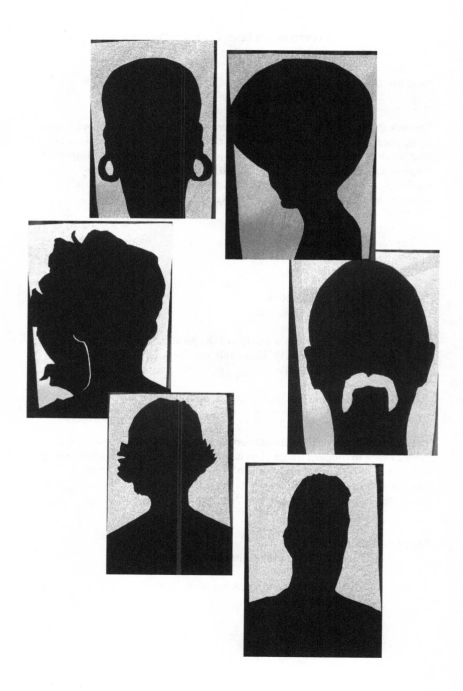

The Zinester Manifesto

a novel of the underground

by
John Dishwasher

six *f* ires.press

Published by Six Fires Press.
Distributed digitally, through a local post office, and by a 1993 Toyota Corolla.

First US Edition September 29, 2022
Printed in the USA, which occupies lands stolen from American Indians.
Interior and cover design by John Dishwasher.
www . johndishwasher . org

Trade Paperback ISBN: 979-8-9860184-0-9

The writing and production of this novel would not have been possible without the understanding and support of my wife Jody.

For Zinesters Everywhere

Chapter One
Sunday, April 29, 4:30 a.m.

Rocky wears the finest lipstick he can afford. On that night he pressed a paper napkin over his bottom lip to pat some of its color away before drinking.

"Those nasty smudges," he lilted, wrinkling his wide nose.

"Even on a soda straw?" asked Blossom.

"That's my grandmother Ong in me," he said.

Rocky's friend Blossom sat in a large brown sweatshirt that swagged at the throat and exposed the tattoo of thorns encircling her neck. Blossom is known for her choker of thorns, and for her shaved head, and for her heavy brown boots -- and particularly for the jangling of the spurs she attaches to those heavy brown boots. She crunched into the taco she held. Blossom gazed down at the fast-food table, crunching.

"I know," said Rocky's lipsticked mouth, "that this is not exactly a romantic setting, but I have to tell you that I love you."

Blossom stopped crunching. She looked up. For the first of only three times in this entire book she smiled. Blossom's smile comes hard and fierce. To those unfamiliar with her, it seems pure fury, even aggressive. But the taut flex in her prominent cheekbones at that moment beamed amusement at Rocky, not ire. Blossom relaxed her rare smile. It disappeared. She continued crunching. She swallowed.

"You love *everybody*," she replied, flatly.

"But I love you especial. You're my woman and I need you to cuddle me like one of your butchy girlfriends. Can I have one of your salsas?"

"Go ahead."

Rocky picked one of the foil packets from Blossom's plastic tray to tear away a corner and squeeze a pool onto the paper placemat. This procedure caused the wooden bangles around his wrist to clank.

"Look," cooed his voice, gently, "I'm so discombobulated. Look, this is really hard to explain. But, look, I'm serious, I think you are the love of my life."

Blossom did not smile. She stared at the edge of her bitten taco, aiming a good bite at her mouth. Her great brown eyes sparkled though as she crunched. She crunched.

"Well, aren't you going to say something?" Rocky paused. "This is mild salsa, isn't it? I fancy the hot. Mild salsa tastes like spoiled ketchup to me. That's the Acevedo in me, you know. My *'buelo* Memo."

Rocky twisted out of his fiberglass seat to step to the salsa bar. His high heels clicked on the tiles. As he waited behind a white man getting condiments there he smoothed the seat of his skirt over his rump and righted his wide patent black belt. He wrapped a tendril of hair behind his earrings, daintily, frilled out the puffed sleeves of his blouse, and loosened the bangles around his wrist. All tidied up, Rocky noticed now the hunched shoulders of the white man getting salsa. The white man turned for the exit and Rocky saw, fleetingly, his gaunt features and trembling manner. Then, as the white man stepped toward a green sedan, Rocky observed the apple shape of his own body reflected in the 5 a.m. window. Rocky grimaced. When he returned to the table he tucked his skirt up under his thighs as he sat, and tightened his black hose over his knees. He ripped a corner of the hot sauce packet and dribbled a second pool onto the paper placemat. With a fingertip, he tapped a dollop onto his tongue.

"More like it."

Rocky squirted salsa onto the corner of his taco. Then, over the salsa, he laid a blob of yellow mustard. He angled the corner of the crispy shell at his yawning lipsticked lips and eyed his future bride. He crunched.

Finally, Blossom responded, joking along.

"I'm not very romantic," she stated. This is a joke for Blossom.

"No worries," Rocky lilted, crunching. "I don't mind. I still love you."

"When did you start putting fucking mustard on your tacos?"

"The day I realized I wasn't doing it just because I had never done it before. Besides, all us Williamses love yellow mustard, hon."

"Like to see you do that at The Baja Zine Fiesta."

Rocky laughed. "OMG. What a party. I honestly don't think anyone would care at that love-in."

"I doubt it."

A delicious intermission passed as Rocky crunched and savored and patiently waited, and admired Blossom's golden skin and her fire-orange ear gauges. Blossom shook her shaved head finally. "I don't know what to say."

"I'm not asking you to marry me. My, my, no. No such conformity for us, my dear. I'm just giving you a heads-up that I want to spend the rest of my life with you. You know all about me. Almost everything. Maybe actually you can help me out of my confusion."

Moisture gathered at Rocky's eyelids.

"You're about to cry."

"Probably."

"I don't understand this," Blossom stated, swabbing her lips with a paper napkin. "You said at the after party you were in the mood for Taco Snatch. Here we are in our fiberglass booth, listening to shitty pop music. So you got some Taco Snatch. Nothing to cry about."

Rocky chortled, "But I love you."

"I ... You love *everybody*."

"Boss, look, I need you to help me."

Rocky lay down his taco on its wrapper. He had taken two ladylike bites from it.

Blossom said, "You know I'm here for you. You can tell me anything."

"This stuff is new."

Blossom sucked strawberry soda through her straw. A gurgling sounded in the dregs of the paper cup. She lifted the cup with her left hand and shook the ice in it, draining more of the soft drink to the bottom. She suck-gurgled again. Then, neatly, she placed the cup back onto its ring of wet.

Rocky said, "I guess we could've gone through the drive-thru. But you know me."

"Mm-hmm."

"Well, I've figured it out."

3

And Rocky straightened his back and squared his chin and drew a breath. He wiped his mouth with a paper napkin. He said, earnestly, "Okay, I'm so enamored with women, as you know. For the past few years I've really been wishing to be a woman, as you know. And yet, I'm confused because I'm so attracted to them physically. I want to be a woman, but, also, I want to sleep with women. It's been upsetting me more and more lately. But at least I've clarified my issue. I need to figure this out."

Blossom squinted, apologetically.

Rocky's eyes wandered the restaurant for a moment. They fell back to the table. He picked up his taco, positioning it between his teeth, and, quaking visibly, crunched off a bite. Rocky crunched. A tear seeped onto his cheek.

Blossom said, "I'm here for you."

Rocky nodded knowingly. He reached for Blossom's hand, clasping it. His Adam's apple rose and fell as he swallowed. He said, "I love you, golden girl. I love that gorgeous shaved head of yours."

Blossom crunched again into her taco.

The hunched white man shuffled to the green sedan. The hunched white man unlocked the driver-side door of that green sedan. He dithered for a moment, as if perplexed. Then, with a determined look, the hunched white man slung a paper sack containing two bean burritos and four hot salsas onto the passenger seat. The door of the green sedan thunked closed. The hunched white man turned then to tread along the sidewalk on a determined stride. Something shook in his pocket. *Rattle. Rattle.* The hunched white man approached an all-night cafe. People occupied sidewalk tables in front of that all-night cafe. A pair of men played chess there, importantly. A woman sat in the glow of a laptop.

A woman.

Flinching, the hunched white man reached for the entrance that divided the serious chess players from the glowing woman. He tugged at the door. In moments he was gazing on the neon orange eyeshadow of a young white woman behind a counter. The young white woman asked, "What can I getchoo?" *A beat.* Then carefully, slowly, the hunched white man answered. He said: "Can I have a decaf Americano, please?" "Sure," the young white woman replied. She tapped a screen; she quoted a price. The hunched white man extended a sunburned hand then as the young white woman extended a pale hand. The hands of the two strangers touched. The young white woman asked, brightening her bright orange eyeshadow, "And what's your name?" *A beat.* Then, carefully, slowly, the hunched white man answered. He said: "My name is Stanley Donner Jr." The young white woman chuckled as a marker scratched this name onto the side of a paper cup. "Okay, Stanley Donner Jr.," she replied. "We'll have that for you in a sec."

And, with thanks, Stanley Donner Jr. backed away from the counter, allowing a second white man to approach the young white woman. The second white man was not hunched. Stanley Donner Jr. returned his attention to the entrance of the cafe. He saw again through the glass storefront there the two men at chess and the glowing woman. The woman. She wore a large afro. From her large afro descended a long elegant neck. Also, she bared two fine shoulders. Stanley Donner Jr. quivered. Determinedly he pivoted away from the storefront and away from the counter and stepped out away from his waiting place to forge through some populated cafe tables to achieve a small alcove. He trembled. Stanley Donner Jr. pulled at one of the doors in the alcove. It was locked. He backed away then and steadied himself, leaning against a green-painted wall. He leaned. Stanley Donner Jr. shook something in his pocket. *Rattle. Rattle.* Gently then he bumped his forehead with the heel of his right hand. Stanley Donner Jr. shook something again in his pocket. *Rattle. Rattle.* But a flyer on a tall rectangular bulletin board distracted him.

"Yoga classes," Stanley mumbled aloud.

"Real estate," Stanley mumbled aloud.

"Lawnmower for sale," Stanley mumbled aloud.

"Lost puppy. Lost puppy. Lost puppy."

Stanley Donner Jr. pushed slowly off the wall and toward the busy bulletin board to bend forward. "Palm Desert Zine Fest," he mumbled aloud. He fixed a fingertip against this flyer. But someone suddenly stood beside Stanley, tugging at the men's room door. It was locked. That someone sank into the shadows behind him. Finally, the door to the men's room opened. Stanley breathed a whoosh of soap scent. But still his fingertip pinned the flyer to the corkboard. A date was announced: May 26. An invitation: "Everyone Welcome."

Stanley Donner Jr. mumbled aloud, to himself, "What is a zine fest?"

A voice behind him answered: *"Zeen.* It's pronounced *zeen.* Like maga-*zine."*

Stanley looked over his shoulder. A brown man. The brown man slouched against the green-painted wall, watching him expectantly. He wore drapey white clothing, like linen. The brown man in linen said, "The can's free, bro. You waitin'?"

"Sorry," Stanley Donner Jr. said quietly. "Excuse me," Stanley said. Then he pulled at the men's room door and stepped through it.

Stanley Donner Jr. splashed his face with cold water. Stanley splashed his face again with cold water. Blankly he gazed into the oval-shaped mirror. Stanley did not care that he weighed 50 pounds less than nine months earlier. He did not care that his features now appeared hollow and haunted. He did not care at all. Neither did Stanley care that his clothes hung off his frame as if off a clothes hanger, or that they rode rumpled and creased. Stanley did not care that his blue eyes peered out of dark circles, that his pink skin had gone sallow, and that his brown hair lie unkempt. He did not care. Not at all. He dispensed a hand towel then and did not care about his unshaven chin and cheeks, nor about the tremor in his hands as he dried them. Stanley Donner Jr. finished wiping his face and left the paper towel, negligently, to drop from the vanity to the floor.

But the cool water had sturdied him. And he had regained a determined expression. Always a splashing of water buoyed his nerves.

Stanley opened the door and stepped out and let the door swing closed as the brown man with the information about how to pronounce the unfamiliar word dodged past him. The alcove was empty again and Stanley pivoted to the bulletin board. He read anew the advertisement for the 'zeen' fest and unpinned it from the cork. He gripped the paper in both hands, squinting over it avidly. "Everyone Welcome," it promised him. He exited the alcove, folding the flyer into quarters and slipping it into his hind pocket.

Now Stanley Donner Jr. waited near the cafe counter, expecting the young white woman with the neon orange eyeshadow to announce his name at any moment. But he glanced to the glass storefront again and still that afro was there, and still her long elegant neck, and those fine shoulders; and Stanley stood so affected by these that, in truth, his breathing became confused, and even a dizziness swirled. He had splashed his face but it had

6

not worked quite well enough. So he could wait no longer. Stanley, trembling, marched to the cafe entrance, jerked the door open, and strode away from the beautiful black woman, away from her. Determinedly he turned rightward, sucking in a lungful of air, pressing the heel of his hand against his chest. Determinedly he trod the direction from which he had come, back toward the Taco Snatch. As he passed the intent chess players on the sidewalk he noticed a young white woman through the cafe's glass. Behind a counter, she stood, with bright orange eyeshadow, gesturing a paper cup at him, her other hand waving energetically.

Stanley Donner Jr. waved back.

"Goodbye," he mumbled aloud.

Stanley Donner Jr. walked on.

The sidewalk tables under the cafe's canopy sat bathed in a faint orange light. Amid that orange light, the blue glow of a laptop screen shined up into the bright darting eyes of a young black woman. Viola. Viola's oval face tops a long elegant neck. Above that oval face, a full afro crowns her fine features like a shimmering velvet halo. Viola's shoulders were set in that darkness, her eyes dancing streetward, then back through the cafe window, then back to computer screen. She typed. As Viola typed she tucked her elbows in hard against her rib cage, a gesture usual for her in those days.

"I get the feeling that white boy wants to shake my hourglass," she typed. "I get that feeling. But there was something about him that was difficult to interpret. When I first saw him I wondered if maybe he was living with *It*."

Viola cast a wary eye across the cafe's smoldery interior. A young couple, arm-in-arm, approached on the sidewalk behind her, their sandals scraping the concrete. Viola twitched a look backward at them and noted their drapey white garb. Slightly she ducked her head. The couple passed. They entered the cafe and veered for the counter. Viola resumed typing.

"Anyways, sometimes you look up and see someone who has it worse than you, for some reason other than yours, maybe, and you ask yourself: Why? And you say to yourself: Well, if I knew the answer to that question probably I would not be sitting on a sidewalk in the middle of the night."

Viola sighed. A weak, hopeful smile wrinkled her mouth.

"Okay, my fays, so we've been communicating back and forth through the comments for some time and y'all make me feel so strong that I'm going to accept your invitations. This blog has been mostly about *us* so far, but I'm needing more support so I'm thanking you in advance for letting it become more about *me*. Partly this arises from how warm and encouraging you are, and partly from Becca insisting it will help. (Thank you, Becca.) Besides, they say being more personal binds your followers to you; though I hope you're feelin' me well enough by now to know I would never commence a thang such as this solely for mercenary reasons.

"Anyways, what I'm talking about will become evident too soon. (The ogre.) For now, let me say this cafe is a good one. No one bothers me excepting the occasional white boy spying my hourglass. And I like to take my time coming down from a fest. The Kensington Zine Fest was just around the corner this evening on Adams. That's why I'm still up here in College Heights, out of National City, out of my territory, so to speak. And look at him -- there's that white boy again, all hunched up. He's bending toward the bulletin board now. What's that? He just took my flyer off that bulletin board and put it in his pocket. And Becca's calling out to him to take his coffee. He's already on the sidewalk, though. Mm-Mmn. Something up with that critter. Something wounded in that soul."

Viola's typing stopped. She gazed into the laptop's blue glow. Her features crowded with feigned concentration as actually she tracked the hunched white man with her peripheral vision. Skittishly she fidgeted, marking him as he turned away. With his frontside averted now, Viola looked up from her acting to assure herself of his departure. Her shoulders loosened. She exhaled. Viola had dressed attractively for the zinefest this evening, and intentionally, to test her inner strength. She considered now she might not be ready for the oglings of a wee-hour cafe, though the oglings of the zinefest had not bothered her at all. The low-rise denims. The flowery crop top. The seashell earrings dangling like bohemian bait. More than one man took more than a second look tonight at Viola's cinnamon-colored skin.

So she was doing better, but,

"I've got to get myself home. I feel time just dribbling through my fingers, precious. And y'all know how true it is for me that time is money. Demetria's making her rent, but I'm getting strange vibes from her. She's flighty. Like she's planning for escape.

I can make it with someone sharing rent, barely. But I can't make it alone. No way. Why I stay out here on the West Coast when so many places so much cheaper, I don't know. Just more opportunity, I guess. I scrap for food and shelter but at least I can scrap that off my art out here. Back in Caro, there's no such thing as living off a little magazine and doing side editing here and there. Not even in Asheville or Chapel Hill. Here, on the other hand, there are zinefests and pop-up shows all the time. I earn some real coin off those. Like today. Sold twenty units. That's a chunk! Add to this the editing jobs I can network out here, plus all your *O, Kindred* subscriptions and I'm good. Barely, you know, but good."

Viola stretched her long neck, peering past two men quietly conversing in Arabic over a depleted chessboard. She could see beyond them the hunched white man crossing now to the Taco Snatch. She relaxed.

"The submissions call for issue nine is almost upon us, in case you're waiting. Just released issue seven. I shipped those analog subscriptions last week, as you know, my fays. If it has not arrived in your mailbox yet, it is on its way. I'm taking seven to Palm Desert Zine Fest soon too. After every release I wonder how many more issues we can get out of a people of color fairy tale zine. And every time my peeps from around the world deliver: From South Asia to South Dakota to South Central. God bless y'all, every one."

But Viola tightened her elbows into her rib cage.

"That wounded white boy just started his car down there at that Taco Snatch. Mm-Hm. Headlights now. Pulling out. Yeah, I guessed it. Here he comes."

Her entire persona sank into the blue glow of the laptop -- apparently. For the corner of Viola's eye watched the little green sedan sidle past, slow. The vehicle hesitated at the near corner. But a second car arrived then, rumbling impatiently, pushing the green sedan on.

"Hmm. If it had not been for those two girls coming up behind, I think that white boy might have just sat there even longer. But nothing scary in his eye, I guess. Hard to judge this one. I feel like he is seeing something in me he has never seen before. I get the feeling he is trying to understand something from me -- like I have a fresh explanation he might need. Well, maybe I do.

"I am going to shut down now and catch the first bus downtown before the morning people get rolling. The sky's turning purple already. Nothing more depressing than seeing freshly-showered just-awaking people starting their busy energetic day when I haven't even shut my eye. Wishing y'all so many Happily-Ever-Afters."

Viola lay her hands in her lap briefly. She reached up then and tapped the computer's trackpad to click 'post'. She glanced back over her shoulder. She glanced back into the cafe. Nobody seemed to be casing her. Again she surveyed her surroundings. The two Arabic speakers sat bent over a newly joined chess battle. Becca scrubbed saucers at the sink. Good time for a getaway. In an instant, Viola had sleeved her laptop, slipped it into her wheeled zines box, and was striding swiftly to the alcove in the back of the cafe. There she pinned to the bulletin board a flyer to replace the one pilfered by Stanley Donner Jr. A moment later, riding an air kiss from Becca, Viola was scudding on an electric scooter under the bright street lights of Park Avenue, her hippy denims and flapping crop top revealing the silky skin of her midriff. That impatient car she had seen before, the one carrying the two women, rumbled up behind her now. Viola felt it pass her as the scooter hummed her toward the bus stop on Howard Street.

Viola watched. Viola listened.

She was watching and listening for It.

"Is this guy gonna go, or what?" Blossom fumed.

"Leave him be," responded Rocky, dabbing his eyes. "People have problems. For instance, my mascara is running. Maybe a stop sign isn't a bad place to solve them. I saw that man inside at the salsa bar anywho. Something's wrong in him. I can feel it."

Blossom glanced to Rocky as they idled behind the green sedan. "It's pretty late, huh?" she said. The words tightened her cheeks with sympathy. "You need to sleep, huh?"

"Yes, I do. Sleep will help. I'm sorry it's been all about me tonight. At least since that blah blah blah after party. I was containing myself before. Oh, look at the sky. It's turning purple already, like a deep crush velvet." Then, after an interval of awe: "What a fancy scarf that color would make."

Blossom punched her horn twice, lightly. The green sedan crept leftward. But Blossom, too, needed to turn left. "And of course the fucking chooch goes left!" she growled.

10

"You got the angries, honey. It's okay."

"Just tired, I guess."

She stalled at the stop sign for a breath, dithering over whether to fucking go straight or to fucking turn left. Blossom did not want to follow the crawling green sedan, but continuing straight would require a fucking U-turn to get to the fucking 163. She glared at the sidewalk, waiting for her mind to decide, and noticed a great afro atop an elegant neck. The arms beneath the afro shifted a laptop into a bookbag.

"What beautiful style," erupted Rocky, seeing the same woman. "Just look at that tiny waist above those generous hips. And she has dressed them to show them off too, God bless her. And that natural! In private the black girls fret to me sometimes about their hair, you know -- Takes *so* much care. But can you beat that fro for a fashion statement? *Stylin!*"

Blossom agreed. Unconsciously she stroked the stubble of her shaved scalp.

Then Rocky said: "OMG, it's Vee! How did I miss that? I didn't recognize her till she turned toward us. Should we offer a ride?"

Blossom murmured, "I ... She lives here in San Diego." And, "We're pretty late, Rock."

"Oh."

They went straight. But Blossom clutched and gassed with her jangling heavy brown boots to hook a U-turn around the next median and rumble them back by that same stop sign. She traced a path to the 163 meant to avoid the creeping green sedan. Viola scootered along the sidewalk now, her elbows tucked in tight against her sides. They passed her.

"She looks a little afraid," Rocky sighed gently. He lifted his eyes. "Daylight's coming on, though. And the street's so well lit. She sure is zoomin' on that thing. Can't imagine anyone bothering her at that speed."

Five minutes later they were northbound. Considering the early hour and the day of the week Blossom did not expect the usual slowdown at the merge of the 805 and the 5. She calculated possible traffic glitches once they entered the hyper-urban thruways of Orange County, however. A foghorn, she heard then. Her ear gauges shimmied with her glance right. Rocky. He snored already, his head fallen back, his pronounced Adam's apple incongruously masculine beneath that exquisitely feminine

11

make-up job. But, yes, his mascara *had* run. Blossom loved this man. But she loved him in a way that defied conventional labels. Not romantically. Not in a familial way, either. As a friend, maybe? No, she thought. Different from that.

Blossom raced them off the 163, along a long westward curve, and onto the 805 North. She commented to herself that southbound traffic was already fucking crowding. And before even 6 a.m.! And on a fucking Sunday! Must be construction back there, she thought. With Rocky in a gone snooze now she ticked up the radio for company. Its noise unsettled her, however, and she tapped it to silence. For some beats after the liposuction commercial faded Blossom rode alone, nearly injured by the smarmy announcer's absence. Slightly her chin quivered.

Her thoughts drifted to Sacheen Littlefeather.

The Academy of Motion Picture Arts and Sciences had recently provided Blossom with her best leads yet. In her possession, she now had a list of every single invitee to the 1973 Oscar Awards ceremony, plus that night's seating arrangement, plus a twenty-inch stack of photocopied paraphernalia related to the event. Blossom acquired this information quite frankly by simply entering the Academy's library in Beverly Hills and enlisting the aid of a serious librarian.

No one there asked Blossom's intent.

From the reflexive glance of Littlefeather when the booing erupted, and the clarity of that booing through the young woman's microphone as she stood on that stage, Blossom deduced that the instigator of the booing must have been seated at orchestra level. The Dorothy Chandler Pavilion seated more than 3,000 guests that year, but the orchestra level sat only about 1,300. Blossom quartered that number by surmising that the perpetrator must have been seated to the right of Littlefeather and forward of the first balcony, which surely would have absorbed and softened the violence of his voice. This reduced the number of potential culprits to 300. Then, from that number, Blossom subtracted all women, celebrities, nominees, and honorees. With these deductions, she had narrowed her list to about 60 men.

Marlon Brando refused to accept his best actor award that year. In his stead he had sent a young woman, an Apache-Yaqui in traditional dress, to decline the trophy in his name. Sacheen Littlefeather she was called. She took the podium with poise, and with an apologetic manner, but with an unapologetic message --

12

that Mr. Brando refused this gracious honor to protest the maltreatment of American Indians in Hollywood films, television shows, and reruns. As soon as the objective of Littlefeather's speech became clear a brazen man seated at orchestra level began booing her. The viciousness in his boo truly startled. Many joined him, though some did support Littlefeather with applause. The young woman maintained her composure throughout, and after an 'excuse me,' completed her remarks with dignity. Then fifty years later Blossom saw a video of the event on SkipTube. She could not forget those images. The clash symbolized too much to just leave in her SkipTube history. Here was a rich, well-connected certainly white man trying to boo into silence a young American Indian woman as she attempted to dignify her oppressed race. The scene contained everything that motivates Blossom: Wealth and Injustice. Ethnicity and Privilege. Power and Oppression. Cowardice and Valor. Instantly she knew a treatment of this historical moment belonged in her zine. That man's outburst, as demeaning as it was, exactly fits the kinds of insults *Apologies In Order* exists to rectify. So Blossom committed herself to, at the very least, exposing the man who booed Littlefeather, and, if possible, confronting him personally and demanding an apology. For months now, fruitlessly, she had been seeking by various slippery means the identity of the elusive offender. But now, after a diligent sifting of the Academy's Oscars History Collection, and a few afternoons worth of photocopying, she could add to her investigation two tantalizing new tools – that register of guests and where they sat, and that two-foot-tall stack of what the dutiful librarian kept referring to as 'miscellanea.' Each of those stray pages related to that night in 1973. Blossom felt anxious to really dig into those materials.

Rocky still snored. The clock on Blossom's dashboard blinked 7:12 a.m. She calculated that since he had appointments in Anaheim that afternoon instead of West Hollywood he could sleep another three hours before leaving for the boutique. She shook him.

"What honey?"

A moment later Blossom had been kissed on the cheekbone and apologized to and was alone again. Another 40 minutes of traffic in daylight passed before she arrived in Inglewood. But by then, because of the morning hour, at least she could expect to find parking in her neighborhood. And today was her day off from the call center; so she need not worry that her sleepiness would compromise her conversion stats.

Blossom idled on Imperial Highway now, waiting for the stoplight at La Cienaga to turn green. She draped her hand over the steering wheel. Her black-green tattoo of a thorny vine winded up from her ring finger to encircle her wrist and then spiral up her arm. A cop blew through the intersection, northward on La Cienaga. Then, a few beats later, an old convertible Impala barreled through too, matching the cop's speed and direction. Blossom ducked her head, looking rightward through her windshield after that blood-red Impala. *There!* She had just witnessed the most famous lowrider in southeast LA! Easy Castillo. From the *SlapDown* zine. Blossom peered still after him. *Goals!* How she relished seeing that warrior in action! She wondered if he was even chasing that black and white. Blossom probed her memory for Easy's presence at The Kensington Zine Fest the previous night. She could not recall him.

Then Blossom was sitting at her desk in her attic apartment on 118th Drive. She rented it from an older cosin. The steep angles of the house's rooftop cramped the room, encasing her in it as if in a honeycomb. The clock said 8:01 a.m. now and Blossom had shed her spurs, boots, flack jacket, and formless black pants to relax cross-legged in boxers and a soft brown t-shirt. Her long highway cogitation over Littlefeather and knowing she had that entire day to herself had jazzed her into percolating a stiff cup of caffeine and attacking that Oscars 'miscellanea' instead of just bedding down. Among the materials she had acquired were reproductions of some amateur snapshots taken behind the curtains in the forepart of the award ceremonies, when the less glamorous technical honors were being dispensed. Many of those images came from a little-known trade journal called *Stagecraft*, which circulated mainly among film crews in the 1970s. Blossom had reviewed maybe twenty pages of her new hoard so far. With her left hand, she paged over the next photocopy. It was from *Stagecraft*.

A dog beside a little white boy. To the right of the boy stood a white man in a fedora, possibly the director. The white man pointed significantly at something and drooped his head toward a camera operator who straddled some tram rails. The dog's apparent trainer held a folded leash and waited half out of view to the left. Blossom stared at the caption beneath the image for a

14

moment but felt heavily sluggish, strengthless, and even stomach-sick from lack of sleep. She laid her shaved head over her tattooed arm on the desk. But then she rose and slogged to her bed. After angling her porcelain ear gauges out of her lobes, and letting them clink onto the area rug beside her nightstand, Blossom sank into her pillow. Soon she snored like a foghorn.

Ezekiel Castillo cocked his chin and hit a chrome switch under the left side of his dashboard. The rear bumper of his convertible 1964 Impala cranked upward, liquidly, rising twelve extra inches off the asphalt street. He checked both side mirrors and continued creeping his *ranfla* along Marine Avenue, tail up. He rumbled to Aviation Boulevard. There he spun right. He knew better than to push this defiant pose across Aviation and into the Manhattan Beach municipality. The code there was ahead of his game.

"Here, piggy, piggy," he muttered. "Come on to Easy."

He checked again both side mirrors.

"Here, piggy, piggy."

The convertible is painted blood red with gold metal flakes. Subdued purple pinstripes accent the clean lines of this vintage Chevrolet, spiking and swirling sex appeal into the hood and the door handles, and the trunk. On that day the Impala's polished mahogany steering wheel slid through Easy's fingers as that right turn straightened him onto Aviation. Alone he rode that morning, partaking of the perfect West Coast air as it curled around his windshield and into his collar. On the back seat waited two video-equipped drones. Of course the top was down.

Then, three blocks ahead, through the intersection of Aviation and El Segundo Boulevard, Easy saw a black and white cruiser cross at patrol speed. It passed too quickly for him to identify the city seal on the door, but ...

"Roger that rabbit," he muttered.

With the hit of a switch, Easy simultaneously dropped his rear and gassed. In three blocks he was whipping right onto El Segundo and peering forward for the squad car. He spotted its lights waiting at the intersection of La Cienaga, in front of a Shaft Burger. Easy accelerated to the speed limit, pushing to catch the cop. But the traffic light turned green then and the cruiser went left.

Just as Easy hooked left after the cop the light changed red. Easy kept his speed beneath 40 miles per hour.

"Sooie," he chuckled.

Finally, after 20 minutes of cat and mouse, and hide and seek, and thread the needle, and just as Easy was making his quarry, the patrol car hit Centinela Avenue and broke right. The Impala screeched to a stop. "Inglewood," Easy blurted. He rolled his steering wheel left to slide the lowrider into the turn lanes facing Centinela.

"*Cabrón*," said he.

And the police car sped away.

Ezekiel shrugged and rumbled left through the green traffic light now. A tightness in his skin relaxed. A flush of thin perspiration followed, and a chuckle in the hollows of his throat. La Cienaga defines the boundary between Los Angeles proper and Inglewood. The municipal code of Inglewood is one of the strictest in LA County regarding drones. To attempt a hit there surrendered too much advantage. Easy had not identified the black and white as Inglewood earlier because, trailing it the entire pursuit, he could not see the city seal on the door.

After a fistful of minutes, Easy stepped from of his legally parked "six-four," strutted his broad athletic frame past a small bike shop and a hair salon, and entered a convenience mart for a fresh pack of menthols. He wore wraparound sunglasses -- 90s style. A full black mustache cornered his lips and reached for his prominent jawline. His hair he combed back *suavecito* slick and shrouded with a hairnet. Easy bobbed his head slightly. A chronic closed-mouth smile warmed his expressive lips.

"Got away from me," he announced to Fredo proudly, standing now before a bulletproof barrier that made Fredo appear as much a prisoner as a bodega cashier. Easy positioned himself behind an old woman who paid for some fresh bolillos. The bread rolls steamed inside the plastic sack she held. Still, he bobbed his head.

"*Ese*, you're asking for it," answered Fredo over the old woman's silver hair. He laid coins into her arthritic fingers. Noticeably Fredo was older than Easy, maybe late thirties. He stood sinewy and strong with flinty eyes and shadowy concave cheeks.

"I'm not just asking for it, foo, I'm out chasing it. '*Toy cazando* the chumps." Easy held the door open for the old woman, nodding respectfully to her as Fredo slid two packs of menthols

16

under the bulletproof glass. Easy tendered a twenty for the cigarettes and a five for the mineral water he had nabbed from a mini-fridge.

"Hope they don't catch you flat-footed."

"Never."

"Mm hm."

"Never leave my house without my angels. Always connected, homes. Only really at risk when the web goes down."

"They'll get onto you, though. That's what *la jura* does."

"Some of them already are. I think the patrol car I was just tailing may have been running from me."

"*E' posible*. How long since you hooked one?"

"Eight days."

"*Simón*. But I fear for you."

"It's a mission."

And Fredo, nodding seriously now with his lips pressed, looked down to a small pile of half-sized magazines on the counter. A glance at the publication gives the impression of a 'gotcha' paper -- one of those gratis compilings of recent mug shots with advertisements for bail bondsmen and defense attorneys. But that glance deceives. Though this front cover did showcase an arrest-style photograph with black measurement lines on a white wall behind an expressionless perpetrator, the image had been manipulated digitally and the perpetrator pictured was actually an LA County sheriff's deputy -- One of Easy's pursuits from the previous quarter. The title topping the mini-magazine read *SlapDown*.

Fredo and Easy slapped palms and bumped fists under the glass and Easy pushed through the sticker-covered door.

"I'll try to set up a hit right here in front of the mart so you can see the show."

"Got the *churros* waiting, *carnal*."

Easy checked his exit briefly, holding open the door. He looked back quasi-professionally then and tossed at Fredo: "Cameras working?"

"Like a dream," came the answer. "Scared off some taggers the other night while chillin' on my couch. That alarm button of yours is tight. Got it recorded if you wanna see."

"Later, 'mano. My day off, you know?"

They nodded farewells as a white man with shoulder-length dreadlocks ducked between them. The glass door stuttered to a close.

Easy, still purging the thrill of the chase, strode to the end of the row of storefronts. He leaned against a metal rail there and reflected on the mental push and pull between him and the police, and on the matching of his skills against theirs, and on their societal dominance and how it felt to toy with it. During these reflections he peeled the cellophane off his new box of cigarettes, knocked the pack once against the heel of his hand, and, striking a match, lit up. A white girl came lumping along the sidewalk then. She pushed a bicycle with a flattened rear tire. An instinct to help the girl rose in Easy, but he repressed it. Can't just go offering assistance to a white girl like that, he thought. Get damned mad. So Easy tracked back to the cop who just got away. Squad car 81? Wonder who that was? Didn't much matter since he or she was Inglewood blood. Easy considered the municipal code of Inglewood and for the hundredth time tried to see a way around it. But then the white girl was veering off the sidewalk and huffing her bike right toward him, stubbornly. The girl wore sunglasses, wayfarers. She yanked at the bike shop's locked door.

"Oh, c'mon," she sighed. Then, complaining at Easy, "You know what time this place opens?"

Ezekiel Castillo emerged from his reverie. He noticed the white girl's voluptuous build and the lightness and poise of her bearing. Moved by her contours, and how she carried them, he exhaled a plume of silver smoke and slipped into what he called his 'newscaster' diction. Easy asked of the wayfarers, sounding like a college boy, "It doesn't say on the door?"

"No. Too faded to read."

"It's still pretty early, I guess. For a Sunday. But that guy opens every day. Raul's his name. Maybe nine or ten." For a beat, Easy watched the traffic on Centinela through his wraparounds. Then, slowly, with a hint of concern, he queried: "What are you doing over here?"

The white girl glared through the door now. Her wayfarers had been removed and she nearly pressed her nose against the glass. She turned a squint on Easy. He saw her ice-blue eyes. Frustratedly she said, "The weather's so glorious today. I wanted to keep riding and tried to go around the marina to get to Playa Del Rey Beach. You ever get sick of using those Maps apps for every little thing? You ever just wanna do it yourself, without help? Anyhow, when I finally gave in and turned my phone back on, I saw that I had turned too early – and in the wrong direction. And now this." She gestured accusingly at the bicycle's flat tire.

The white girl still attracted Easy. As he dwelled on the redundancy of the words *"Playa* del Rey *Beach"* his hidden eyes toured her curves.

She continued, "But I don't feel like pushing that flat all the way back to Venice. Oh, whatevs. I guess I could lock it up and just come back later."

Easy's desire ebbed.

He nodded. He backed off the metal rail, politely, making room so the white girl could chain her bike. She looked to her phone then and Easy heard her grumbling something about a Diet FizzBang as she corrected the balance of her wayfarers on her nose. Soon he was pondering again the Inglewood municipal code.

Even after the white girl moved off though Easy still felt her contours lingering in his blood.

The word 'unibrow' floated among Clare's thoughts as she assembled her explanation. Or was it a complaint? But if a complaint, against whom? Against life? Here was her problem, she told herself. Time to get over this. Inconveniences are not insults. Who was she to expect uninterrupted progress through every little thing she attempted? Especially as she was beginning something so new for herself, something so brave and courageous, even heroic.

Yes, a unibrow, she repeated. This man sported a rather flattering unibrow. And also, thankfully, a kind attentive face.

Clare firmed her nerve. She puckered up her features. She complained, "I was going to fix it myself. I watched another guy fix it last time at a bike shop and it looked easy enough. Then I went along with a SkipTube video the next time, right? But I couldn't do it. I had to take it to the shop again. The video didn't say anything about what to do with my long fingernails. Does everyone get flat tires like this all the time? It's only been two weeks for me. No wonder everyone drives cars."

The unibrow nodded, as if he understood only too well. This man's kind face controlled its smile, seeming to hold the expression in reserve for a more opportune moment. Clare went on to elucidate for Raul, at length, how she was traveling everywhere

19

on a bicycle now, that she had decided to be more self-sufficient, less dependant on things, that she wanted to be tougher as a person and that giving up her vintage Saab for a while seemed a daring and obvious way to begin. However, this hassle with the flat tires was interfering with her efforts to harden herself. She was determined to deal with such hiccups, but only up to a point. Eventually her strategy had to actually work or it was not really a strategy at all.

"The whole idea is to ride a bike," Clare said. "So if I don't have a bike to ride my plan falls apart. I need to go places. Without a bike, I'll resort to my Saab or something. I just started this. I'm not ready to give up yet."

After several minutes of detailed explanations like these Clare sensed, because she is in fact a very sensitive person, that she might be impinging upon Raul's valuable time.

She squinted. "So sorry to go on like this. Do you have a bicycle that I can buy so that I can have two bicycles? I was thinking as I was pushing this one down the sidewalk that with two bikes I would always have one to ride around while the other one was getting its flat fixed."

The unibrow rose. The contained smile broke free. Raul stepped quietly then from behind the counter, his great brown eyes alight. He ushered Clare into a small pasture of handlebars. The aging man said he offered many types of bicycles, bicycles for all challenges, and that certainly Clare could find one to suit hers. He asked to what extent she rode? How long was her commute?

"I will be riding it to Palm Desert soon. I plan to ride it out there."

Clare placed her hand on the saddle of another beach coaster, one resembling the bike she had just wheeled into the shop. Her fingers squeezed the saddle affectionately, already claiming it.

"To Palm Desert? From here?" replied Raul. His brown eyes shined with surprise.

"I live in Venice Beach," she addended. "From there, actually."

"A bicycle like this one is not really suited for such a trip, miss," he informed, kindly. "They call these coasters because that's all they do. They're really just designed for boardwalk coasting and relaxation. A trip of the kind you are describing – that's probably a hundred and fifty miles. Wait, are you carrying anything with you, or is the trip just about speed and distance?"

"I'll be taking stuff."

"Alright, cyclists use touring bikes for that kind of trip. I have several to pick from, as you can see. This blue one over here for example has a high-tech chrome-molybdenum frame. Very light. Nine speeds. Touring bikes can be quite expensive."

Clare's features puckered. Fondling still the coaster's seat she protested that probably she could handle the trip on a coaster, that part of the journey, in fact, would be accomplished by commuter rail.

Raul protested in turn that no knowledgeable cyclist would even contemplate a ride to Palm Desert on a coaster, even from the terminus of the train lines, that beach bikes are not designed for the climbs involved.

"Oh, c'mon. Is that so?"

"I'm not just trying to sell you a bike, miss. If you're commuting a couple of miles to work or maybe to some bar on a Saturday afternoon this one will do you fine. No problem. They're built for that. A tour to Palm Desert, on the other hand ... that requires much more sophisticated equipment."

To the old man's great surprise Clare listened to his words carefully now, squinting, and, with her look resolving into utter belief, accepted his advice without further hesitation. After some minutes of dawdling over which color she preferred, she declared, "Oh, whatevs. That rad pink one, I guess." And then she inserted her debit card to pay $1,050 for an extra bike -- for an extra bike to ride while having the occasional flat tire repaired.

Clare stopped squinting at Raul then and her ice-blue eyes grew round. Again she began to detail for the old man her determination to live without a car. For a long time, she would do it! At least six months. She described how she had given up her vintage Saab despite it being a truly darling ride, how she had stashed her car keys in the freezer behind her frozen cinnamon rolls, as a reminder not to cheat, and how she was tired of being so soft. That was the word she used: "Soft." Clare discoursed further then, at some length, but never again gathered from Raul's interested unibrow that his time might be wasted.

"That's Old America," she finished. "I'm tired of being like that. I'm thinking of myself as New America now. So it's time for me to become stronger. I can do it. It'll just take a little time and effort. I am having one other problem, though. So sorry to go on like this but can you give me some tips on how to bring home groceries from the supermarket? It has been exceedingly awkward. I can't seem to figure that out. And is there such a thing as an insulated cup holder for bicycle handlebars? My Diet FizzBangs keep going warm."

So that is how it began.

Many have asked how we all met in the first place. In the beginning, I thought this question natural, a logical, off-hand query to be expected during any introductory conversation. But later, as the question kept being put to me, and with such sharp-eyed interest from even seasoned acquaintances, I began to realize that, yes, there is more here than just small talk. The short answer is that we all tabled near each other that year at The Baja Zine Fiesta in Tijuana. The problem, however, is that this simple answer, though factual, leaves out so much of the story that it robs its factuality of any real truth. For it was not just that suddenly we were together and talking face to face that seems so significant now, but instead the many coincidences that led us to those particular tables on that particular day. The six of us were like the tributaries of a hidden river, continually flowing toward each other, crossing and re-crossing different terrains until finally we poured into that last broad channel of common forward motion. As I presented this historical puzzle to the others, and carefully we retraced our memories back along the many ephemeral threads involved, we agreed that our meeting in Tijuana that day as much ended one process as began another. Across that entire season of zinefests we had been funneling toward each other as if by the pull of gravity. We've talked this through now. In remote hotel rooms we've discussed it, and in 24-hour diners, during after parties, and in campgrounds, and oftentimes over the road. I'm going to try to put it all down correctly.

In general, our initial intersections seem mere chance, just the random meetings of passing strangers; but all of us have noted, in retrospect, the feeling of orchestration running through those accidental encounters, maybe even of intent. None of us have gone so far as to propose a source for that intent, a who or a what which might have been guiding our paths toward convergence; but considering what has happened since then it feels dogmatic to blindly reject the possibility that fate was deliberately moving through us. Thinking back we all agreed that probably that late night and early morning of that final weekend in April -- that night and morning just described -- was the best place to start. If we wanted, we could trace these markers back to before some of us even arrived in Southern California. But it was during those eight hours which began in the wee hours of that April darkness that we all first crossed paths in a way that set the stage for the following six months, and, if you will, for every day that has passed since then, even up to the hour that I write these words.

Chapter Two
Friday, May 11. Afternoon

The stack of photocopies on Blossom's desk had shortened by more than half. Not two feet tall now, it stood less than one foot. Blossom turned over the next copy to see a Hollywood actress in grotesque yellow headgear offering the camera an exaggerated pout. In this candid shot of Lynn Redgrave in costume, the actor telegraphed her camp as a faux Elizabethan queen. Then Blossom turned over another sheet: A man gripping a power tool and staring up at a barber's chair bolted to the ceiling. The man leaned back, off-balance, in serious study. The blobby contrast smudged any hint of his identity. Blossom turned another page: That upside down barber chair again, but now from that *Stagecraft* journal she kept encountering, the little trade publication for show business stagehands. The journal's occasional blasé inclusion of the famous had provided Blossom with several exciting but ultimately fruitless leads concerning the man who booed Littlefeather. She planned to examine original copies of the publication from all of 1973, if not at the Academy library, maybe at UCLA. In any event, *Stagecraft's* reproduction of this upside down barber chair was more sharply rendered than the previous one, but clearly a duplicate of it. This led Blossom to wonder if the shot was actually a publicity still of some sort. The image did not offer a detailed caption like many of *Stagecraft's* photos. This one read simply: "Robert Donnelly at work on the inverted set for Ernest Borgnine's latest vehicle."

Blossom sighed. She raised her eyes to gaze out the single square window of her tiny Inglewood attic apartment. The window was gabled to accommodate the angles of the roof and the honeycomb quality of her room. Blossom had two hours still before having to leave for the call center. Her bare feet crossed up under her thighs as she sat in boxers, her soft brown t-shirt riding her shoulders loose. She raked her palm over her shaved scalp, thoughtfully. Then she fiddled with her navel stud. Blossom tried not to worry about the non-profit donations she needed to convert tonight in order to make this week's quota at her job. She pushed the thought away, along with the contiguous fact that missing quota would mean having to work an extra 'voluntary' shift tomorrow morning. Then, with the skin over her cheekbones tight and tense, she dropped her eyes back to the photocopies.

There waited Robert Donnelly's upturned profile. And his power tool. And his white flesh. As Blossom leafed to the

25

succeeding page she noticed a shaft of sunlight balming the skin of her left hand. Then she named the color of her skin: Golden, as Rocky called it. Blossom laid her golden hand over the photocopy and noticed again, as she had many times now, how thoroughly white folks dominated the entertainment industry in those days; how every single one of these pages she reviewed exhibited white people, nothing but white people. She turned over another photocopy. She rested the golden richness of her skin across it. Above her hand laughed now the image of a white man wearing a blazer and thick-rimmed glasses. He fingered a martini glass and arced his spine in an open-mouthed guffaw. The man wore a spotted cravat. Blossom paged two sheets forward, quickly, then three more, then four more. Every single one of these faces was white. Even in the background -- that guy there lugging that phony beehive toward some set -- even that guy was white. Blossom flipped over four more copies but finally halted. She could pore through these pages all day long and see nothing but white people, or really, *white men*. True, these images were fifty years old, she sniffed. True, times had changed -- nominally. Probably if *Stagecraft* existed today you might find a Mexican carrying that fucking beehive, she thought, or some black brother securing that upside down barber chair. And certainly more token people of color were represented in Hollywood now, not to mention the fetishized. But do those really count?

Blossom recalled the video of Littlefeather assuming the stage in the Dorothy Chandler Pavilion in 1973. Probably only two or three persons in that entire audience of thousands were non-white. What? Maybe Rita Moreno? Sidney Poitier? Bruce Lee? Surely no American Indians. How that must have felt, Blossom considered. To face them so fucking alone, the sole fucking member of your race; to walk out into the midst of one of the white man's religious rituals, one of his celebrations in which he called himself good and holy, and there, completely alone, with no one for support, call him fucking evil to his fucking face. Where did she get that courage? Well, Blossom articulated inwardly, she did not subscribe to his religion. That would be part of it, I guess. I suppose it's easier to desecrate a religion you don't believe in. Would I go into such a black mass and piss on its altar? That's where Littlefeather stood. That's an altar if there ever was one. Or could I invade, say, the president's state of the union address beating some sacred drum? I mean, even if you hate them I still think it would be hard to fucking insult thousands of people to their faces. Seems almost superhuman. So much poise. Brando must have really loved us to do that. He took a stand for us on that day. And he couldn't know SkipTube would come along later to prove him so superior to the other power brokers of his age. And he couldn't know what Littlefeather's undaunted dignity would mean to a Payómkawichum woman like me fifty years later. He did something very beautiful that night. They are not all of them evil, I guess, those white devils. Bless you, Marlon Brando. And then all the rest too -- What's not shown in the video: Littlefeather had to leave that altar then. She had to walk out of that ritual she had just defiled and move among its believers backstage. What did the white stagehands do? Did they stare? Did they fucking laugh at her traditional dress? Or her 'costume' as they probably fucking called it? Blossom glowered. So much dignity. So much dignity. Could I do that? she asked herself. I guess you would prepare yourself. One cannot know when an opportunity to make things right might come. One can only prepare -- so that if the opportunity arises one is solid enough to endure pushback from the wrong-doers. And with dignity, Blossom affirmed inwardly, with dignity. Without dignity resistance forfeits half its force. How white people fucking degrade themselves, she thought. Who among them could do that? They don't realize their weakness. The societal power they have diminishes their inner strength, warps it instead into a kind of petulance. So few of them have the courage of a Littlefeather! What strength that brave woman gives me!

Blossom had been paging past white man after white man, through copy after copy after copy, without really examining the content of the sheets. She realized suddenly she had been doing this. The angles of her face hardened. Her forward momentum died. One by one Blossom began placing the copies back atop the stack, repairing to the point where her thoughts initially strayed. Soon she faced again that laughing man holding the martini who wore the blazer and spotted cravat. Two pages further back waited the blobby set technician beneath the upside down barber chair. Then Lynn Redgrave with a yellow vulva on her head.

Blossom had been paying attention here so she quit her retreat. She flexed her spine against her seatback and swiveled her arms behind her to stretch her shoulders. She rolled her head then to loosen her neck and felt the empty lobes where her ear gauges fit brush against her shirt. Then Blossom inhaled a concerted breath.

She started forward again. Here was the fuzzy reproduction of the man with the power tool staring up at the barber chair. Blossom studied the copy. She paged it over. Here that better reproduction of the same, with its routine caption. Next Blossom looked down on the photograph of the man in the blazer, with the spotted cravat. He fingered that martini glass, arcking back in his howl of merriment. That image came from *Stagecraft*. Beneath the photo the editors had printed a terse, uninformative caption: "Boo Boo in action."

Blossom sighed. She leafed the copy onto the read pile. The following page presented to her the same photograph of the laughing man in the blazer, but this time in miniature, and worked into a news article. The headline read: "Boo Boo Strikes Again." Facetiously the article described the laughing man's exploits, painting him rather pointedly as one who continually looked for reasons to agitate. Then it referred to some recent flourish of his that the article would not name. The flourish was left undescribed, like an inside joke that everyone in the industry knew about but no one would repeat. The end of the article reminded that "Boo Boo's" nickname arose from his willingness to take the lead in booing stage performers.

Blossom read the entire article again.

She checked the Academy's guest list and seating chart.

Blossom read the final paragraph two more times. She studied "Boo Boo's" photograph with scrutinous intensity. Then, breathily, she said, "Oh my fucking God."

Ezekiel Castillo crouched on a wheeled stool and leaned toward a door-sized mirror. He turned his head from left to right, critically, as his printer zuzzed out self-adhesive address labels. His sister Linda sat in a swivel chair behind him, between his photocopier and his light table. Linda swiveled side to side, alternately watching the printouts eject and watching Easy fastidiously groom the rounded arc of his full mustache. The prescription glasses Easy wears are thick. She was late twenties at the time. He, about thirty.

Snip. Snip.

"Are you even cutting hair off that bush?" Linda cracked through her perpetual grin.

"Just waiting for my printouts."

She glanced again to the zuzzing machine.

"How many you mailing this time?"

"Five hundred and change," Easy answered, "but only addressing 200 tonight because somehow I let myself run out of labels. I think I'm getting to where I need an assistant. My efficiency is slipping. At any rate, those envelopes there on the light table -- Once I seal them and print the postage we can ride. What happened? Where's my homeboy Koji?"

"Had to stand me up cause the sushi chef's sick."

"Friday night and no date. Well, well. What was the plan?"

"Nothing really. Probably another superhero flick."

"You're not going in?"

"Why?" Linda snapped. "*I'm* still off. Besides, I hate running the front of the house when he's the Itamae. *Not* good for our relationship. Okaasan can handle it just fine."

Still Easy groomed, his mouth flexing an oval.

Snip. Snip.

Behind him, spread beneath the window of this once-bedroom, sat the workstation for his home office. It featured, most prominently, a six-foot-wide desk upon which stood a 48-inch computer screen. That day Easy had been drafting a security system design for a new several-million-dollar home in Pomona. The computer screen portrayed a three-dimensional image of the home in question, along with a flowchart. Easy's office had once been two separate rooms. He and his friend Mario had knocked out a wall to let Easy manage his various pursuits in a single space. This meant that against the wall directly opposite his security systems design business a large art table sat with a separate desktop computer. There Easy built his zines. Above the computer, in narrow shelves, several shades and qualities of gray paper were stacked, from newsprint to cardstock. Also, there was a long-arm stapler and a broken pencil.

Snip. Snip.

Between these opposing desks, against the wall, rested Easy's state-of-the-art photocopier. Next to the copier sat the light table with the aforementioned envelopes waiting to be labeled for *SlapDown* subscribers. It was between that photocopier and light table that Linda swiveled back and forth in her chair, smiling ironically. The fourth wall of the room framed two entrances and the door-sized mirror into which Easy still leaned.

"That mustache."

"Multi-purpose. As authentically me as it can be, *sabes*, but simultaneously a decoy."

"And *'ama?*"

"Let the cops think I'm rough, a threat, *amenazante*, like she used to say." He quoted the words with pride. "That's part of my act. You've seen their faces when I turn off the barrio cadence. How it shocks them when suddenly I code-switch into college boy."

She giggled. "Yeah, it's pretty hilarious. They can be so pathetic. That CalTech routine totally puts them on pause. *One Three One Two.*"

A chuckle rose from the roots of Easy's throat. He gave the mirror a cocky bob of the head: "Yeah, *One Three One Two.*" Then, after a snip: "They see me in the low low and decide I'm a cholo. Like they think I got a record. Like they think they can push me round since a record means they can accuse me of anything and make it stick." His muscular shoulders flexed. He twisted his neck sideward. "It's worth all the effort and risk just to see their disorientation when suddenly, with perfect newscaster diction, I am citing the municipal code at them. Almost as good as checking their authority in general and exposing their casual abuses." Easy smiled. "Besides, the 'stache looks cool."

"Yes, *'mano*. A cool *bigote*. That mustache is so bomb that all the girlie girls swoon for you when you enter the room. So when are you going to scoop up one of them *mamacitas* and make her the mother of my nephews?"

"Not ready, sis. And it's gonna be nieces. Or German Shepherds. A man of war waits to have his children during peacetime. I am a man of war."

"When did you last cruise for a hit?"

"Yesterday. In Florence. *Nada*. I'm needing to shift my *tierra* farther east, looks like. The cops patrolling south LA might be wise to me. This mustache don't fool all of them. You think my piggies have a photo of me on the wall of their locker room? Or maybe of the six-four?"

"So they can fap?"

Ezekiel did not respond to this, did not chuckle.

Linda said, smilingly, "Red convertible '64 Impalas are not everywhere, *mijo*."

"*Ándale*."

Linda's smartphone dinged. She shifted leftward in the swivel chair to pry the instrument out of her skin-tight pockets.

Above her denims, Linda wore a loose red blouse with a palm frond print that covered her arms but left her fine collar bones exposed. Her long black hair was pulled into a ponytail, and her spontaneous and fluid way of wriggling her limbs demonstrated her electric youth. Linda has large brown eyes which still she accents with thick eyeliner that comes to a point outside her eye corners. Cat eyes, they're called. In that moment she turned her cat eyes on her phone screen, inquisitively.

"I'm thinking of trying Riverside," Easy continued. "I haven't been around there at all. Virgin territory. I already looked over its code and it's not so different from Bellflower in terms of drones. More stringent than Monterrey Park, but not as open as Downey. Inglewood, on the other hand, is over and out. I'm giving up on that shit."

The zuzzing of the printer had ceased. Easy rose from the squat stool and stretched his veined biceps behind his back to loosen his shoulders and neck. He lifted the stack of labels off the printer tray and carried them to the light table where he evened their edges neatly and laid them down. He half-sat against a barstool. Easy affixed a label to an envelope. Then another. He reached for a cigarette that teetered over the edge of an ashtray there. He did not light it.

"If you fit in, you have given in," he proclaimed, peering at the tip of the menthol through his thick eyeglasses. He smirked up at the seven drones hanging off ceiling hooks. "It's the grating against their asshat norms that keeps me *vivo*, Lindy: That push and pull between them and me. What I really have to offer the world remains to be seen, I think. But whatever it is I know this zootsuiting in their faces is going to make it *más auténtica*." His proclamation ended. He replaced the menthol at the ashtray edge, unlit. Then, looking over his shoulder: "You feel like helping? We can get out of here faster. What do you wanna do, anyway?"

"You're right. You're right," Linda answered, springing off the swivel seat. "You know I'm just razzing you, *cariño*. Maybe a food truck? A Tecate? We could What's Upp *Chingoncito*."

Linda began to affix addresses and Easy, with a wink that seconded her food truck idea, strode three paces to his zine table to boot the postage printer on its computer. He indicated First Class, entered the weight, inserted a count of 200 units, and clicked print. As the printer again started to zuzz Easy found again Linda's side. She labeled an envelope and he stuffed it with issue 16 of *SlapDown*.

In this issue, Easy published photos captured by his drones of a cop stopping him without cause. The zine described the incident in detail: That it occurred on Sepulveda Boulevard near the corner of Washington Place in Culver City at 8:09 p.m.; how, according to Easy's onboard computer log, there was no reason for the stop besides his brown skin and flamboyant red lowrider. But, since ultimately the officer neither violated any laws nor infringed upon the police code of conduct, Easy refrained from publishing the man's name and mugshot. In his opinion even less inflammatory *SlapDown* issues like this one challenged law enforcement. Knowing you are under scrutiny tempers your behavior, Easy believes. A cop who fears he is being recorded will ride more lightly. In this manner, *SlapDown* seeks to prevent abuse as much as expose it.

With a sponge pen Easy moistened the adhesive flaps on the 6 x 9 envelopes and sealed them. Their reshuffling of roles had dammed the flow of his and Linda's conversation. For a minute they stood mute, hearing only the noise of the printer and their own scuffling of paper and envelope.

Then, bending over her phone, Linda said, "Looks like the woman at *Apologies In Order* found her man."

"Which one?"

"She posted today that she knows who booed Littlefeather."

Easy hiked an eyebrow. "Roger that. She's been hunting him awhile."

"Yeah."

"I liked her Standing Rock issue. And that March 4 Life one."

Linda reflected, "Yeah, she's been focused on American Indians for a while now. This seems to be like her biggest find." Still she studied her phone. "She's kinda freaking out on Twitagram but the symbolism *is* pretty potent."

"Her zine's rad." Easy nodded. "Well, well, some zinester over by Sofi plans to make some noise for the Apaches. Who is the chump?"

"Doesn't say. Says she's putting it in a zine for Palm Desert."

"Nice tease. I'll have to look at that one. Is he still alive?"

"Don't know."

"I like that girl."

Linda remarked flatly then, turning her head in a way that flipped her ponytail, "So buy her a drink."

"What? She's a lesbian. With that punk haircut?"

"Bi," corrected Linda.

"De veras?"

"I've read her perzine. She's got a real revealing one about being a bisexual rez kid. Bi dyke."

"I like her. I do," Easy shrugged.

"So?"

"But not that way. I admit she's got the sexiest shaved head I've ever seen. And that golden complexion of hers is something. But still ... not my style."

"Riot girls might surprise you, big brother. Any kind of woman's going to redirect that testosterone of yours."

"Not ready for that."

"You know I love what you're doing. Just afraid. Why you think I'm always coming around? I'm your witness."

"I've got thousands of witnesses."

"That's so true."

Stock reports scrolled across the bottom of Clare's television screen as she slouched on her cute little Venice Beach loveseat. A slow Reggae rhythm pulsed quietly as a notification pinged her smartphone. A half-block away local folk and tourists strolled and rolled and skated along Ocean Front Walk. Clare could glimpse the beach, barely, if she rose to her doorway right now, but none of these worldly elements mattered to her at the moment. Clare sat suspended, afloat in an altered state of being.

Though she could not see it, Clare sensed a leaf on the blank page of the sketchbook on her lap. Then Clare found the outer tip of that invisible leaf with the point of the pencil she cradled in her fingers. Downward the leaf pulled the pencil point and Clare had drawn into existence suddenly one edge of a leaf. The opposite edge of that leaf came into being then beneath her pencil, a slightly curled mirror image of the first. Clare detailed over this curled edge a few evenly-spaced sharp points, or leaf teeth, and, flowing inward from those teeth, some leaf veins. The soft curves of the leaf flushed Clare with pleasure; and so, to challenge that pleasure, Clare countered those curves with a straight dark leaf stalk.

33

She breathed evenly.

And now ... the flower.

A stem suddenly arced up and away from the leaf stalk and Clare crowned it with a plump ripe ovary, and surrounded the ovary with some erect quivering stamen, and then enveloped them all with silky enticing petals. Under her willful pencil the bloom's pollen tube grew very very swollen. She stalled. Clare was waiting now for the flower's next command. Meanwhile, she enriched the drawing's volume with shading. Ah! The bloom needed company! That was it! Clare quickly sketched two additional examples of this impossible blossom onto the page. The flower seemed like one which might exist, and Clare knew eventually the curious would ask her to identify the species, but this flower does not exist. By imagining, Clare had fashioned a bloom so large it could never ride atop a stem so slight. Nature's physics would not allow it.

The playlist, more than an hour long, timed itself out before Clare came out of her suspended state. She felt satisfied with this spontaneous blossom, and also cleansed somehow by her journey into the mystic world of her sketchbook. Clare sat her pencil aside and her mind flickered forward through a cleaning up of the pencil lines and an inking of the sketch. The back of her hands pressed down on the open book, absent-mindedly smoothing its pages.

A peaceful quiet surrounded Clare. But she realized then that, no, it was not quiet at all. She heard the grind of skateboard wheels over concrete, and then, above that, the babble of humans relaxing along the boardwalk, and, still beyond, a faint churn from the day's heavy surf. She felt a sea breeze curling through her window. Clare stretched her neck, trying to see between the vacation condos that obstructed her view of the beach. Then the television caught her attention. Idly she watched the stock ticker scrolling along the bottom of a newscast. That green notification light blinked still on her smartphone. Clare had not yet realized the Reggae was done.

Clare shut her sketchbook. She rose. A lyric by The Pinche Cabrones drummed through her mind. *"... Podrá nublarse el sol etérnamente ... loo haa loo"* was all she could repeat so far, since, at the time of this scene, Clare did not yet understand Spanish. She fingered a glop of hand lotion from a pot on her kitchenette table and began massaging it into her palms and fingers. She swayed her hips and shoulders liquidly then as the tune still swirled through her thoughts. Like a sorceress Clare moves, as free and as potent when she dances as when she sketches. She exhaled finally, letting the arms she had raised float back to her sides. Her door she pulled open then to lean against its frame contentedly. Squinting at the bright glare there, and puckering her features against it, Clare donned sunglasses – Wayfarers – to more comfortably peer through the narrow gap separating the vacation condos. Beyond them, she could barely see a volleyball net, and palm fronds, and the sunny beige of beach sand. The breeze off the Pacific cooled this warm afternoon to soothing, even to sublime. The day, Clare mused, just begged for pastels.

Her gleeful mind jumped past the inking of her latest blossom now to eagerly deliberate its color. Magenta? In a beat she plopped again onto the loveseat, sans shades, pulling her knees up against her breasts and digging her feet into the cushions. The sketchbook lay open over her toes. Clare dried the greasy feeling of her palms on her shorts and leafed over a page.

Like, she thought. Perhaps: The Flowers of Cygnus X, or something. Alpha Centauri at Noon. Huh. Flowers from the Outer Rim.

Passingly she flipped through all the extraterrestrial blooms she had inked over the last two months. She counted the best ones: 12. That was enough. Clare envisioned each occupying its own two-page spread. On the right page, she always places a color reproduction of the flower. On the left page, she always lists its fictional planet and biome of origin, its pretend genus and species, and some alien cultural significance -- like how it figured into a Galactic poem or served as a symbol of royalty on Exoplanet 36-24-36.

Might she finalize and collate these 12 before The California Zine-O-Rama? Should she color them again with paint markers? Or did that make it too easy? Clare complained to herself that even painting had become easy for everyone. What did she have to know about egg yolks and wet plaster and brushes like artists back in the day? And what about *technique*. Did she have any technique to speak of? Truth be told, Clare did not feel exactly skilled, just very well-practiced and constantly inspired. Ideas she had in droves, and a cockiness, and an insatiable hunger to draw the visions down. But, she thought,

Every time I turn around there's something new to put aside. No Saab. No paint markers. What next? Do I stop sleeping on my bed now and start sleeping on the floor? Oh c'mon! I mean how far do I go with this making every little thing hard? Seems unnatural. So sorry, but we're not built for this. Paint markers. They're just paint markers! Where did that thought come from anyway? I am so irritating myself!

Clare unpuckered her features. She coached herself to just keep at the struggle until she no longer felt soft. *Soft.* There was that word again. Yeah, she really hated that word. Soft. She was so tired of softness.

Could I actually sleep on the floor? Huh. I just wanna see that I can live without all this ease. I need some friction or something. I can take it. I know I can. Why not? I don't need all this stuff. Got it in me. Oh, whatevs.

But paint markers?

I haven't driven in three weeks now, right? I've learned how to fix a bicycle flat too. I think. I even bought tools for fixing those flats. Love that. If that's not strong, I don't know what is.

Having killed now the spell of her creative jag with these several perturbations, Clare realized a craving for a cinnamon roll. She rose for the refrigerator and mulled the possibility of making a zine out of this roughing-it thing she was attempting. Like a self-help zine. Lots of kids made those. Her friend Kulani did one about quitting porn. And those drug-recovery ones always empower her.

"Perhaps it would motivate me," she mumbled aloud. Then she thought: It would be harder for me to quit if I felt like all the kids were watching. But my *Moon Bloom* zine ... They like it. They're always looking forward to my space flowers. Perhaps I should stay focused on those. *Bouquets from Triton* might work as a subtitle for this year's Zine-O-Rama edition. And *Glandulus Gonnapopus.* That's right. There's a fine name for the bloom I discovered just now. Why not?

Clare noticed the notification light blinking on her smartphone finally. She jerked open the microwave door to withdraw her smoking cinnamon roll and buttoned the phone's touch screen to life. Upon reading the email she murmured, "Littlefeather? Who the hell is Littlefeather?"

Only as she sank her teeth into the moist cinnamon roll did she realize the Reggae had stopped.

Stanley Donner Jr. climbed out of his green sedan. His legs felt cramped. He stretched them. He shuffled across the asphalt, pulling and twisting at the stiffness in his lower back. Stanley gripped something in his pocket. He shook it. *Rattle. Rattle.*

Now Stanley stood at the foot of his stairway. He hunched there, waiting. A beat, he waited. Then another. Soon several minutes had passed but still Stanley stood, hunched. Finally, he lay his fingers over the handrails. He did not look up. His left foot he lifted to a step. His right. Stanley forced himself to ascend.

Stanley Donner Jr. refused to be destroyed. He wished for his destruction, yes. How Stanley craved his torment's end! *Rattle. Rattle.* But let it come with dignity! He would not go out crushed, a nothing. No. For this alone he ascended these steps to occupy the living area of his three-bedroom condominium. He switched on its overhead lamp. He found his home exactly as he had left it, exactly as he had feared. The room was as disheveled and unattended as his own physical person.

He trembled.

Threading through the many cardboard boxes on the floor he arrived at the kitchenette. Coffee cups in the sink and frozen goods containers on the counter. A flyer on the refrigerator and he was opening a faucet then to fill his hands and splash his gaunt visage with the watery coolness spilling over the bowl of his palms. Stanley drew a glass to drink. He shifted to the sofa then as his face and fingers still dripped. His left hand was sun-burned red, his right hand pinkish pale.

He sat.

"Andorra," Stanley mumbled. He had heard a well-spoken somebody describing a tiny country far away. On the news. On the radio. As he drove for hours and hours and hours. In his green sedan. Stanley reached for his laptop and opened it and suddenly sat studying a map of Andorra. He priced a flight to the country. He goggled 'Andorra citizenship.' He learned that probably he would never be a citizen of Andorra, an Andorran.

Stanley Donner Jr. hunched over the flyer he had taken off the refrigerator door. "Palm Desert Zine Fest," it read. He fixated on the promising words "Everyone Welcome. Everyone Welcome. Everyone Welcome." Along the bottom of the flyer, with other bits of data, a web address appeared in plain typeface. Stanley felt welcomed enough by the words "Everyone Welcome" that he visited that website.

He gazed.

"What is a zine anyway," he mumbled aloud. The question sharpened his curiosity but the homepage did not answer it. Stanley scanned for a blurb, for some boxed definition somewhere on the page to anchor him, to orient him forward. Nothing. A menu pointed to 'exhibitors.' He followed the link. The exhibitors page showed him a black and white illustration of two feet descending steps. The two feet were weighted by thick chains. A description said: "*Cardiac Erect* examines the life adjustments required of persons living with a super-fast heart rate due to Atrial Fibrillation."

"Ah-ha."

Stanley's gaunt aspect stared at the chained ankles.

"Zines must be related to medical care."

The top of another image teased the bottom of Stanley's laptop screen. He scrolled to it. Here a bearded Asian man sat with his elbows on a rectangular table. On the tablecloth before him lay three groups of booklets, each fanned into a semi-circle. The photograph on the cover of one booklet seemed to depict the aftermath of a riot. Was that looting? A political protest? The webpage description said, "*Lollipop Shotgun* is about the contributions zines and zinesters can make to societies in transition."

Stanley scrolled on.

"What?"

Here another photo and description, and another. He reviewed several of these presentations studiously but even after some minutes could not articulate exactly what was a zine.

"How do *Bananafish* and *God's Pussy* and *Walking Men* and *A Death Disco Playlist* relate to one another?" he mumbled aloud.

But Stanley Donner Jr. had forgotten his troubles. And he sat alert and focused and not trembling. Stanley hunched over his laptop and scrolled and gazed through the surreal compendium. Here was a pattern of tarot icons, and images of an old cassette tape deck, and a man wearing pants too big for him, and some kind of three-headed being with an arm growing out of its stomach. Bewildered, Stanley felt. Finally, he opened a new browser tab and just typed into the search engine the words 'zine definition.' Soon he was reading this:

"A zine is a self-published booklet through which independent makers distribute their art or ideas."

Then he read this:

"Zines are usually printed in small-circulation editions and produced to be sold at low cost, traded in kind, or given away for free."

Then he read this:

"A zine often serves as a forum for information, perspectives or voices under-represented or not represented at all by mainstream media."

Stanley sat gazing. He tabbed back to the Palm Desert Zine Fest page. "I'm getting it," he mumbled. "So that man made a magazine, or no, really a booklet about some political cause. And that other woman. Here, she made some sort of pamphlet, or maybe a booklet, about issues related to a chronic health condition."

Stanley skimmed down to where he had stopped, just past *God's Pussy*. He noticed now that a link accompanied each presentation. He clicked the link beneath the following presentation and found behind it a photograph of an older white man in a dark blazer leaning back in a big guffaw. The man held a martini glass in one hand and wore thick-rimmed eyeglasses and a spotted cravat. The title topping that page said *Apologies In Order*. Beneath the title, in a smaller font size: "New America won't be real until Old America has said it's sorry." And then, under the photograph itself, this caption: "This is the fucking chooch who booed Littlefeather."

"Well," Stanley mumbled aloud, as he tabbed back to the zinefest page, as these many disparate elements began to finally assimilate into a coherent understanding. "We got politics here, and people walking around Chicago, and a long insistence that God is a naughty housewife, and some kind of ... revenge activism?"

He checked the date on the flyer: May 26. Two weeks away.

Stanley sat aside his laptop and rose from the couch. He strode to the kitchenette. He did not shuffle now, he strode. Stanley picked up his feet, advancing surely. His working through this *zine's* confusion had suspended his troubles. But then he glimpsed the closed door, that closed door ending the short hallway off the kitchenette. The door was closed tight. Very tight. Stanley flinched. A stab punctured his chest and his troubles swarmed now back over him. Like a wave, his troubles came. Like a warm current rushing his being and dissolving the strength he had just ramshackled together. Zines went forgotten. "I'm so sorry," he mumbled to the closed door. "Please," he mumbled. Stanley looked for the clock: 2:41 p.m. Those few minutes of relief, of being distracted by his curiosity, fell into ancient history. Suddenly they had never really occurred. Stanley refixed the flyer to the refrigerator door. His eyes swept the condominium. The space lay even more unkempt than he. Garbage surrounded him, and half-filled moving boxes. Sunlight broke through cracks in the blinds that covered the glass door of the balcony. He had not thought to pull those blinds open today.

He trembled.

Mechanically Stanley shuffled to a bookcase at the foot of which waited a cardboard box. Stanley sank to his knees. He pressed the heel of his hand against his temple for a beat, collecting himself. Then, determinedly, he placed an anonymous book from a neglected shelf into the lifeless box between his knees. One, two, three more unremarked books he placed into the box. But finally Stanley just could not keep on. A moment later his car keys bulged his pants pocket and dazedly he was descending his stairway yet again. Yet again. He plodded the parking lot, making for his green sedan.

Viola kept her blinds shut but their slats open. The warm glow of the bayside light cheered her, along with the soft airs breezing through her screen. Automobiles loudened the boulevard while she composed this blog entry. The cars roared, just two buildings away. She sat at her desk in her apartment, typing at a sprint.

"Demetria assured me that nothing is up."

With a headband, Viola had pulled her hair up off her brow and tied it into a high puff. She had crisscrossed a white scarf over her baby hairs and edges then, letting the twill cotton rest semi-loose and comfortable against her cinnamon-brown forehead and temples.

"I came right out and asked if she is staying here. I told her I need to know if she is bolting because I need to make plans to cover her side of the rent, to find someone else. But she said not necessary. A couple of weeks ago I started to suspect. And I've only gotten more signals since then as ya'll know from recent posts. So today I just plain asked. Friendly like. She's not my sister but we get along. Some of the boys she brings round are rough but that's okay. And she abides by our agreement that they stay no longer than overnight. So we're doing alright. She says she has no plans to leave. I asked her to just let me know when she decides to move on; that we both know we're not going to spend the rest of our lives together, so when the time comes the time comes."

Viola had shut her door tight despite Demetria being out. Her private space was dominated by a full-size bed which presently served as a platform for two overstuffed banker's boxes and several manuscripts which lie crisscrossed atop each other. Viola's room was close and cluttered, but its restricted area and busyness let her feel safe. She sat relaxed, her elbows resting on the desk. At home, on a sunny afternoon like this, she felt no urge to crimp those elbows up tight against her ribs. Still, she fretted.

"I've had four submissions come in so far and one of them unacceptable. I can't have some non-fairyland interlopers throwing down some fays. I don't mind stories that reflect the times we're surviving, but I don't want to reinforce our traumas. Not down with that. The second story tells of an elf, a teenage elf who assumes the form of a dragon-lobster. He does this to bluster his way out of his hometown, which is described in the story as a giant prison yard. Blew my mind. How's that for a tease for issue nine? Hmm, and another subject line just popped into my inbox: A 'Littlefeather' something. Maybe an American Indian angle.

"I'm sweating some because I need 10 to 12 worthwhile pieces to comprise a zine that's not going to piss ya'll off. I know you're trusting that I am publishing a solid 15 dollars worth of material. If I cheat you, you'll drop me. And that's fair. Then what happens to October rent? So I'm sweating. In the meantime, I snagged a proofreading gig with *Moxie Girls*, out of South Texas. A one-off job. Some college gals down there trying to turn a collaborative zine they had in high school into something more professional. They do this edgy stuff tinged with the sweet. I like how they ride that in-between. Girls who are nice to you as long as you respect them, but who, if you don't ... well ... we all got those daggers in us."

Viola's gaze drifted now off the computer screen and up to her window and then sideward to the work-mussed bedspread. Her nose twitched. Anew she looked through the window and, widening her eyes to its sunbathed blinds, fell to daydreaming. Her small sensitive hands crossed and stroked at her silky biceps. She returned to the blog, eventually.

"Now, when I'm in the moment, I'm fine. In other words, when I'm editing, reading, drawing, laying out -- even printing or shipping -- no problems. It's only when I take a break and think about my situation that *It* starts to come over me. Like now. I feel a drag, a kind of sluggishness as I contemplate all the work spread out across my mattress and I start to worry about getting a job, and then *It* comes. My dear precious fays, a question: Have you ever faced *It* head-on? You know ... *It*. Yeah, *that*. Have you? I'm realizing I gotta stop pretending *It* is not there. I can't keep running from it. Who am I fooling? Only me. Like I said: When everything is going well, when I could take a job or not, when I have a choice, it doesn't freak me out the same. I tell myself I can handle it. When I'm on the shakes, though, and it looks like I might *have* to take a job, well, *It* really starts to get to me. *It* starts to break me down."

Viola pulled her elbows across the desktop. She drew them up close to her ribs, confining her breasts. Her forehead bent then to a raised hand. The twill dryness of the cotton scarf absorbed the damp off her palm. After a beat Viola reached for a large seashell she kept on her desk. She held it over her ear. A hollowness, she heard. A screaming. She rose nervously then to her window to see schoolboys on scooters speeding over the parking lot asphalt. They hopped the speed bumps with daredevil flare. They twirled the footboards of the scooters like turbines. A few seconds later she sat again.

"And then there's this: All this stuff happening on the street has been very triggering. I've had to stop watching news reports. When I'm online I exercise extreme self-discipline now to avoid them. Cookies and algorithms and all that trap are my ogre suddenly. I click on some news story because I want to see that the horrible headline is not true. And then they start feeding me more news stories that make me feel even worse than the first. Ratchets up my freak and suddenly I'm doomscrolling. Besides, what can I do about all this stuff? I don't see how my worrying and sweating changes jailhouse suicides or beautiful black boys being gunned down for nothing. But then I feel obligated in some way to pay attention, as if I'm betraying our struggle by not constantly agonizing. I tell myself our fairy tales address these problems, indirectly. And it's true. Anything that puts us out there in any kind of guise other than The Man's stereotype, anything that dilutes misconceptions of us, helps to break down the mindset that leads to our murders. A jet Cinderella with jerry curls does just that. I've known that since Creation. Always been my theory. But ultimately you *know* that that is not what *O, Kindred* is for. Our zine is about *us*, my fays – proactive. Not about *them* – reactive."

Viola leaned back and crossed her arms again. Though intentionally she kept *O, Kindred* a zine for people of color and by people of color, she *was* considering the possibility of placing it in some white spaces, strategically.

"Anyways, I think I'm doing my part. In my own little way, I am fighting this regression we're resisting. I don't see why I have to watch all these war reports every day and ingest all that blood and guts when all it does is agitate me to the point of immobility."

Inhaling a deep breath Viola shut her great brown eyes. She leaned forward, straight-backed, and fixed her doubled fists onto the prominence of her hip bone, just where it scooped into waist. Viola sighed out the breath and parted her glistening eyelids. She re-read the blog. Before clicking post, she added:

"The trick is to understand what part of *It* I can, in good conscience, ignore, and what part of *It* I *have* to wrestle with honestly for my own personal growth. If I am to offer as much as I can to our struggle, my fays, I have to understand this."

The little dressing room was plush and cozy. Rocky sat on a tufted velvet ottoman between swags of crushed gold curtains as Isabel preened before the mirrors in a sleeveless cardigan waistcoat, testing its fit. She stood in her panties and her socks, with her shapely backside displayed for the mirrors, and her bosomy frontside turned to Rocky. Isabel was a white girl. She cocked a hip and slid her fingertips into the vest's watch pocket, runway style. Rocky's knees leaned sideways out of his short skirt, ladylike.

"That fits just darling," he lilted, breathily. "Hold your left arm down at your side for me, hon, and bend your right arm as if you're carrying a fancy flap bag over that shoulder."

"Like ... there?"

"Yes, yes. Oh! And definitely with an open-neck top under! So becoming. I do believe I'm starting to get excited. And one of those skinny pants we found. Do you see what I'm thinking?"

"Maybe."

43

Isabel chortled, wonderingly. The woman managed a wind power company by day so that she might nurture her passion for the arts by night. She delighted in bohemian attire for the casual fundraisers she often attended. Rocky and she picked through the form-fitting chinos they had unearthed in their digging spree along Melrose Avenue. He encouraged her into a pair, pulling the fabric up over her luxuriant hips and cinching it for her at the waist.

She asked, "And the purse pose again now?"

"Okay, sure," Rocky replied. "But really, doll, that pose is just to help me with perspective. We'll worry about the accessories in a minute. Right now we're going for proof of concept."

Then, proof of concept established, they worked Isabel through a range of color combinations, always referencing that same sleeveless cardigan waistcoat. Finally they decided on cropped olive chinos and a washy orange v-neck tee. The sing-song quality of Rocky's voice thrilled at the resonance in this combo.

"Usually v-necks are problematic for me, sugar, but something about that cut and the lay of this cotton really shows off that lovely bosom of yours. Not many gals could make this vibe work, you know. If you're comfortable with it, my dear, you really should flaunt your talent for crisp casual. It flatters you so. One of my philosophies is to accentuate qualities we have that others do not. I consider it our cosmic obligation. And, look, that slight decolletage of yours is really just glorious for this ensemble."

Isabel beamed. Soon she stood completely fitted out, accessorized, and beholding her reflection. Her sky blue eyes swam with astonishment. She gazed on Rocky like an idol to be worshipped. She said, "If you had any idea how much I love you right now." And then, "How did you know?"

"Oh, and I love you too. You know that, my sweet. Look at you. Sometimes when I freestyle like this with a woman and we find something so original and natural to her it just makes it all worth it ... life I mean. Do you know what I mean?"

She did. But Isabel paused her girlish circling before the mirrors. Still admiring her reflection, she uttered: "When you say that, Rocky, you sound a bit sad." She smiled, inconsistently.

"Oh, please excuse," Rocky murmured. And he ducked his wide nose behind the sheltering fingertips he had raised. Rocky swallowed, his Adam's apple hiking and falling. He studied Isabel from the corner of his eye for a beat, perking his manner with a naive titter. Breathily he confessed, "Maybe just a tad tired, my dear. Or maybe some little identity crisis, you know, my many shades of brown blood confusing themselves. These things ... they come and they go. I really would love to photograph this outfit, Bell. Do you mind?"

He asked if they might make a picture outdoors, in the day's perfect golden light. Then he queried did she want her face included in the shot or would she rather retain her anonymity. As Rocky expected, Isabel, in this sparkle of garments, preferred her face *seen*.

Rocky was the only male ever hired by that West Hollywood ladies' boutique. Eventually, his regular clients always asked (even if belatedly as Isabel just had) how he got started in the trade. "Dressing friends," he sang. "But then there was this day..." And Rocky described an 'Inquire for Position' sign he saw one afternoon in the window of an Anaheim boutique. "I still work with that establishment, you know. I still consider it my home base." Anywho, he had entered the Anaheim boutique to inquire after the sign only to observe a winsome young strawberry blonde traipsing toward the cash wrap with a blouse he *knew* was just *awful* for her. He checked her oh so gently, with a veritable torrent of compliments praising her luminous aura but also bemoaning how that orange fabric would render her complexion just plain invisible. "I couldn't help myself, you know. She was full of so much beauty and she was about to smother it. It was Rocky to the rescue." That soul needed to be known to this world, Rocky believed. And that emerald chiffon mini-dress hanging in the corner would let it be known so very much better. He explained this to the girl in terms of fashion, you know, not in terms of *soul*. "People just clam up when you talk that way, don't they? Anywho, I learned she was going to one of those Mulholland Drive swimming pool shindigs and in a few minutes we had her all dolled up in a way she didn't know she was capable of. A little necklace, we added, dear, and a mini clutch for her clove cigarettes and lighter and personals." Rocky kept her card still, in fact. He considered it a good luck charm since that was the day his new career commenced. "And it has not stopped since. OMG, what a handsome, handsome girl!" They even held hands all the way to the register, like besties. After an exchange of contacts there, and the girl's payment and departure, Rocky recalled his original motive for even entering that Anaheim boutique. Rocky related then his approach to the manager: "My my, I almost forgot, ma'am, that I came in here because of that sign you have in the window. It says there that you just might be seeking fresh personnel." Rocky then raised his eyebrows for Isabel. He lilted, "And do you know what Pretty Mister Jane said to me that day?"

"What, love?"

"She said these words: 'You're hired.' Fancy that! Short and sweet and exactly what I wanted to hear." Rocky tittered, shielding his nose with his fingertips.

And that was how Rockford Williams-Ong got his start dressing all these oh so inspiring lovelies, and helping them to represent to the big round world outside them the tender but indomitable souls they carried inside them. The key to his genius? Why, if you must call it that, there is one. Most importantly, Rocky tells me, one must stay abreast of the norm. It begins there. First, you have to know what everyone is expecting from you, even demanding from you. Then you contrive some mischievous little way to not conform. Something very tiny even. A simple formula. Probably easier said than done. But it works, he says.

"Like that pearl brooch we used for your belt buckle," Rocky explained that day. "You may not realize it, sweet, but that is the linchpin to this outfit. The rest is a variation on the norm. The brooch is your moment of non-conformity. A passer-by or some partygoer on a dance floor sees that and is just thrilled! Absolutely thrilled! Surprise! Something novel! And if the rest of the ensemble sings along to that tune, which this outfit does just righteously, then you've won them over. They belong to you in a way. Bell, honey, you *do do do* look stylin'."

And the photographs were snapped.

Rocky actually had more tangible demonstrations of his philosophy if Isabel cared to see. And since she did, back in the dressing room he pulled one out: Some sheets of paper folded into a booklet and stapled along the bend. The title across the top said *Shake Me The Boom Boom.*

"Why yes, you're not the first to call them paper dolls," he agreed, responding to Isabel's initial blurt. "Except that already they are dressed, I suppose. And glued to the page. I call them instead my *figures.* But it doesn't matter what we name them, does it? We get so many magazines here. A hideaway like this just has to have what's on the catwalk lying around or it isn't taken seriously. But *so many of them?* Once they're passé I just cut them all up when I'm bored. I rearrange, see? That's where the *Shake* in the title comes from. Look, you can see here where I play with my philosophy. This business casual is the norm, isn't it? And look, here is your one dash of non-conformity -- That splash of fancy fuchsia in the shoe clip. If you make it all non-conformist it's too much, love. You disturb people. They don't find it relatable and just go blah, blah, blah in their head. It's necessary to tease them along slowly. Little by little. One brooch-buckle or shoe clip at a time."

And Rocky would love for Isabel to take this little booklet with her. Many like this he had constructed. Sometimes he even sold them. "No, no, this one is a gift." A dear friend, in fact, would be displaying several of his *Boom Booms* at an informal art gathering in Palm Desert, in two weeks. It would be just lovely if she could come. Rocky could not be there himself, however, because of work. Saturday, you know, was just his busiest day. But knowing an old acquaintance found his philosophy as engaging as his penchant for fashion flattered him indeed. Rocky did not feel he deserved so grandiose a compliment. Isabel could always follow his Twitagram too. Sometimes he posted the more shocking of his rearrangements there. You know: Motorcycle helmets meet Gianni meets bowling shoes meet Victoria.

Isabel tapped alive her smartphone for Rocky's @, marveling at not having followed him previously. He shook loose the wooden bangles around his wrist as she bent and pecked. Slyly Rocky spied his own notifications to see he had received a voice mail during his and Isabel's rather extended confab. Always he kept his devices silenced, or off while attending to a darling -- So that he might offer to her the whole of his being. He prinked the shoulders of his blouse. After a flirty exchange of currency then and a parting stroll to the door he and Isabel kissed cheeks. The door shut behind her. Rocky felt then deflated, even forlorn. Always he suffered this depression when one of his princesses left his side. He raised his phone to douse the melancholy.

His pumps clicked now back toward the cash wrap.

Blossom! OMG! She call-called. Is something wrong?

He dialed back.

Blossom answered immediately: "Did you see my email or my post, Rock?"

"No, dear. I've been absolutely overwhelmed by a buxom little gem for some hours now."

"Rock, I found out who booed Littlefeather. I know who he is!"

"You do?! Who?"

47

"Brunton Howell."

"Really? Why, who's that?"

"Some white-ass fuckhead."

Chapter Three
Saturday, May 26

Almost all of us were in the same place again, by coincidence, toward the end of May – all of us except Rocky, who had to work that day. With the giddy feelings of the new zine season having been smoothed away by the first fest in the Kensington neighborhood of San Diego, at the end of April, the mood that permeated Palm Desert was noticeably mellow, despite its being a brand new fest and strangely venued off the grid.

Every year, through the winters, no zinefests took place in those days. Zine makers worked on their projects privately through the darker months, quietly and alone. Part of the reason so many folks had stayed up so late that night in April – at the Taco Snatch and at the cafe – was that the first zinefest always engenders a kind of euphoria, and people need time to come down from it. An impromptu after party had occurred in the parking lot in Kensington, where maybe 70 people just loitered and reconnected. Then someone took up a collection for pizza, which was delivered. Then someone else suggested a midnight movie at the nearby art cinema. Each time the gathering evolved the crowd shrank. But even after the long and incomprehensible Danish film ended folks were still wandering about and winding down, filtering away one by lonely one to different all-night establishments around San Diego and northward.

By the time we all arrived at Palm Desert a month later, therefore, the intoxication accompanying a new zinefest season had dissipated. The difficulties of suitcasing one's products from home to venue and back without damaging them had returned to preeminence; that, and musings on the most attractive arrangement of one's zines for table display. In other words, the edge was off. Routine, though a glad and congenial one, had channeled zinester vigor. That was the mood at The Palm Desert Zine Fest that year. Only really the arriving offered anything noteworthy since several of us experienced the unusual just trying to get there. For now, I'll focus on that.

They were late –

Because the top was down on Easy's convertible and the lights of a police cruiser twirled cherry red and cobalt blue behind it. He and Linda sat on 3rd Street in Riverside, wire wheels and white walls against the curb, waiting for *la jura* to do something. A fair breeze tousled strands of Linda's long brown hair in the daylight air. Easy's do, pomaded and netted, did not move.

With some defiant bounces of his lowrider's nose Easy had solicited this stop on a flippant whim, and before Linda could object. But, with the hit now unfolding, he watched his rearview mirror with gravity. When it seemed the cop had typed his license plate number into his computer terminal Easy would give his angels wings. Night hits were different, more dangerous. For those encounters his angels launched right after Easy slipped his gearshift into park.

The cop stared down. The pivot and slight quiver in his shoulders suggested typing. The typing ceased. Easy chuckled in the depths of his throat. He tapped the *go* button on his smartphone. The PX58 Kirkos drones resting on the Impala's broad back seat began to buzz. They hissed. Then, in a beat, just as the policeman swung open his patrol car door, the drones wavered slowly off Easy's naugahyde upholstery and then rocketed straight up into the air. They stopped at an altitude of forty feet. One drone then floated twenty feet to starboard. After checking their positions with a glance Easy looked to the shoebox-sized computer screen mounted beneath his customized dashboard. Five separate video streams appeared on that screen: a stream of his lowrider from directly above via drone 1, a stream of his lowrider from a thirty-degree angle via drone 2, a stream from the wall-eyed camera affixed to his side mirror, a stream from his dashboard camera, and a stream of his Faustbook page where all of these videos were now being broadcast. A red box in the corner of the Faustbook page blinked the word LIVE. A sixth space remained blank. Easy referred to that last space as *room to grow*.

"Sorry, Lindy," he apologized. "But it's just a day hit."

The cop approached, bulked out by a flack jacket. The viewer counter on the Faustbook page read 23 but ticked upward. As the cop arrived the counter read 50.

"License, registration, and insurance, please."

Drawling out his voice *muy suavecito,* Easy answered: "Of course, officer." He gave his head a cocky *vato* nod and handed over the ready papers with a shrug. The cop received the documents without comment, retracing his steps to his car.

"Well, well," swaggered Easy. He turned full-face to his dashcam now. Not a hint of fear colored his tone or grin. Easy was so merry, in fact, that his ominous wraparound sunglasses seemed

51

even cheerful. "Ladies and *caballeros*, Officer *5.26 stroke 1* is making sure I'm legal. Just so you know, I am supremely legal. Just so you also know, 100 percent of my daytime hits ask for my paperwork and go back to their cars once they see my drones. On the other hand, only 25 percent of my nighttime hits ask for my paperwork. The nighttime chumps usually deal with me before positively identifying me. Do you think that might be because they can't see my equipment as well as these daytime chumps?"

The viewer count had leapt to 300.

Easy and Linda sat wordlessly then, waiting. Finally, Linda muttered, "I'm not feeling this. I'll never get used to it."

"You do."

But Easy watched his rearview mirror intently.

A woman pushing a baby stroller squeaked by on the sidewalk. Then, wiggling around them on the street side, a bicycle rolled past. The bike looked expensive. It was pink, with a rack over its rear tire that held two saddlebags. Easy did not notice the bike but Linda did. She said, quietly, "That white woman's wearing a West Coast Zine Feast shirt." Easy glanced forward. He said nothing.

Then, "Here he comes."

The rubber soles of the cop's shoes approached again. His black uniform and gear-laden belt streamed through Easy's side camera. When the officer stopped and looked down at Ezekial the dashcam included both the cop's head and Easy's. The airborne cameras broadcast a routine traffic stop, seemingly, except for the blood-red convertible. The policeman returned to Easy his documents.

"Mr. Castillo," he said. "I got the impression you were following me. Is that what you were doing?"

"Officer," Easy drawled, shrugging with cholo aplomb. "I was just out showing off my ride. I spend a lot of time keeping this car nice, you know. It's a classic. '64 Impala. 409. Turbo Fire. Hand pinstriped by Derunio." Easy described the car with pride, and in an intimate tone, as if he and the cop were lifelong homeboys and Easy was just updating the man on his ride's latest tricks. "At any rate, since I was barely passing through Riverside I just took the opportunity to share this beauty with my neighbors. You've got a nice downtown area here." Broadly Easy grinned. His bright teeth showed beneath his full mustache, friendly-like.

The policeman smiled in response, even laughed a bit. He hooked his thumbs into the armholes of his flack jacket. He said, amiably: "Just a heads up, Mr. Castillo. Not all law enforcement officers are as tolerant as I am." And without waiting for Easy's honeyed expression of gratitude, the cop pivoted away, marched back to his car, ducked through the door, and, a moment later, lurched off the curb into traffic.

The viewer count had reached 1,021.

Easy exhaled.

He looked rightward to Linda, who sat stiff with unease, unsmiling. When he spoke to the dashcam his tone matched exactly his previous tone. The policeman had not fazed him at all: "That, ladies and gentlemen, was a classic hook and reel. I got him all the way to the shore, *sabes*, but I could not land him. He did everything legal, that one. Sorry, *damas y caballeros,* unfortunately, I cannot complain about Officer *5.26 stroke 1.* Or probably that is fortunate, no?"

A cloud of smiles and hearts floated up the right side of the Faustbook feed.

"Adios, for now, hipsters. Linda and I are on our way to The Palm Desert Zine Fest. We will be streaming from our table in a couple of hours. In the meantime, we're as hungry as *chupacabras* and about to dine finely at the Shaft Burger near Riverside's entrance to the 215 South on 3rd Street. Anyone nearby wanting to scarf with us come on over. But hurry. That's a roger rabbit. Over and out."

The red 'live' button blinked off. While the four streams were rendering into fixed videos Easy bent his head back for the sky. He tapped his smartphone and his angels descended slowly from the heavens to gently occupy the back seat of his lowrider. Linda stated again, "I'll never get used to it."

Easy opened his hand and offered it. Linda's ever-ready smile flashed happy again as she took Easy's bait. Brother and sister slapped palms and bumped fists. The Impala was rumbling.

"Enough day hits like that, *'mana*, and you can take a night one, though it is definitely a different animal. You even get to liking the push and pull of power between you and them. That said, I *am* going to enjoy this smoke."

He craned his mustache forward, drawing on the menthol as he struck a match.

"I guess Officer *5.26 stroke 1* doesn't warrant a zine of his own, huh?"

"Not even close. That one only goes to prove a Riverside day hit fits the pattern of Monterrey Park and the others. He didn't even mention the drones. He either knows the municipal code himself or is just plain afraid of the cameras. Hard to believe my rep has spread this far east."

Then, sighing smoke, "Look there." And Easy pointed to the bicyclist who earlier had passed them. He and Linda were en route to the Shaft Burger. The white woman pumped strenuously at the pedals of a pink touring bike. "That girl in the Zine Feast shirt again."

"Maybe we know her," Linda said.

"I'm hungry. Gotta eat."

Time was running out. Blossom's chin quivered as she realized she was not going to fucking finish. The image she had of Littlefeather's verbal assailant from that backstage journal *Stagecraft* just did not satisfy. And this zine meant too much to her to throw together carelessly, with lazy filler. Besides, though she might print a few copies and bring them along, still she would have to collate, fold and staple them. And all this when she should have left ten minutes ago. So, though Blossom had assembled this zine as rapidly as possible: "The Man Who Booed Littlefeather" would not debut at The Palm Desert Zine Fest as advertised, but instead at The California Zine-O-Rama in two weeks. Blossom growled. Today she would take only earlier issues of *Apologies in Order*, and some of her older personal zines. But she planned to promise a big Los Angeles reveal to the folks who visited her table.

Blossom leaned her chin into her left palm. Her tattoo of blue-black thorns spiraled down her forearm and then back up around her bicep and under her shirtsleeve. Her desk sat against the gabled window of her Inglewood attic apartment as the window's deep recess deflected a watery light across the tiny room. Blossom's decision relaxed the tension across her cheeks. That zine was on hold now. Leaving it for later was the right thing to do even though her failure to finish fucking bitched. Hurriedly she wiggled and rolled porcelain gauges into the holes of her two earlobes and click click clicked to shut down her computer.

Behind her on the floor waited a large plastic crate in which she stored her zinefest paraphernalia. She had learned to put absolutely everything in the same place and to bring absolutely everything with her every time she rode out to a fest. This made it impossible to forget some obscure necessity.

She stood.

Blossom's heavy clothes fell into the shape of a black rectangle.

She bent over the plastic crate, double-checking its contents. As she picked past her tablecloth, and over the boots box which encased her zines, and behind the folding vertical display she used to draw attention to her presentation, Blossom reflected on how fortunate she was that this vile perpetrator still lived. The moment she learned this fact she had experienced a surge of disgusted rage followed by a razor-cold determination. He was old, in his latter seventies surely, but still she had time to demand an apology from him and to right that wrong he left behind. The instant Blossom identified the man she had craved to fucking confront him. Now she knew she could make this happen.

Brunton "Boo Boo" Howell was his name. He had schmoozed the Hollywood elite primarily in the 1970s and 80s, beginning as a publicist in the offices of Polygon Talent Management in 1969. There, after impressing a personal friend of rising star Peter Fonda, he had hustled a gig as a talent agent for some lesser-known actors. In 1973 he wangled a seat at the Oscars through connections, scheming to amplify his exposure and credibility by appearing there among the American royalty of the day. He could never have predicted Littlefeather would provide him so perfect an opportunity to curry favor with the establishment. Howell's outburst convinced Blossom that even just four years into his career "Boo Boo" already enjoyed enough leverage in Hollywood to feel psychological back-up. She felt certain of this. Timid newcomers did not behave that independently. Blossom assumed he was loaded on fucking whiskey sours as well.

She checked her money box for ones and fives, confirming that she had adequate change. She located her card swiper, too, and reminded herself to lay out her Paypal and Venmo welcome mat. Finally, she searched out breath mints. Reassured, Blossom strained the bulky crate off the wooden floor and penguin-walked it down the creaking stairs to the rear doorway. She returned then to her closet for her collapsible wagon.

Blossom envisioned the neighborhood Howell inhabited: That picturesque collection of avenues just south of the Los Angeles County Museum of Art: all those architecturally eclectic three and four-bedroom multi-million dollar bungalows. Regtin Street. 1205. Privacy Invader told her all this. And some Faustbook creeping had shown her that Boo Boo still lived and breathed, though apparently not as shrewdly as in his youth. The man existed and was connected to some plebian friends and family, but lacked the savvy to keep his profile private. But maybe he considered that precaution unnecessary since he never fucking posted anything anyway. Blossom un-ghosted herself finally and sent a few messages through Faustbook, inquiring benignly for an email interview. No response. And her ferreting had overturned no personal email addresses. She wondered what Howell looked like now. She wondered if he even remembered that night back in 1973. Then Blossom wondered what Littlefeather looked like now. Was she still alive too? Why had she not asked herself that question yet? Her obsession with the victimizer, Blossom realized, had obscured from her the victim.

She donned her flack jacket. She attached her spurs to her heavy brown boots.

With her wagon uncollapsed outside on the sidewalk, Blossom penguin-walked her crate through the rear door, her thin arms straightened by its weight. She fit the crate into the wagon, took up the wagon's handle, and realized that definitely she would be late. Blossom marched along now in her dark garb, a seemingly curveless woman, dragging the wagon over the thumping seams of the concrete as her spurs jangled on her heels. She considered a heads-up text to the organizers but calculated she would arrive before they bequeathed away her table.

Here was her car. Last night she had finally found a parking spot a quarter-mile from her attic.

Blossom popped the trunk and hefted into it her crate and wagon. As she did so she committed herself to visiting that neighborhood south of LACMA. Of course, she would! How not? Howell had stiffed her online. And a nice up-to-date photograph of "Boo Boo" would flesh out the zine and ensure greater accountability. Suddenly the idea of confronting this fucking chooch right on his fucking doorstep seemed absolutely fucking necessary to Blossom. Yes! This oppressor would be deprived of the anonymity of time! This man would be remembered for his transgression! He would repent it – if not with an objective apology to the human beings he denigrated, at least with private regrets. I'll fucking see to that, Blossom thought. She felt glad now to have not finished the zine. It wasn't ready.

She slid into the driver's seat of her brown '95 Accord, panting slightly with her hurried efforts. She whipped out her phone, punched a text to Rocky, and mounted the phone in its dash bracket.

"Sure you can't come?" she asked.

Her shaved scalp tilted then through her window and into the day's glorious sunbath, checking for traffic. Nothing. A tight U-turn she hooked out of her parking spot. About the time Blossom engaged her right turn indicator to pull off 118th and out of her neighborhood Rocky's response dinged.

"Working, dear. Sorry. Did you finish it? Are you already in Palm Desert? Good luck, golden child."

Blossom accelerated onto Aviation Boulevard, heading for the 105 West. She would answer Rocky from the zinefest.

"See this isn't so hard. I'm running a little late, I guess, but I'll make it. Eventually. No worries."

Clare rode Vine Street in downtown Riverside, pedaling along the sidewalk. About three blocks ago a Metrolink porter had helped hoist her bike off the commuter train's bicycle car and now she was steering for Interstate 215 South. She did not know interstate highways forbade the use of bicycles. Never had Clare cause to even wonder about such a prohibition, or to remark the absence of cyclists on highways. So, blissfully unknowing, she rolled on quite confident.

She cornered Third Street, about a half-mile past the commuter depot, and felt already quite misty. A midday May morning makes for fine riding in West LA, perhaps. But out easterly toward the desert, here beyond the train terminal in the Inland Empire, the sun burned already hot, portending its summer fierceness. Eighty degrees at barely 10 a.m, and so bright Clare was almost squinting behind her wayfarers.

Clare now thought that kind gentleman with the unibrow in Culver City sublimely knowledgeable and imminently professional. He had insisted she purchase a touring bike for this trip. How right he was! The rear tire mount and pretty lilac

57

saddlebags he had sold her also worked perfectly for groceries, and they were attachable to either of her bikes. Panniers, he called them. But why call them something other than saddlebags? That's what they looked like. Right now her saddlebags hung laden with all the accoutrements of her zinefest table. Clare had packed her *Moon Bloom* zines in there, and a pastel green cloth to cover the tabletop, and two orange ceramic planets with which to ornament her display. Clare also had her candy dish and free sweets. And she had remembered this time to bring change, thank God -- lots of fives and ones, along with a card reader for her phone so she could swipe plastic if necessary.

Sixty-seven miles to go.

So Clare was zooming along now and feeling quite in charge and very self-sufficient. She cranked at the pedals hard since her maps app said she was running late. She rode toward the on-ramp through some scattered gravel and gutter clutter until a sluggishness pulled at her. Clare squinched her face. For a beat, she wondered. In the next beat, she told herself surely that drag she felt was nothing, was imaginary. But then, cranking on, she sludged to a slow and finally impossible go. Clare tried to force the bike onward.

The front tire was flat.

Sixty-six miles to go.

Clare dismounted, toed out the kickstand, and stared, arms akimbo.

She deflated inside.

Maps said she had just enough time to get to Palm Desert if ... wait, it said she had just enough time to get to Palm Desert *if she were a car! What?!* Clare's heart tumbled. *What?!* She palmed her brow. Only just now had Clare noticed the bicycle icon above the map's traffic view. She touched it. *Six and a half hours?* The zinefest would be way over by then. What kind of goof is that? Clare had never known Palm Desert was like a whole state away. She swayed on her feet for a beat, glaring in astonishment at her phone screen. That's too far, she thought to herself. I mean, I'm already misty and it's only been like fifteen minutes.

Honk. Honk.

She looked over her shoulder.

Honk. Honk.

I guess I'm in people's way, or something. So sorry. But then: Wait, these car people can just get over themselves. Clare handled her touring bike up over the curb and dragged it to a plot of dirty grass that framed the sequoia-like signpost of a five-story tall Arco marquee. There she toed out again the kickstand.

"What now?"

She calculated a few numbers in her head, wiped the mist off her brow, and plopped down on the grass to tap the Uber app on her phone. Of course. The solution. Her fingers hovered then, however, hesitated. Almost she touched "set pickup location" but checked her intent. Her hand trembled.

C'mon, this is when it counts, she was telling herself. Hailing Uber is soft, she scolded herself. I have to deal with this myself. My mistake. Face it. This is what it means to be strong, right? The zinefest is off. So accept it. Perhaps missing it is the punishment I deserve for being such an asshat. I do know how to fix this tire, though! And I brought my tools -- that third-hand contraption. I am ready for every little thing, I am. Flexy. That's me. After the repair, I'll make myself ride all the way back home without the help of Metrolink. There. A mixture of punishment and training, that will be. That's what that ride will be.

Clare palmed her eyes.

Six and half hours?

Total defeat.

But she did swipe away the Uber order page, steady her hands, and rise. To her left, in the near distance, a man sporting a flack jacket took a squared stance before the Arco. He examined Clare too aggressively. Irked to womanly defiance, Clare matched his steady gaze through her wayfarers and approached the mart's glass doors on a poised and dancerly stride. She wore today her lucky West Coast Zine Feast shirt. The shirt was lucky for having entered her life at her very first zinefest. Besides the miracle of being accepted to The Feast on her first attempt three years ago, that day Clare had actually sold out of *Moon Bloom*, her premier issue. Also the t-shirt was pink.

After acquiring an ice-cold Diet FizzBang Clare swilled a few gulps of its tickling carbonation and ambled again to her saddlebags. She rummaged for repair tools, feeling much in command now. Another swish of FizzBang then and Clare buttoned on her phone. In the SkipTube app she touched history and, for a memory refresher, scrolled to a previously consulted "How to fix a bicycle flat" video.

"I gotta turn your pink ass upside down, I guess," she sighed. "Okay, so I gotta unhitch my saddlebags, I guess."

Clare contemplated her long fingernails, squinting at them with concern. But that feeling of command rose in her again. She felt resourceful.

Honk. Honk.

"Oh, whatevs," she thought, bending to her saddlebags.

Honk. Honk.

"Oh, c'mon. These car people." From her stooped pose, looking upside down through the triangle of her hiked elbow, Clare saw an old red car. Its chrome bumper shined like a pristine mirror as the vehicle sat diagonally behind her, its exhaust pipes grumbling.

"Hey, don't I know you?" called a masculine voice.

Clare straightened, pivoted. A guy spoke from the driver's seat of the old convertible. He wore wraparound sunglasses and a dark mustache which brightened his grinning teeth. In the passenger seat nodded a girl, smiling also. Her ponytail hung long and straight and black, and even from that distance, Clare could descry her heavy eyeliner. Clare's first impression of the couple mixed a vague familiarity with an instinctual fear for unknown men who give uninvited attention. Her features puckered. She felt glad of her sunglasses. She was hiding behind them.

To buy a few more seconds of assessment, she uttered, weakly, "What?"

"Is that a West Coast Zine Feast shirt?" asked the cat-eyed girl.

A little confounded, Clare answered, "Yes."

"Hey," said the man, more gently. "Are you stuck? You going to Palm Desert?"

Clare tensed, visibly. Confusion muddled her. Her mind was a row of numbers trying to add themselves up but failing. She said, "So sorry. I don't really remember you. The zinefest, you mean?"

"Yeah, Palm Desert Zine Fest," he said. "I swear I recognize you from somewhere. We're on our way there."

The pony-tailed girl offered, smiling, "Jump in. We'll give you a ride. You weren't riding your bike out there were you?"

"I was going to."

"No way," said the girl.

"I was going to," Clare insisted.

The gear shift on the steering column of the dark red antique drum rolled into park. The girl leaned over the passenger door now, her arms hanging down, her ponytail dangling free, a big happy grin on her face. The guy with the mustache stood over her touring bike suddenly. He smelled like spearmint.

"You fixing that?"

The spearmint awakened Clare. The guy removed his wraparounds, unveiling two great brown eyes. Again he seemed familiar. Clare glanced to the girl in the car, groping for some reference that might help her identify them. She said to the guy, "I was going to."

"Tough. If you want, you know. I can put it in my trunk. That trunk's the size of a garage. You can worry about the flat later."

"Jump in," said the girl, laughing. "We're okay. We're going to Palm Desert Zine Fest. You look familiar but I can't remember your zine."

"Well, thanks," Clare replied, gaining confidence. "It's called *Moon Bloom*."

"Yeah, yeah. I remember now. You shared a table with *Lollipop Shotgun* once. You did The South Bay Zine Bazaar last year."

"Yeah, okay," Clare said, at ease. They had friends in common. She was safe.

"No sweat," announced the mustache. He wedged his wraparounds back over his nose as his broad frame strode to the pinstriped trunk.

They had to detach and stow the bicycle's front tire and pannier rack in the corners of the trunk before the guy could angle the rest of the bike around the lowrider's hydraulic pumps and batteries. But before 10 minutes had elapsed Clare had plopped onto the sofa-sized backseat with her saddlebags and the blood-red Impala was rumbling in a left turn lane, about to ramp onto the 215 South. The guy had topped the convertible so they could hear each other over the wind.

The girl said, "*Lollipop Shotgun* was our tablemate in Tijuana last year, at The Baja Zine Fiesta. You know Koji?"

"Tia-juana?" Clare said.

"You done that fest before?"

"No."

"It's so bomb."

"Koji? Yeah, I know him." Clare was massaging her hands with a moist towelette now, cleaning them deeply. She squinted at

61

the large flatscreen computer monitor on the seat beside her, along with the box of apparent zinefest materiel on the floorboard there. "I know Jeremias better, though – his illustrator. Jerry helps me come up with phony scientific names for my space flowers occasionally. We kind of collaborate when we drink and draw."

"*Órale*," put the mustache. "You really were riding that bike out to Palm Desert?"

"Yeah," she said quietly.

"Tough. What route were you taking?"

"I-10 all the way to Cook Street, I guess, according to maps. Definitely it was going to be my hardest ride of all time."

"I-10?" he questioned. "You know it's illegal to ride a bicycle on I-10, don't you?"

"Oh, no," said Clare. "It is?"

"Yeah, nothing lighter than a motorcycle on the highway."

By now the chrome exhaust pipes of the lowrider roared with exertion as the Impala gained elevation toward high desert.

"Oh, I didn't know that."

Clare squinted at the mountains before them.

White dust clouded up from the rolling of the green sedan. The runnels grooving this unpaved desert road jarred and thunked the car. Stanley Donner Jr. rode slowly, bouncing. He felt no urgency to arrive even though he knew the zinefest had begun hours back. His left arm rest over the open window of his driver's side door, its flesh broiling in the sun. No other vehicles tracked this road right now. Stanley drove it solo, creeping the green sedan along, thunking, raising the white dust.

A lonesome structure rose on the horizon, visible through clusters of creosote, through staggering Joshua Trees, between solitary sentinels of yucca. From a distance, among that austere flora, the structure appeared squat and rectangular. But as Stanley closened and parked the building resolved instead to two different structures, both square. He heard a drift of live music off the far edifice. People loitered in front of both buildings. Stanley unbent his gaunt frame from the green sedan. He twisted his bony spine and stretched forth his cramped legs. He straightened the shoulders of his rumpled shirt then. Stanley Donner Jr. stood appraising the scene rather numbly.

Carefully then, tentatively, he hunched toward the nearer edifice, the quieter one. A sandwich board announced "Palm Desert Zine Fest" with an arrow directing him toward two open doors. A few unimposing tables sat outside the building. Behind the nearest of those tables, a young white woman gazed out at the Mohave mountainscape while a young Korean man sat next to her and frowned rather severely into an open book. Many tables were inside, Stanley saw. In his hand he gripped, nervously, the bulletin board flyer from the San Diego cafe. The words across its bottom encouraged him. "Everyone Welcome," they said. "Everyone Welcome. Everyone Welcome."

Stanley Donner Jr. hesitantly shuffled up to the outdoor table. It was covered with booklets, or pamphlets, or these so-called *zines*. The young white woman gave Stanley a sharp but inviting smile. The young Korean man glanced up too, though offering a more removed and distant mien. Neither shied from Stanley's unkempt appearance, nor his skeletal aspect, nor his disturbed look. They just accepted him. In fact, the white woman even made eye contact with Stanley, and then held that eye contact. When she did this Stanley felt like a person. When she did this he felt truly welcomed. Finding confidence in this first contact Stanley hunched closer now to the young white woman, bending over the table between them. After a few moments, he spoke.

"Did you make this?" He pointed at a booklet. He did not touch the booklet.

"Yes, I did."

Thoughtfully: "How did you make it?"

The young white woman picked up the zine and handed it to Stanley. Her sharp smile warmed and her green eyes sparkled. She said, "Here you go. Have a look. Flip through it. It's easy. Just an idea and a copy machine and a stapler and boom you're there."

Slowly, Stanley began turning the pages of the zine he now reluctantly held. The disturbance in his eyes softened, and their lids widened. He viewed some drawings of a red cat sitting on a window ledge, and of a street littered with overturned trash cans.

The young white woman asked, "You ever been to a zinefest before? Or made a zine?"

Stanley did not look up from the drawings. He turned another page. A little dazed, he answered distractedly, "In truth, no I have not."

"There's a schedule on the wall inside. They have a zine-making workshop at 2:30. Try it out if you want. You can make your first zine right here."

Stanley looked up then. He saw the double doors standing open behind the white woman's gesture. Rows of tables walled that space. And other tables had been arranged, mid-room, into an island. A dozen or so persons leaned or milled among the tables, perusing the zines or conversing. The wail of an unintelligible lyric floated to Stanley on a punkish riff. The sound faded out then beyond the distant building.

"2:30?"

"That's right."

Stanley Donner Jr. dropped his attention back to the booklet he held. Each page he turned carefully, skimming over speech balloons that quoted oddly spelled versions of a cat's meow. He could not comprehend the plot, he realized, without a thorough reading, so he asked the young white woman: "What is your zine about?"

She explained, amiably: "It's a comic about a girl who is following her cat around just before the end of the world. Her cat *knows* the world is going to end even though humans do not yet know. And the girl understands her cat intuitively, right? So it's this unsettling story where you watch her following around her cat and sensing through the cat's strange meows how everything is about to go to shit. There are a lot of overturned trash cans in this story because the world is about to become a giant overturned trash can."

Stanley was squinting, suspicious. He felt himself distrusting the young white woman. He pressed, slowly, abstractedly, "You made a booklet about that?"

"Yeah, sure," she answered. "Zines can be about anything. Things you love: Sharks. Polyamoury. Rocket ships. Things you hate too. Like acne, or maybe my menstrual cramps, or Karens. Sometimes people work through their personal problems in them. Self-help zines and such. Whatever."

Stanley flinched. His shoulders hunched a little more and his cheeks rose against the startled globes of his eyes. A hand entered the pocket of his ragged pants. Its fingers gripped something there. The shaking of a container full of loose, hard objects was heard. *Rattle. Rattle.*

"And you sell it?" he breathed.

She leaned back, offering a good-natured arch of eyebrow.

"It's not about selling, really, though that happens. It's really more about sharing and being a part of the community. Most folks just hope to break even. You know, like a self-supporting hobby."

Stanley's flinch smoothed, but now he slightly trembled. Laying down *The Lap Cat of the Apocalypse, Issue One,* he bent over issues two, three, and four studiously, inching rightward until at last he stood in front of the white woman's tablemate. The Korean man still frowned into his open book. But the youth had nodded during the woman's explaining and had seemed even to participate in their conversation without ever looking up or interjecting even a grunt. On the cover of his zine appeared a frowning character who obviously served as a self-caricature. A speech balloon above him said: "I Do Not Have A 12-Inch Dick."

Stanley scratched at his mussed hair. He shoulder-wiped the sheen of sweat that the desert air had already leached through his gaunt features.

He said, "I think I'm starting to understand. And then you all get together maybe once a year like this. Like a generalized market."

"In some places that's how it is," the white woman said. "But around here there are a lot of zinefests. This is actually a small one, and quite out of the way as you probably noticed. One of the biggest zinefests of the year is in just two weeks in Los Angeles. The California Zine-O-Rama, it's called. I didn't get accepted to that one but a couple of zinesters here did."

She gestured backward, vaguely, still smiling.

"I'll attend it, though. The other big ones are in Long Beach and San Diego and Anaheim."

Stanley, directed by the woman's indistinct wave, considered again the building's interior. Maybe 15 tables inside showcased 30 or so zine makers. He stood close enough that a few of the exhibitors nearer the open doors noticed his interest and matched it, staring back at him. A mustachioed man with thick eyeglasses was one of them. That guy looked past a man in a red and black hoodie who handled something in a frame. From the back of the room too, another face emerged. Its features seemed familiar to Stanley even before his mind recalled their identity. Stanley recognized the afro then, and the long elegant neck, and the fine shoulders. He flinched. In the distance, a rough cover of a song by The Smiths began.

Stanley stood slightly bewildered now, unsure. And the young white woman peered at him with her own sudden uncertainty and caution. He stared. Slowly, hoarsely, he asked, "They have these in Los Angeles too?"

"They're all over SoCal," she said. "There's like twenty of them. From LA, to way out here, even down to Tia-juana. That's one of the more famous ones."

"Tijuana?"

And Stanley Donner Jr. gulped air at this. Visibly his bewilderment worsened. Suddenly, in fact, he swayed on his feet. Stanley put his hand down on the zine table. His red hand he put down, the one sunburnt by all his driving. Stanley steadied himself against the table.

"Dude, you okay?" blurted the Korean guy. "You need to sit down?"

Stanley kept his balance. "What's that about Tijuana?" Again he coughed, dryly.

"Here you want some water?" the young white woman quickly offered. "You look like you're about to faint."

Stanley accepted the water bottle. He swallowed from its plastic mouth. He exhaled. Alarm possessed the young white woman, he saw. He wished she would talk more about this Tijuana zinefest, but he could not bring himself to beg the question. *Tijuana.* Stanley pressed the heel of his hand against his chest then and swallowed more water. He said nothing. This determined effort firmed Stanley's stance. It hardened and cleared his expression. His recovery gave the young white woman the confidence to prompt, "That workshop starts in a few minutes, just in the back of the building."

Stanley Donner Jr. shook his head negatively. He breathed: "I need to splash my face." Apologizing then, with grim purpose, he hunched away from the zine table. Stanley used the water bottle to freshen his face beside his green sedan. Then he got into the car and slowly thunked away.

The Palm Desert Zine Fest had ended hours ago. Viola sat in the all-night diner opposite her apartment complex, in a corner booth abutting the window. The server Lupe did not mind her ordering only a decaf and sitting forever, clacking at her keyboard like a steamboat making time. Sometimes, late like this, the two women indulged long confabs about anything: Teaching English in Tegucigalpa, the belligerent line cook, Disneyland. Right now Viola further tightened her earbuds. Their bright blue color complemented the ribbon knotting the low ponytail into which she had hurried her afro after the fest. The buds filled Viola's ears with the sounds of river rapids, canceling out the soul-starved pop music that possessed the diner. Her deft hands fell to the laptop and set the cursor racing left to right across the flat white screen.

"The Zine-O-Rama is coming up in a couple of weeks which is timely since I will be needing coin and that is always one of our biggest sales dates. I tabled at the new Palm Desert fest today. I'm here tonight coming down from that high. I just can never sleep after all that razzmatazz. Shoutout to my homegirl Vivian for riding me all the way out there. The fest was small and I sat in a back corner, unluckily, out of the natural flow of traffic. But it was a true zine crowd, nobody pronouncing the word wrong. This can be either good or bad, depending on what part of your audience you're itching to cultivate. Some folx recognized me and one brother I haven't seen in a minute brought himself up to date by buying two back issues. This was Palm Desert's first year and though I would not call the fest a grand slam, I would call it a home run. Renee and Igor did us right by advertising, even flyering Palm Springs, and it's always dope to see the community growing. Next year I'm sure they'll get more attendees. At the end of the day I felt my regular weariness and that dry throat I get from all those hours of explaining and pitching our work.

"Today was profitable, in any event, and I'm deciding because of it to prep heavy for the Zine-O-Rama in LA. Last year we sold almost one hundred units there, my fays. At year's end, I saw that that was the day that kept me in the black. But that big bump has always come from somewhere. The year before it was The Feast in Long Beach. I've ordered another run of issue six since interest in our cross-dressing reverse centaur continues, and might even be growing. Wouldn't I love a sequel to that story! Two issues moving like number six would be lavish."

Warmly smiling now, even showing her teeth, Viola nodded affirmatively to a gesturing Lupe who splashed her coffee cup full. Lupe stooped then in an approving way, almost maternally, to peek at the computer screen. Viola did not mind. The old woman's white waist apron hung forward with the weight of her ticket book for a few seconds. The decaf smoked. Finally, Lupe placed her finger on the screen. "Cross-dressing reverse centaur?" But before Viola could tug out an earbud to reply Lupe had skipped away.

She typed on: "Sometimes I remember when I was desperate for submissions in the beginning and I get so afraid of suffering it again that I think: 'Just send me any ole thang, for God's sake, any kinda fairy tale will do.' Okay, not there yet. I have eight workable pieces, just so ya'll know. But I'm getting so accustomed to this fanciful genre that everything looks the same to me. I wait and wait for something fresh and everything looks the same. No offense to my beloved fays who are sending me your love and craft. It's an editor's problem. Here, let me put it in perspective. I even felt like this about issue six. And, as we all know, issue six *kills*. Ziggy even told me he saw a graffiti stencil of our reverse centaur on a bridge over the LA River. I have not, however, seen that tag myself, and that is just too flattering a compliment to accept without having seen it myself."

Viola stalled her galloping fingers. Her eyes darted off screen. They crossed five lanes of broken traffic then to land at her apartment complex. There, she could just make out the building she and Demetria inhabited. It backed the building which fronted the street. A tall brick wall divides those apartments from the public sidewalk and in that moment of that night a man sat leaning against that brick wall, among the shrubs, with his mismatched boots propped up on the bottom rack of his top-heavy shopping cart. Viola recognized him -- An angry white man full of defiant, aggressive stares.

"Feeling stable. Things are semi-solid right now so I'm not troubled by *It* the way I am sometimes. I haven't had to consider getting a job lately so my sweat attacks have not come. This is the best time of year for me. At this time of year I feel like I have some control over the direction of my life. And laying off internet news reports has been a great plus. Seems like it takes 10 days or so to get those traumas out of my being. But as soon as I purge them I can look forward and really try. I paddle along smooth as silk then with our work, precious, and really feel productive. In other words, I have no idea what horrors have happened in the streets in the past couple of weeks and I feel very steady and strong and engaged because of it, doing my part."

Viola scowled now. She felt grateful this diner did not hang a dozen television sets in your face like so many others did. The news reports which disturbed her so profoundly, she had begun to believe, amounted to a kind of propaganda. Someone somewhere was purposefully using them to paralyze people like herself. Viola's elbows tucked in tight against her rib cage. Her great brown eyes swept the dining room cautiously. She found Lupe leaning her hip against a stainless steel counter near the emergency exit, holding her weight on one locked leg, the other slightly bent. The brown old woman puckered her lips in concentration, the tip of her tongue walking the fence line of her upper teeth. She scribbled on a slip of paper. A pile of cash lay on the counter before her.

Viola eased her shoulders.

"I've been considering distributing unsold back copies of *O, Kindred* in some white spaces where people read a lot. For free. I thought to just give them away at zinefests, but that might cut into sales. Anyways, if I can't seem to sell a particular issue (uh, hum – issue 3), I might as well use it to abide by my own philosophy and break down their stereotypes by spreading our truth. Taking on these problems deliberately makes me feel like I'm swimming somewhere in particular instead of just being pushed around by the currents of my fear.

"There, I said it. I finally named *It* for you. I guess I can talk about *It* right now because I'm feeling so together. Are you disappointed when I tell you that for me *It* is just fear? F-E-A-R. Well, if that simple word disappoints you, it's because that word means something different to you than to me. Sometimes I call it my ogre, my demon, my terrorist. Hmm. How can I put it that makes you feel what I feel? Maybe that to me fear is that nightmare you only have a couple of times a year. Or less. That one where you wake up panting, out of breath, in a sweat. That's fear to me. But it doesn't just happen to me a couple times a year. Anytime I'm out of my apartment it might happen. Or, especially, put me in a job where a bunch of people are always hounding me, or looking at me for some reason -- like one of these beleaguered diner waitresses here -- then it's triggering all the time. *All the time.* The panting never really stops inside me then. When I work those jobs people ask sometimes why do I look so uncomfortable? But they just don't know how much control it takes to look just *uncomfortable.* Anyways, to me, *It* is fear. But *It* might be something else for you. *It* can be lots of things. Don't wanna think about it no more."

69

Viola pressed together her plush lips and suddenly folded closed the laptop. She sagged into the vinyl cushions of the diner booth then, scanning the restaurant for her girl Lupe. The decaf sat smoking, two plastic creamers just beside. Lupe had refilled it with a motherly wink before her exit. *Sweetheart. Is it that late? Just a single server remained on the floor. Must be after 3 a.m.,* Viola thought, confirming this with her phone. Through the window, she saw that angry white man still in the bushes, but sleeping now. Through the window, she saw the darkness that separated her from home.

Rocky tried to imagine the Palm Desert Zine Fest: *Wonder what it was like out there off the grid?* He took up his scissors. He lay down again his scissors. Rocky sighed. He took up again his scissors. But, before laying them back down again, he thought: *You need to make sure you don't blow off the Zine-O-Rama, son. You need that connection to community. That's what's wrong with you tonight, you big brown recluse.* Rocky chided himself for ditching Palm Desert. No excuse. He knew how to wheedle Pretty Mister Jane out of an unexpected day off, even on short notice. *When is that darling ever going to hire another floorwalker?*

Rocky mulled playing some music.

Okay, some music. Put some music on, you. Some nice cathartic melancholy stuff with a moody background and some reverb bass. That would soothe your blue. Look, reverb bass. That's it.

"Okay," Rocky said aloud.

But instead, he remoted the television to life. The idea of chatting human beings drew him irresistibly. Friendlier, it felt, less lonesome. The screen flickered and Rocky dimmed its volume enough that he could not clearly understand the give and take between Bill Gates and an obviously very skeptical journalist. He took up again his scissors.

Rocky sat on the floor in his panties, cross-legged, in the drone of the TV, with his fashion magazines and antique look books in haphazard array about him. He had hiked up his skirt to his waist, very neatly. He had refit the wooden bangles of his right wrist to his left – to quieten their clank as he snipped. Out of a celebrity mag, he carved now a pair of crayon yellow lips. Some recent starlet. *Oh, I don't know her name.* But Rocky just adored her yellow mouth. He lay the lips aside. Now around a pair of rangy

70

legs, he cut, careful to retain their bobby socks. *Ahh. Love these sneakers. Love the bendy gym energy in these gams. Ahh. Why, this is suburban pep club stuff, really.* Rocky reflected on how his scissoring removed brands, and how so few shoppers could reliably distinguish between brand A and brand B without tags or logos just spelling it out for them. *What does that say,* he wondered. *Are styles really defined by actual style or by the* brainwashing *of marketers?*

Everything seemed so blah, blah, blah.

But I suppose they don't have much choice, poor fellas. If they want to make money, that is. People want *to conform. So you gotta make attire that helps them conform or they just won't buy it. Why else would people patronize malls? So what's a poor soul like Neiman Marcus to do? And that fancy pants boy Chico? They are just downright barred from following your rule of style, Rock. And, besides, are you really any different, you big apple-shaped freak? Are you really so original? Look, people at zinefests seem to like my figures. Maybe if I branded myself like the big boys ... Look, how about your idea of giving outfits names the way bartenders name cocktails? I could start doing that. What would a Mint Julep look like on a person? Or a Hanky Panky? And what would you name, say, these yellow lips over these tweeny gym shoes? How about a Gangly Smooch? Now there. Now that's just stylin'. Who wouldn't want to drink a Gangly Smooch? And then, after drinking it, dress themselves in it. LOL. I suppose you would have to add a nice long necklace to that cocktail, one with a fancy plumb bob on the end of it.*

Rocky threw down his scissors.

His hands rose to cover his wide nose.

They shook.

"Okay, okay," he mumbled aloud, shaking a bangle off his wrist. And, "So strange to be me. Not working. This isn't working. Do other people do this? I mean, you *know* you're not going to start naming your outfits! That would not last one single day!"

Rocky barked these words at himself contemptuously, aloud, with a deep-seated savagery that no one besides him would ever hear. He adjusted a bra strap. He adjusted the other. He counseled himself then, in silence: *None of this is lightening your depression, Rockford. Contain that Williams in you, for Pete's sake. Maybe if I fantasized about yesterday's husky little lifeguard. What an endearing laugh she had. And how those lovelies always assume I'm gay. It just turns their self-protection radar right off, doesn't it? But that Indonesian darling from last week needs to get away from her boyfriend.*

Still, she haunts me. I've never even seen them together and it's so obvious he's chipping away at her confidence.

Usually, Rocky's clients disrobed right in front of him. Just two days previous, for example, he had occupied dressing room 1 with Caroline, a professional black woman of five-four height with a buxom cup and uncommonly pretty knees. She worked in gaming somewhere. A technical designer. Instantly she had just peeled off her clothes – eager for Rocky to redress her into the diva they both believed her to be. Rocky had curated a debonair blazer that gathered to her curves just right. Vintage. Red. With velvet collar. And its fine vertical pinstripes stretched her proportions attractively. Caroline was thrilled. All very last minute. And just what she needed, she said, to calm her nerves for a Friday presentation concerning some new first-person shooter.

If ever that sweetheart knew I was straight and moved by the perk of her nipples, I'm afraid she would just feel violated.

Guilt, Rocky felt.

You can never let that happen! OMG! You must never never never let your desire show!

But also trapped, Rocky felt.

For he adored the clients he catered to. In fact, he just lived to buttress the assurance and pride in these women, to coax them into an indomitable strut. Their initial trust in him, however, always sprang from their reading him as homosexual. And he had learned that disabusing the darlings of this misconception cost him dearly. *Straightness* killed his appointment calendar. It hit his pocketbook. For some reason, his *gayness* just drew to him so many regular gals. So imposture and shame had become an integral part of Rocky's livelihood -- an occupational hazard, so to speak.

I bet some of them don't even undress like that for their husbands. How can you sit in that boudoir, son, in that sacred little bubble with these precious souls and deceive them like you do? Is this part of your problem? Yes, yes, it must be: That you're carrying on with the dears in such dishonesty, and so incessantly -- Just clamping down on that passion of yours -- Not being yourself -- Just lying about it all the time -- Not being yourself -- Not being yourself -- Acting. It's warped me. Got me twisted inside. Can't stop thinking about it. If you really cared about the darlings you would be honest with them. But of course I cannot do that. They would abandon me. Look, maybe I should turn the question around and put it this way: What would I have to do to sit in those

72

dressing rooms with my princesses and have my presence be completely and totally and absolutely honest?

Rocky quit snipping. A naked sternum lay on the carpet before him. He had cropped off a perfume model's head, and her shoulders and arms. He had severed her at the waist too. Only the open flesh between the button plackets of her undone blouse remained. That's all. A woman's breastbone. Just the skin over a woman's heart. Rocky's daydreaming had ruined this cut-out, he realized. This triangle of flesh was hardly recognizable in isolation. It meant nothing.

He thought: *What a roundabout way to come to the point. Always it comes back to this, doesn't it? This: That I've got a woman's heart. Really I'm a woman. I'm just a woman who loves women. When am I going to accept this?*

Rocky lay down again the scissors. He handled the remote control and transformed the unbelieved pandemic warnings into a dead black screen. His eyes lingered over this fresh collage material -- over the crayon yellow lips, over the gangly ninth-grader limbs, over the anonymous womanly sternum.

That's all me. I am that disassembled figure. In pieces. Disconnected. Unarranged. What difference does it make that I'm attracted to women? That I want to sleep with them? I need to bring myself together now. Become whole. I am a woman. I need to let myself be a woman.

Rocky leaned back, bracing his shoulders against the seat of the sofa. He stretched his torso then and reached past his hiked-up skirt and into his panties. With a thumb and two fingers, he took a hold of his warm cock. He pulled it forth. Rocky gazed on that appendage as if it were a completely foreign object suddenly, as if it were a riddle totally inscrutable. Staring at it, he said, "This isn't me."

Chapter Four
The California Zine-O-Rama

Stanley Donner Jr. stood bug-eyed. The roar of the convention hall swamped his senses. A buzzing of writhing bodies moving and bending as zinesters sat or leaned and attendees shifted or angled through people around or against tables colored from fuchsia to pastel to black with blazing booklets. And noise. The voice noise. Cackling and hellos and spiels shouted over other spiels and goodbyes and chattering. It smothered. Stanley hunched toward a large rectangular map, examining its floor plan and legend. He sought to orient himself in this melee, to establish some point of reference from which to process the happy mosh. The table nearest him, the one busy with black t-shirts, was the information table, according to the map. Beyond that Stanley saw the enclosure broaden -- the walls swept back, the ceiling rose higher, and the depths of the space retreated out of focus.

This was The California Zine-O-Rama.

"Nothing like what I saw out in the desert," he mumbled to himself, aloud.

With his mind still acclimating to the chaos, Stanley recalled his principal reason for attending this fest. The legend along the bottom of the map named and numbered each exhibitor; and the numbers were plotted across the floor plan. Stanley looked for names like "afro" and "elegant neck" and "fine shoulders," but read instead titles like *SlapDown* and *Vomiting Plastic* and *Lollipop Shotgun* and *How to French Kiss Oprah While Reading Proust*. He reviewed the entire list. The bizarre amalgamations of imagery mesmerized his reason. Finally, he gave up on locating the beautiful black woman through the map.

Stanley Donner Jr. stepped away from the floor plan. In just minutes the over-stimulation of this fest had purged from him all his troubles. Tranquilly, for an extended moment, he lay a long wondering gaze over the vast central hall. An arena, it seemed. With his shoulders hunched, with a tug at the waist of his ragged pants, carefully, slowly, Stanley shuffled into the roar of the Zine-O-Rama. He would begin his search for the beautiful black woman at table one and just go from there. There were 135 tables.

Three years now participating in these and still every time a body approached her table Clare felt a stab of shyness. Her great

75

blue eyes rose to this curly-headed man. She smiled for him, with effort. Clare had grown accustomed to most idiosyncrasies of a zinefest except this part where a total stranger stops before you, picks up a zine into which you have plowed a little less than your soul maybe but much much more than your spare time, and then, indifferently leafs through the zine page by page, reading your words, judging your art, with you right there to witness their frowns or laughter. And folks are so habituated to perusing merchandise impersonally that sometimes they go through these motions without even acknowledging the zinester before them, as if he or they or she is irrelevant to the artwork they hold. A truly poignant psychology to endure. Clare had never decided whether to ignore her table visitors altogether, avert her eyes from them by pretending fascination with something in her hands, or monitor their browse attentively, which risked making them feel as self-conscious as she. And there are other approaches too. Some zinesters become borderline aggressive with attendees. Others display downright contempt. In any event, often during these encounters, Clare yearned to hide behind her sunglasses, even while indoors. After three zine seasons and some dozen fests she had only arrived at this:

"If you have any questions, I'm happy to answer them."

She offered these words to the curly-headed youth, her features puckering faintly. And then: "Take a candy, if you'd like." Clare rose slightly with a stretch and plucked a piece of butterscotch from the candy dish at the corner of her table. The candies were her ice-breaker. She plopped again onto her chair.

The man seemed Pakistani and sported a veritable bush of curls as a hairdo. If tighter, the thick loose ringlets might be termed an afro. As they were, Clare had heard them called jerry curls by Becca. I dwell on this insignificant detail because Clare insists the hairstyle absolutely defined the man, that everything else about him disappeared into it -- Except maybe the bright orange button on the strap of the canvas bag over his shoulder. That button portrayed the skeleton of a fish.

The young Pakistani paged through *Moon Bloom 3*, sucking now on a red and white peppermint disk. "Glandulus Gonnapopus?" he laughed with delight.

"Yeah," Clare replied, flattered. She was savoring her butterscotch.

"These based on real plants?"

"No, I invent them."

He peeled back another page. His great brown eyes enlarged. Then, ironically: "Oh, Ha! Are some of these maybe intentionally erotic?"

Clare smiled coquettishly. She drawled, "Perhaps."

"That's so cool," he said, and replaced the zine on the tablecloth. The curly-headed guy bent closer then to examine a button made by Clare.

"That *Phallicus Giganticus* again."

"Yep. Lots of people like it."

"I imagine so. Awesome." He unbent and drifted to Clare's tablemate, Steph, scanning the offerings on that side of the table. Steph did not look up. Steph followed the school of invisibility in these transactions, where one remains dormant and speechless unless addressed. Clare had tried Steph's approach, but it did not feel natural to her. Steph also refused to price his table, complaining that tags looked too Capitalist. The Pakistani youth faded backward finally, away from them both. "Thanks for the candy," he offered with a wide charming smile. Clare's sexy "you're very welcome" capped this adieu. The jerry curls blended then into the stream of zinefest regulars, unknowns, and wide-eyed rookies.

Steph said, "People love that cock one, don't they?"

At The California Zine-O-Rama tablemates are drawn randomly. Organizers of smaller fests sometimes let vendors request specific table partners, or even leave the seating arrangement to a first-come-first-served scramble – but not at this big one. The Zine-O-Rama organizers carefully map everything on the premises to help alleviate the considerable chaos and confusion caused by the fest's mammoth size. So while occasionally they might pair zinesters well-known for being inseparable, like Rocky and Blossom, it was only fortuitous that Clare drew a writer she followed on Twitagram, and who also followed her. Steph is lithely built with ethereal facial features, naturally lush lashes, and a moppy black mane which he combs from a right-side part to look like a 1950s schoolboy. Steph tabled a personal zine detailing his mother's refusal to acknowledge his gender fluidity. In the zine he argues cogently and movingly for addressing individuals by their chosen pronoun, expounding on what such address means to a person's self-esteem. Steph is not a *she,* Steph insists. Steph is a *he.*

"I'm a sucker for curly hair like that," Clare said. "Besides, Desi boys are hot."

They both glanced again for the young man. The Pakistani jerry curl had migrated to a table opposite them which offered a tall pinboard covered by dozens of buttons. From this angle they now commanded a full view of the canvas bag draped over his shoulder. A kaleidoscope of small buttons decorated it. They knew then why he had come.

Clare gave her last sliver of butterscotch a good crunch.

Already Blossom's throat felt hoarse. This was the busiest zinefest of the year and the swarm of attendees vibrated through the venue like bees in a hive. Everyone who passed Blossom's table noted her upright display for *The Man Who Booed Littlefeather*. Its damning title with the enlarged photo of the white man laughing over his martini was frequently contemplated, and many paused to discuss it with her.

Wearing her flack jacket over her lucky brown sweatshirt, Blossom stood with her great brown eyes alight, anxious to expound on the import of the zine to anyone who would hear. How she described the perpetrator of the offense depended upon the appearance and attitude of the person before her. At the moment an angry femme with drilling eyes leaned attentively, paging through the zine, listening.

Blossom was saying over the crowd noise, "Your general 1970s patriarchal oppressor. Brunton Howell. Very rich. Very well-connected. And so intolerant that he could not hold his tongue for two minutes. He was intent on defending a needless form of maligning, on defending an unnecessary form of degradation because it made him a lot of money. He wanted the cash from his obscenities to keep rolling in."

Blossom was saying: "He was incapable of seeing other races as truly human. Who knows, maybe he doesn't even see people other than himself as truly human, as deserving of respect and dignity. Watch the video. I put its URL on the back. She is the stand-up example of a dignified human being."

Blossom was saying: "That moment was a symbol in itself of the very point Marlon Brando was trying to make. A complete encapsulation of Hollywood's every insult to my race. They would not allow her sixty seconds to defend us without trying to subjugate her as she did so, without lording over her their devil's power."

Blossom was saying: "Why did he find that statement so offensive that it deserved his vocal insults? Was it because it killed his buzz? Interrupted his good time? Isn't that why they've always pushed us aside? Because things are going so well for them and they don't want to deal with the inconvenience of having to do what is right?"

The angry femme with drilling eyes bought the zine.

Rocky was of the school that engaged the attendees who browsed his table. He had found that interacting with folks increased the likelihood they would carry off a *Shake Me The Boom Boom*. He would elaborate on his philosophy of non-conformity and emphasize how his zines really were just inanimate expressions of it. He would explain that, actually, he practiced his rule of style in real-world settings, too, in boutiques where he made his living; that in fact, he clothed private customers according to these precepts, *and, mind you, to just dazzling effect.* Twice Rocky had attracted new clients who had wandered into fests accidentally and fancied his zine. In terms of personality, however, and perspective and values, those two business-lady strays little resembled the zine makers he loved and sought for company. They were decidedly Old America. Regardless, they were affluent and Rocky would not refuse their custom. Besides, as he often says: Every soul deserves beauty.

This predictable and more or less famous gregariousness of Rocky's made his stewing silence at the Zine-O-Rama doubly remarkable. Zine fanatics came and went and hardly he uttered a word. His *Boom Booms* were offered across his yellow tablecloth like always, but only barely moved. He had sold maybe half his usual haul. Rocky just brooded, micro-adjusting now and then the lay of his golden skirt.

Blossom, his tablemate, was thoroughly absorbed in her own mission -- so much so that hours passed before finally she noted Rocky's moody reticence. Minutes more passed before she extracted herself enough from her own focus to respond to it.

Edgily, her tough angular face said, "Okay, Rock. What up?"

But Rocky only glanced from the corner of an eye. Blossom watched his Adam's apple rise and fall. Defenseless, Rocky seemed to her, but also strong -- a fluid mixing of triumph and bald vulnerability. Rocky smoothed his dress over his thighs.

79

Stanley Donner Jr.'s skeletal shoulders had bent thoughtfully over thirty tables already but still he had not seen the beautiful black woman. He had encountered other interesting things, however. For example, Stanley did not know that poppy seed bagels had a fan club. He did not know that knitting could be a means of political rebellion. Stanley did not know that a criteria existed for gauging the sex appeal of 19th Century balloonists. Before attending this zinefest Stanley had never witnessed a man vociferously defending his right to be overweight. Nor had he realized that physically-challenged people were so tired of ostracism that they had organized against such *ableist* treatment. Stanley Donner Jr. had cruised some sixty tables by now. His winging his way through this flow of attendees recalled to him being on a highway, among a flock of cars, driving. The analogy strengthened him, gave him comfort, and through this comfort Stanley sensed now ideas of his own wanting to crystallize. Earlier he had paused at a table displaying comics that involved stick men. Stanley knew he could draw a stick man. At another table, a woman with pink hair spoke to him frankly about being sexually assaulted. He did not know what to say to that woman, but from her he learned, among other things, that discomforting personal stories can be told in zines. This affected Stanley Donner Jr. deeply. He considered the story he himself might tell. He trembled. Stanley felt an unsteadiness then, a shifting of ground within his being, a weakness presaging collapse. Softly he pressed the heel of his hand against his sternum, girding himself, determinedly. Stanley Donner Jr. dwelt for a moment on the color green. He liked the color green. Then he eased away from the table with the green tablecloth that held the orange lava lamp. He raised his unshaven chin to gaze up the stairwell he would now climb. Stanley might draw a green stick man. Stanley could do that. Stanley might discuss other things, perhaps, things besides his troubles. Like books. He had lots of books. He had passed table 80 now. Stanley climbed the stairs. He did not think about the beautiful black woman as he climbed. He thought instead of his home library, and of a stick man, and perhaps of a zine based on his writings. Stanley Donner Jr. hoped the woman who had been assaulted was okay now. She seemed to be okay now. He thought: I never would have known she had been assaulted without her telling me. He thought: I suppose I've met many women who have been assaulted without knowing it. He thought: That's probably an important thing to realize. Stanley Donner Jr. thought about assault victims. He thought about books. He thought about the color green. And then he saw Viola.

Clare and Steph fidgeted silently. An unexplained quiet had fallen over the swarm of attendees before their table so they gazed across the venue, benumbed by the day's stimulation. Steph finger-combed some boy bangs out of his long eyelashes. Then, rather distractedly, he offered, "So how's your mission coming?"

Clare awoke. "Hard." She squinted and swigged from a plastic bottle of Diet FizzBang, relishing its icy bubbles.

"But that's what you wanted, right?"

"Yeah, but I didn't expect the hard stuff to be so hard. I am soft. So soft. I don't know. But my calves have toned up quite a bit already. You can't really tell by looking at them but it's true. I expect I'll be lasting longer on the dance floor nowadays."

"Ah."

Steph's attention drifted inconstantly through the milling heads as his and Clare's shared silence descended anew. Clare noticed that the Pakistani jerry curl guy had shuffled back left to pause over a table opposite them. She examined his manner and moves as she pried into her purse for a pot of moisturizing cream. A liberal dollop, she fingered then and began to massage it into her hands, ruminatively.

"I'm thinking of making a zine about it."

"Like text?"

"Perhaps a photozine, like some pictures of me trying to fix a bicycle flat. I'm going to have to cut my nails because of this, you know. I don't know how short I need them to be yet. I'm still trying to work around it. But, in the end, you can't change a bicycle tire with fingernails this long. Did you know that?"

"No."

"Perhaps I'll call it *Bike Hike*. Or, hey, *Bike Fight*. That's better. You know, like *Moon Bloom*. Like branding. *Bike Hike* doesn't make sense, I guess. Perhaps *The Wheel Deal*. Or how about *Spoke Croak*. I definitely feel *that* way sometimes. Oh, something like that. Whatevs. Something that rhymes."

Unconsciously Steph checked his fingernails. Clare explained then that in the final stages of repairing a bicycle flat, just

81

before one pumps up the newly inserted inner tube, one has to tuck the rubber edge of the tire back under the metal rim. That act, she insisted, is simply impossible to accomplish with long fingernails. The precision and force of the human fingertip become an irreplaceable tool at that critical juncture.

Clare screwed closed her pot of skin cream then and dropped it into her purse. She finished, "I got a flat trying to ride to Palm Desert a couple weeks ago."

"You rode a bicycle to Palm Desert from Venice Beach!?"

"I was going to. I only made it to Riverside."

"You rode a bicycle all the way from Venice Beach to Riverside!?"

"Well, I put it on the train."

"Oh."

Clare glugged from her Diet FizzBang. Two young women slowed up before Steph's zine display. Steph's eyes fell to the table. Clare gulped again.

"I rode the Metrolink with my bike all the way to Riverside. Took forever. That's what I mean. This is so hard. Then I learned that basically I had to take the 10 to get through the mountains."

"On a bicycle?" Steph said under his breath, still facing downward. "That's impossible."

"I got a flat. So much easier when the fests are somewhere here in LA."

An awkwardness filtered through the two young women standing before Steph as the one holding his baby blue zine carefully replaced it. The woman's expression apologized for not buying it as she looked to Steph to say thanks. Steph just kept peering downward, however, his fine features in decided retreat. Without offense, the two women accepted his reluctance to engage and shifted to the next table upstream. On that table waited homemade coloring books featuring inventors of color. The table was ornamented with a miniature traffic light, a pacemaker, and some strands of fiber optic cable.

Clare continued, "There's lots of stuff on the side of the road that you never think about that can give you flats. A bicycle guy with the coolest unibrow in Culver City told me all about this. I was trying to get around Marina del Rey one day without Maps and ended up way out there on Centinela where I met him. Real adventure. Sharp stuff like glass, yeah, but also random nails and screws and things people drop. Worst of all, goatheads. They're a kind of thorn. Anyway, you know that zine *SlapDown?*"

"Yeah, yeah, I know about Easy. They're sitting back in the corner today. I saw the table when I came in. He does that tech stuff. With monitors and drones."

"That guy and his girlfriend saw my pink West Coast Zine Feast shirt and stopped and offered me a ride. Nice girl. She smiles a lot. They were on their way to Palm Desert."

"No way."

"Yeah way. She said my shirt caught her eye and then she kind of recognized me. They were pulling out of a Shaft Burger. If it hadn't been for his girlfriend with him I would have declined, I guess. He's got a dope kind of antique gangster aesthetic going. Love that. And lowriders are the coolest, sure. But all that's a little scary to a girl alone."

"His sister."

"What's that?"

"It's not his girlfriend, it's his sister."

"No kidding."

"No kidding."

This information checked Clare's rhythm. Her gaze, which had been tracking still the migration of the Pakistani jerry curl, suddenly left him. She squinted. She said, distantly, "That Easy guy. He's cute."

Zinesters are more or less loners. Basically, a zinefest is an event where many loners assemble to be loners together. As loners, zinesters are highly sensitive to the psychological space of others. With uncanny intuition, they sense the barriers erected around a person's interior world. At one table a browsing zinester might interact with a tabling zinester for a full five minutes if the subject appeals to both and both have relaxed their mental defenses enough to share. At the very next table, however, there may be a zine even more perfectly tuned to that same browsing zinester's interests and goals, and yet she will not say a single word to the tabler. This because she recognizes that the second tabler does not welcome conversation. Zinesters honor each other's space. And usually, when you see discomfort at a table it is because a non-zinester is taking interpersonal liberties that a zinester would never take. Zinesters accept these liberties and forgive them and answer them willingly and with goodwill because part of putting yourself forward at a zinefest is accepting the risk of innocent obtrusions and prying. Having to occasionally share more than you like is the price a zine maker pays for engaging with the community and the event. For this reason, rarely do you see the same zinesters tabling at all the different zinefests. Sometimes they need a break.

In Rocky's case, both of these circumstances applied. Since purposefully he was showcasing himself here, he felt not only willing but even obliged to indulge the pressings of whomever might pause before him. But the true zinesters scuffling through saw in Rocky's signaling a barrier. In other words, though he occupied this public space, and therefore, by default, had accepted its rule of participation, he would prefer to be left alone. So by zinesters, Rocky was left alone.

These dynamics of sensitivity did not apply to Blossom, however. Discourse between Rocky and Blossom could never be inhibited by such external mores. They were too intimate for that. So at hour four, with Rocky still uttering only courteous expositions to curious passers-by, and sometimes even mere monosyllables, Blossom finally emerged from her all-consuming determination to disseminate the infamy of Brunton "Boo Boo" Howell.

During a lull in traffic, she said, "Okay, this is super weird." She extended her shaved head over her table and turned it. "I've hardly ever seen you like this. What's happened?"

Rocky peaked from the corner of an eye.

"Are you sick?"

Rocky glanced away.

"Did someone die, God forbid?"

Rocky shook his head.

"Are you ever going to tell me?"

Rocky just looked down.

"Talk to me, Rock. Is it that problem? That confusion that's been bugging you?"

Rocky lifted two soft eyes to her. He murmured, with breathy gentleness, "It's scary stuff to say aloud, Boss. Do you love me, dear? Do you promise you won't stop loving me?"

Viola had woven her hair into some protective jumbo braids. Heavily now they framed her fine cinnamon-brown features, like velvet ornaments. The flow of attendees before her table had streamed until minutes ago. Now it only trickled. Viola glanced side to side, cautiously. She swung open her computer. She jacked into the venue's wifi.

"So there's this quiet time that happens about now at Los Angeles," she typed. "The fair starts a little slow, building gradually as the on-timers show. These fade out a little, like now, and then a crush will come soon which will not abate until quitting time. On track for a good day. I've already matched last year's numbers and we still have the busiest hours ahead. Thank the Lord for that.

"Ya'll remember that white boy I mentioned in that cafe way back in April? Remember the one I said looked like he might want to shake my hourglass? Well, he just cruised by. At Palm Desert a couple weeks ago I saw him, too, standing there holding that flyer he stole off the bulletin board in College Heights. It didn't occur to me to mention him then. But a minute ago I looked up and there he was again. I might have felt stalked, but that boy is so intent on the whole scene that I don't feel like his attendance is about me. And, since he went by Palm Desert without saying a word to me (he pulled a Houdini without even entering the room), it might just be he's dropping into the scene as people do sometimes. From nowhere. Suddenly some little old lady from Pasadena wants to talk about the succulent garden she keeps on her balcony and you got a beaming new zinester sitting next to you with pretty photographs sewn into a quilted notebook, and maybe a few cacti adorning the table. Or a burlesque dancer, maybe you'll meet, who enjoys sketching her golden retriever. Or some anarchist gay couple trying simultaneously to spread radical literature and make a nearby skate park safer for queer folx. Those sorts. Scheming. Ranting. Sharing their love. You see them here and there through a season, and then they disappear again, moving on to some other interesting thing in their lives. I like those come-and-goers alright, though I never fully adopt them as my own. Hard for me to get close to a bird on the wing. So anyways there was that white boy a few minutes ago, looking things over with a keen eye, like he couldn't stop himself, like it was touching something hungry in him, or kindling some untapped fire. I watched him discovering our community, my fays. Table by table, he went. One at a time. Studying. He passed on the other side of the aisle from me, checking out the *Robots in Underwear* guys, and *My Dildo's Zine*. Gotta hush now, tho. People comin."

Viola tapped the send button. She closed her laptop. She looked up through her great brown eyes to a tall Asian woman dressed in multiple tones of orange.

Blossom knew this punk. A dude. A coyote's toe bone pierced his eyebrow. A pink ribbon frilled from the toe bone's knuckle. He held *The Man Who Booed Littlefeather.* For him, Blossom described "Boo Boo" Howell as a "fucking pasty-faced piece of patriarchal trash. The perfect example of his era and class and white racism. And the bloodsucker's still alive. So if you're looking for something to vandalize just ask and I'll give you his fucking address."

"You know where he lives?" asked the punk dude.

"I've walked by his three-bedroom mansion. Westside. By LACMA."

"You stalking him, Boss?"

"Not yet."

As the guy turned a page Blossom pointed out an image. The indicated photograph depicted a face old enough to have lost many of its distinguishing characteristics, its contours having settled into a mush of seamy flesh. She explained, "I got that picture there by leaning over his back fence at night and shooting through his back fucking kitchen window as he filled a glass of water to take his fucking Geritol and laxatives and shit."

Blossom knew this punk dude well enough that she felt tempted to admit she had not found the nerve yet to confront Howell personally. The confession swirled in her, but since she was having difficulty even articulating this truth to herself she suppressed it. In her mind, she had excused her ongoing casing of Howell's residence as "preparation." But really it was a stall. Blossom knew that to demand the apology that she and all American Indians deserved, she would have to knock on Howell's front door; that to right that public wrong and avenge Littlefeather, she would eventually have to stand face to face with the chooch. But he so completely embodied everything she hated and saw as unjust in the world that knocking on that door had grown into a heftier fucking proposition than expected. In her mind, Howell had become larger than life, the totality of what oppressed her. Brunton Howell was the machine who had crushed people like Blossom and Littlefeather for the entirety of the existence of modern society.

This daunted. This constricted her throat. So the time she was taking to reinforce her nerve was time she needed to take.

Attendees sidled through, remarking her display as the punk flipped pages. Instead of admitting these complications to the guy, she said, "I ... It's still fluid. I haven't knocked on his front door yet, approached him directly. But I got enough to make the zine."

The punk looked dubious, eyeing Blossom with suspicion. "Just walk up and beat on the fucking door, Boss."

"Yeah, I know."

"Make sure you got your camera and just kick the fucking door in with those goddamn big brown boots. Maybe drink something first. Go to a show. Go to a show and slam for a while, get your testosterone going, then put on your magic spurs and smash his fucking door. That'll get you the balls."

Blossom winced. Her skin tightened over her cheekbones. Defensively, she protested, "It's not that. It's not that." But she knew it was.

He held the zine open still. "This shit through the back window is weak shit. Use it, I guess. But it can't be your anchor for an outing like this." He pivoted his shoulders, grumping down at Rocky:

"What you think, Rock?"

"I'm helping her how I can, Mill. I offered to go with her. To drive the getaway car, right? She'll do it, though. I can see it coming."

Rocky's comment sounded distant, vaporous. Then the punk dude laid down the zine. Blossom objected to these two friends of hers talking about her as if she were not there -- and right in front of her. Her chin quivered. Edgily she snapped, "I'm on this. This is my fight."

He smirked. "You got the fucker, Boss. Just make it legit. For us and for you. That asshat needs to know you've burned him. And everyone who reads this wants to see him hang his head and say he's a sorry dogshit. This apology angle of yours is so superior to a crud like this. He doesn't deserve the chance. When you get that fucking picture, though, goddamnit I want to see it."

"Thank you, my fays, for reading this, my very first live blog. Your questions and suggestions have been so important to me all along. Why else would I be doing this?"

Viola gazed over the keyboard into the glow of her laptop screen. She grinned delight and surprise while nestling her hourglass back into her chair and adjusting the waist of her low-rise denims. She had just been on her feet and conversing with an attendee. They had sported a bushy goatee and golden hoop earrings.

"Yeah, since some of y'all have been DMing me about this, I can tell you that once I find my tabling space, and I'm established in my seat and I got *O, Kindred* laid out and ready to sell I really relax. It's roughly true I'm an agoraphobe, as Sanjay so tenderly asked in the comments here last week, but only roughly. Actually, to be accurate, my problem is more of an intermittent agoraphobia complicated by what I call site-specific performance anxiety. This means I can handle being around people for a while when they're decent; and that my anxiety only comes on me when I'm forced to perform some task for which I am not trained, or at which I am not adept. I just cannot handle the way people judge my mistakes in those situations as if they reflect on the entire black race.

"Hmm. So I sit here in my spot at the California Zine-O-Rama and I have no problems because the people are decent and I know what I'm doing. For several hours I can sit here behind the fruits of our labors and watch people like or even dislike our zine. I can sit here and comfortably observe all us loners relating to each other, and complimenting each other, and creating a positive vibe for each other. For some reason, until now I have never really realized how much I rely on this community for my mental health. I feel much less isolated because of these fairs. And feeling less isolated makes me less a prey to *It*. A zinefest gives me strength internally. And having everyone be positive and encouraging gives me the gumption to keep on keepin' on. I realize that my work is part of a bigger work and that together, even without intending it, we are all of us zinesters working to help build a New America that everyone can share in. *That's no small thang.*

"I'm glad y'all are liking these updates and so props to Rankrushna for suggesting this live blog to me. Now Sanjay is saying I should go the next step and even live *Vlog* one of these events. Maybe I will. Ole Viole here is not so shy about her face. But y'all need to remember that people don't always talk the way they write and that a girl from rural North Carolina may not always prefer to speak like some BBC newslady, even if she know how. So you might just hear my origins comin' right out of my mowf, y'all. I'm right comfortable with them origins. Just a heads up. For now, though, signing off. Happily Ever After, V."

And Viola posted the blog, cheerfully, to look up then into the giggling green eyes of a plus-size attendee gripping issue six. The man was saying to himself, "What the hell?"

Clare squinted at a polished bald head. The man bent at her, reflecting fluorescent beams from the overhead lamps into her eyes. He had browsed the table left of Clare's, one offering a travel zine, and had inched sideward to stoop now over her space flowers. Clare had not interacted with the travel zine kids – *The Love Speeder.* They tabled a tall, rather complicated display decorated with photos of the many vagabond types they had encountered in their summer automobile tours of US byroads. The title of the zine derived from their nickname for the old Dodge station wagon they drove. *The Love Speeder's* presentation blocked Clare's view of the actual zinesters themselves -- a white man and his teenage son. This made conversation unnatural, and Clare was not so friendly as to be friendly unnaturally.

"Moon Bloom," the bald head spoke at Clare, neutrally.

His shiny white flesh blinded. Were he to stay too long Clare would be reaching for her wayfarers. As it was, obviously he had pronounced the zine title for himself, not to Clare, so she did not respond. The man opened issue three and leafed through it, flower by flower by flower, pinning the zine to the pastel green tablecloth with one hand as he paged on with the other. He clucked at *Glandulus Gonnapopus,* startled at *Phallicus Giganticus,* and gave every single fictional description in the issue a studious read. "Interesting," he finally said to himself. "Very interesting. Redon. Your style reminds me of Odilon Redon ... Except for the names and the ink outlines." Then he inched to his left, to Steph's side of the table. "He, Him, His," the bald man quoted, neutrally. He articulated Steph's title only for himself. But that satisfied Steph just fine since he preferred to be ignored. The bald man gave Steph's zine an exhaustive review. Then he shuffled again leftward, inching on to study a coloring book that featured on its cover George Washington Carver.

With that polished head now away Clare rose off her seat to stretch for her candy dish and pluck out a cinnamon lozenge. As

89

she plopped again backward and untwisted the candy's wrapper she decided Easy had lain dormant long enough that she could reintroduce him as a topic of conversation without appearing obsessed. She said to Steph, "That guy at *SlapDown*, Easy. He like seems very tough, you know. But when we were driving to Palm Desert he started talking about his zine and little by little his street facade kinda dropped away and, like, there's more to him than just some in-your-face style. It's like a whole philosophy is behind his zine. He's thought through the implications of what he's doing to the end. It's so dope. Have you seen what that zine is really about?"

"I guess not," said Steph.

Clare tongued the cinnamon candy judiciously, knocking it against the insides of her teeth. "He deliberately lures cops into stopping him and harassing him so he can document it. He's got these drones that he programs to hover over him and film every little thing that happens and broadcast it all live on Faustbook. He calls them his angels. He says that if everyone did what he's doing, the police would never ever stop anyone without cause."

"What table number are they again?"

"Let's see." Clare unfolded a map of the convention hall and smoothed it between her and Steph. Her features puckered. "112. In the corner. Like you thought. His sister was telling me about The Baja Zine Fiesta, in Tia-juana. Have you done that one?"

"No, but people are still talking about last year's. It's kinda famous already."

"Isn't Tia-juana dangerous?"

Steph nodded affirmatively. He said, "Don't go there." He said, "Tia-juana is very dangerous." Then, "I'm heading to the restroom. Will you cover for me? I want to check out *SlapDown* too. I'll see what's on their table today."

Clare assented, knowing Steph would cover for her absence in return. She would cruise by *SlapDown* herself then. For sure, she would -- To say hello. Clare reflected on Easy's other passenger that day on the trip to Palm Desert, on that cat-eyed beauty who actually was his sister. Spearmint. He had smelled of spearmint. Still Clare remembered. Then she reconsidered Easy's behavior as they conversed on the highway. A few things she interpreted differently now -- Like his dwelling on her apparent familiarity, like his constant glancing into the rearview mirror. And it was true Clare had begun to look around again. Yes, she had recovered enough from Becca's move to San Diego, and from Becca's very practical but painful suggestion that they start seeing other people. And definitely she was feeling *the need*. Clare sighed. Like that curly-headed Desi boy. He had warmed her thighs up alright ... for a male. Clare lifted her head to scan for the Pakistani kid. Just one row over now. A small plastic bag he held in his left hand. He had found something he liked. Clare reflected then on how Easy's appearance and style contradicted his rather intimidating intelligence. She wondered if that was a racist thing to think. Then she wondered if perhaps Easy was intentionally creating that illusion, like a decoy, using people's prejudice against them, as a tool of advantage. He would know then what *they* were thinking, wouldn't he? But they would be misjudging what *he* was thinking. Huh. Clare was still contemplating this question and crunching up the last of her cinnamon lozenge when Steph suddenly descended upon the table in alarm.

He panted, "Hey, Clare! Easy's not there. Only his sister is. But check it out: They've got a huge monitor set up. And it's live! And Easy's gettin' shaken down. Right now! It's live!" He gestured imperatively: "Let's go."

Clare sat startled. She said, "The table."

"Don't matter. Gotta see this."

"At least grab your change, yeah?" And Clare grappled an envelope full of ones and fives into her purse. She strung her purse up over her shoulder then and jerkily rose to her feet. When she and Steph rounded the corner toward *SlapDown* they found a crowd gathering before a table behind which stood a large screen television. Between the TV and the table sat a cat-eyed girl over a laptop. Easy's sister Linda. This time Linda was not smiling.

A college guy in a Long Beach State t-shirt stood before Blossom holding *The Man Who Booed Littlefeather*. As he listened to Blossom's spiel his eyes drifted from Blossom's shaved head to her ear gauges to her lips studs to her blue-black choker of tattooed thorns.

"An exemplar of his times. That's who we were fighting against as women back then, and that is who we are fighting against right now. A man with power who is comfortable in his position and is going to do everything he can to keep that position from being compromised. He is so well-established that he can even hoot like an imbecile in front of thousands of his peers and not

91

have to feel the least fear of being taken to task for the insult. Just the opposite – he is celebrated for it, nicknamed with affection 'Boo Boo.' "

"Seriously?"

"Yeah, that's where his nickname comes from. Because he boos people."

The college guy glanced up from the zine again, squinting critically into Blossom's great brown eyes.

"That's the most difficult thing for us to uproot, to fight against," Blossom continued. "That entrenched power. I ... With it comes a hubris and confidence that disheartens anyone who would oppose it. Believe me, it is subtle in one way. But in another way, it is as solid as a prison wall. This is the wall women have to break through if we're going to find justice. Its hugeness prevents us from acting sometimes. It feels like we're assaulting a well-defended homeland, right? But it isn't their homeland, it's ours. And we're not invading, we're just trying to recover what always should have been ours in the first place."

The college guy folded shut the zine. Blossom pointed at it with her left index finger.

"There," she said. "By herself, that woman confronted three thousand oppressors intent upon destroying her. In my eyes, because she even attempted it, and then while doing it maintained her dignity, she succeeded. I'm just making sure everyone knows about her victory."

The young man in the Long Beach State t-shirt opened up his wallet and pulled out a five-dollar bill.

Stanley Donner Jr. could not be certain, of course, but it seemed to him the beautiful black woman recognized him. When finally, after considerable hesitation and circumlocution, he had carefully approached her table, she had received him with an air that suggested he was not completely unknown.

He hunched over a booklet upon which appeared the figure of a human male body topped with the head of a horse. This man-horse thing wore a flowing red dress with flamenco-style skirts. Stanley wondered what the configuration signified. He opened the booklet seeking quick explanation, and, leafing the pages, considered that the creature might be allegorical like in Dante, or a genetic mutation *à la* H.G. Wells. But the red dress? And

Flamenco? Did this horse-man dance with the imperious seduction of an Andalusian gypsy? Did it employ castanets? Often cover illustrations belied the actual text, Stanley remembered. Then he closed the booklet and stopped his stalling and looked at the beautiful black woman.

His creased shirt draped off his shoulders like from a clothes hanger. Whiskery, he hunched there, and sickly-skinned. Only the sunburn of his left forelimb hinted at any health in him. Stanley Donner Jr. gazed on Viola. He mumbled, questioningly, "I think I saw you at a cafe in College Heights in San Diego a while back."

The beautiful black woman met the directness of Stanley's hollow stare. She wore a yellow crop top that enlivened her reddish-brown complexion to a smoldery glow. Her hair fell around her face today as ropey dangles. She searched Stanley's cavernous blue eyes briefly and wisely, and then, weighing the implications of various answers, replied decisively.

"Yes, you did. I remember. You took our flyer off the bulletin board."

"That was your flyer?" he startled.

"Mm-Hmn. For the zinefest a couple weeks ago in Palm Desert. Organizers sometimes send me flyers to put up around San Diego."

"Sorry. I ..."

"No, it's alright. You took it out of interest obviously. I saw you out there at the fest. I put up another one anyway. That's what those things are for."

"You saw me in Palm Desert? I saw you too."

"Yeah, I saw you. You cruised by the door and then left right away. I wondered why."

"In truth, I wasn't feeling well."

Stanley pronounced these words haltingly, hardly articulate, trembling slightly as the syllables escaped his breath.

"Did you get a chance to at least visit the other building?"

"No."

"And after all the razzmatazz of that drive?"

The beautiful black woman softened then at Stanley's reaction to this question. He flinched. His skeletal frame contracted. And his trembling grew more visible. Viola checked herself. She withdrew. Stanley felt her wondering at the effect of such a benign query, but sensing, too, his incapacity for engaging it further. Viola gave him suddenly a lot of room.

She smiled.

Stanley raised a hand and waved farewell.

Viola nodded.

Stanley Donner Jr. stepped away then. His meeting and speaking with the beautiful black woman had buoyed him, undoubtedly, had flushed him even with a kind of liquid euphoria. But also it broke open a broad vulnerability in him, a vulnerability he lacked still the fortitude to confront. Stanley Donner Jr. felt a deep stab of guilt. He felt a scraping begin in his chest. A scraping. He could not feel any upswell of happiness or even the lightest fog of hope these days without having to weather that stab of guilt and that feeling of scraping.

People crowded toward a large video monitor behind a table ahead. The buzz there encouraged Stanley their way, compassing him out of the disorientation his sudden parting from the beautiful black woman had wrought.

But, "Sir, sir," he heard.

He turned.

Viola.

She stood now. Stanley felt instead of saw the deep contours of her narrow waist.

"You dropped something."

She pointed at the pill bottle Stanley had rattled a couple of times and then fumblingly misplaced over the loose pocket of his ragged pants. A backstep. He stooped. Erect again now, gripping his pills, he offered a smile to the beautiful black woman, weakly. He mumbled aloud, "My name is Stanley Donner Jr."

She gave a thumbs up.

Stanley shuffled then toward the attendees pressing around the video monitor.

"That was so out of this world, Rock. You should have come over there. That guy at *SlapDown* is out of his fucking mind. It's like he's trying to martyr himself."

Rocky felt Blossom's jitter. Her excitement was genuine, he saw, electric; but also he recognized her leveraging that energy against his withdrawn funk, angling it to derail his morose track of mind, to draw him out. They played this game with each other once in a while. Today Rocky did not accept Blossom's gambit. He just gazed on. She sat now, gathering in the tendrils of her fading thrill. Rocky noticed her flack jacket off, and the quivering in her chin. He twisted some straying hairs around his ear.

"Did anyone come by?" she asked, catching her breath.

Rocky said no. Then he said, "Look, I've been thinking."

"Thank God," blurted Blossom.

She turned then to face him, her features blunt compassion. She might have seized Rocky's hands but checked herself. Instead, she balled her fists against the golden skirt over his knees.

"So let's get this out," she encouraged. "You know I'm with you, Rock."

"It's dumbfounding, I tell you."

"I believe you. I know it's big. You've made a decision. I can see this. I've known this since you got here today. Whatever it is, I am here for you."

They both flicked a glance sideways as a pair of zinesters sauntered by. The zinesters considered browsing their wares, but, sensing the intimacy of their converse, footed on.

"You will be speechless, I'm sure."

Blossom sniffed. "If it's made you speechless, I'm sure it will do the same to me. But I can't be speechless until you tell me."

"True, I suppose," Rocky said. Then, looking from the corner of an eye, "Promise you love me?"

"Rocky, I love you. You know that."

Rocky twitched his head. His Adam's apple pumped with a swallow. He half-smiled. Unconsciously now he rattled the bangles at his wrists and tucked his skirt seams under his thighs and smoothed his hose against his calves. Then, all at once, he spat as forcefully as his lilting voice might: "Why, I should feel happy because I have an answer. And I am happy, I suppose. It's just that I don't think I can do this by myself. I really need support." And then, before Blossom could promise that support, he said: "Look, so you know I've felt like a woman for a few years and have been confused by my physical attraction to them. Why, it's simple..." Rocky cleared his throat. "I am a woman inside. Truly. Just because I want to be intimate with women does not necessarily make me a man, now does it? So I've decided to become a woman. I want to be a woman who loves women. I want to be a woman, and, when the time comes, I want to make love to women as a woman."

Instantly: "I'm with you, Rock. Of course, I am." But Blossom paused then. Rocky felt her watch him as he stared into the lap of his skirt. She remarked, seriously, "You're not alone, you know. There are others. But I do understand your confusion better now. That would be a total mindfuck, I guess, until you figured it out. In any event, I'm here for you all the way, Rock. Just tell me what I need to do to show up for you."

Rocky opened his palms to Blossom and she put her hands in his. He said, "They make categories for you to fit into." He gripped her tightly. "But I don't fit into *any* of them."

Viola frowned now at her desktop screen. She sat fatigued, shaken. Her elbows gripped at her rib cage like the retracted wings of a stormbound heron. Viola wrung her hands. She frowned. She dropped her fingers to the keyboard.

"I'm home now, precious. Sorry my live blog clunked, but the final hours of a zinefest are its busiest and luckily I stayed hoppin' till time to pack up and leave. I will report to ya'll now that, on the whole, this zinefest was more or less routine except for two things. One, that wounded white boy finally came by my table and actually talked to me. Just like when I first saw him in that cafe in College Heights, I felt that there is something off about him – but not threatening. It is strange: As a person with inner problems I can tell you that he is struggling with It (whatever It is for him) and that he is at the edge of controlling it, but I can also tell you there is nothing to fear from that man. If he is going to do anyone any harm, it is probably going to be himself. I spoke gently with him, trying to give him strength in my own way. He may be a white boy, but he is still a human being. When someone is suffering they lose their skin color. For most of us, this is true. I've seen this go both ways. Blacks are less oppressed than we once were and it is partly, I think, because human beings have a hard time watching their neighbors suffer. Let them see that suffering and they are more willing to let things change. Maybe that will happen now also since our suffering is so publicly evident at the moment. Number Two (and I saved the worst for last): Easy is up to his razzmatazz again, and it will probably take me days and days to get over what I saw at his table this afternoon. An inner setback to be sure. Unfortunately, I learned from viewing that trauma that It is permanent, and that even though I might shield myself from It, as I often do, it will never go away. I keep repeating this truth to myself, but for some reason, I just cannot seem to internalize it. I gotta stop trying to make *It* go away. At least if I want to be a person who is going to make a difference. And I want to make a difference. These are times when people gotta stand up and be strong. I am gonna be strong. To do that I gotta face *It*. My fear as I call it. My ogre. I gotta take *It* on. These little personal commitments matter right now. If I can face my fear, I will make a difference. If I can't, I won't. So I am going to face my fear. Anyways, seeing what happened to Easy reminds me why he and I loved each other once but also why we could not stay together. I respect the path he has taken, even envy its strength and courage, but I cannot be a part of it. I don't belong in the streets. Not strong that way. I'll post a link to what I saw at his table later, after I recover some and find the bravery to track it down on his website. My darling Linda (that's Easy's sister) sent me a text saying she has seen him since those horrors I witnessed today and that he is okay, even stronger than ever. She knew it would bother me, that precious girl. Still, I will have nightmares. That was worse than a news report. That was a friend."

After a deep breath, Viola added a crying face emoticon to the end of the blog entry. Then, signing off with an ironically lowercase *happily-ever-after*, she clicked the 'post' button and immediately closed the browser tab.

Her hands were shaking.

That hat year Linda managed *SlapDown*'s table at The California Zine-O-Rama all by herself. You're about to see why.

A display rack behind Linda held a 50-inch television screen at about head height. Sideways Linda sat over *SlapDown's* table, glancing to and from that TV screen, her dark brown hair falling almost to her waist in that attitude. She tapped a laptop. With the laptop she controlled which of the five video feeds on the screen was larger, and which was smaller, and which audio source got volume, and which did not.

She tossed her head in mystery. She thought: What a rookie! Is this cop blind? The drones lift off and he just doesn't notice? Or doesn't care possibly? No acknowledgment of them at all. Well, I guess this is what Easy hoped for. Let's see what he gets.

97

"Boss!" Linda suddenly snapped into the loosely assembling crowd. A golden young woman with a shaved head reacted, returning to Linda an accommodating nod.

"Can you help me spread a trigger warning, please? Can you tell these folks that this is being recorded? If some shit goes down people need to know that Easy wants this to happen, that he's in control. So they don't stress."

Blossom agreed, readily and seriously. She knew of Easy's exploits and did not want people traumatized by them unnecessarily.

Linda enlarged Easy's dashboard camera then, giving it predominance on the TV screen. Hundreds watched on Faustbook. Maybe twenty straggled around *SlapDown*'s table, fanning out from it like branches off a tree. Some lifted their phones to record the process of the recording.

Before them now Ezekiel Castillo's profile looked up through his wraparound sunglasses to a man in a black uniform who looked down through aviator sunglasses. The two men discoursed, tensely.

The cop was accusing: "I backpaced you driving 50 in a 35."

In barrio cadence, proudly pronounced, and bobbing his head, Easy countered, "With all due respect, sir, I was doing 35 miles per hour in a 35 miles per hour zone."

"Were you following me?"

"I was showing off my ride, officer. I was cruising Crenshaw Boulevard and showing off my lowrider. This is a 1964 Impala. Very rare. With a plumb red paint job, as you can see, and some classic pinstriping by a historic automobile artist. It gets lots of looks on The Shaw. People like it. And I like giving people that thrill."

"You were doing 50."

"I was not."

"Are you disputing me?"

"Yes I am."

This answer electrified the live observers at the Zine-O-Rama. The chatter among them instantly ceased. They stood rapt. That sudden silence slowed more passers-by. The branches of the tree grew crowded. The police officer fumbled for a second at Easy's unintimidated reply. Easy did not elaborate. His mouth remained flat beneath his full mustache. Then, nettled, the cop said, haughtily, "Your identification says you live in Norwalk. What are you doing over here in Leimert Park?"

"On my way to the Pasadena Convention Center. Just pulled off for a little sightseeing."

Titters.

"Just pulled off? I would say that's quite out of your way. What business do you have at the convention center?"

"That business is my business."

Murmurs.

The policeman folded his arms across his chest now. "You seem quite sure of yourself, Mr. Castillo. Do I smell marijuana in your car?"

"*In* my car? This is a convertible, officer. Besides, marijuana is legal."

"Driving under the influence is not legal."

"I am not high. And I have not been high for years, which I can prove." Easy's diction had turned college boy. The cop did not seem to notice. Easy added, crisply, "There are no illegal substances in this vehicle."

"You're giving me attitude."

"I am just stating a fact."

"A *fact?* For *me?*"

"I am stating a verifiable fact."

"I need you to step out of the vehicle, sir."

"Why?"

"I have cause for suspicion."

"Suspicion of what?"

"I need you to step out of the vehicle."

Easy brushed his mustache with his hand. Finally, he shrugged, and with a shove of his shoulder, popped open the heavy door of the Impala.

Fifty or so wide-eyed viewers drew in closer to Linda now as she shrank the stream from the lowrider's dashboard camera and enlarged the two videos broadcasting from the hovering drones. With a click, she sourced the audio from Easy's phone, which he had dialed into the system upon being stopped, and which he had just slipped into a chest pocket. From the drones, the two men stood now visible beside the blood-red car. Easy, in his athletic brawn, was appreciably larger than the police officer.

"Put your hands on top of the hood."

Easy obeyed.

"Spread your legs."

Easy obeyed.

But Easy had not spread his legs wide enough, apparently, because the video showed the cop kicking his left foot farther to the left.

The cop frisked Easy.

With his feet so far apart Easy began to lose his balance, tottering slightly backward; and then, a beat later, Easy had been slammed to the pavement with his arms behind his back and his face in the asphalt as the cop knelt on his back. The weight of the policeman compressed his chest, making it difficult to breathe. Easy's phone had jogged forward onto the blacktop. With his elbow, the peace officer ground Easy's cheek against the street. The cop growled these words into Easy's ear:

"Fucking punk. High as you can be. You're floating. And that blunt in your ashtray is all I need."

Easy said nothing. But he heard an automobile speed toward them and screech to a halt. A car door was opened. A rapid trod of rubber soles.

"Got him, Sarj," the cop on Easy's back called to the newcomer. "Banger had some lip on him. Smartin' off. Resisting arrest." The cop on Easy's back panted with adrenaline. So did the observers in the convention center.

Easy could only hear now. He saw nothing but the pebbly grain of the asphalt ahead of his left eye, and a curb beyond the cop's elbow. His cheekbone hurt. He worked to breathe.

Then the cop on his back said, "What's wrong, Sarj?" And, after a prolonged silence, emphatically: "He's high. He was exceeding the speed limit and DUI. I tried to search him but he resisted violently and I had to restrain for my own safety. I had reason to fear he was armed." Then again: "What's wrong?"

Suddenly Easy sucked a deep breath. The cop had moved off his back. Easy could see the rubber soles of the officer's shoes a stride off his head now. He had not heard the second policeman say anything yet, but the fidgeting in those near shoes suggested to Easy doubt -- The cop seemed to be gathering that he had made a mistake.

Ezekiel said from the ground, in crystal clear standard American diction, "The sergeant knows better than to say anything, chump. What he's not saying is that you're fucked. You just totally fucked yourself."

A scattering of handclaps filtered through the Zine-O-Rama audience. By now a hundred had gathered.

"Shut your mouth," the cop barked, with unconvincing authority. He nudged at Easy's shoulder with his toe, threateningly.

"Look up," Easy coughed. "About forty feet above you will see two drones which have recorded everything you have done since the moment you pulled me over. There are two cameras inside my car which also recorded it, audio included, not to mention my phone which has been live all this time and recorded at the other end by people I know. Once a week I get tested for drugs, and I've been undergoing drug tests long enough to prove I have not been high in years. Most cops in your precinct know about me. I guess warnings about me have not arrived at the point of being included in your training manual. The crimes you have committed here include assault, battery, and the use of excessive force. I might include racial profiling and unwarranted search in my complaint if I feel like it. Your days as a *peace* officer will soon be ending."

A car passed.

For some beats, Easy heard nothing more.

"What the fuck are you talking about? Are you internal affairs?"

"You wish," Easy answered. "Welcome to New America, chump. You're Old America and I'm here to shake your crooked ass out. Sergeant, could you please uncuff me so I can get up?"

Easy heard a stealthing of rubber soles. Those aimed at his head did not move. The new shoes stopped near. Then, quietly: "Your collar, Donner. As I see it he is not resisting at this moment and you do not need my backup. If you book him, you book him. But his tricks are known. Everything he just said is true. If he's guilty, he's guilty. But if he's not ... well ..."

And the shoes of the sergeant rubbered away, back to the second car. That door was opened. It thunked closed. The car whipped a turn and gunned off.

"Fucking shit," Easy heard as the handcuffs were loosened off his wrists. By the time Easy had risen to his knees the cop was in his car. By the time Easy had stood and leaned against his lowrider, to reset his equilibrium, the cop had sped away.

Easy caught his breath. He looked up to his angels with a grin.

He raised a fist.

The crowd in the convention center burst into cheers.

Chapter Five
Tuesday, June 26

More than anything else it is the balance and interplay of our varied personalities which has made us effective. We all recognize this. Remove one of us and we as a group are nothing. Only together, both feeding and feeding off each others' strengths, have we accomplished something remarkable. Not many humans can face down authority with such a fearless self-possession. But that kind of personality does not always offer the insight and sensitivity another might. And while one of us might feel an inexhaustible affection for every soul they meet, another provides a force of will that sometimes pulls the rest of us along, through whatever difficulty, over whatever obstacle. Others of us excel in our sense of objectivity and detachment, or in our artistic aptitude for blending everything we touch into a cohesive whole.

We could not know, at that point in our history, how we would complement one another. We could not know how our conflicting personalities would provide just the friction needed to make a real difference. But it was true. Long before we were really paying attention to one another we had begun to influence each other in tangible ways that still repercuss. We had begun to lay the foundation for what we would become and what we would accomplish.

Easy was walking.

It was 7:35 a.m. in Norwalk and he was walking down Rosecrans Avenue to his drug screen. Three times a month, on Tuesdays, Easy paid for a urinalysis. The fourth Tuesday he paid for a hair follicle test. All of this because he knew one day they would get him. He knew they would. Ezekiel would check Authority for as long as he could. He would bait Authority into exposing its abuses as many times as possible. But someday its tolerance would crack. Someday one of its little piggies would lose his cool and rumble Easy in for nothing. And he was certain the frame would be a drug wrap. Some contraband in his trunk, they would plant, or claim they found on his person. That day would come (as it almost had with Donner) and that day the chumps would be surprised. For on that day his attorney would produce a ream of drug screens that proved he had not had any illegal substances in his veins for literally years. Easy's architecture of defiance wobbled without this foundation of weekly drug tests. Neither did it stand completely defensible without him keeping receipts for each of his cash transactions, and producible documents for all of his card activity. His home computer log, too, Easy minded assiduously and kept quickly accessible. Not to mention the data logger he had installed in the Impala. All of these were Easy's backstop. The drug screens and the document trail would provide air-tight alibis the day some *pendejo* finally lost his shit and went to squealing. These and the fact he could demonstrate such an obvious motive for whatever false charges were trumped up: His zine *SlapDown.*

Sometimes, walking Rosecrans like he was now, Easy felt vulnerable. For he knew that when away from his angels he lacked their guardian eyes. So sometimes, while walking and feeling this vulnerability, Easy questioned why continually he put himself at such risk. He reflected on his family. Had someone among them triggered his anti-authority trip? *Trip.* He acknowledged it as such. No illusions. But nothing at home had kindled it. Not *'apá.* Not his *tíos.* It was just seeing that swagger, he thought, seeing some white-faced cop come parading down a brown-black street, or even *through* a brown-black *home* and acting like he owned it. Like he *owned* it. Something in Easy... his dignity... He just cannot submit to such hubris. And for Easy to ignore that hubris is to submit to it. Ezekiel Castillo was born to resist it.

He watched his homeboys challenge that swagger at school and get thrown down. And he watched and identified the school system as just a smaller branch off a bigger tree, a mere offshoot. And if this mere offshoot could ground men as strong and as *hombre* as his homeboys, no person alone could hope to battle that entire tree -- If that is, they fought on the tree's terms. To prevail in his resistance, Easy concluded, he would have to redefine the terms of the battle, create new ones -- his own.

Ezekiel witnessed his friends, one by one, get silenced, get taken down, get put away, get buried; and he studied their defeats. He saw that the only way to effectively check that swagger was to outwit it. That's hundreds of years of dominance, he told himself. Strut all day, stand as tall and proud as you deserve to stand, but still those monsters can flatten you, and effortlessly. *Foos can't push against that weight. Fronting achieves nothing there.* And to engage the chumps on their terms is just plain fronting. *So you work around them, homes.* For the weight of that ancient swagger, in fact, is also its weakness.

It was all those electrifying phone videos from the twenty-teens that finally enlightened Easy. It was also rewinding back to Rodney King, as he investigated, and seeing the extraordinary difference those images made. Easy realized that to neutralize the monsters one need only capture their misdeeds on video. Moving images hold them accountable for some reason. By making it impossible for them to deny their behavior, they would cease denying their behavior. They would be forced to confess it and maybe even change it. Easy's mission started there. The rest was merely technical: Child's play for a brain that encased an engineering degree from CalTech.

So Easy was walking. He was walking to his weekly drug screen: The principal outwork of his impregnable defense, the very lynchpin to his outsmarting and denying those monsters any swagger over him. Authority is not faceless, he had gleaned sitting in the gallery behind his homeboys at trials. There is a place where it has two eyes. And when, eventually, they dragged Easy before those two eyes he would stand ready to meet their stare, directly, without shrinking. To beat Easy down, to silence Easy, or bury Easy, they would have to acknowledge first their hypocrisy and swallow it. He did not think they would do that. It is the system that oppresses, he believes, rarely the individual.

Except for people like that dog who assaulted him a couple of weeks previous. What a zine he was making! Jerry Donner. First month on the beat cop. Nothing would officially arise from Donner's botched traffic stop until *SlapDown* started appearing around Southeast LA with Donner's mugshot on the cover. That would be happening soon. Easy refrained from filing a complaint with the LAPD Internal Affairs Group. Neither did he circulate his videos among news outlets. Only those who watched it live or who were viewing it still through shares knew of the brutality. But that was about to change. Easy had assembled his data. People Seek and some rudimentary Goggle and Faustbook creeping had informed him thoroughly of rookie Donner. Some tight spreads, he had built, from stills of the illegal stop. The sergeant who arrived later had yet to be identified. With his face against the pavement Easy could not see the man. And possibly that sergeant had even disguised his voice when schooling Donner. Easy's angels had captured the sergeant's car number off its roof. But deliberately the man had refused to look up at the drones, and knowingly he had stayed out of view of the lowrider's cameras. Easy could not name that accomplice with any confidence. But Donner -- That chump was *jodido* -- Over. And. Out.

Easy envisioned the content of this *SlapDown* spread across its sixteen pages: A description of the scene in Leimert Park, a verbatim transcript of their discourse from first word to last, stills of him being bodyslammed. Potent. Plus the SkipTube and Faustbook addresses where readers could witness it all for themselves from four different vantages. Every slur. Every twitch of the sucker. Well, well, that cracker really screwed himself, Easy mused. Sure I got a bloody nose. Some abrasions on the face. But those heal. This would never heal for Donner. He probably could not work as a security guard after this reveal, or even a crossing guard. *Imbecile.* Maybe he could re-enlist in the military. In any event, the chump should never again hold power over other human beings.

All of *SlapDown's* regular outlets would receive this issue. From Fredo's convenience mart in Cypress Grove to Highlight Books up in Los Feliz. From Bango Wango in Chinatown to the next zinefest in Long Beach. Easy expected the zine would filter through to the mass media too. If he let that process play out organically those bullhorns were more likely to blare that song. All of Califas would eventually see this rabbit run. And then, of course, the zine would be placed guerrilla-style throughout the washrooms of police headquarters itself. He had an overnight dispatcher friend eager to handle that troll for him. This chump was so fucked. He so deserved it.

Easy strode past the entrance of the drug test facility, past the large red brick building, bobbing his head with proud self-assurance. He donned an FCLA cap instead of his hairnet for these early morning strolls. And blue jeans and tennis shoes, he wore, and his thick prescription glasses instead of wraparounds. Police patrols never seemed to recognize Ezekiel in this guise despite his mustache and brawny build. They drove right by him. A chuckle rumbled in the back of Easy's throat. His mouth kept flat, though, unsmiling. He dropped the empty bottle of mineral water he had been carrying into a trash barrel. Easy walked on beyond the medical facility's 20-foot marker -- the smoker's line -- halting finally at the railroad crossing which always seemed to start clamoring about then. There he sparked a menthol.

As Easy stood smoking he contemplated Tijuana. Applications for this year's Baja Zine Fiesta had barely opened and still the buzz around last year's event simmered in the community. Folks raved, actually. But his material felt less relevant to Mexico. Lots of Americans would attend, he expected, so there was that. But did he really want to take his electronics over the border? And the six-four? He did not relish bringing along the lowrider, though plenty of foos itched to cruise *Revolución*. Maybe just zines, he wondered, nothing but zines. Easy questioned the effort. Was it worth it? On the other hand, *SlapDown* existed to stoke resistance, to encourage folks to check Authority's power to abuse. That message applied in Mexico as well as anywhere else. Easy imagined some *Tijuas* artist cruising in a ride equipped like his, and how the cameras would deter those green-uniformed *perros* who aimed to tap a bribe off him or even to take the groceries off his passenger seat.

How would it feel now to cross that border? To find himself in a land whose Authority was not *his* Authority? Years since he had crossed to the other side, since his early twenties. Would his anti-Authority trip maintain its traction over there? Might his urge to resist fade a little? Because a Mexican cop meant something very different to Easy than a US cop. The push and pull between them certainly would tilt, maybe even evaporate. Easy wondered how that would feel. Those little piggies were not his little piggies. Then he shrugged. He did not have to decide yet.

The cigarette was done. The smoke has ceased to rise. Easy contemplated its burned-out tip. For a beat he stood blankly, thinking of nothing. The railroad crossing began its clangor then, as predicted, with the automobile gates lowering to secure passage for the coming commuter coach. The Pacific Surfliner chuffed slower than usual that day. But Easy had seen it do so before. Countless times the train had rocked by just as he moved to enter the testing facility at almost exactly 7:58 a.m.

A profile through a train window caught Easy's eye. As the train screamed away he groped at his memory for a possible name. Then, turning, it struck him: Well, well, that girl looked just like Rocky from *Shake Me the Boom Boom*.

A cigarette butt depository waited exactly 20 feet from the testing office. Easy angled the filter of his menthol through its aperture. Directly he approached the building then, intent upon his Tuesday urinalysis. For the dozenth time, Easy noticed the security cameras mounted off the corners of the edifice and inwardly criticized their obsolescence. A woman in red scrubs appeared

107

behind the glass door, rolling over its lock. She smiled a greeting. They recognized each other. *Ay, mamacita*, Ezekiel mused. Mona was her name.

Rocky was walking.

His West Hollywood shopping spree with Fernandinha had gone quickly. She was easily dressed for her engagement -- one of those Tuesday afternoon cocktail parties that only a socialite connected to 'the business' would think to arrange. As *Dinya* was a personal fitness coach and yoga instructor her natural look smoothed off half the challenge for that gig, or, in other words, *the slimming*. Rocky accentuated her long Brazilian legs with crepe palazzo pants, some flat sandals beneath, and a loose cotton tank above. It did require almost subliminal coaxing to convince the angel to tie her hair up, and maybe ultimately she would ignore Rocky's counsel. But that was his master's touch. All would expect her chic boardwalk vibe to ride below long free tresses of shiny brunette. If she arrived like that everyone would remark her stirring beauty, of course; but if she followed his advice and non-conformed by wearing an updo, windblown, with some tendrils hanging across the brow, that afternoon tea would just *buzz* at her freshness. Both women and men would migrate from room to room to view her. They would not know why, but that updo would be why. Rocky hoped Dinya listened to him.

And Rocky was walking.

With Fernandinha styled to wow and no further appointments after that late morning rendezvous, Rocky kissed his client on the cheek and ducked away to the "car" he claimed to have parked in a garage around the corner. He always professed this possession to prevent his affluent clients from feeling guilty about his meager means. He knew that if he allowed that guilt eventually they would stop consulting him. His white grandfather Williams had drilled this truth into him as a youngster: That poverty is not shameful, but that flaunting poverty does no good. Secretly then he walked down Fairfax, dodged right onto the Sunset Strip to catch the #4 bus which connected to the #1 bus which deposited him at the foot of his favorite parade ground. In the preceding month Rocky had fully internalized his decision to transition, and day by day he had felt it empowering him. Self-knowledge! What a superpower! Little by little, waking up morning after morning and glaring down at his cock as he urinated away his night's heaviness, Rocky had felt stronger and stronger and surer and surer about his womanhood. So he walked. Rocky strutted really down the Venice Beach boardwalk.

And Rocky was walking.

He wore graceful leather ballet flats that a client bought him in a fit of gratitude. He wore an orange blazer over a tight white mini-dress of tulle that hugged his ass and highlighted his muscular shiny-shaved legs. And that ass of Rocky's was just shaking that hugging skirt. Above these he had thrown around his neck a fancy yellow scarf, signaling his brazen good feeling. Rocky was strutting down Venice Beach boardwalk, totally unselfconscious. He peeled away his blazer soon, revealing the fine lines of his shoulders and arms. Boldly he exhibited his glam do as it framed his confident, dauntless smile. He let his wrist bangles clank. He let everything ride as it might, naturally, adjusting nothing. Today Rocky was perfect! Even the hated apple shape of his body was perfect, and the wideness of his nose! And here were his sunglasses. And his yellow scarf. And Rocky was just strutting like he had never strutted before.

After midday now, bright, and the muscle men pumped iron under a perfect sphere of sun. The tourists swarmed at this summer hour but the local color felt true to Rocky too. He resisted his giddy urge to engage with passing strangers until an on-coming brownish darling approached, just as voluptuous as she could be. She strolled hand-in-hand with her man. The woman seemed half-dazed by Venice's t-shirt and gimcrack drag, and by the carnival of weirdoes who peopled it.

Rocky decided to become one of them.

"Hey, Mamma!" his voice caressed, adoringly. Almost they passed each other but Rocky leaned into the woman's broad flowing dress in a kindly way which hitched her ambling forward motion. The garment was dark purple and violet with a fine pattern of flowers in airy fabric. Deep-necked, her dress cinched at the waist to let its sleeves drape indistinguishably into its skirts.

The woman stood flummoxed at Rocky's address. She held back her head, not knowing exactly how to react.

"What a beautiful muumuu, my dear," Rocky lilted. "You, my love, have found your color. And you have found your look. OMG. I have seen so many people today, but I do not think I've seen one other person on this boardwalk who has so convincingly found their style."

The woman's neck had craned forward. She peered down across the bib and knees of her dressfront, not yet feeling complimented. The dress was Hawaiian style -- but more Maui local than Waikiki tourist. Just perfection for any boardwalk on a shiny day. And just plain crying for a sea breeze and some hipsway. Flatteringly the dress swagged off the woman's broad curves. Above it, she wore a floppy sun hat with a band that wooed the fabric's purple.

"Now, you tell me," Rocky continued. "This is not by accident, now is it? You have been working on this style, now haven't you? Things don't come together so fine without a little time and experimentation. Am I right, mamma?"

Finally, the woman smiled. Finally, Rocky's buoyant mood had persuaded. He was euphoric, but not frighteningly so. This was love in him -- not an amphetamine high. Unmistakably Rocky meant what he said, his voice lavish and gentle.

"This style is almost all I wear," the woman confided, adopting the tone of a fellow connoisseur. Then, removing his sunglasses, Rocky squatted. He kept his knees together and draped an arm over them. He touched the material of the dress, fanning it slightly to appreciate its pattern and cut more critically. His pinchings and pullings arrived with such acumen and objectivity that the woman did not shrink from him.

He asked, "But with variations? And this is ramie, isn't it?"

"I have more than a dozen of these dresses. Yes, ramie. I have one for every possible kind of engagement."

"Stylin!"

"You're correct. It took me a decade to pin down this cut. But I've always thought it suited me very well. You really agree?"

Rocky released the fabric and flexed upward to match the interest in the woman's gaze. She removed now her sunglasses too. Their eyes met, both of them beaming. These two knew one another so well without ever having met.

"Mamma, I am not lying. Beauty is beauty and you have found it. Balance, proportion, fit, personality. And it's got the authentic you just woven right through the pattern. OMG."

"I'm telling you a larger woman can do things with a dress that a smaller woman simply cannot."

110

"True. True. In this, dear, I would put you on a runway next to a ninety-pound waif any day. You would kill."

"You know I would."

"God bless you, sister."

"You've got quite an eye."

"A goddess like you makes it easy."

And with a wink and a spontaneous clasp of hands Rocky let that diva from somewhere back East glide away toward her evening on Venice Beach, or maybe in Santa Monica. He suspected she would carry their encounter back to Baltimore or maybe Pennsylvania just as he would take their tale to Blossom and maybe even his zine.

You should have photographed that wonder in this golden daylight, Rocky reflected. *She just inspires,* he thought. *Perfection.* And her confidence was *so New America.* Palpable agency.

But Rocky kept strutting. He strutted on until the boardwalk proper unraveled into a more common stretch of sidewalk that fronted a row of vacation condos abutting the Marina del Rey. His ballet flats were newish and he felt his toes chafing toward a blister so he pivoted there for Washington Boulevard, heading for the bus stop where his West Hollywood trips occasionally died. Still his yellow scarf bounced freely. By the time he sank onto the bus bench on Palawan Way the sun was burning at about 2 o'clock and his long parade had tranquilized his high. Rocky felt cleansed.

He decided: *It's not so rude to compliment strangers, now is it? Whatever blah, blah, blah conformist made up that stupid rule just doesn't know how to be nice to people.*

Clare walked an alley off Venice Beach. It was late afternoon, a golden Southern California day. Hers was more of a saunter than a walk, really. Contentedly she strolled, noticing the weather's aquamarine sky, its diffuse brightness, and the brushy kiss of a sea breeze. The lilac saddlebags straddling the rear wheel of her touring bike held fruit and vegetables and some crispy morsels for crunching later with her teeth. Last week she had amplified her carrying capacity by acquiring a handlebar basket and at this moment it contained a sweating half-gallon of milk and a box of orange juice.

111

This had been a pleasant day for Clare. After waking late she had coasted the boardwalk to Santa Monica Pier, brunched in that little cafe on Ocean Avenue with the lavender awning and elegant dolphin logo, pedaled herself a mile farther north to boutique row on Montana, found herself an airy peach and white blouse of madras, and, after hesitating briefly over the price, a pretty new ring for her left thumb. She biked leisurely back down the boardwalk then, engaged in a flirtatious telephone chat about the agonies of her bicycle mission with her old girlfriend Becca, microwaved a cinnamon roll to steaming, and then sketched rather unfruitfully but still satisfyingly while nodding her head to K-pop. Clare napped for a half hour. She woke to discover she lacked milk for her daily post-siesta latte and so sallied forth for a grocery run. She never once thought of her Saab.

And all of this while the stock market was plunging.

Clare had just rolled off 28th Street and dismounted. She was pushing her handlebars those final 20 yards to her rear step. Clare liked walking her touring bike right up to the back door. She would hoist it over the wooden threshold then and kickstand the bicycle right inside her kitchenette. She found groceries easier to unload from her lilac saddlebags when she parked them beside the refrigerator. So Clare pushed and hoisted. Then she lay her wayfarers on the counter. Then she stepped through the cute little arch that delineated her kitchenette from her living area. Clare buttoned on the television with the remote control and turned away as the screen warmed toward resolution. She opened her refrigerator door.

Clare hummed a K-pop tune as she placed carrots and celery in the bottom crisper. She torqued her shoulders to the tune's imaginary beat as she tumbled tomatoes over the counter. Clare swiveled her hips like a belly dancer as the milk found its place on the bottom shelf. This woman moves like a sorceress. Everyone who sees Clare dance remarks on the compelling power she exudes. She had just begun to snake her arms in the air, sinuously, while pivoting toward her espresso machine, when she saw the muted news announcer looking more serious than usual. The graphic beside his head described a stylized stock ticker jagging downward, downward, downward.

She stiffened.

Clare marched through the arch of her kitchenette and lifted the remote off her cute loveseat. She unmuted the talking

112

head. He told her rather coldly that she had just lost a shit-ton of money.

Now Clare was walking quite differently. The balmy ease of the day had gone. The 500 square feet of her tiny abode certainly embodied smallness, but, in a circumstance like this, they provided plenty of room for pacing back and forth. Clare was walking and her keypad was being touched and Clare was listening to a warbling on the country's other coast. That warble hailed her long-time broker: His personal line.

"Oh, c'mon," she finally huffed.

Clare paced.

She murmured, "He always works late on days like this."

Clare itched to check her holdings on the STOX app but her shellshock stayed that impulse. Moreso she needed Donner. The man had a commendable talent for reassurance. Oh yes, Donner would put her at ease. He would know what to do.

"Hi, Don?" she cried out in a false lightness. The features of her face puckered. "Clare Luanne Taylor. Oh, I know you know. How are you? How bad was it for me? Yes, I'll wait. So sorry."

It was pretty bad but not tragic, Donner reassured.

"Tech stocks are like hella important to my portfolio, you know. Do you think they'll bounce back? Should I drop them? Or something? Perhaps?"

Donner knew Clare's portfolio extremely well, he reassured. And a rebound he predicted, indeed. Fallout from a big data hack announcement hurt the social networks and triggered a sell-off, but the circuit breaker put everything on hold and a quick recovery was expected in the morning. He was taking good care of her.

Clare felt less panicked after this chat and tapped the STOX app for the closing numbers on her three largest holdings.

She winced.

And on such a pretty day, she thought.

She dipped a finger into the pot of hand lotion on her kitchenette table and began massaging the balm over her knuckles. A beat later she was rubbing the greasy feeling off on her baby blue shorts. Clare pulled open her door and leaned against the doorframe, training her sight betwixt the vacation condos and toward the glad pedestrians enjoying the boardwalk. She noted the sun sagging past meridian, and the masculine carriage of a woman wearing a happy yellow scarf, and then a skinny shirtless skater.

Clare scooped another dose of lotion and rubbed it into her palms now, nervously. Automatically, mechanically, she had crossed back beneath the arch to her kitchenette, feeling the thuds of her heartbeat crowding out her breath. Clare saw that her hands slightly trembled. She wiped them again on her shorts. She looked again at her hands.

I'm just not accustomed to such shocks, she told herself. I should learn more about these financial things. I need to take more agency over my life, over *every little thing* in my life. If I had real command, I would not feel so rattled.

Clare fished from her saddlebags the Guatemalan Highland she had ground at the gourmet market around the corner. Then she lifted a filter off the top of her espresso machine. She studied and admired the new ring on her left thumb, but doubtfully now. Clare's face puckered tight. She bent stiffly to brew herself a latte.

Blossom was walking and the early evening avenue was lined with rich people in their rich bungalows watching their rich televisions and Blossom was walking and at her every stride the spurs of her heavy brown boots jangled on her heels, angrily.

Blossom was walking and she had walked around Brunton Howell's block three times now and she had noticed a maid watch her through some neighboring curtains and probably recoil from the blue-black thorns snaking up her arm, and the determination stretching her unsmiling cheeks, and her flack jacket, and her shaved head.

Blossom was walking and on this fourth circuit, drawing a deep breath, she shunted off the sidewalk to follow some flagstones leading to a doorway and she stood now on that doorstep and she stood now before the monster's den. Brunton Howell. *Boo Boo.* The assaulter of brave Littlefeather.

Blossom stood. She raised a fist to knock. She took a full breath. Blossom knocked on the brown door.

She was standing.

She was waiting.

Some beats passed and Blossom was gazing then at her heavy brown boots as her dark clothes fell loosely off her womanly curves, straightening them. Over the past month, she had attempted this approach many times. Finally, she had given up and forced herself to keep off this street for two complete weeks, to divert the current of fears and hesitations which drowned her will every time she neared this domicile. Then, walking the street fresh again, just now, consciously stoking her righteous rage and invoking the courage of Littlefeather herself, she had done it. She had seized agency. Here she was, waiting for this brown dam to be removed. And then, creakingly, a crack widened between the brown door and its frame. The hinges sounded and Blossom looked up from her boots. Her camera hung around her neck; she adjusted it. The breach widened more and more and now Blossom beheld a woman's face and heard a woman's voice. White. Elderly. Grayed strings of hair tied back from powdered cheeks. She wore a clean apron.

"Yes?"

Blossom's breath stopped. She swallowed. She inhaled. Relief, she felt, that this person was not Howell. The detour smoothed the way somehow, momentarily. Her chin quivered.

"I ... Hello. I would like to talk to Mr. Howell, please."

"And who may I say is calling?"

"Blossom."

"Blossom? Does Mr. Howell know you? Is he expecting your call?"

"Blossom from *Apologies in Order*. *Apologies in Order* is a small independent publication."

"One moment, please."

And the woman retreated out of the door's opening which promptly contracted, and heavily.

Blossom stared at the imposing brown door. She stared at its paint and its molding differently now than over the past four weeks, with almost an ownership. She sniffed. Having started this interaction relieved her. Emboldened, she felt. Blossom would begin with this brief question: "Why did you boo Littlefeather?" And, capitalizing on Howell's astonishment, snap a photograph of his guilty grimace. That's how it would go. And then, on behalf of all the indigenous peoples of both North and South America, Blossom would insist upon an apology. She had done this before. In the name of Russell Banks, she had done it. In the name of Standing Rock. Now it was this fucking chooch's turn. Taking two weeks to rebuild her nerve had been wise, indeed. Here she stood: Ready for what must be done to make this wrong right. Light-headed, Blossom stared, but inspirited. She believed the woman had not sensed her anxiety.

115

The brown door cracked open again. The grayed hair leaned outward. "I'm sorry we are not interested in a subscription."

"This is not about a subscription," Blossom put immediately, countering the sudden fracture she felt in their rapport. "I would like to ask Mr. Howell about the 1973 Academy Awards Ceremony. I'm writing about it … "

"I'm sorry … " But the words were unsure, the door not shutting.

"I … uh, Mr. Howell was in the audience of the 1973 Oscars and if he would be willing to answer just one question about his participation in it, I would certainly be fair to him. I'd also like a photograph if possible."

Blossom tapped the camera lens with her left hand. She did not smile.

The door eased more open.

"Fair?" This word came warmly, with curiosity, even humor. Blossom pressed her advantage.

"He started the booing of Littlefeather. I would like to ask him about it."

The woman's powdered face betrayed frank interest.

"Blossom, you said? Was that your last name?"

"First name. Silver is my last name."

"From … *Apologies in Order*, you said?"

"Yes."

For several beats the old woman's blue eyes absorbed this young lady on her doorstep. Blossom felt her ear gauges being scrutinized and her dimple piercing and her shaved scalp. Then, "And, Miss Blossom Silver, your publication is online also, I presume?"

"It has a website."

"Could you give me a moment, please?"

"Sure."

And the brown door swung shut and Blossom felt plain relief. The sheer length of that dialogue, and the nearly losing the connection with the woman but by persistence regaining it had purged from Blossom every residue of fear. That was a call center trick, actually, for outgoing solicitations. You just keep talking until they ring off. Occasionally it worked, like now. She felt giddy. Blossom pressed her lips confidently and studied the windows of the house. Translucent white curtains hung in them. She glanced above to the picture-perfect suburban tree drooping over the urban rooftop. Other trees stood in parallel rows along the avenue, like servants in livery. The house next door was built like a Swiss chalet; across the street rose a stucco facade, Southwestern style, next to that an Art Deco number flaunting polygonal designs. Each of these dwellings squatted behind immaculate lawns that smelled somewhat of manure. So that's the odor of privilege, Blossom thought. Minutes passed. A lot of them. Night approached. Blossom began to wonder if she would be ignored now. She kept herself coiled, though, poised to strike with her question, to snap her photograph. Blossom gazed down at the tattoo of thorns encircling her ring finger, at how it wraps around her wrist from there and then winds up around the golden flesh of her forearm and bicep. Proudly her eyes traced the spiral. She reached up to adjust her new nose ring then and was concluding she had in fact been abandoned by these cowards when the brown door swung open and the gray-haired woman leaned out. This time she held a computer tablet.

The woman asked, presumptively, "Is this your website, Miss Silver?"

She positioned the tablet between them. The homepage of Blossom's simple X-Template site colored the screen. The site exists primarily as a contact point for people seeking her zines. Blurbs, she posts there, and images from *Apologies in Order,* and links to her networks and online store.

"Yes, that's me."

Still anchoring her splash page was that original clipping of Howell: the one from *Stagecraft,* the one which portrayed the chooch guffawing over a cocktail. The old lady, therefore, and presumably Brunton himself, knew now about her crusade.

The woman touched the screen to change tabs. "And you are Blossom Silver, as the index of Internet Assigned Names shows? With an address on 118th Drive in Inglewood?"

Blossom swallowed. The skin across her cheekbones drew tight. She narrowed her eyes, drilling the lady with a searching glare. What's fucking happening? Her chin quivered as the woman tabbed again. "And this is your Twitagram profile?" Blossom was stunned. With a crackling voice that mixed surprise with defiance, she blurted: "Is Mr. Howell going to talk to me? Boo Boo. Is Boo Boo here?"

"Good day," the old woman said.

The door shut.

"I am a-walkin', my fays. Got my phone up here in front of my face ... experimentin' with Sanjay's vlog suggestion. Hmmm. Now if ya'll don't like what ya see here, don't put it on ole Viole, alright? -- put it on Bangladesh. But I think it's a promisin' idea. So here I am talkin' to ya'll and a-walkin'. Just to arrive here, for instance, where I am finally just now gettin' to sit down this heavy-ass backpack of mine, I had to go walkin' from a bus stop just north of Balboa Park, you know, to that distro I was pimpin' at ya'll in my last blog post -- Zine Cognito. Here. Just let me sit down a spell and catch my breaff. Ahh. Mmm. Now, I got to that joant a good long minute before they were supposed to close, but Phil (who some of ya'll SoCal peeps know) had already skedaddled. Our Lonno (who more of ya'll SoCal peeps know) told me *O, Kindred* had at least a dozen transactions this quarter and likely Phil'd be dealin' out my coin any time. Thank you, my fays, for buyin' up all those issue sevens. I left behind lots of issue eights just so ya know. And subscriptions went off in the mail this mornin'. If you're half a planet away don't be feelin' forgotten, digital issues go out tomorrow. I walked miles more sidewalk after that, precious, with a few of my brown boys honkin' at what I presume to be my intelligence along the way, until finally I made it here to this super chill all-night cafe of ours. If you had any idea how much work I've done under this white canopy at 3 a.m. on a Tuesday! Gotta go in and get myself an Americano from my girl Becca. Decaffeinated, for now."

"Hello again, my fays, an hour later now and I've turnt my phone camera round again aksin' myself whether I'm gonna stay here to work the night through. More culling and possible sequencin' for issue nine needs doin'. Last bus don't roll south till 1 a.m., though, so I got five hours to decide. Lonno, by the way, tells me someone took one of our zines today and sat in *Cognito's* corner armchair readin' it cover to cover. Who was that? One a ya'll? She says she only thought to say somethin' cuz the boy was in no way leisure readin'. Uhn-Uh. Like he was studyin' the joant hard, she tells me, or lookin' for somethin' specific. Reminds me I been thinkin' about placin' back copies of issue three, see, in some of those 'take a book, leave a book' boxes you find round. Those 'little free libraries' are not exclusively white spaces, I guess, but hit the right neighborhoods and, dern, they may as well be. Say, hey, La

Jolla. So Lonno's story's got me thinkin' about this all over. Always feelin' your feedback, my fays. The golden hour here as you can probably see in that sky behind my twisty half updo. Well, *if* you can see behind it since I teased it up so proud this mornin'. I'm hauntin' that sidewalk table I always take when it's available – the one that fronts the window off the entrance? But now you can actually see this famous spot with your own beautiful eyes. You can thank Sanjay for this idea. So, look, this is that very table where the focus of our blog shifted from pure fairy tale talk to some fairy tale talk mixed with me, myself and *It*."

"Hey, again, my fays. Another two hours gone already and here I am talkin' more whispery at ya'll since a frownin' white girl two tables off from me keeps on distractin' with this lookin' over her shoulder errytime a person pass. Might be her *It*. Looks like she might be fearin' some lover isn't comin' who she just really really wants to come -- at least that's my interpretation. So I am not alone in my wrestlin' with how to deal with *It*. Hours now pickin' over all these submissions for issue nine and I'm wonderin', let me tell ya, if there is *any*body out there *any*where who ain't runnin' from some fear, or tryin' to dampen down some big burnin' hurt, or in some subtle or even unconscious way revolting against *It*. For instance, here's a tiny preview of issue nine: Some onyx-skinned fairy in a neon pink tutu is fightin' to break a curse set on her by some shapeshiftin' warlock. Now, the warlock is shadowy, usually invisible, and the fairy's only hope is to cop a counterspell off a talkin' ivory fungus. To me, that's about *It*. Or there's this leprechaun here. But an evil leprechaun, see, who's chasin' a three-legged Japanese sprite who has the power to summon blustery storms. What's a leprechaun doin' sneakin' round 1700s Japan, you ask? Well, that's my point. In the 1700s Japan was hyper suspicious of all us so-called Westerners. They fought dern wars to keep away traders. I don't think ole Ireland was sendin' out traders back then. If memory serves correct it mighta been the Dutch, maybe, or was it the Portuguese? In any regard the message is the same: This tiny green leprechaun creature from some other land makes me afraid so I'm gonna kill it. I don't recognize this freak. It's not like me. So let's kill it. And now I'm suddenly whisperin' at ya'll all over again cuz that white girl, my fays, is just lookin' at every single body that goes walkin' by these tables. Still. And she *ain't* just people-watchin'. Mm-Mnn. That girl needs somethin' from someone. Precious. She is lookin' for her Precious. Considerin' how long we've been sittin' here I guess she does have reason to fear her Precious ain't gonna show. So, clearly, I am not alone in my wrestlin' with *It*. Do you too, my fays? If so, I guess I'm not the exception; I am more like the rule. I am errybody. And if errybody is strugglin' the same way I am strugglin', is *It* our natural state? And if *It* is my natural state, should I even be fightin' it?"

"Okay, my fays. So it is many more hours later on now and I am sure enough slog tired. Goin' on home, I guess. Decided not to work here through the night. Gonna rent-a-scooter over to that midnight bus now and trolley home. So ends this vlog experiment number one. Let me know what ya'll think. Wishin' you my precious fays so many Happily-Ever-Afters. A-walkin' now, a-walkin'."

Stanley Donner Jr. woke that morning to the feeling of something scraping out the inside of his chest. Then he was walking, walking the floor of his three-bedroom condo from one corner to another -- and back again. Then he was shaking his pill bottle. *Rattle. Rattle.* And staring at his pill bottle. And gripping his pill bottle. Stanley did not understand the scraping feeling. He had never understood why sometimes it plagued him and other times it did not. He just knew that sometimes it came suddenly to scrape out the inside of his chest and that when it came he had two alternatives. Always Stanley chose to flee. He fled because the other alternative meant surrender, and still he refused to surrender.

He gazed on the pill bottle.

Stanley Donner Jr. ceased walking to and fro. He faced the closed door now, that door ending the short hallway off the kitchenette, that tightly closed door. Angry he felt at her, and trembling. But it was his fault, yes. His fault, not hers. His anger melted to guilt. "I'm so sorry," he mumbled to her. Stanley stood pressing the heel of his hand against his sternum.

He turned from the tightly closed door then, quickly, semi-dazed. He bent over the bathroom sink to scrub his gaunt features but found no soap in the dish and so dug in a packed cardboard box on the floor for soap to use but found no soap there and so splashed his gaunt features with cool water over the bathroom sink.

Ninety minutes later, unwashed and unshaven, Stanley Donner Jr. had put 79 miles on his green sedan and was walking into the Long Beach Public Library.

"I read that you have a zine library here."

Ninety minutes later Stanley Donner Jr. had put 109 miles on his green sedan and was walking into the Baldwin Hills Branch of the LA Public Library.

"Someone told me you have a zine library here."

One hour later Stanley Donner Jr. had put 124 miles on his green sedan and was walking into The Book Circus.

"I would like to buy all these zines."

"All of them?"

"Is that okay?"

"Yes, of course"

"I'm a millionaire. I just got a life insurance payout."

"I'm sorry, or congratulations. Not sure which I should say."

He flinched. "In truth, sorry is better."

"Sorry."

Stanley Donner Jr. said nothing. He trembled.

Three hours later Stanley Donner Jr. had put 247 miles on his green sedan and was walking into Zine Cognito. He knelt before an anarchic rack of images and textures and sizes and colors to pluck forth a single zine that presented on its cover a male human body topped by a horse's head. The man-horse thing wore a red dress. Stanley carried the thick volume to an armchair in the corner of the shop, and there, in the afternoon sunlight, hunched over it fervently, scouring the entire issue from first page to last. Then he approached the counter.

"See all those zines?" he told the clerk named Lonno. "I want to buy them. Could you perhaps put them in a box for me?"

"All of them?"

"Well, not the duplicates, I guess."

Then Stanley Donner Jr. was walking the sidewalk. He felt dazed and he was turning a corner now. And he was walking around the block now. And walking. He was rattling his pill bottle now, distractedly. And he was walking and walking. And he was trembling.

Stanley gazed on the pill bottle.

Two hours later Stanley Donner Jr. had put 313 miles on his green sedan and sat parked on the shoulder of the I-15 highway. His left arm hung over the car door, its flesh burnt. A California Highway Patrol car idled behind Stanley. That car's cherry red and cobalt blue lights twirled. The officer stooped finally beside Stanley's window, his aviator sunglasses looking past the sun-burnt arm, his semi-oval badge glinting.

He said, "Mr. Donner, I'm just issuing you a warning today; but you need to update your registration as soon as possible." The cop handed a rectangular white sheet through Stanley's window. Then he offered Stanley a business card. "Take this too," the cop said, humanely, "And, uh ... Mr. Donner ... Happy Birthday."

Stanley read the card. It said: "Riverside County Mental Health Services." Beneath this, the officer had circled a telephone number next to the words "Crisis Line." Stanley Donner Jr. stretched his neck to see his reflection in the rearview mirror. He found there his eyes swollen and pink and his gaunt features bathed with tears.

Chapter Six
The Weekend of July 7

"Oh, whatevs!"

Clare tried again.

She had removed her lilac saddlebags from the rear pannier mount and dropped them on the tarmac in front of the city bus. But still the bike weighed too much. Now she even unclamped the pannier mount itself, setting the aluminum frame behind her. But still she could not lift the coaster high enough to slide it into the bus' bicycle rack.

Clare was stuck. She puckered her features in a puff of defeat as the bus driver tromped down hurriedly, turned out of his folding door, and said,

"Let me do it."

"I guess I can't," she grimaced. "So sorry. Next time I'll use my lighter bike, I guess. So sorry."

He angled the wheels into the run of the rack. "I'm actually not supposed to do this but my supervisor's at lunch."

"Thank you so much."

"When you take it down roll it out. It'll come off easier than trying to lift it."

The driver secured the bike in place with the rack's spring-loaded tire hook. A beat later he had leapt back up into his bouncy bucket seat and was strapping himself in. The passenger coach sat in the Fullerton Transportation Center, Dock 1.

Clare stood beside him then, ready to pay her fare. Her saddlebags hung from the end of her straightened arm. The frame of the bike's pannier mount leaned against her shin. She kept on her wayfarers, hiding behind them. "I'm mortified. It's my first time trying to put my bike on a bus. Next time I won't bring my coaster for this type of thing. You won't have to do this for me again. I promise. I'm really trying to take care of myself right now. But right when I start trying it seems like suddenly I'm needing more help than ever; I mean for *every little thing*. It's been a struggle, but I'm not ready to give up yet. Gotta stay pozzy."

"You're good," he said. "Don't worry about it." And the coach lumbered out of its slip then, wallowing through a broad slow arc that crossed the spacious blacktop and found its exit onto Santa Fe Avenue.

Clare plopped into a seat near the front. Frowning and dejected, she noticed a graffito on the seatback in front of her. It said: "nRageD." Then she buttoned on her phone to track through her maps app where she sat in relation to where she was going. Clare palmed her forehead. Her brow was misty. Various satellites had transformed her into a blue arrowhead that ticked upward on the screen of her phone. A 21-minute bus ride from Fullerton into Anaheim, it told her.

She squinted.

What a mess.

If the fiasco stopped at her bike-lifting inabilities she might not feel so defeated. But there had been the original plan to pedal to Union Station and then to train from there to Anaheim. Union Station is only 16 miles from Venice. But she had gotten hella tired after only like three miles. Then there had been the new strategy to ride by light rail from Santa Monica College, where she pooped out, to Union Station, and then train on. That had started alright as she had managed to wheel the bike onto the platform and into the rail car. But then a young black man with a twinkling smile had insisted on talking sweet. Not all forward young gents irritated Clare, to be sure, and it certainly was true this one had some *appeal,* and she *was* feeling *the need* more and more, but did he not see that she was pushing around a bicycle? And that she was misty with fatigue? And that probably she might not feel exactly sexy right then? Men! Then there followed the problem of having to switch to the purple line subway after pedaling 25 minutes north to Wilshire from the last Expo line stop. That meant plenty more mistiness, followed by the strain of fighting those steep staircases. *Ugh.* But I did it, she reminded herself, grimly. Two long flights of steps holding back the weight of my bike and saddlebags so they didn't go cartwheeling down. See? Just conditioning perhaps. Perhaps that's why I couldn't lift the bike onto this bus. That's it. I'm tired, or something. Probably I could have lifted the bike if I had not blown so many carbs on that ride and those stairs.

The coach stopped and Clare watched a hairy old man in Capri shorts deboard to remove his bicycle from the bus rack. He rolled it off, using the driver's suggested technique.

I can do that.

Clare dove into her saddlebag for a bottle of Diet FizzBang. It bubbled and hissed when she broke its plastic seal and still was sweating with a coolness that refreshed. Love that, she sighed. The cold felt good against her palm. As she gulped Clare recalled the beautiful brunette standing beside the vending machines in the Fullerton station. Some Russian girl, perhaps? She was hot.

Delicious.

She should start just riding her light bike, Clare mused. This lifting part would be easier then. Clare pondered the limited usefulness of a coaster. Just a kind of heavy two-wheeled pleasure craft, it was, neither for the plow nor the stagecoach, definitely no pony express. She chuckled at the analogy. A bike as a horse? Why not? I call these things saddlebags, after all.

About the time she finished leisurely draining her soda, and perking her acuteness and verve, she was a couple of blocks from her destination and had regained her wind and confidence. Clare stood, hefting the saddlebags to her shoulder. The frame of the pannier mount clomped against her calves as she stepped along the aisle to the driver. She was hiding behind her wayfarers again.

"I should be able to get it off myself. I watched that other guy do it."

"Alright."

Clare directed, "I'm stopping in front of that Taco Snatch. Oh, someone else rang the bell."

The signal had pinged and the commuter coach was slowing up. Clare lay her bags and pannier mount in the grass beside the curb and, in a moment, with little strain, had rolled the bike off the bus rack and was kickstanding it on the sidewalk. She turned and beamed up at the driver a victorious grin. She offered a thumbs up. Unsmiling, the driver waved politely and lurched back into the traffic of North Harbor Drive.

See?

Clare clamped again the pannier mount to the bicycle frame, refit her saddlebags over it, and buttoned her phone for the time of day.

A little late.

For some yards, she just pushed but finally straddled the cushiony seat to cross the deserted avenue and hang left onto Broadway. She was pedaling away from the zinefest, actually, detouring for a tasty treat. Her maps app indicated the presence of a bistro in this direction, beyond two boutiques and a luxury laundromat. The Anaheim Museum of History and Art, which was hosting the zinefest, fell farther and farther behind Clare now as she coasted by a woman aiming a smartphone at a second woman in magenta who posed grandly in the sun. Clare rode a curb cut then onto the sidewalk and edged around a brown hippy couple in drapey white striding across her trajectory. She looked for a place to

126

lock up. Finding neither signpost nor rack nearby, Clare kickstood her bicycle before the bistro's large windows, leaving it untethered. She shouldered her lilac saddlebags. She entered.

Clare plopped onto a barstool. She ordered fried mushrooms and pilaf and, as she dined and delayed, flirtatiously revealed to the cute bartender with red hair that her bags were full of impossible space flowers which were about to be tabled for sale. Then she mentioned her uber-adventurous ride from Venice Beach.

"You rode that coaster all the way from Venice Beach to Anaheim?"

"I was going to," she squinted. "But actually a lot of the trip was on public transportation."

"Oh. Do you always leave it unlocked like that?"

Clare was licking her fingers. "No. You guys have big windows, though. Hey, can you give me some change, maybe? I need like twenty ones if you can spare them, perhaps some fives. I forgot all about bringing change for my table. I so irritate myself when I do that."

"You know, I'm so excited. I'm going to be a woman soon."

"You are?"

Tina was a regular, a long-time client of Rocky's. Cozily they conferred here in their accustomed boudoir, in this corner dressing room of the Anaheim boutique. Tina had the habit of lingering through specialty clothes shoppes alone for a few months, in whatever metropolis she happened to find herself, and then spiriting her acquisitions to this private cloister for a few-hours review with Rocky. He matched right with right, and offered a few additions, and awoke her tactfully to which cuts should be tailored and why, and suggested subtle accessories and complementary hairstyles. Tina took notes. Rocky tended to the darling between customers. She purchased few items from the boutique itself anymore, but always *gifted* Rocky a handsome fee. This had been going on for three years now, since Tina *discovered* Rocky one day while browsing West Hollywood and he had dressed her for some sort of boardroom tiff in Burbank. She worked in publicity. If Rocky were well-off and well-connected they would have been close friends. But even without the broad affection of a fully-developed friendship, they were still something of intimates.

Tina had texted this morning with a last-minute request for one of their tete-a-tetes. Rocky agreed, warmly, and gave up his table at the Anaheim Zine Fest, which was occurring just blocks away from the boutique. Steph had taken his spot since by the time Rocky received Tina's text Blossom was already hopping distros down Interstate 5.

Right now Rocky rested his elbow over his crossed knees with his forearm dangling forward and his bangles loose against his wrist. He swallowed, his Adam's apple rising and falling in his throat. Rocky's soft breathy voice lilted then:

"How does it feel to be a woman?"

"Well, I don't know. I've never known anything else so I have nothing to compare it to."

"I suppose then I'll be able to answer that question better than you in a while, won't I?"

"I think you will. If comparing my behavior to my husband's is any guide, we certainly have different feelings about sex."

"Ah. Look at you, darling. He must come after you every day."

"He used to if I let him. Now it's more like every other day."

"I'm not clear yet on how large I want my breasts to be. What would you suggest?"

"Do you like mine?"

"Sweetheart, I've seen so many breasts in this room, and every single pair has been beautiful, of course, but yours really are stunning."

"Well, that's just to look at, not to carry around with you everywhere you go."

"Ah."

"I would suggest something somewhat smaller than mine."

"Maybe a B cup? You've got some pretty Cs. And such wonderful areolas."

"You think so? B cups are about right, according to me. Larger than that and there are some ... well, let's say ... you start to feel some limitations on your movement."

"But they're so voluptuous."

"Yes, you see you can't lose, really. It depends on what you want. If you want to attract a lot of attention, the bigger you go the more you get. If you want less attention, the smaller cups are easier to hide, to keep people's minds off them. But, you see, a lady can always turn a B cup into an attention-getter, if a lady wants to. Straight men especially are very predictable in these matters. Poor things."

"Poor things, yes. I know what you mean about those cishet boys. They can be beasts and brutes, can't they? Sometimes it's adorable. Other times it's quite blah, blah, blah. I'm leaning toward the more modest sizes like you suggest; but somehow just the idea of finally being a woman, bodily, makes me fancy something more *striking*. You know what I mean?"

"I think so. At least you have a choice. And you're old enough to think about it reasonably. I knew a volleyball player in high school who so cursed her Ds."

"I know a woman who would kill to be a stripper but her As are an obstacle. And she is so afraid of surgery. Sometimes she's very WTF about it, other times she's quite LOL."

"So you get it."

"Thanks for chatting with me about it."

"When does the process begin?"

"I've really just decided. Just over a month ago. But the longer I think about it the more certain I become. I'll be taking the next step soon."

"You have support?"

"A friend."

"Good. You do what you need to do. If they can make you on the outside what you are on the inside, why not?"

"Yes."

"You're a beautiful person, Rocky. You've helped me so much to feel confident. I leave here feeling like I can conquer the world."

"Oh, thank you, Tina."

"I have a couple of outfits that we worked out together that I reserve for those days that I know I'm facing a battle at work, and that I'm going to have to kick some real ass. It's like putting on armor."

"Oh, thank you. You deserve it. You're precious."

"So how's that?"

Rocky gave a quiet sizzle of a whistle. Their unbuttoning of a light shirtwaist over an asymmetrical avant-garde dress just killed, he insisted. So much so, he said, that he must beg she allow him to photograph her outside on the sidewalk in the golden sun.

"That is a sunlight ensemble if I ever saw one, hon. That cut could be so Steampunk, but the magenta disguises that. Remember it on cool bright days. And, look, I know just the little pin to add to that lapel. It will blend everything from your eyes to those shoes."

"Give me a hug," Tina gushed. "You deserve to be happy."

Stanley Donner Jr. sat on the steps of the Anaheim Museum of History and Art. His wrinkled shirt draped off his hunched skeletal shoulders. He scratched with his sunburned hand at the pink flesh of his bony chest. He streamed his fingers through his tangled hair. Today his pill bottle rested in the breast pocket of his shirt. But today he was not dwelling on his pill bottle. Not at all. His troubles seemed far away.

Stanley Donner Jr. sat on the steps of the museum reading a paragraph that identified a rather gaseous-looking flower as native to the Andromeda Galaxy. The description claimed that at one time this vivid bloom served as a poison among nobility there, and then, later, after several millennia of revolutions, as a laxative among the bourgeois intelligentsia. Stanley Donner Jr. doubted the exact accuracy of this zine; but certainly the shape and suggested texture of the flower implanted not only these outlandish scenarios in his mind but many more he could not quite articulate. Stanley reflected on the woman from whom he had bought the zine. Open, she seemed to him, approachable, despite an air of urbanity, of poshness. He wondered whether she developed and executed this material alone. For the writing was as refined as the art was accomplished. Did she have a collaborator? "I should have asked her that," Stanley mumbled at himself, aloud. In any event, the zine reminded Stanley that one can say anything one wants to say in a zine, and in any particular way.

Suddenly Stanley Donner Jr. decided to make a zine of his own.

Stanley paged away from the zine's final spiky specimen to look on its back cover -- A sunflower grinning inside a space helmet. He filed the space flowers back into the slippery bundle of zines on his lap. He had bought one at every single table inside the museum, slowly combing through the rows of exhibitors in the basement, greedily unloading his pocketful of dollars. The fairy tale zine was not in attendance, though. And in questioning about its

130

absence Stanley had learned he could keep abreast of the doings of most zine makers through Twitagram. Before tackling this loot on his lap, therefore, he had downloaded the app onto his smartphone, created a profile, located the fairy tale zine, and learned from its stream that the beautiful black woman's name was Viola and that just days ago she had accidentally sliced her finger open with a kitchen knife. Then Stanley saw that she would be tabling her fairy tales at the upcoming South Bay Zine Bazaar, which would be taking place in San Diego ... Tomorrow! Stanley followed Viola's profile. Then, one by one, he checked the back and front of every zine on his lap, following every @ he could find. Stanley felt proud to have met all these creatives in person. He unhunched his shoulders. He stood from the museum step.

Stanley Donner Jr. lifted his cavernous eyes upward now, gazing into the deep blue sky. Bluer than usual today, clear -- weekend clear. He inhaled and the air tasted fresh to him, and the normal weekday crush of traffic was absent, and a light breeze curled around him, cooling, as the sunlight warmed. Until this moment he had not realized the perfect feeling of the day -- neither the unaccustomed quiet nor the occasional waft of perfume from the museum's Hawthorn bushes. Stanley drew a fully aware breath then, giving the afternoon surrounding him all his attention, wondering at it. His eyes strayed and tripped over his green sedan parked against the far curb. Stanley felt no need to go to his car. He felt no need for traffic today. He turned away from the green sedan then and pointed himself nowhere, toward nothing, descending the museum's steps.

He sauntered by a Shaft Burger. He strolled by a boutique. Then he entered a bistro.

A red-headed bartender loaned Stanley a pen with green ink. The need for a writing utensil titillated Stanley mildly. Usually, he noted ideas for essays and book reviews in his smartphone. But this idea was not about writing, it was about drawing. A paper napkin lay folded into a rectangle before him on the bistro table. As he waited for his fried mushrooms and pilaf he unfolded the napkin. After a moment's thought, he drew across the soft paper a grid -- five squares by five squares. He did not know how many pages his first zine might need, but 25 seemed plenty.

Stanley had been thinking about stickmen for a month now. Not only did he know he could draw a stick man, which was important, but sometimes he felt like a stick man himself. He had been noticing the color green lately too. "Good omen the bartender gave me a pen with green ink," he mumbled at himself. "How often would that happen?" Then Stanley Donner Jr. looked down at the grid of 25 squares and felt a phantom knife begin to scrape out the inside of his chest. He resisted what came next. *Scrape. Scrape.* He resisted. *Scrape.* But finally, pushing the heel of his hand determinedly against his perspiring temple, Stanley defied that scraping feeling in his chest and plunged on through his guilt.

He trembled.

Hunching over the grid he drew a stick figure into the first square. That was himself, Stanley Donner Jr. So there! Page one! Cocking his head Stanley inked two stick figures now into the second square. Page two. Then, still on page two, he gave those two figures big hands. The hands touched. The two stick figures were holding hands. Stanley now gave the second stick figure long hair. That hair was brown, though no one but him would know this given the green ink. Stanley smiled, faintly. On the third page, he drew a heart. He passed over the fourth square quickly, leaving it blank, and drew in the fifth square a lone stick figure. Himself. His smile faded. He left that stick figure completely alone. Stanley Donner Jr. stared at that lone stick figure for a long time.

He trembled.

Stanley left squares six and seven blank. In the eighth square, he sketched a door, a tightly closed door at the end of a blunt hallway. He attached to that door a heavy lock which he did not know how to draw correctly. Here was the door. The door. "Traitor," he mumbled at himself, viciously. Squares nine and ten Stanley left blank. In the eleventh square, he drew again the lone figure from square five. Himself again. Alone again. Over this lone figure which was himself, he sketched a heart this time -- a heart larger even than the figure's head. Then Stanley mussed the heart with some harsh dark markings, suggesting the heart was not right. Stanley felt unwell suddenly. Not right. He did not feel right. At all. In truth, Stanley craved to swallow his oval pills. All of them. Together. All at once. His usual answer to this craving was to determinedly locate the nearest restroom and splash his face with cold water, but this time he opted instead to finish this tentative plan for his first zine.

Many blank squares remained on the napkin but only two more were needed. Stanley envisioned and sketched the thick door again, that thick door from square seven. He envisioned himself forcing that door open and entering the room behind it and finding in that room the second stick figure, the one with long brown hair. She had been absent now for so long, for so so long, since way way back in square two. Stanley wanted to draw her behind that tight door, waiting for him, smiling there and expectant like before. But this was an impossible lie. So, in the last square, Stanley Donner Jr. drew nothing. Neither the door did he draw nor the brown-haired figure. Instead, he just penned these three words: "I miss you."

Blossom always wondered at the music in this bookshop. *Puter's* was one of the more radical literature outlets in San Diego but always for some reason playing Chopin or some other fucking establishmentarian shit. As she threaded from the side entrance through a hive of stacks, her spurs jangling on the heels of her heavy brown boots, she saw Becca raise her head to locate her unusual clanking. A beat later Becca recognized her. Becca stood, excited, her lime green eyeshadow glowing over a toothy smile.

"Another LA zinester just left," she greeted, with warmth.

"Yeah? Who?"

"See if you can guess. Horseshoe mustache. Matrix sunglasses. Mischievous wink." She ducked while describing the man. From beneath the counter, she retrieved a zine. "This one. *SlapDown.* I adore this boy."

Blossom knew of Easy and said so.

This shop was not a true distro like Zine Cognito, but rather a bookstore. However, besides new books and choice used ones, and a few t-shirts featuring Hunter S. Thompson and Kerouac, the shop also reserved a front corner for zines.

"I ... Should I leave these with you?" Blossom asked, brandishing a copy of *Apologies in Order.* "Or shelve them myself like last time I was here."

"Who's apologizing this time?"

With her left hand, Blossom placed the zine on the counter. She scratched her fingers over her shaved head and sniffed. "Or not."

Becca's lime eyelids fell downward. She took up the zine with that absorption fellow zinesters give each other's work, devouring its content, of course, but also, just as actively, trolling for subtle tricks that might stimulate or enhance her own zine making. Becca commented immediately on the martini glass and donkey laughter that animated the cover. She adored, as opposition, the regal quality of Littlefeather in her braids and traditional dress. Patiently Becca leafed on, inquisitively, as Blossom observed her, as Blossom twisted her bridge piercing, as the tension across Blossom's cheekbones tightened with self-consciousness. Becca finally finished by remarking that the color shots of Howell's rich neighborhood demonstrated a lifetime of impunity for that crime, even of reward for it. She asked, "You sure it's him?"

"Yeah. Took me a long time. But I'm sure."

Blossom thought to detail her confrontation on Howell's doorstep two weeks ago, to explain how though unfruitful in her initial aim, it had underscored her already persuasive evidence. No disinterested person would react that combatively, especially to someone just trying to right a wrong. Howell disliked Blossom's reminder. As did his wife. Or was that his daughter? Or his servant? Or would the wife of a man like that be his fucking servant? Blossom had not decided on this question. In any event, neither of the two wanted her giving fresh attention to that long-ago evening. According to Blossom the motivation for their pushback was self-evident: Howell was the culprit.

She tugged at the frazzled collar of her stretched t-shirt, unconsciously highlighting the inked choker of thorns that encircles her throat, and its tail that trails off over her golden shoulder. "He's still alive, that fucking chooch. I went to his house to demand an apology but he was too fucking cowardly to come to his own fucking door."

"For real?"

"I knocked on his goddamn door. He sent out some old cunt to take care of it for him. Wouldn't even deal with me. Brushed me off with this ominous like 'we-know-who-you-are-leave-us-alone' type shit."

Becca nodded. Still she fingered the zine. "Rad. LA zinesters be makin' waves right now. Easy's shit is over-the-top too."

"No doubt," replied Blossom. She hooked her thumbs into the armholes of her flack jacket. "You hear what he did at the Zine-O-Rama?"

Becca had not so Blossom told of Easy's day hit and how all the zinesters in the hall watched it live on those big screens he always sets up behind his table; and how everyone went fucking Geronimo when he stood up and raised his fucking fist. She promised Becca that in terms of zine lore this growing fame surrounding Easy might eventually eclipse Dishwasher Pete's phony appearance on the David Letterman show back in the day. And Pete's gag was just a goof, not socially impactful like *SlapDown*. Blossom related how she was right there at his table, how she tried to keep folks calm at Linda's request, spreading a trigger warning, informing everyone that ultimately Easy had control of the situation since intentionally he had coaxed it and was documenting it.

"That dude is out of his fucking mind," Blossom opined. "But he's on a fucking mission and I can identify with anyone on a mission. That zine he dropped off might detail all this."

The story inspired Becca. She folded closed Blossom's latest issue and turned toward the shop's zine rack, energized. Scores of bright creations lay haphazardly cast atop and within and along the foot of the rack and bookcase. They were a variform kaleidoscope, a multiplicity of traumas and storylines and celebrations just waiting to breach their dam.

She held up Blossom's zine.

"This is tight."

"Thanks. I'm reluctant to tell everything online. The curiosity might fade. I wannu sell a bunch of zines first. Then I'll do a reveal. I talk about it in my networks, right? To generate interest. But I only print his name and photo here in the zine."

Becca nodded approvingly, "Smart strategy." Then, "Why everybody stopping in today, anyway? Besides Easy, there was another dude too. Skinny white boy who looked like he was strung out, or like he'd just been driving 100 miles per hour or whatever. He asked about stickmen zines? Then he spent like hours looking through the whole corner. Bought like twenty. But when he finally paid he kept mumbling at me 'too much, too much, gotta go home now.' I'm like ... Watchu sayin', foo?"

"South Bay Zine Bazaar is tomorrow. Some LA peeps using the trip to crash distros, I guess. Saving gas. Don't know about that white dude but that's why I drove down early. I'm surfing Rocky's cousin's couch tonight in his Chula Vista barbershop. You know Mario?"

"Don't think so. I should be up on that South Bay fest but I'm still learnin' the ropes down here. Lying low."

"How you like it so far? I guess I haven't seen you since you left LA."

"Good. More tranquil. I needed that like you know. You doing Tijuana?"

"Just submitted my app this morning. I ... It was the first thing on my list today."

Becca said she also had submitted her application and certainly hoped to be there. She could only table a couple of zinefests per year because usually she worked at least one of her three jobs on the weekends, but she tried to ensure The Baja Zine Fiesta was one of them. Becca described her latest zine -- a perzine about helping her uncle find his way out of an opioid addiction. It was called *Fentanyl Fucks Your Soul (Totally) (Not a joke)*. Blossom nodded through the explanation, with interest. They agreed then that nothing compared to BZF. One of a kind. Then Becca held up Blossom's zine, her limey eyes shining with undiluted cheer. She said:

"This one, sista. I'm puttin' this one right here on the counter. When I've got the register and old Putt-Putt is out the first thing I do is change the music. Now, the second thing I'm gonna do is put this zine right here." With a disdainful wrist, Becca dismissed an antique copy of *Ham on Rye* which occupied a prominent counter display. "Fuck this Bukowski shit."

Blossom sniffed. "Becca, you're The Bitch."

"No, Boss," she answered. "*You're* The Bitch."

Easy's blood-red Impala hugged a long curving slope toward the 163 South. Gaining momentum with the gradient, he roared downhill, checking traffic as he yielded and then swerving leftward for the fast lane. He raised his voice over the winds buffeting the windows of the lowrider. The top was up.

"That takes care of College Heights," he called to his sister. "Sold quite a few at Zine Cognito last quarter. Wonder how this Donner one will do tomorrow at South Bay. Now I guess to Barrio Logan, no? But we've got extra time. We could backtrack and try to put some La Jolla cop in his place."

Linda was shaking her head. "This is San Diego, Eaze. And that's not even San Diego -- that's La Jolla."

"*Eso.* I've never gotten a hit there."

Still Linda was shaking her head. "Of course you haven't. You're not *stoopid*. It's not like LA. You know all the codes around LA. What do you know about the municipal code of La Jolla?"

Easy shrugged.

"Sooie!" he crowed, nasally. Then, laughing: "Here, piggy piggy. Come on to Easy."

Linda crossed her arms decisively and said with matter-of-factness: "If you don't mind, no. You know that if it comes *yo esté contigo*. 100 percent. *Como ves*. But I don't especially relish going looking for it while at a disadvantage. Do that alone. There are ways *la jura* bothers me that you can't understand. To you they're cops. To me they're cops, but they're also power-tripping men. One Three One Two, you know."

Easy nodded. Confident and brassy was his nod, but still he kept his compass pointed southward, toward Barrio Logan. Linda's reluctance made him circumspect. His wraparound sunglasses hid this. Ezekiel conceded:

"A C A B, sis. I'll admit it. I can't be as mouthy around here because I can't quote shit at them." He sped on for a mile or so. Then, "I guess that might glitch my stare some, which probably changes the whole chemistry. Half of what I do I do because I know I can match them on technicalities."

Linda said, "I read that gamblers playing for fun are more likely to win than gamblers trying to make a living at it."

"For reals?"

"If they're at equal skill level, yeah. They say that having something to lose changes the way you play. More doubts, they say. Afraid to take that chance that wins you all the *lana*."

Easy considered that the top was up on the convertible anyway. He dislikes long highway runs with Linda's hair flapping all over the world. And a roof makes it possible to smoke at higher speeds without the risk of blown embers marring his naugahyde upholstery. He had navigated the drones out the windows before, sure, but the process is cumbersome -- Just another handicap to compound his disadvantage.

"I haven't driven the Saturday Lowdown in a while, since back when Vee and I were kickin' it. Lots of the Logan foos are waiting, you know. Everyone wants to see the Donner zine. Word spread damn fast on that one."

Linda approved of this. "It's a good one, Eaze. Maybe your best."

Big grin. And that cocky *vato* nod. With theatrical swag, Easy smoothed the side of his hairnet, *muy suavecito*, as he chuckled deep in his throat. They were rumbling under the Balboa Park

137

bridge now. The evening sun gilded the bridge's Roman arches with its glittery haze. The windows of the Impala stood halfway closed so brother and sister could better hear each other. Still, they had to slightly shout.

"Like you'd think they'd be satisfied just viewing the footage online, no? But people ... they really want this zine in their hands."

"Evidence," Linda called. And, since she can hardly be heard over the wind, I'll paraphrase this part. Linda described the intangibility of the internet and its inconstancy. Today a webpage is there. Tomorrow it is not. Today a webpage says one thing. The next day it changes. "All those ones and zeros you make so much money manipulating to protect the mansions of rich blood are going to disappear one day. And your website and social avatars with it. That box of zines in the trunk, though. Those might exist for another hundred years, right? *Son artefactos.* They're not going to evaporate as if they never happened."

"Good one. Kinda creepy."

"That's mostly a Koji rant, I guess. But, yeah, our whole age would just disappear from history without electricity. That part's mine. You ever thought about that, *'manito?"*

Easy squinted behind his wraparounds. He clicked on his right turn signal. "No. Guess I haven't."

And then they were exiting onto Logan Avenue.

After a pair of stoplights: "Look at that purple Monte Carlo," Linda cried, pointing.

"That's Mario's new G-Body. Just got that new skin."

The purple Monte Carlo honked. Easy honked back and raised a solidarity fist for Mario. From separate directions then they both passed the Taco Snatch that abuts the ramp onto the San Diego Bay bridge. A park has been constructed beneath that bridge among and around the concrete pillars that support it. Each of the many pillars is decked out with its own blazing, rebellious mural -- all of them celebrating *La Raza*. Right then, inching along a stretch of asphalt between those pillars, lifting their rear wheels into a dog leg stance, or three wheelin' it, crept a line of lowriders. Spectators milled close, admiring the cars' rumbling parade. The lowriders rolled as vividly as spilled Skittles.

Linda said, "Nothing like Chicano Park. You could scrape a low low through this barrio for years and no cop would even look twice at you."

Easy replied, "Feels good."
His front end began to bounce.

Viola's left hand was bandaged. Even so, it hovered over her laptop keyboard. She occupied one end of a six-foot table. This afternoon three feet of that table belonged to *O, Kindred* and offered issues four through eight. The other three feet belonged to *Santa Puta*, a zine produced by two determined advocates for the rights of sex workers. These two tablemates of Viola's wore white from head to toe. They had not sat down all day.

"Alrigght, my fays," Viola tapped clumsily, pinning her elbows to her ribs. "So I had to go to urgengg care because I almosg cutt my finger off slicing tomaggoes. If ig was my leg I would have been tempgged to chance infecggion and let nature take igs course. But I use my hands constanggly. I have to have my hands to do our work. Withougt thag finger (left, index) I would have to get a job, which I am going to have to do anyway to pay the bill for my stiggches (five). As it is sometimes I am higging the 'g' when I want to hit the 't' because of the bandage. I'm leaving the 'g's as evidence of my pligght. I may seem calm frrom y'all's side of this blog but I am sweagging profusely. A job! Ole Viole does nogg have a good time at jobs! I can usually make igg two weeks before I start fantasizing about different wways I might remove myseelf from this world. My agoraphobia and performance anxiety become acute at jobs. Thag's why I figght and scrap to make my coin off our artt. I'm not doing it for the sake of art, precious. I'm doing itt because that's the only skill I have thag makes it possible for me to not go to a regular job!"

Viola and *Santa Puta* faced a wall of glass that gave on to a sunlit flagstone courtyard. The afternoon light refracted through that glass, washing them and the zine makers surrounding them in a dilute summer blue. Above, exposed iron trellises and wide wood beams shouldered the venue's vaulted roof. An antique warehouse, this space recalled, or some old manufacturing edifice. At present, the building housed a community center in the Chula Vista municipality of San Diego County. On the courtyard patio, under a white canopy, a garage-funk band fronted by a female singer with brilliant red hair and thick thighs covered a Ramones tune. The fest and the tune rattled the swarming room.

"Okay, I'll go more careful now with the 'g's. I need to tell ya'll that getting a job means I will be seriously squeezing the pipeline of fairy tales that usually keeps me solvent and independent. I work a good 16 hours a day doing everything I can to keep stories flowing into *O, Kindred,* and *O, Kindred* flowing into your mailboxes -- electronic and otherwise. Take away six to eight hours a day as I do something like launder dirty rags or whatever, and then what? Will I be able to keep up with the zine? I fear. I can make a part-time job last me two weeks usually. I've hustled this razzmatazz before. I work two weeks. Quit. Recover. Work two weeks somewheres new. Quit. Recover. Like that. But it's not sustainable. You run out of jobs. And if I didn't live in a giant metropolis this trick just would not work one bit."

Viola slouched backward and crossed her long cinnamon-colored arms. They were bare to the shoulder today as her right hand rose to pick and pat at her black velvet natural and then daydreamily bob at a dangling seashell earring. Idly she reflected on the *Santa Puta* zine. The two activists interviewed female-identifying prostitutes and discussed with them everything *but* prostitution. Art. Politics. Child-rearing. Their intent was to present the womyn as multi-dimensional individuals. Viola agreed sex workers should be free to ply their trade legally and safely. She knew, however, she could never offer those services herself. In light of her problem scanning groceries for strangers, she considered herself laughably incapable of providing for them even more personal attentions.

"Y'all probably cannot tell by what I've written here that I'm actually sitting in the middle of a zinefest. The South Bay has changed their fest to a two-day affair. This is tight for lots of folx because it lets more participate. But you can only table one of the two days so someone like me ends up getting less traffic on their single day. People are moving through, though, and I've chalked enough units today to justify my coming. I might have done Anaheim yesterday, but I just cannot manage two zinefests in the same weekend without a car. Just can't. The wheels on my box of zines don't spin that fast. Anyways, with it being relatively tame so far neither has this event helped take my mind off my plight. Probably today I needed that more than anything else: A good distraction. A lot of uplifting busyness would help me restart my mind and come to grips with my new reality. A job?

"I should say all of your suggestions over the last four days have been good timing. *Banjaroo* told me to just envision people in their underwear when I'm feeling overwhelmed by them. As I scootered by a Shaft Burger earlier, wondering if I'll end up working at its counter, I pictured those folx in fishnet hose. This actually helped for a minute. And *SuperMexican* told me to just remember that *It* is a figment of my imagination. But my imagination is in my mind, precious, and so telling myself *It* is in my imagination doesn't keep it from being in my mind. But thanks for the input. I hope you're feeling me when I say just because an idea doesn't work for me doesn't mean I don't appreciate it. I'm taking all suggestions seriously. I'm experimenting with *everything*."

Viola looked up again to the *Santa Puta* gals. The two women in white insisted to everyone who paused before them that any person of sound body and mind who, given a choice, can willingly assume the most maligned role a society offers, and then carry out that role with dignity and self-respect, transcends the conventions of that society so fundamentally that their execution of that role can only be regarded as an act of saintliness. From that premise, they took the title of their zine. The more times Viola listened to them repeat this position, the greater the idea inspired her. But its very potency also left her self-conscious. Should she be more iconoclastic like them? Her great brown eyes darted across the aisle then and down the run to Easy and Linda from *SlapDown*. And she remembered Blossom from *Apologies in Order*, who sat just behind her facing the opposite wall. Radicals! She counseled herself that different souls had different contributions to make, and that actually sometimes *O, Kindred* was inflammatory too.

"My selections and sequence for issue 9 are set. I'll probably be sending out form rejection letters later today when I get home. We've got 10 solid fairy tales all born out of races of color. This time I'm really happy about a Hawaiian tale involving Maui. Many know Maui merely as a place where rich people and surfers go. Actually, the island is named for a mythical Hawaiian hero. As a tease I'll tell you there's a typhoon in this story, and some penguins, and that the guy who wrote it has Maui speaking in Hawaiian Creole. He said he wanted to write it in Hawaiian itself, but that that would make the story inaccessible to too many people. So he wrote it in that rhythmic island pidgin. I will probably put Maui on the cover. Hmm. Later today I need to send out those rejection letters. Really hate that. I don't like telling folx their piece wasn't right for the zine. But not everything fits everywhere. And I make my rejections as impersonal as I can by sending out form letters. It stings less that way. I think. For most."

Viola wondered if the Santa Puta ladies were ever going to sit down. She wondered if she should stand all day too. Then her wandering attention again welcomed in the yelping voice of the brilliant-red wailer of garage funk. Viola realized her fro had been nodding to that band's bass line for half an hour now. She thought: That singer gives me strength. She thought: That singer is doing her part by giving me strength.

Viola finished, "Aspirin keeps my finger from throbbing. I wonder who's wage slave I'm about to become. I wonder what ogre of a boss is about to start beating my brow. Thank you, my fays, for your continuing positive feedback on my first live vlog a couple weeks back. I hope you understand why I didn't feel like doing another one today even though a zinefesg is ideal magerial."

Chapter Seven
Monday, July 23

Clare plopped into the driver seat of her baby blue Saab, clicked her garage door opener, started the sedan's engine, and turned up the vintage air conditioning. She pressed her face into the cotton shoulder of her pastel orange blouse then, napping off her mistiness. A smudge of make-up remained.

"Oh, c'mon!"

Her features puckered.

But Clare swiveled her chin before the rearview mirror to find that the smudging had not appreciably altered her appearance. So, with the back of one hand, she squeezed away still more sweat as the fingers of the other hand aimed the cooling vents more precisely. This cold air felt good. Soon Clare felt better. She exhaled and gripped the steering wheel with both hands. Tightly she gripped.

Looking across the dashboard and feeling the bucket seat cupping her rump, Clare realized she had not manned this cockpit for over three months now. Its well-known interior of black leather and hard black plastic felt strangely new to her -- fresh and unspoiled. But how weird to be capped by felt and steel suddenly, to sit so enclosed and restrained. Clare had become accustomed of late to feeling unconfined, to having just wind envelop her, and sunbeams, and the commotion of street.

The air conditioning soothed and emboldened Clare, tempting her to gear the car into drive and gas out for Long Beach. How easy that would be! But she did not. She awoke her smartphone, touched the Twitagram icon, summoned the list of profiles she followed, and tapped Dorothy's picture. Next, she activated the message arrow.

The cursor blinked.

In a few seconds, she was squinting and speedfingering.

"Hi, Dor," she tapped. "I was going to bus down to help you guys flyer for The Feast but I didn't get like three blocks. I was drenched with sweat. And I was even on my light bike. So sorry, but I can't come. Total facepalm but you know about my mission and I'm actually sitting in my Saab right now. That's how tempted I was to break my pact with myself and help. It's been three months now! Three whole months without a car! Love that! I'm feeling stronger and more self-reliant and I don't want to give in. I LOVE The Feast and will be there for sure. Email me a PDF of the flyer, okay? I'll copy it and hang a bunch around West LA. I didn't see in the news if you guys are under this wildfire smoke like us. The killerest sunsets! So sorry again. Say you still love me."

Clare laid the phone on her armrest but did not touch the send arrow. The Saab idled under a tin roof. Her rented house once had enjoyed a cute little backyard until someone, as an afterthought apparently, plunked this rough-hewn garage atop it. Only the garage's paint matched the parent edifice, nothing of its architecture. Clare always backed her Saab in. So right now, as she dithered for a minute before sending her message, as she mused into her rearview mirror, she saw through the garage's back entrance her touring bike leaning against her backdoor. There, an air conditioning unit spun and hummed. Forward, through her windshield, Clare saw an older black man in a heavy rastacap slowly flip-flopping by with a leash around his wrist and a panting dachshund following. The dog's tongue lolled as the man's sunglasses acknowledged Clare familiarly. Clare nodded hers in return, with a smile. She took up her phone again then, re-read her message to Dorothy, changed the words "the killerest" to "killer," and finally tapped send.

A beat later the Saab sat dead and ticking as its engine cooled and Clare was wheeling her touring bike away from her backdoor and back into the garage to be kickstooded next to her coaster. She secured the two garage doors shut, both the bigger and the smaller, to keep her vintage Saab and bicycles safe. It occurred to Clare that her message to Dorothy left out some stuff. Like how biking had become just a part of her routine even though sometimes it might be hella hard. Like, actually, how she little noticed bicycling nowadays except for in exceptional circumstances like this heatwave. Like basically she was getting used to it or something.

Her phone pinged as she twisted and pushed at her flat's back doorknob. Dorothy. She had replied with three red hearts and this exhortation: "Don't give up! You are goals for me!"

Clare laughed and removed her wayfarers.

Soon she had plopped onto her loveseat and was recuperating from her venture into the stifling, suffocating, enervating temperatures. Hungered by her several exertions, Clare handled her phone one time more, now to open the SUBS app. She would have a sandwich delivered from the Cluster Mart, and some potato chips, and … oh, whatevs … a cookie too. After touching the pay button she ratcheted up some Electro Swing. Clare felt exhilarated by not having surrendered to the temptations of her automobile, and, unleashing some sorceress gyrations, shagged her way to the refrigerator for an ice-cold Diet FizzBang. She would not leave her flat again, she resolved, until the heat broke.

Viola sat in a white cinder-block room the size of a walk-in closet. The square tabletop beneath her elbows held some loose paper napkins and a soggy paper cup with a plastic straw rising through its plastic lid. Red lipstick stained the tip of that straw. The lipstick was not Viola's.

She was on break.

"So today I started yet another job," she typed into her laptop. Her elbows dug at her ribs. "You know those places that you think are a gas station, but then you get closer and realize it's a convenience store, but then you go inside to find out there's also a fast-food joint crammed in there too ... And that the fast-food joint serves not only submarine sandwiches and tacos, but also pizza? Well, that's where I work. Behind the fast-food counter. Around here we call those capitalistically modified organisms a Cluster Mart. I'm 'building sandwiches' right now while I train. But probably I won't even last long enough to learn the register well. Mn-Mmn. I bailed on that last job I was telling y'all about at the Filipinx supermarket. I tried to razzle-dazzle more like you folx suggested and started shoving the sampler tray at people more forcefully when they passed. The problem was that people actually started sampling the hams and then asking me about them. But I don't speak Tagalog. (At least I think that's what they were speaking.) My performance anxiety kicked in and I freaked. When they realized their weekend sampler girl was now deliberately avoiding the customers they fired her. 'Very very bad,' the guy told me. This wasn't a case of Impostor Syndrome, ya'll. I really was an impostor. Becca gave me the idea to try a temp agency next. Then I won't have to go through the humiliating traumas of faking earnestness while being interviewed only to slog in all hangdog a few days later for my sole and last paycheck. Thank you Becca for your very practical suggestion. The pay at this Cluster Mart is minimum wage in case you're wondering. At this rate, I should have my urgent care bill paid off sometime in the year 2250 A.D.

"I look into these people's eyes as they stare at the menu board, or down through the sneeze guard at the pickles and the pepperoncinis, and I ask myself why do they scare me? What is it that makes me want to run and hide? Well, to me it seems like everyone is walking around wearing a scary mask. No one seems to be who they pretend to be. One guy who left just now seemed like maybe his inner self matched his outer appearance (12-inch Cold Cut Mambo, lots of mayonnaise). But most folx give off the opposite vibe. What the hell does that mean? And how can I know that? But I don't know that. It's just a feeling. But it's that feeling that fills me with anxiety, with fear for them, with *It*. Are they even human beings? Am *I* a human being? Do I wear a mask too? Everyone seems to me an ogre. Or I am the ogre. Or my fear is the ogre. I've realized this kind of thinking, this trying to think away my fear doesn't work. Besides the fact I never find any logic to soothe my trembling (as ya'll can see from this scary mask confusion), all that labyrinthine deliberating only fixes *It* in my mind. I'm tired of being afraid and cowering and, believe it or not, I've really started riding myself about this. Yesterday after coming in here to get a uniform and this stupid fucking hat that totally disses my fro, I was suddenly afraid to get on the bus back home. Suddenly I just started barking at myself inside: 'Bitch! Watchu afraid of! C'mon, now. Why you actin' like some little girl? Like a squirrel running from a dog when there ain't no dog to be seen. This *ain't* no *thang*. Pull up them britches. Get on that bus. You be strong, now. Time to grow up.' This ranting at myself helped a little. I mean, I did it. I hiked up my britches, so to speak, and got on that bus and looked around a little defiantly, angry-like. I actually saw a shaggy old man in the back turn his head away, like he was afraid. Well now, I thought. This is more like it. I sat down and felt proud. Maybe this is how you beat *It:* With anger."

Viola saw again the enamel white walls enclosing her. The break room seemed a cell block suddenly, or a jaw of clenching teeth. Halfway through her first shift and already she craved early release or extraction. She contemplated her anger, the surprise of its power. She noticed the soggy cup on the table, the ring of moisture encircling its base. Beyond the door, she saw a product display teetering with potato chips and motor oil. Viola heard the beep-beeping of the cash register then, and the nauseating radio music, and the squeaky churr of the hotdog rollers. Her attention dropped to keyboard:

"Once upon a time there was a Cold Cut Mambo, an Italian Meatball, and a little black girl rocking a fro. Then the pushy manager insisted the little black girl memorize the menu before she even started her job. That means she spent an entire night committing sandwich ingredients to memory even while The West Coast Zine Feast was only a couple of weeks away and she needed to find an artist for the cover of issue nine. Maui. I'm seeing him knee-deep in the surf, looking up at a mountainous wave. I could use Leticia again but her style doesn't suit the musculo-flowery subject matter. I need someone who can do heroic and menacing, but in pastel.

"Hmmph. My precious, so now I work in an industry that often is the setting for grainy footage of heinous assaults. I'm there. On the front lines. So you know I been coaching myself away from news stories! And the heatwave! I'm afraid the heatwave here is going to provoke the crimes. People are irritated. You can see it when they come in sweaty and wiping their faces and cursing Exxon for causing it. If the heat doesn't break soon, they're going to go berserk. The thermometer is about to bust its nut, I'm saying. And when it does where are people going to go berserk? At the Cluster Mart!"

Viola's great brown eyes darted forward then, alert.

"My supervisor just peeked his head around the corner -- and *not* to spy ole Viole's hourglass. I guess not many Cluster Mart grunts spend their breaks typing at a mad pace."

She clapped shut her computer, wobbling the small square tabletop and its soggy paper cup. Viola wiggled the laptop into her bookbag and zipped the bag safe. She stood. Two transparent plastic gloves she fished from her apron pocket. As she shuffled out of the break room, slowly, Viola snaked one glove over her left fingers and then the other over her right. She wondered nervously when she would finally get the recipe right for that Double Deluxe Gullet Smasher. Just too counter-intuitive to easily remember. And it seemed like every other fool was ordering that shit.

The sweat was dripping over Easy's brow and he suggested to Mario that they duck into that Cluster Mart over there to snag something cold. Mario agreed, saying his ride needed gas anyway if they planned to drive down to Huntington Beach and back. So Mario coasted his CRX 2000 to the fuel pumps, killed its engine, and Easy stepped out of the passenger side to head in for refreshments. Just as Easy strode away from the CRX a police car cruised by, suddenly slowed, and then jogged right at the next corner.

The handballers had been dope despite the heat. Neither Easy nor Mario could believe the players going so aggressive in the swelter. Even just sitting on the nearby park bench, spectating from under a tree, they had been soaked with sweat and flat-mouthed with discomfort. Once in a while, they lurked a match when they knew the two-on-two summer tournament was underway. They had participated in those for fun when younger, with the park midway between their childhood homes in Torrance, and with Hops and Opie always around. And so whenever Ezekiel and Mario felt like reconnecting, and Mario could drive up from San Diego on one of his Mondays off from cutting hair, they sometimes ended up there with taco shop fare in their laps. They would talk of the old days as they lunched, which were only about 10 years old, and riff aloud on what Opie would be doing if he were still alive, and how Hops would be killing it if he had not ended up Inside for being in the wrong place at the wrong time. The two men felt themselves fortunate and eyed each other with wonder, astonished that they had survived long enough to succeed, that they had sidestepped so many deadfalls. Mario would cringe at the latest *SlapDown* and ask Easy when he was going to stop pushing his luck. And then, with Easy chuckling in the roots of his throat and Mario swaying his lanky frame, they would shamble off to a nearby spot for a couple of icy drafts. Today they decided, instead of the drafts, to cruise down the Pacific Coast Highway to Huntington Beach to visit an old friend -- to meet her new man and see her infant son. Easy argued for keeping it non-alcoholic at least until they arrived at Dani's condo. Also, he preferred to take Mario's CRX instead of his Impala so they could travel more anonymously and safely. So Easy had just stepped out of the Cluster Mart with a sweating cold bottle of mineral water and a lemonade for Mario when the cop hit him.

Like a meteor.

A blur of black.

A sudden silent heavy descent of a speeding being with its arm cocked and its flashlight breaking Easy's eardrum and choking his falling form and driving his head to the blacktop.

Shouts erupted behind the Cluster Mart's glass front. A window slammed open above the mart's entry. And then Mario, internalizing what was happening, registered that Easy was down and that a cop had grounded him.

149

Mario lost his breath.

A beat later two other patrol cars raced around different corners and halted violently, to swing their doors wide and grip their holstered sidearms and crouch as if Easy or Mario or someone else on the scene brandished a weapon.

Easy lay semi-conscious.

The policeman stood akimbo over his limp form, panting. But Easy began to stir then and the cop handcuffed his wrists and yanked hard as Easy pushed to his knees and was dragged stumbling toward the police vehicle. The two other officers straightened from their crouching positions, reassessing the scene with blatant surprise and confusion. A hurried exchange passed between the first cop and the other two. Then the first accelerated northward up Hamilton Avenue with a woozing Ezekiel Castillo in the back seat. Mario glimpsed Easy's strong neck and shoulders drooping forward.

A clerk from inside the Cluster Mart had taken several stunned steps out onto the tarmac by now. Her white face had blanched, and she covered her mouth with a flat hand. An itinerate preacher from Austria who rented a room over the mart had also descended his stairway, to cautiously approach the scene in a traumatized, disbelieving air. Mario strode toward the remaining patrol car. The second cop had already fled, in a seeming panic, and so this third cop stood alone, still in the frame of his open door. Mario examined the city seal on the door to establish which police station to seek out. The officer appeared slightly disoriented, unsure. He was young. He was brown.

Mario asked, his voice quavering with purpose, "What was that policeman's name?"

The cop, hesitating over whether to speak, gazed about to find himself alone. He sat into his cruiser then quickly, backed the sedan around for flight, and, through his open window, made eye contact with Mario. He said, "Donner."

Then he squealed away.

Mario's heart thumped in his throat.

He turned toward the clerk and the evangelist on the pavement. He neared them, uncertainly, striding.

He asked, "Did you see that?"

They nodded, still shaken.

He asked, "Will you help us?"

They nodded, vigorously.

150

Mario scrolled the contacts in his phone for Easy's attorney. Every one of Easy's friends kept Easy's attorney in their contacts. By the time Mario touched the dial button he had already bent his lanky build into his CRX 2000. A beat later he was speeding for LAPD's South Bureau.

The mineral water and the lemonade still lie sweating on the blacktop.

Stanley Donner Jr. stared at the screen of his smartphone as into his mouth he mushed a last wad of submarine sandwich. The wad was fat and tasteless and it squirreled his cheeks as he scissored his jaws to cut and crush the loaf-end and vegetable and not lick away that drip of mayonnaise at the joint of his lips.

Stanley Donner Jr. hunched over his phone, studying his maps application and glad the red line of traffic he watched had finally turned *blood* red. This meant that when he mounted the 405 South again he would be joining a parade of inchworms. Speed limit: 65 mph. Speedometer: 5 mph.

He sighed with relief.

Stanley needed that slow traffic.

Stanley did not smile at this happy luck but instead zoomed out his map to fantasize about other jams or bottlenecks or accidents he might sit through or behind someday. He licked now the joint of his lips, wiped, and crumpled his napkin into the sandwich paper. Stanley's gaunt frame rotated off the squeaky barstool, passed the trash can, and stepped out of the Cluster Mart toward his green sedan. He might just survive, he thought. Traffic would help. He would make it till tomorrow, he thought. For he had somewhere to sit now for the rest of the day. And maybe she would be there. Maybe.

If she forgave.

His skeletal shoulders wore his neglected dress shirt the way a clothes hanger would wear it. Its rumpled fabric hung from him as limp as a rag as he passed through the Cluster Mart's glass doors, as he found his driver's seat and ignition key, as a CRX 2000 coasted up to a gas pump just as Stanley rolled his green sedan away. Stanley entered street traffic headed for the 110 North, which would take him to the 405 South, and spied a police car cruising opposite him. His rearview mirror showed the cop braking twice and quickly slowing and redirecting his vehicle. Stanley sensed that

151

by driving on he forfeited a chance to witness something dramatic. He crossed under the interstate then and eased a left onto the 110 on-ramp. Stanley did not want dramatic. About three minutes later he was sitting on a twelve-lane highway and going nowhere.

Stanley shouldered the sedan into the sludge of congestion, finding a position behind a plumber's van. He rolled down his window, manually. His sunburned arm rested then on the door in the sizzling daylight. A brown haze to northeast spoke of wildfire. The heatwave seethed through the green sedan's interior and drew threads of sweat from him, dampening his joints. Stanley might switch on the air conditioning but did not. He preferred the discomfort. It shunted his mind to the physical. Discomforts of the body distracted from disturbance of the mind. They helped him to manage his troubles, to keep them below nose level. The hotter and sweatier and more oppressed and miserable Stanley Donner Jr. felt physically, the less submerged he felt psychologically. Besides, he deserved this inferno.

The plumber's van inched onward and Stanley noted its unmeaning license plate and the name of the Santa Barbara dealership studded on its back door and the plumber's water drop logo and an oval window sticker that said "SB." Beside that sticker, another showed the silhouette of a surfer holding a longboard vertically and looking out to sea. Stanley heard the chugging and humming of the vehicles that encircled him and smelled their puffing and coughing and decided to leave his radio as silent as his air conditioner. The cars traveling in the northbound lanes tooled along at the speed limit. Stanley pitied them. A traffic jam was safe in its no-going. Something to do. Or to not do. Somewhere to put his mind, to suspend its manias. A place to fix his attention that simultaneously dulled his thinking. A boredom that captivated, and so soothed and steadied. A blessing. He felt lifeless in it, beautifully lifeless. And there was no better place to watch for her.

The plumber's van rolled. Its lurch and braking acquired now a sustained forward pace. Reflexively Stanley swerved into a slower lane. He trembled. He idled now behind a royal blue Jaguar with a black and gold license plate. If he played this swerving right he could spin a 60-minute delay out to 90 minutes. Already today he had inchwormed through two different pile-ups. There had been the morning rush on the 10 West which he joined near Ontario. He had dog-paddled with those cars until they cleared near Santa Monica. He had doubled back then to mount the 405 South and sit for two hours and tap at the brakes and tap at the gas and feed on that highway's endless monotony of endless lines of cars as they seized his mind without engaging it, as they occupied his thoughts without letting them drift. But the 405 had loosened around noon and compelled him to drive at speed. Sometimes as he drove during this middle part of the day Stanley felt amid a flock of birds. Each of the autos around him, he noticed, responded to another auto, which in turn responded to another, and on. The flock sensation reassured him. It provided a feeling of community, as if he were a part of something bigger than himself. But eventually, the safeness of that feeling allowed for too much daydreaming. So today, like normal, Stanley had finally ducked out of that flock and onto a city street to fuel up the green sedan and order a submarine sandwich and stall there on a barstool as he waited for the afternoon cars leaving LA to amass so he could insert himself into their creeping. Next would come the third leg of the day's journey. By maintaining his lane-switching tactics vigilantly Stanley could usually stretch this third leg past 5 p.m. After he passed the merger of the 405 and I-5, near Irvine, it benefited him nothing to return north so he always just rode the I-5 on to Oceanside. There, turning onto the fourth leg of the trip, he would follow the 76 East back toward his condo where his eleven-hour circle of a drive would die. Often, even that late, luck granted him a nice slowdown on the home stretch up the 15 North. The cars entering the flow at Temecula, where he lived, frequently retarded all forward motion to a tortoise-like crawl for miles and miles and miles. Stanley always hoped for this slowness.

But at that point in that day's journey, Stanley Donner Jr. still sat on the 405 South. In fact, he has hardly covered two miles since this scene started, and all of that in his initial sprint up the 110 North. Unfortunately, even the miseries of being stalled in a field of steel and asphalt amid a blazing heatwave did not help Stanley that day. Before a few weeks previous he had no recourse when this occurred -- when the traffic jams provided no succor. Back then he had to just bear his troubles unmitigated. Or *rattle rattle* his pillbox and fantasize about the little blue ovals within. Sometimes Stanley would moan or chant or even weep. Always he trembled. But on his birthday a highway patrolman had given him quite a gift – a business card. And now when these distractions failed him, when he felt his soul collapsing even as he hunched fervently over his steering wheel for hours, Stanley reached for his smartphone to call the number printed on that business card. He was doing so now. Calling. For Stanley Donner Jr. was determined not to kill himself. Not yet.

Always a kind voice answered.

"Hello? Riverside Intervention. Can I help you?"

"Hello," Stanley responded carefully. Then carefully, slowly, "A friend told me I could talk to you if I needed someone to talk to."

"Yes, you can," the kind voice assured. "What's on your mind?"

And, as Stanley Donner Jr. tried to keep to the slowest lane on this stalled highway, as he pressed the heel of his hand against his chest, as he trailed closely still the royal blue Jaguar, he started to talk about why it helped him to sit in traffic.

It was night.

The jangling of Blossom's spurs against her heels drew the glances of two stout men approaching a Cluster Mart. The men were conversing, heard her spurs, turned to see, noted Blossom's seething rage, and then stepped on through the glass doors to escape both her and the sweltering heat. Ever so briefly, with sweat running along her spine and soaking her soft brown t-shirt, Blossom considered following them and grabbing a veggie sub for Rocky. That man never seemed to eat. But her fury, searing her, instantly converted that sympathetic urge to vapor. A growling she heard then. It came at her from the Cluster Mart's rear dumpster. A disheveled white man stood there with defiant, aggressive stares. He leaned against a top-heavy shopping cart. Blossom growled right back at him, menacingly.

Blossom had stomped a half-mile from her parking spot. Ten minutes stomping those heavy brown boots and still her fury went unpurged. She stomped on along the nighttime sidewalk, jangling, dampening her shirt still more with her cascading sweat.

Boom, boom, boom.

She hammered Rocky's door with her balled left fist.

Boom, boom.

A sheet of folded paper she clenched in the fist not hammering the door, the right.

"Hello? Who's there?"

After a moment Blossom pounded again.

Boom, boom, boom.

"It's me!"

"Boss?" A pause. Then, "For Christ's sake, honey, I'm masturbating! Give me a second to finish and get my skirt back on."

"Rock, let me in. I need to talk to you," Blossom called. "I want to fucking scream."

"Me too. Hold on."

Blossom grrred inarticulately. She grrred again.

Boom, boom, boom.

The deadbolts clicked and rolled and clicked. The door cracked. Cooing at Blossom breathily Rocky begged, "Hey, sunshine, let me put on some clothes."

Less than a minute later Rocky set the door ajar and Blossom shouldered through to find him in a mussed green suede skirt and an unpresentably wrinkled pink blouse. On the coffee table, a laptop sat open with its browser showcasing a phony fashion runway with semi-nude models strutting it. The women wore outfits that covered everything but what Rocky liked to refer to as "their stylish parts."

"I'll put this away, dear," he purred. Rocky folded the computer closed and backhanded some perspiration off his temples. He exhaled thoroughly. "Now ... Why ... You left out your ear gauges."

But this comment was just diversionary. For Rocky sat alarmed. Never had he seen Blossom's face so chiseled and drawn. Was the darling starving herself? The golden skin stretched over her high cheekbones as if over a drumhead. She looked feverish. Nothing but blood and steel in those features.

"I want to scream, but he doesn't fucking deserve it. I ... look at this." Blossom jammed the folded page at Rocky. She perched on the sofa corner, bending forward over her knees, fists doubled. She jolted up again. She paced. Blossom ground her teeth, stalking in a venomous steam.

She said, "You know what he's doing? He's doing the same fucking thing to me that he did to Littlefeather. You see? I ... It's the same fucking thing. I'm speaking for my people and he is fucking silencing me."

Rocky balanced on the sofa's edge now, pressing the expensive paper open over his closed knees. "What is this?"

"Can't you read?" With a step Blossom loomed, dropping her finger to tap italicized words in the text. She resumed her

155

pacing. "It's a fucking cease and desist letter. They're saying my zine is harassment, an invasion of privacy, and libelous."

"My God," hushed Rocky.

"See now?"

"What does this mean?"

"It means my new *Apologies in Order* is fucking roadkill. I can't sell it online. I can't table it. I can't fucking do anything with it."

"Sure you can. Freedom of speech and whatever."

"No, I can't. If I had the money, I could ignore this and go on and let some attorney help me. But that's a fucking official cease and desist letter, Rock, from a real fucking Hollywood attorney. I looked. Probably it's bogus, but how am I supposed to know that? And where do I get the fucking money to hire an attorney to tell me whether it's bogus or not? For fuck's sake, I'm a headset slave, a call center grunt. I'm barely making it. Chooch. Fucking asshat chooch! And I didn't convert shit tonight! And Mondays are usually a clutch-ass shift."

Blossom paced still through this diatribe. But then the clomping boots halted.

"I guess I could ignore it. Hiphoppers ignore these things a lot. I think."

She leaned against the arm of the sofa, grimacing over Rocky's shoulder as he scoured the two terse paragraphs beneath the imperious letterhead. The thorns of Blossom's tattoos curled then over her eyes. She covered the angles of her golden features with her hand. She raked her golden head. Blossom slogged back to sink opposite Rocky on the couch. He had never seen the woman look so helpless. Her chin quivered.

"He's got everything. I can't fight him on his terms. He's won. He's doing the same fucking thing to me that he did to Littlefeather. I ... it might as well be 1973."

Rocky folded in half the print-outs for his new *Shake Me The Boom Boom*. He held the edges against the tabletop with his left fingertips as his right thumb crimped the fold tight. The heel of his hand smoothed that fold then. On the cover smiled a breast that had been smudged into position beneath a floating top hat. Fancy, that breast looked. A perfect sphere. Rocky liked the cupro blouse he had picked to hang below it -- A jaunty red ivy pattern over ocean blue. He unfolded the print-outs again, flattening them enough to fit through the jaw of the long-arm stapler. He aligned the crease of the fold just under the bite of the stapler, squared again the print-outs, and then, carefully, pressed down to bind them. *Thunk.* He stapled the print-outs twice more: Once at the middle of the fold. *Thunk.* And once again near the bottom. *Thunk.*

Rocky thought the cowboy chaps he had arranged beneath the red and blue blouse gave his breast-faced model real vitality, a sort of rough-and-readiness. He had cut the chaps out of an old tobacco advertisement just yesternight. That ad, which featured a scruffy white gay man on a stallion, had offered only a single leg, the left. Rocky had photographed that leg close-up and then flipped and sized the jpeg to print as a right leg. It did not quite work: Too bow-legged. But to Rocky, this imperfection pleased.

Shouldn't have done that now, should you? You're going too far. But that's why you did it anyway, isn't it?

Rocky held five new print-outs now, the next set. He pressed their edges against the tabletop with his left fingertips and doubled the sheets over, crimping a nice tight fold with his right thumb. He smoothed them then with the heel of his hand.

"Okay," he said aloud. *Aesthetically this cover figure is not one of your better ones, son, but in terms of ideas, there may be something to it. Look, visually it's forced ... contrived ... too much like you're trying to startle or be non-conformist, which flagrantly breaks your rule of style; but there* was *that Swedish beauty from Mission Viejo you dressed who could probably pull off a pair of chaps. But you couldn't make them real chaps, now could you? They would have to be* chaps-like -- *only cut like chaps, worn like chaps, but not actual cowhide. That's it. Some nice worn denims maybe, with the back of the legs cut out, and worn over hose. Little chains could hold them to the leg from behind. Denim chaps. My, my, that is a fancy idea.*

Rocky had flattened this second set of five print-outs again to fit them through the jaw of the long-arm stapler. He aligned the crease of the fold just under the bite of the stapler. *Thunk.* Scoot. *Thunk.* Scoot again. *Thunk.* Rocky extracted the bound sheets and folded this twenty-page zine one last time, into its final form. He smoothed the fold with satisfaction and sat the copy aside. Next to him on the floor lay a pile of slippery new *Boom Booms* folded and stapled. He reached for the succeeding set of five collated print-outs.

Rocky felt just luxurious in front of his little air-conditioner. Even this late in the evening, with his boutique day behind him and darkness having fallen still he could see folks outside his window pacing the sidewalks of Fullerton in search of a night breeze and some respite from the heat.

Imagine that! So many of the houses around -- even all the multi-million-dollar ones! -- don't even have an air-conditioner. And here I am: Chill.

The window unit thrummed. He had found it in storage at The Lido. His continuously bewailing how the heatwave wilted his hair and made sleeping fitful at best, which gave him horridly baggy eyes, had encouraged Pretty Mister Jane to let him borrow it. Rocky had angled the a/c into his garage-apartment window and then secured the window by wedging it tight with an aluminum broomstick bent to size. That way the bad boys couldn't get in. Rocky fancied himself the envy of East Valencia Drive with his rickety old coolness blower. To take full advantage of it he slept on the sofa.

It seems that in a bind I can do the odd he-man chore. Rocky had never felt entirely confident with suchlike tasks. *You're just so resourceful and self-sufficient, aren't you? That's your 'buelo Memo peeking through again, isn't it? That saintly charro could fix anything.*

Rocky reconsidered the cowboy chaps before him and concluded he just plain adored this boob-faced freak. He had pasted his figures erratically this issue, onto whatever slab of paper lie at hand: A green and yellow sandwich wrapper from the nearby Cluster Mart, a burger sack from the McDonald's, a shipping sleeve from Amazon. He had sized these random backgrounds to 11 x 8.5 with a pair of scissors, applied his figures, and then scanned them so that the printed PDFs had a uniform texture.

"Okay," he said aloud. "A couple more copies and I'll have a stylin' new *Boom Boom* for The Feast."

Every single figure in his latest zine was bald. Only now did Rocky realize this. *That's Blossom on your mind, son,* he told himself. *Blossom.*

Rocky swallowed. His Adam's apple pumped in his throat.

I suppose you're not going to get over the dear. You think you've solved all your problems by deciding to become a woman only to realize that you want to become a woman so that you can make love to your best friend. What will she think when I tell her that? Thunk. Look, should you say it that way? I must say something. I can't pretend about anything anymore. Why, I'm in the vein of getting over all my inner hypocrisies right now. Thunk. *How's that for non-conformity, huh? Was there ever a conformist alive who wasn't full of her own hypocrisies? If you want to buck the system, honey, you gotta buck your own system. No system lies to you more than your own.* Thunk. *I suppose it's not polite to go about telling people you love them, though. Folks just aren't down with that, are they? How's this for non-conformity: I love you.* Re-fold. Rub. *Who says that, anymore? Why I do. How it bothers people until they get used to it! Then they just crave it! Those words will not surprise Blossom, I know. She's heard me say them enough. Look at all these bald heads!*

Rocky swallowed. His Adam's apple rose and fell in his throat. He smoothed the fold of this newly-stapled copy with a final rub.

Making her understand how I really mean those words ... Why, I'm guessing that's going to cause some blah, blah, blah. *Am I ready for that? The woman is totally unpredictable when offended. Lord! And I promised this would never happen between us. Ugh! And if she sees it as a betrayal ... Why, those grudges of hers...! O my depressing my! But you have to say it, girl. Look, you can't hold back now, you big coward. For God's sake you might just scissor off your junk, you. Before you do that you gotta come clean 1000 percent. About everything. This isn't a time in life when one hedges about stuff. Now's when to be truthier than ever. But do I really feel like a woman inside?*

Rocky held the edges of the final copy he would staple tonight against the tabletop. Usually, he printed only ten at a time to avoid stressing Pretty Mister Jane's little copier at the boutique. But this afternoon he had run two extra copies since a pair of new followers had messaged him through Twitagram requesting his latest by ground mail. With his right thumb, Rocky crimped the fold tight. The heel of his hand smoothed the fold. Then he flattened the print-outs again to fit them through the jaw of the long-arm stapler.

Usually. But sometimes I feel like a man. I suppose. Sometimes you don't feel like anything, though. Sometimes you have no gender at all. I love the way women look. Thunk. *They can achieve an elegance that is simply barred to the male of the species. Look at this waif in this sternum-bearing cut-out on the back cover. I have removed her face because I only want her bald head and her sheer crop top. Still, though, I can see in her chest a breastbone I will never enjoy. Look at that wonderful clavicle and those high ribs. Ugh.* Thunk. *And look here at this arm. Okay, I cut out that emaciated arm because it makes a nice*

159

triangle bent like that. That's a nice complement to those bow-legged
chaps on the cover, isn't it? But my elbow will never look like that. Males
cannot get that angularity. Triceps ruin everything. Ugh. Thunk. *When*
you change your sex will you look like her? Shoulders too broad. And
you'll never have a woman's hips, you, no matter how much progesterone
you eat. Or is it estrogen? Wonder what that stuff tastes like? This is all
about Blossom, isn't it? Bald heads all over this zine for Long Beach. Has
she ever thought of me romantically?

Then, just behind him, Rocky heard a pounding against his
front door.

Boom, boom, boom. Boom, boom.

My, my what is that?

"Hello? Who's there?" he called.

Boom, boom, boom.

Rocky rose. Protectively he swathed his silk nightgown
around his front. His fingers hovered over his wide nose. Quiet
alarm, he felt.

"It's me!"

"Boss?" and the wind-up of tension in Rocky released then.
He eased, but flustered. He blurted the first put-off that leapt to
mind: "For Christ's sake, honey, I'm masturbating. Uhhh, Give me a
second to finish and get my skirt back on."

"Rock, let me in I need to talk to you. I want to fucking
scream."

But ... Rocky thought ... and without even texting? WTF! And I
can't let her see all my bald-headed fantasies. Not yet. You'll blow her
mind that way, girl. You need to say it differently. Maybe at The Feast.
You could use the zine to bring it up, though, couldn't you? I have no idea
how she's going to react to this. Is the darling capable of canceling me?
We've been friends for so long. Blankly Rocky gaped at his pile of
zines, briefly immobilized.

"Uh ... me too. Uh ... just hold on."

Boom, boom, boom.

Rocky cracked the door, revealing a cross-section of his
pallid face. Blossom quivered there, a torch of sweating fury.
Cooing at her breathily he entreated, "Hey, Sunshine, let me put on
some clothes."

WTF, he thought.

Rocky shuffled his newly bound zines under the sofa. He
opened his laptop to flutteringly click on a nude fashion site he
occasionally patronized. While the site loaded he lifted his

long-arm stapler and walked it to the cabinet beneath his kitchen sink where he stowed his gear. There, he washed his hands, dropped his nightgown at his feet, tugged from his clothes hamper yesterday's green suede skirt and pink blouse, and hurried them over his curves. A deep breath Rocky drew then, and exhaled, to appear relaxed. Then, looking at his hands, he reached to swing open the door.

Chapter Eight
The West Coast Zine Feast

We all recognize that The West Coast Zine Feast served as a turning point for each of us personally, and therefore, by extension, for us as a group. Our lives had intersected before then; we had crossed paths with one another while navigating our zine scene. But on that day in Long Beach, we began to come together in a way that set the stage for our finding a common forward motion. We arrived at the fest oblivious to this, of course, but also, I dare submit, craving its advent. We each had been drifting alone and detached for too long. We each had felt alienated from a collective purpose for too long. We sought a bridge to others, a connection. We hankered for a congealing.

The venue that year was new for the community. The space suited smaller conventions well with its gymnasium-sized hall where the zine makers were housed, a cozy triangular room in the rear that served for panel discussions, a separate performance area with a stage and raised seating, and an area for workshops against the front windows. Blossom and Rocky tabled together that day, as usual. Viola occupied a propitiously busy corner. And Clare had ended up seated across an aisle from Easy. Stanley attended, after having spent most of the previous night driving around in circles.

Among the documents provided to me as I assembled the materials for this testament was a blog entry by Viola. Long Beach meant extra travel expenses for her -- a worry -- but the fest remained irresistible for the traffic it promised. She began her blog that day: "I should not have quit that job ... " But, by the end of The Feast, as you will see, she felt much less doubtful about that decision.

Viola typed,

"I should not have quit that job, Precious. Mm-Mmn. I am so screwed. But that was the only way I could be ready for The Feast today. And yesterday I finally sent off an email to that artist who does good Hawaiian-style stuff. I hope he's available. I was getting freaky behind schedule. Last night until 2 a.m. I was printing freebies and bookmarks. Traffic to the online store has dipped from those minimal numbers I was worrying ya'll with last week to flat nothing. But there should be lots of people in Long Beach today. (I sincerely hope you are one of them.) I'm on the Pacific Surfliner right now, riding the Amtrak up from San Diego to the Santa Ana

163

terminal, laptop plugged into the wall of the train, lucky orange hip huggers tight, my moisturized natural picked and patted. Just passed San Clemente and we're starting to hang inland away from the view. People enjoying themselves on that beach there, strolling along for seashells, for peace. My finger is better. The urgent care bill came. I go forward today feeling lost and defeated and empty inside, and helpless; and did I say lost and defeated? At least the Tijuana people received my application. I can't believe I applied for that fest. I've never been across that border. Why am I even considering it? I'll tell you why: M-O-N-E-Y! Today I'm praying for goodness. Gotta rent an electric scooter for the home stretch from the train station to the venue. Gotta crack my winning smile there. No one's gonna be buying no fairy tales from no frowning black gal."

Stanley Donner Jr. hunched before Viola, determinedly. His rumpled shirt looked to have just been picked up off his bathroom floor. His complexion was frankly sickish. In that moment his appearance might have been described, at best, as neglected. He spoke slowly, with quiet words carefully pronounced.
" ... hmm ... Hello."
"Well, hello, Stanley. You're back."
He smiled, unsteadily. "Can't stay away."
"That's fine. That's fine."
A sudden quiver animated Stanley's coat hanger frame. His cavernous eyes glanced about -- back and forth, to here then there. A frowning Korean man sat to Viola's left. He stared into an open book rather severely. The zine on his table proclaimed: "I Do Not Have a 12-Inch Dick." Stanley remembered that guy from Palm Desert. To Viola's right lay some zines covered with photographs of hairy armpits. The chair behind those zines sat vacant. He reacted to neither of these tables. Stanley's wan lips pressed together, his features thin and gaunt.
Suddenly, as if having thought of something energetic to share, Stanley said to Viola, hoarsely: "Busy?"
"Yes, The Feast is one of the busiest of the zinefests."
Stanley Donner Jr. turned to appreciate the volume of bodies coursing across the space. They flowed in a kaleidoscope of channels and currents and swirls. The roar matched that of the

Zine-O-Rama. He noticed through a side door hippies near a tiki bar, and a wailing of live music found him from somewhere.

Adventurously he mumbled, "Selling stuff?"

"Yes," Viola smiled. "I've already covered the cost of my table and transportation and it's very early. Everything else I make goes to keep a roof over my head."

He raised his eyebrows. "You live off this?"

Viola shrugged and laughed. "If you wanna call it that."

"Your hand better? I learned about Twitagram and started following lots of zine people."

Viola smiled kindly. She lifted her hand off the table. The puffy swathe which had previously wrapped it had been downsized to a mere band-aid. The swelling had disappeared too.

"All better."

"You know," he offered, slowly, "I tried to get into this fair. I learned from a SkipTube video how to make one of those little eight-page zines that you fold from a single sheet of paper."

"An eight-fold, you mean."

"That's what they're called?"

"Yeah, some of my favorite zines are eight-folds."

He nodded. "Okay. Yeah. So I applied to this fair at the last minute with my single eight-fold zine. I didn't get in."

"This is one of the more competitive fests. Even the Zine-O-Rama is less exclusive."

"Why is that?"

Just then a broad-shouldered woman in go-go boots floated up to Viola's table with a harumph. Stanley Donner Jr. backed away a half-step. The woman posed a quiet question to Viola about *O, Kindred* and Stanley stepped rightward, allowing the two women more space to talk. Relief, Stanley felt then. He did not want to leave Viola's presence; no, not at all. But still he felt relieved to have been excused from it by circumstance. Stanley stalled, uncertainly now, before the frowning Korean man. He reached down to turn over a few pages of the "I Do Not Have a 12-Inch Dick" zine. The guy continued reading his book, though. The zine interested Stanley, but a second woman stopped in front of Viola then and he found himself backing away with real commitment, sinking into a side swirl of the milling hoards.

The wailing of the live music gave Stanley Donner Jr. direction. As he cornered a post and approached a double-wide doorway the sounds of the band became more discrete and

165

intelligible. Stanley paused outside the performance space, listening. A nearby sandwich board proclaimed: "Now Playing: The Anaphylactics." Stanley pivoted away, drawn to the tall windows against the front sidewalk where a loose crowd assembled. Folks dipped paper into a solution there. They placed dead leaves or car keys or whatever objects might be in their pockets on the paper and then covered it. Outside, on a table, they exposed the paper to sunlight for a few minutes. Back inside they treated the paper with a second solution which turned the page a rich brilliant blue -- except for where the objects had blocked the sunlight. Different participants managed different stages of the process simultaneously so the entire protocol was observed by Stanley in about a minute. The final products were white shapes decorating vivid blue. A Persian woman invited Stanley to try his own design. He declined.

Wandering away, Stanley Donner Jr. slipped the zinefest program out of his rear pocket and unfolded it. Cyanotype, that process was called. He wondered if they had solutions that could turn paper green instead of blue. The zinefest program excited Stanley's interest now. What else was there? Another workshop for zine-making started in an hour, he found. And after that, a poetry reading later in the day. Also, a panel discussion about history zines. Stanley had not realized zinefests offered such functions. But then he mumbled to himself, aloud: "Wasn't I invited to a zine-making workshop once? Somewhere?" Later he remembered it was Palm Desert.

The first couple hours of a fest hum with contradictions. The tablers have just set up and sit woozy from a long night printing and folding and stapling last-minute zines. Yet the fresh open-eyed attendees passing through have a wired-on-espresso air to them or a just-having-jogged look. The energy glitters in those first couple of hours, but also droops; it is morning-like in its mixing of the sluggish with the keen. But then an evenness seeps in. The zinesters brighten as the attendees calm and after two or ten sales everyone glances at their phones to realize four more hours remain. The excitement drips away. Suddenly half the tablers in the hall hold a sketchpad on one knee and a pencil in their moving hands and bounce or sway their heads to whatever music moods the talky background. Zinesters fall into various creative

166

visions then and let the eager loner side of their personalities come to the fore, leaving behind their reluctant social sides, or holding them, maybe, in suspension.

Like others, Clare balanced a sketchpad on her knee now and gripped a pencil with her fingertips. She did not draw, however. For despite having turned her chair to train her sight off of Easy, still she found herself twisting her neck to watch him. He sat only strides from her, directly across the aisle, and *the need* in Clare had been just tightening and tightening. In fact, her *need* felt more like an *ache* now, a chronic, itching *ache*. She gazed on Easy's broad muscular shoulders and that virile mustache, on that self-assured nod of his, on that retro hairnet that imbued him with a streetwise mystique, and on those thick prescription glasses which kept him eminently approachable. Attendees obstructed Clare's view of Easy at times, but nothing severed her awareness of him.

Clare noticed that Easy's table stayed busy, that usually at least one person stood picking it over. In terms of attendees, he attracted the same attention as any other tabler; but in terms of fellow zinesters, it seemed everyone in the building knew of him and was willfully strolling by to keep abreast of his doings. Probably, Clare thought, they were asking him about what happened on the day of the Zine-O-Rama. Sometimes though a kid's approach did seem urgent enough to touch something more recent. In any event, Clare theorized that people felt drawn to Easy because of the clarity of his objective, and because of his defiant but rational methods of achieving it, and, of course, because of his balls.

His balls.

As susceptible as anyone to Easy's charisma, and feeling strangely proud at having personally ridden in the lowrider which executed his 'hits,' Clare found herself suddenly and spontaneously pretending to accidentally glide by his table.

"Well hello, Mr. Ezekiel," said she.

His chin rest in his palm as he leaned toward a laptop. He glanced over the rim of his thick glasses. Then he removed them. Easy smiled. A quiet chuckle emerged from the depths of his throat.

They exchanged zinefest pleasantries: The quirkiness of the crowd, trends in sales, the chutzpah of the punk band thrashing beyond, and the idiosyncrasies of the day -- like the organizers' decision to designate all restrooms as gender-neutral.

Finally, Clare said, "I guess I haven't talked to you since Palm Desert."

"Yeah, I guess that's right."

"I was at the Zine-O-Rama but missed you because of your big to-do or something."

Easy dropped his look from hers. Clare interpreted this withdrawal to mean he had retold that dramatic story just too many times already. But Easy seemed maybe unsure, too, like he did not know exactly how to proceed. He said, "Yeah," and shrugged. He reached up and brushed distractedly at his mustache. Clare stooped to his zines to let the subject die.

She and Easy's sister had traded only friendly glances so far, and half-smiles. Linda had stayed mute through their awkward opening, seeming to restrain herself, consciously. Now Linda said simply "Hi," and broadened her smile to full, and widened her cat eyes to bright. Clare side-stepped with an answering hello and picked up Linda's zine *Ashes to Ashes*. She read Linda's name near the bottom: Castillo. Then, pretending to realize something remarkable, Clare turned back to Easy's zine. She lay a finger below his name: Castillo. With feigned surprise, Clare squinted. "Huh. The same last name? You two brother and sister?"

Linda replied, significantly, "That's right. Mr. Hero here has only got me watching out for his wild ass right now."

Easy chuckled.

Clare stared now. She stared without blinking into Easy's great brown eyes. She gave him a flirtatious wink finally and enhanced her tease with a dancy twerk of shoulders. Easy stared right back, though, unfazed by his sister's innuendo or Clare's sexy self-confidence. Clare had not expected this stoic reaction from him. Her features slightly puckered. She contained a blush.

Blossom slouched back from her table into her chair. She folded her arms across her stomach. The tattoo spiraling her left forearm snaked around her elbow, twisted up into the arm of her flack jacket, and reemerged from her collar to enwind her throat with blue-black thorns. Blossom wore fire-orange ear gauges that day which complemented her golden complexion. She jutted forward the soul patch piercing above her chin. A few attendees sensed Blossom's seething anger and marked some extra distance from her. Nearly empty, her table sat, a lusterless brown veneer.

Atop it lay a square of cardboard upon which a sheet of paper had been taped. Just that. One sheet of paper taped to a piece of cardboard was not normal for Blossom. It was not normal for anyone there. People were noticing it because it was not normal.

Koji ambled up. Koji authors a comic zine in which he draws out storyboards for irreverent plots based on famous pop songs. He calls it *The Anarchist's Jukebox*. He is also well-known for *Lollipop Shotgun,* a political zine that brainstorms, analyzes, and extols zine activism. His table anchored a rear corner of the room, but at the moment he stood dawdling nearer the entrance, before Blossom. Koji is Okinawan-American, and one of those heavier rounder men who move with assurance and athletic grace. He wears a Zeus beard that frequently he tugs at.

"Hey, Boss," he said, breaking into her angry silence. "Missed you at South Bay because I was in Anaheim the day before. And I didn't go to the Zine-O-Rama this year because I had to cover for our sushi chef who keeps calling off. Anyway, found you on the venue map today on purpose."

With one hand Koji gestured to Blossom's table, questioningly. The other pulled at his beard.

"Where'd that Littlefeather thing go? I was gonna buy it. What is this?"

Blossom tensed out of her slump and unfolded her arms to straighten them and grip her seat edge. Slightly her gauges shuddered as she shook her shaved head. Her face tightened over her cheekbones. Disdainfully she nodded at the sheet on the table.

Koji bent.

She said, "A cease and desist letter. If I keep selling the Littlefeather issue of *Apologies* they're threatening to sue me for libel. Since I can't sell it I'm making sure everyone here at least knows why I can't sell it."

"Who's suing you? The guy who booed her?"

"That's right."

Koji's expression crinkled. His brows pinched together with worry. "They're coming after us, aren't they?" he muttered. "They don't like that we don't play their game so they're trying to make us either play along or shut up."

Blossom grunted, angrily. "*Me.* They're coming after *me.*"

Koji bent still over the letter. Uncomprehendingly he skimmed the legalese taped to the cardboard. Shaking his head, he grabbed at his beard more manically now. "You, yeah. But who's

169

next? This is just the tip of the iceberg. Am I next because I turned Billy Joel's 'Big Shot' song into a 'Pit Stop' song and made his hero into some joker who needs to take a shit?"

Blossom stared grimly. The harsh angles of her face did not slacken. She did not care that Koji interpreted this threat to her as a threat to himself. And she did not want to hear him explicate the wider political nuances surrounding this second silencing of Littlefeather. Blossom understood them better than he, she felt. Besides, constantly Koji was ranting on about The Man. It grew tiresome.

Blossom had internalized this line of thinking: The cease and desist letter represented the simple fact that fucking Old America had never wanted, and still did not want American Indians to defend their dignity. Period. They wanted American Indians abject. Forever. Well, she thought, It's time we exchanged Old America's blue eyes for New America's brown ones.

"Not making this about me," Koji continued, still grabbing his beard. "I'm just saying if they can come after you, they can come after any of us. People take liberties. People borrow. Half the time that's what art is. Look at pop art, for Pete's sake. This is like suing Andy Warhol. Maybe. How'd he find out about it, anyway?"

Blossom's flintiness dulled. Here was the one question that diluted her rage. For always its broaching reminded Blossom that she had provoked these complications herself. Her tension lessened. She positioned her elbows on the table and slumped into her shoulders. The blue-black thorns around her neck throbbed. Blossom knew she was stuck -- that she had to explain it all. So she explained it all.

Koji responded that The Man was starting to notice their little zine world and that The Man's attention should be met with utmost caution. "People love our energy. They love it when it's rough and underground. But once it starts to pip out of its little egg and become a big brown rooster than can crow every morning and be obstreperous, like you, suddenly everything is different."

He opined further that while most zines exist unnoticed by the mainstream, at every fest he attended he encountered zines that, given wider circulation, could "command the popular ethos" and "influence the tilt of history."

"Everything about a zine is subversive," he enlarged. "Even the ones that seem really tame. Because every minute a human mind spends on a zine is a minute that it is not eating the blue pill.

You know, like from The Matrix. The Man wants society drugged and blind. But every time someone picks up a zine and reads it, for those few minutes they have stepped out of their drugged and blind existence -- They have puked up The Man's poisoned kool-aid. You know, like Jonestown."

Blossom stared at Koji.

"Besides, look, we are empowering each other. And we are the last people they want empowered."

Blossom stared.

"I'm tellin' you, Boss. The Man knows that the right mix of a few zinesters deliberately trying to reorient just one of his wobbly cogs could change everything. You know that's what *Lollipop Shotgun* is about: We play like we're a *Lollipop*, but really we're a *Shotgun*. That said, I guess this particular *nisei* is not gonna be knocking on some record label's door anytime soon and flauntin' my *Jukebox* at them. Love your balls, but I'm not calling those bloodsuckers out. Given what they can do to us, of which this threatening letter is an example, there is something to be said for staying under the radar for as long as possible. I mean, we can't avoid a collision with them forever. We will have to lock horns with the mainstream eventually. Maybe this letter and what's happening with *SlapDown* is the beginning of that. But I think until we're pulled into open warfare with them we should avoid full-frontal assaults. They're too well equipped for us. We gotta stay guerrilla."

"I disagree."

Koji grinned. He released his beard and let his hand drop to his side with relief. "You inspire me, Boss. I've got the theories, maybe, but you're the one charging with the bayonet and throwing the Molotov cocktails."

"You misunderstand me, Koje. I'm saying that's all just Big Warrior talk. You're way off base. We're not some kind of revolution, we're just zinesters."

Koji shook his head meaningfully. He whispered, wisely, "It just seems that way."

Easy stood up to slap palms with a Chinese *foo* called Ra. They bumped fists. Ra, gripping a handful of zines, looked at Easy carefully and with concern, meeting Easy's great brown eyes through the thick eyeglasses, reading the twist in Easy's mouth beneath the full mustache, watching Easy's expression beneath the hairnet. All told, Ra sensed the slightest slackening in Easy. His usual stalwart posture seemed ... maybe ... tired?

"How's the ear?"

Ezekiel Castillo smiled. He turned his head, pointing his right profile at the man.

"A little muffled still, but better," he answered. "The doctor says it'll be normal soon."

Ra twitched, in awe. The two rehashed Easy's Donner hit. And then the Donner zine. And then the Donner retribution.

"And it's all right here?"

He held the latest *SlapDown*.

"No. That zine just details the first stop. The attack at the Cluster Mart that all the media people are talking about came after this, as revenge for it. If internal affairs had acted on this zine when they first saw it, I may have been spared the attack. The zine had been circulating for about a month by then. But they say they can't open a file without an official complaint. Official complaints are not my style."

"Gotta be the most famous zine I've ever held."

Easy remarked, "What's that you say?"

And Ra glanced up. He spread his eyes wide. Easy was leaning his ear toward him, chuckling in the back of his throat. Ra chuckled too, uncomfortably.

Easy said, "Not without a cost."

Rocky watched Blossom breathlessly, through the corner of an eye, until Koji floated away.

She would have to be like this today, he thought. *But I suppose I don't have to tell her just now.*

He turned his head, fixing both eyes upon the woman, directly. Blossom leaned back in her chair, arms across her chest, sneering at the correspondence taped to the square of cardboard. She clenched her jaws, zigzagging the muscles of her face through her temples and up into her shaved scalp.

Why, that is just not a face one pours one's heart out to, now is it? But she looks like that all the time, I suppose. OMG, I have seen her at her happiest just frowning like she wants to murder. Oh, well. I suppose I can hold my tongue about my feelings for another day. I've waited this long. That's what you do, isn't it, son? You wait and wait and wait. And even after altering this yellow blazer for the occasion. Look, no lint on these sleeves. At least I know I look good.

"I wonder if *Kindergarten Knife Fight* is here?" offered Rocky, gently, teasing at Blossom's train of thought. *Knife Fight* is a violent crayon comic featuring chubby children with switchblades. Blossom loves it. Rocky saw the humor of the zine sneak through her mood and slightly temper her sneer. But then, as clearly as reading a billboard, he saw Blossom realize that he was trying to interfere with her anger. She resented this so she said nothing. The sinews of Blossom's face kept tight, defined. Whether she chafed at his imposition or not, though, Rocky knew he had tracked her focus off the cease and desist letter, even if only briefly.

A man bent now over a *Shake Me The Boom Boom*.

"Fashion?" asked the man. He wore an overcoat.

"That's right, honey. Fashion," Rocky lilted. "I'm a fashionista. I even dress people for a living. These collages I do in my spare time. Keeps my imagination fancy. Some of these are pretty exotic, but some might actually work in the right setting. All of them buck the norm, though, hon. I don't see the point of doing this stuff unless I'm doing something you would never see on the street. Are you interested in style?"

The man shrugged. He did not seem particularly taken with the *Boom Boom*, but neither was he walking away. He paged on. "I come to these things looking for the unexpected."

"You keep looking through that one your holding then."

"Oh, I see. Yep. A crocodile."

"You know sometimes people walk around with snakes around their necks? I realized you could deliberately use a reptile as an accessory. But if you're going to do that, why tie yourself just to snakes."

"Yep."

"That's a kind of a fantastical outgrowth of that realization. If you've got a yellow snake, wear purple. If it's a snake with a pattern on its back, wear a nice solid to counter its lovely markings. In that one there you've got a green crocodile. Obviously, you would dress yourself in reds to complement him. Wouldn't it be just stylin' to see that little old lady with her 15-foot croc in some suburban mall? That leash is just to make the whole thing look plausible. I don't really think a leash would work on a crocodile. But who knows?"

173

The man shook his head. He closed the zine, vaguely speechless. He did not lift his eyes to Rocky. Leafing through another issue, he stated, indifferently, "All the models in this one have shaved heads."

Rocky nodded. "Yes." Then, very meaningfully he turned toward Blossom. Then, very deliberately he articulated, "That is my homage to bald women."

The man replaced the zine on the tabletop. "Thanks," he said, moving off.

But Rocky did not reply. Rocky just kept staring at Blossom. He stared at her until the man in the overcoat was well away, and until his beloved Blossom finally turned the sharp angles of her face toward him in answer. Their eyes met. He said, "Aren't they just beautiful?"

Rocky swallowed. He knew then he was about to tell Blossom that he loved her.

Red braids framed the dubious face that gazed down over Easy as pensively he sat behind his table. Neon red eyeshadow accented the great brown eyes. They watched Easy petting at his mustache with a finger and thumb, distractedly. How could the man not notice her approach? She woke him: "You done now? Isn't that it, Eaze? What else you got to prove?"

Ezekiel Castillo looked up. He chuckled a welcome. "You sound like my sister, Becca."

"Your sister's a wise woman. You beat your head against a brick wall eventually some hard damn thing's gonna fall on that head. What else you got to prove?"

Easy shrugged.

"People talking about you all over, hon. I'm even hearing about you down in Daygo. You like all this attention?"

"No."

"Hmph," she hmphed doubtfully.

Easy had known Becca for a couple of years. She is a light-skinned black woman who easily passes for white. She is *from* South Central, Lynwood to be precise, but was a sort of gypsy at the time of this story: Living light, staying unattached and moving frequently to seize whatever opportunities emerged. A very practical and resourceful woman, Becca openly admits to leveraging her 'ambiguous racial presentation' to cop the white

174

man's privilege in situations where it suits her and does not compromise others. All she has to do, she explains, is 'talk like them.' Part of what drew her to Easy during this period was seeing him use the values of the white man against the white man, somewhat like her. She did it with her fair complexion. He did it by taking their high-class book learning and re-purposing it against their favor.

Standing now, Easy reminded Becca that fame had never been his motivator, as surely she knew. Always his aim had been to demonstrate the limitations of Authority's power, and to check Authority's abuses, and to force Authority to acknowledge and address those abuses. Most importantly, though, Easy insisted, he strove to empower others to challenge Authority.

"I think you done that."

He bobbed his head.

"But that angels shit is theatrics, honey. Cameras on the car is all you need. Don't need nothing over your head. And them cameras don't cost nothing no more. Anyone can put a cam on the dash and on the side mirrors. Not even as big as a dime. I know this to be true because half the homies in Skyline went and bought that junk when your shit went wild last week. Or stole it." Becca paused, grazing Easy's table now curiously. She plucked off the Donner issue. "Can't say it surprises me, though -- that the *poh*-lice waited to act on this zine until *after* that freak-ass white boy jumped you. Theys some messages they just *do* not want to hear."

He bobbed his head.

She fingered the pages. She paused over the photograph of Easy with his hands on the hood of his Impala. The next page presented a series of stills that reenacted Easy's takedown, frame by frame.

"So this is the famous zine," she hushed. "We saw you on Anderson Cooper and I told everybody that I knew yo crazy ass. Honey, I'm proud of you; don't get me wrong. But I think you done accomplished what you set out to accomplish."

"I'm listening, Becca," Easy said quietly. "I just don't know yet."

"Gimme a hug," she ordered.

Stanley Donner Jr. sat among an audience of three. Before him, on a slightly elevated platform, three panel members perched on fiberglass chairs with chrome legs. Stanley liked that there were as many panel members as audience members. He reached to scratch his gaunt unshaven jaw. He dried his perspiring face into the short sleeve of his wrinkled shirt. Stanley hunched forward.

According to the program this panel had convened to treat 'historical zines.' However, once the talking commenced Stanley did not recognize anything historical being discussed. One panel member, a soft-voiced Latinx who wore many black rings, published an interview zine that documented the 'homeless camp' experience as lived in Southern California public parks. Next to her sat an energetic Armenian woman whose smile never dimmed. That woman employed zines and zine workshops to provide at-risk teens in her community a means toward creativity and accomplishment. The third zine-maker cocked a purple beret back on his blond head. He photographed the cultures of communities being lost to gentrification, recording fleeting landmarks like informal sidewalk markets, or the daily route of a beloved popsicle seller. Even in the introduction the moderator never actually invoked the word history.

Stanley did not understand.

During the question and answer period a white woman asked for advice on a zine she hoped to make: She wanted to embolden people to keep aquariums.

Stanley squinted.

When the panel concluded he checked the sign outside the door to confirm he had been in the right place. The announcement read: "Panel: Historical Zines."

"Here I go again, my fays. Vlog experiment number two – per your continuin' requests. Can ya'll see me alright? Been bloggin' a lot lately but not happenin' today. Too much business in this joant to be just sittin' and writin' like that. Need our eye contact ready. I can talk, though. You *know* I can do that. Can't believe how busy I been. Gave me the idea to run a Faustbook Live of me massaging this razzmatazz of a zinefest. You mind, Jenny? Jenny's my tablemate today."

"Just don't point it at me, Vee."

"Okay. Jenny says don't point my phone her way. I can honor that. Ya'll see all the people shufflin' by? This is one of the busiest zinefests of the year. See that man in the white hoodie walkin' yonder? *Hey, Reggie!* Old friend from Escondido. Ain't seen that boy in a minute. I'm wavin'. Here he comes. Hey, Reggie, I'm Living this, you mind?"

"On Faustbook?"

"Yeah."

"I hate that shit."

"I'll point it down, hon. Sorry. How you been doin'?"

"I'll be back soon, Vee. I'm feelin' that righteous fro, though."

"That didn't work so good. When I told him I was Living he just up and skedaddled. Hm. But what's wrong with me? Shoulda known better with Reggie of all people. Just turnt up, I guess, cuz I'm sellin' so much more than usual. Feelin' strong. How about this -- I point the camera down. That way it doesn't invade anybody's privacy but still my peeps can hear me talkin' to folks, and maybe see a belt buckle or someone's purse or somethin'. I don't think that jacks anyone. Better idea, Jen? You think?"

"Yeah, that's better."

"Jen says it's a better idea and I'm whisperin' now cuz yet another attendee is walkin' toward our table. Excuse me while I put on my white peoples' voice."

A pause. Then,

"You write all these?"

"No, not all of them. Each issue is a compilation of pieces by different writers from around the world. I take submissions from everywhere. Like, one of the tales in that issue you're holding there is from Bangladesh. Dhaka. That's one of my favorites. In it, a maiden has a magic wand that can turn water into milk. But not just any kind of milk. A single glass satisfies your thirst and hunger for an entire day. She uses it to ease a famine in Siberia until the UN can bring truckloads of Doritos."

"Siberia?"

"That's right."

"From Bangladesh?"

"Yeah."

"How does she get there?"

"Read and see. But the magic wand has several properties. Not just water to milk properties. For instance, it can make carpets fly."

"Like a magic carpet?"

"No, a magic wand. The carpet's just normal until the wand comes along."

"That's a sick vibe. Feels sorta psychedelic."

"You could read it that way, yeah."

"I like this one. Not as many literary zines down here as up in the Bay Area. Seems like most stuff in SoCal's visual. You say fifteen dollars?"

"That's right."

"You take cards?"

"Of course."

"You got lots of these zines?"

"Eight issues so far. Just five on the table today. I'm working on issue nine right now. You can subscribe if you decide you like it. The web address is on the back. Here, take this free bookmark."

"Oh, shit. I got cash. Here you go. Thanks."

"Thank *you* ... and there he goes. Hope ya'll could hear that joant. He was aksin' about our issue seven. The one some a y'all certainly remember with the milkmaid and that magic wand. There was also that pole-sitter man in that issue. Remember the fool whose words came out as real live speech balloons which floated round all silent till they popped? And only then could ya hear him bemoanin' his situation atop that pole and beggin' passersby for a ladder? Folks, that's our sixtieth sale today and we ain't even hit halftime yet. Don't know what's goin' on, but I'm feelin' it."

"Vee, anyone actually watching you?"

"Jenny just aksed if anyone out there is actually watchin' this vlog. Lemme look ... Yeah, hey. Check 'er out, Jen. Lots of 'em. Like 152 people."

"Tell them about my body hair, why don'tcha?"

"Y'all, Jenny's got the bombest zine about women gettin' over this whole body hair complex the media and commercials drill into us. Why do we worry so much about our armpits? That hair is natural. Her zine is called *Shave it Up Your Ass*."

An aging man, conspicuous, lurked through. Unattached, he seemed, to the fest, incorrigibly out of place – almost as if deliberately he did not belong. One zinester appraised him as undercover security. Another postulated plainclothes cop. Many noticed him and wondered about this power-tied misfit; but just as many shrugged him off since nothing underway warranted any kind of law enforcement.

Studyingly the man prowled, canvassing the crowded cells of this zinester beehive, methodically, totally flopping in his attempt to appear at ease, relaxed. He was white, blue-eyed, hard-faced, and wore a brown leisure suit. He looked irritated, but also keenly attentive. The entire venue, he walked. After completing his circuit he tracked back to Blossom's table. He pretended his return casual, even accidental; but zinesters are observant souls, and more than one discerned in the man a specific motive: He had come there to visit Blossom.

The man stopped before her table, glanced down at the cease and desist letter taped to the rectangle of cardboard, locked his icy eyes on Blossom's great brown ones, and then exited, abruptly.

The tabler to Blossom's left, from *Maimonides Does Tik Tok*, watched the man stride off. He turned to Blossom then, visibly affronted by the man's behavior, and uttered, "Rat."

Blossom sat strong but also unnerved. She raised her left hand to rake her fingers over her naked scalp. Her chin quivered. "I … You think he came here just to make sure I wasn't selling that *Apologies*."

Maimonides answered, "Without a doubt."

The midway point of the zinefest had passed and Clare had just plopped onto her seat after a slowdance around the main room to exercise her legs, to buy a chocolate donut from the snack counter, and to say hey to Koji, who was paired with a disgruntled registered nurse who tabled a zine called *Other People's Piss*. That woman hated on whiney, ungrateful patients.

Clare had never met her own tablemate Kelly, but they bonded right away. Kelly had just been covering Clare's *Moon Bloom* display. Now Clare was returning the favor so Kelly could view the punk group on the performance stage. Kelly called her zine *Kelly Like Beat Drum*. In it, she interviewed drummers from local bands. She would send them handwritten questions by ground mail which she begged they answer in handwriting as well. Then she published photocopies of the handwritten responses, claiming it was mystical to see words inscribed by the same five fingers which wielded drumsticks.

Clare smiled through Kelly's fourth issue, pinching a last bite of chocolate donut between her lips. She considered the hands of drummers. Strong, Clare guessed. Deft. Accustomed, she guessed, to manipulating things. Clare considered her own hands with a glance. She began to read then the penmanship of Joey Spek from the San Bernadino band *The Golly Wallys*. She sat alone.

Until Easy appeared.

Clare looked up to find Easy holding *Moon Bloom 2*. The blush she had contained at his table earlier did not rise now. Embarrassment was not Clare's style and had been provoked only by that surprise innuendo from Easy's sister, and by Easy's immunity to her impulsive, campy flirtation. Clare's throat did tighten, however, a little.

She said, automatically, "If you have any questions ... " but clipped that sentence. It felt contrived to lay her catch line on an acquaintance. "Want some candy?" she offered instead, nodding at her dish. She plucked out a green and white spearmint disk and plopped back onto her chair.

Easy had paged mostly through the zine by now. "I like how soft your drawings are," he answered, thoughtfully.

Clare winced. She drawled, "I think they're getting harder. I can feel it." She was sucking now.

Easy did not look up. "Do you like that? That they're getting harder?"

"I think it's important for me."

He nodded.

Easy put down Issue Two and picked up Issue One. Clare admired the breadth and bulk of this man's shoulders, and the virility of that full mustache above his strong jaw, and those intelligent brown eyes that caressed now her drawings. Clare watched him put down Issue One then and pick up Issue Three, her latest. This one featured *Phallicus Giganticus,* she recalled, and *Glandulus Gonnapoppus*. Involuntarily her expression puckered. After a beat, though, Clare shrugged. *This is me*, she sighed. Easy made no comment as he paged, did not even chuckle. He lay down the third issue on the tablecloth again and lifted anew the second.

"See this pastelish green one," he said. "This one I like most."

"Oh, *Courtus Contemptuous,*" Clare replied. Her expression relaxed. "It was important in Extrasolar Planetary System DDD, near Sirius. Its nectar is alternatively poisonous or a hallucinogen, depending on the mood of the plant itself. Using it was kind of like Russian Roulette in that culture, and only practiced by semi-suicidal youths, and, of course, the justice system. Accused criminals were forced to drink a brew made from the petals of the flower. If they died they were considered guilty, and if they lived they were considered innocent of their alleged crimes."

"Doesn't sound very fair," Easy said. He was smiling largely, bobbing his head.

"Turns out the people who were forced to drink it on Wednesdays were always guilty, but those who drank it on Thursdays were always innocent."

"Ha!"

"Most legal battles were fought over which day the drinking would take place."

"That idea all yours?"

"Yeah, I dreamed that one up without help from Jeremias."

"I'm gonna buy this one."

"Tight."

Easy tendered from his pocket the same ten dollar bill Clare had handed to his sister an hour ago when buying Linda's accordion-fold poetry zine about "descansos," or, those makeshift memorials one passes on roadsides. And Clare returned to Easy as change the same five-dollar bill Linda had given to Clare as change.

"There you go."

Their eyes held. Clare smiled. Easy cocked his head, as if sorting through any number of replies or gambits or overtures. A breath he drew then, to formulate his statement, but finally just shook his head. He said,

"You weren't at South Bay, in San Diego."

"The heat."

His brows lifted questioningly.

"That heatwave, you know. I'm still going everywhere on a bicycle."

"*Órale.*"

"And I'm still not used to it completely. I'm okay when it's like normal, but the heat waves kill me. I couldn't go all the way down there. Hella hard. Even with help from the train. I was disappointed. I let *Shrink* take my table. He missed the application deadline. You know him?"

"I think so."

"That comedic Satanist stuff."

181

"Yeah, yeah, that's right. Where the horns on his head are actually tongues. What'd you do instead?"

"Sat on my loveseat, drawing, listening to *The Pinche Cabrones.*"

"Well, well, you like *The Pinche Cabrones* too?"

"I love reggae."

"Word. You understand their lyrics?"

"No. But I can sing them anyway."

And Clare's shoulders began to roll then seductively as her lips rounded for a song's refrain and her tablemate Kelly returned, wiggling through the narrow gap separating their table from their neighbor's table. "...*podrá nublarse el sol eternamente ... loo haa loo ... podrá secarse en un instante el mar ... loo haa loo.*" Clare and Easy chuckled together. He wagged her zine in a farewell wave, saying thanks. Easy drifted off, turning finally to sidle through the narrow space between the tables on his side of the runway.

Clare purred to herself, needfully, "You are *very* welcome."

Easy had taken a butterscotch candy.

Blossom clomped back from the restroom, sidewayzing her steps to squeeze through the narrow gap separating their table from their neighbor's table. Rocky plucked non-existent lint off the sleeves of his yellow blazer, nervously. He complained, "Blossom, sugar, I worked so hard on my new zine and you have not even looked at it one second. Now I know you're upset. I know you've been busy. But at least take a look at my figures and give me some feedback. They're a little different from usual."

Blossom stalled, backstepped. She squared herself before Rocky's presentation. Rocky's zines are so well-known to Blossom that she identified the fresh one instantly and picked it out. She wiggled then between the table edges and resumed her chair. With this new *Boom Boom* lying flat before her, Blossom bent to it, leafing over each page one by one. She viewed Rocky's figures savoringly, her gauges hanging forward. She grunted approval. She uttered sniffs. "Very nice," she said. And she meant it.

"Do you notice anything strange about this issue?"

Blossom did not. It was strange the way all of his *Boom Booms* were strange. That's what gave them their awesomeness.

"I mean. Why, look at the models I chose. Do you notice something fancy about them?"

182

"That they've shaved their heads?"

"That's right. They are all you, darling. Do you realize that? Probably not, but now you know. How does that make you feel?"

Blossom did not feel any particular way about that particular style choice. Tons of women ... well, not tons of women, but a lot of women are bald.

"Look, that zine is inspired by Blossom. The one and only Blossom Silver. Look, you are my love, Blossom. I've told you this before and you just dismiss me. Look, I can't take it anymore, I've got to tell you that I love you."

"I know you love me, Rock. I love you too."

"I don't know how to make you understand, dear. Maybe it's not the best time but it is important right now. I am coming clean about everything and I need to tell you how I feel. I'm not joking now, Boss. Please feel what I mean. I am serious. Look, I mean this in the way you don't want me to mean it. But it's true. I really love you. I've been waiting to tell you this. And I'm telling it to you right now." Rocky paused. Then he cooed, "Will you look at me, please?"

Blossom raised her face to Rocky. Her great brown eyes were blank spheres of searching shocked injury. Definitely she had been yanked from her rage -- but only to land on a dead place. Blossom seemed to comprehend the words just spoken to her, but also to resist the words just spoken to her. Her anger kindled then at this betrayal by Rocky; but her anger would not flare. Confusion. Blossom closed Rocky's latest *Shake Me The Boom Boom* and handed it back to him.

"I like the zine, Rock."

"Is that all you have to say?" he whispered.

Blossom shuddered. She was conflicted.

"Right now that's all I can say."

Rocky flushed. Tears seeped around his eyelids. He had hidden his wide nose behind his fingertips, but bravely now stouted himself, straightening the lapel of the yellow blazer he had selected for these moments. Rocky resigned his hands to the tabletop for a beat. He crossed them then over his forearms. The shimmering fingernail polish matched his jacket. Deeply he inhaled.

"I feel so much better now that I've confessed it to you," he said, exhaustedly. "Oh, how I needed to say that." Then, after a pause. "That's my great-grandmother Ong in me, I suppose. Just like one of those blah, blah, blah Manila soap operas."

He stared forward.

He felt Blossom staring forward.

They sat on in silence.

Å twenty-something white guy sporting a Groucho Marx mustache drifted up. He idled for some minutes, perusing issues of *SlapDown* as Easy soothed his throat with a bottle of mineral water. Lots of talking that day. Several parties jogged around the white guy as, at length, he scoured the five separate numbers arranged across Easy's tabletop. Finally, he alighted on the newest, the Donner issue. He ventured at Easy, "I saw all about your situation. What's happening now, if I may ask?"

Easy grin-swallowed. Automatically he spoke college boy to this guy, but amiably. His tone even went familiar: "My hearing is coming back."

"You lost your hearing?"

"Only partly. From when he hit me with his flashlight. Other than that I still have to wait for the system to run its course. He actually arrested me, you know. My attorney says the DA probably won't charge because the evidence against me is so weak. All of the witness statements are in my favor, along with that famous closed-circuit video." He chuckled. "I actually design security systems for a living, you know. Don't tell anyone, but that's how that cashier learned how to download the footage. Anyway, my attorney says I might know the DA's decision as early as this week."

"What was the charge?"

"Armed robbery. The so-called evidence is a handgun I've never seen in my life. The chump says he stopped me before I could get to the door. That's why he acted before backup arrived. He's claiming it was predictive policing."

Groucho shook his head incredulously. "Crapola."

"Yeah, the dude's a lunatic. I still had to post quite a bond to get out of custody, though, and I'm under pretrial supervision even as we speak." The white guy flinched. "A ton of press inquiries came after *The Times* put together that the events in that zine you're holding there actually happened *before* I was arrested. Newspaper people love that kind of discrepancy. That zine describes the first time he stopped me: On Crenshaw, in Leimert Park."

Easy explained then that all the media attention had never been his aim, that the point of his endeavors had always superseded his own ego, and that *SlapDown* had never really been about his cowboying. "But, in the end, I have to figure into the story if the point I am making is going to be relatable. And without some showmanship, you know, you're invisible nowadays."

"Are you going to write up something more?"

Easy gestured to the zine Groucho held.

"I'm following that one up with a second zine that describes his revenge attack. Lots of people asking for it, right? Despite there being a Wikipedia page about it that probably is more thorough than my zine will be. Right now I only have photos of my injuries, and a folder full of screenshots from that viral SkipTube video. But I'll be adding background about the few minutes leading up to the assault, and commentary from my friend Mario who was there. I should have all that on my website soon, and certainly ready for The Van Nuys Zinefest next month in the Valley." Easy screwed the cap back onto the water bottle. He expelled an unguarded sigh. "Honestly, something about all this attention has satisfied my hunger for it all. I'm not actually sure what that means."

"I think I understand," said Groucho.

"To keep on with my cruising would seem like a caricature now that it's gone so big."

Easy shrugged.

Groucho offered an affirming nod. Then, after a thoughtful pause, the white guy said: "I'd like to buy one of each of these, please."

Easy smiled. "Sure. Great. Twenty-five bucks."

B lossom had seen this woman floating around the community but had never actually met her. She stood maybe six feet tall, wore her long cascading hair the color of purple grapes, and exuded a stern mood that somehow never rang of judgment. Her approach to Blossom's table felt anticipant, like she came for a reason in particular.

185

"I heard about this cease and desist letter," she announced through a Latinx accent, tapping the cardboard with a firm index finger. "Koji was telling me about it."

Blossom nodded.

The woman said, "You applied for The Baja Zine Fiesta, no?"

Blossom nodded again. "Yeah, I did."

"I'm an organizer for BZF. You're in. We haven't made our final decisions yet, but I'm going to make sure you're in. You bring that zine to Tijuana, 'mana. Their stupid letter don't mean shit in our country. Bring it to Mexico. A lot of these people will be there and you can sell it to them there."

Blossom sat stunned.

The woman raised her fist. *"Órale,"* she said. She marched off.

Then, for the second of only three times in this entire book, Blossom smiled.

Stanley Donner Jr. described for Viola the cyanotype workshop he observed and the history panel he attended. The wrinkles of his clothing had smoothed somewhat with his canvassing of the fest; and a pinkness colored his flesh now from all the walking and stimulation. Stanley hunched before her. Carefully, he continued:

"I don't remember this kind of thing from the other two zinefests I've seen. Do they have panels at all of them?"

"Well, usually at least workshops. You just didn't see them."

Stanley shook his head, faintly. He mentioned then his confusion concerning the history panel, how the zines in question did not seem to him exactly historical.

"The way it goes," Viola smiled, "is that right now those zines really just describe those communities as they are today. But in 50 years, see, those descriptions will be part of the history of those communities. That's what they mean by 'historical.' It's a kind of forward-thinking activism. Folks like those in the homeless camps have been invisible to history forever, except as maybe some kind of impersonal statistic. They're trying to change that by creating primary resources about real human beings for future researchers."

He nodded. "Oh," he said. "I never would have thought of that." And Stanley's searching expression told Viola that indeed the idea intrigued him. Then, slowly, "You had a lot of people buying I saw."

She grinned. "I've had a good day, thank the Lord."

"You were telling me this is one of the more competitive fairs and that that's why I didn't get in. Why is that?"

Viola leaned back. She relaxed her reddish-brown arms across her tight bare midriff. There was no impatience in her. Her manner put Stanley at ease.

"Just a lot of people want in," she answered, smiling. "And they always have a big crowd. So the organizers try to make sure serious people get in -- People making a life out of it."

Stanley Donner Jr. watched Viola's mouth.

"Like you remember on the application where they asked you to list the last five zinefests you had participated in?" He nodded. "That's about seeing if you've been doing it long, if you're serious about it. But they're open-minded too. They look at the material of new people. First-timers get in every year."

Stanley gave another nod.

He said, "I went ahead and sent an application to that Baja Zine Fiesta in Tijuana even though the deadline had passed." He bracketed the word 'Tijuana' here with quavering pauses. Instantly he regretted having mentioned the city at all. Stanley's cavernous eyes sank deeper into his skull. He yearned for a sip of water. Clearing his throat, he backtracked: "I guess I don't have a lot of material. At least not enough for this big one."

"Everyone starts with one."

"In truth, I have to confess I was disappointed about not getting in here."

"Keep trying. You started by applying to the hardest. There are plenty of others around. You still have a chance with BZF even though you were late. They'll put you on the waitlist. The zine world is extraordinarily welcoming."

No other topics occurred to Stanley now and he felt guilty hoarding Viola's time. Still though she sat patiently, not rushing him. He considered a casual turn toward the Korean guy next to her, the guy with the 'Dick' zine. Such a gesture would relieve Viola of his presence, he thought. She would not feel obligated then to engage him further. But, just as he pivoted toward the Korean guy, Viola leaned forward and asked,

187

"What's your zine about?"

And Stanley Donner Jr. flinched. He swallowed. After a startled breath, he replied, hoarsely, "I brought it ... actually." A pregnant silence followed this, and bewilderment. Stanley's frame shivered as unconsciously his hand probed his pocket for his pill bottle. He needed to splash his face.

Viola noted these reactions. Tenderly she went.

"If you ever feel like sharing it," she said. "I'd love to take a look."

He flushed.

Determinedly Stanley pulled from his pocket his hand and reached for a blue piece of paper tucked under his sunburned arm. The single page had been folded, workshop-style, into an eight-fold zine. Slowly he offered it forward.

Viola took it.

For a beat, she read. Then, immediately, her features pinched with sympathy. Viola looked up to Stanley quickly. He was swaying now, in a daze. She said, "Stanley, my friend. Here. Come sit down next to me for a minute. You look like you need to sit down."

He stood staring, trembling.

Viola said firmly, "Come on, now! Sit down!"

So Stanley Donner Jr. sat beside Viola for a while, watching her sell several copies of her fairy tales. His zine lay on the table between them. On the cover was a stick man. Above the stick man was this title: "How It Feels When Your Wife Dies."

One minute the great hall swarms with humans responding to a multiplicity of visual and aural and olfactory cues: Bright table gizmos, electric zine imagery, bumping beats and yammering and cackling and candy breath all inside a smothering generalized voice-roar. The next minute a megaphone announces *that's a wrap* and *we gotta be outta here in 30 minutes*. The music stops. Within seconds a modular display buckles itself into a wheeled box. Next to it, a spread of handmade patches disappears. Tablecloths are folding now. Collapsible wagons arrive. Clunky backpacks unzipped and zipped. Plastic tubs from budget stores. Containers of whatever breed. Inside an hour the venue has hemorrhaged its vibrancy, its humanity, and pales again to a dead impersonal slab of tile. It is élan extinguished, like toys off a playroom floor.

Clare idled outside the entrance to the hall. Easy spent more time than most disassembling his presentation because of the electronics involved. She had stalled for a while -- hunting down her ex-girlfriend Becca for a friendly reconnect, wandering then the long way round to her table, taking in passively the flurrying elbows and athletic attitudes of all the departing zine folk. When Clare saw that only a monitor stand and a few cables remained on Easy's table she shuffled every little thing of hers into her lilac saddlebags and scurried out onto the sidewalk to, again, stall. Finally Ezekiel's broad frame came striding back from a trip to his lowrider. Clare began a saunter in his direction, infusing each step and sway and sigh with a convincing nonchalance. She wore her wayfarers, shielding her great blue eyes from Easy, hiding from him her jittery nerve.

Then he was close enough.

Clare jolted her shoulders slightly, with feigned surprise.

"Oh, hey," Easy chuckled, also surprised. "Already packed up?"

"Hey, to you too," she replied.

"You doing The Redlands Zine Fest?" he asked. He pressed his wraparounds tight to his brow.

"I was going to, but I don't think so. I am going to the Valley, though. Van Nuys."

"Same," Easy said. "See you in the Valley, I guess."

And then the two of them dithered a beat, grinning beneath their sunglasses, unsure in their garbled body language but ready to let the other notice that uncertainty, offering it even as a subtle but meaningful signal.

Clare gripped the bags over her shoulder. Her fingers fidgeted. She said, "... uh ... I got another flower similar to that green and blue one you like on my workboard right now. I'm coloring it. I'll be posting it soon."

"I'll look for it, yeah," he said.

"Tell me if you like it, if you want," Clare ventured. "I'm not sure about it really."

"Okay, I'll look for it. Yeah. What color is it?"

"They're getting stronger, you know." And Clare shifted to step away, disoriented, flustered.

Easy answered, "Good. I like that color."

To track back to her bicycle without being seen by Easy Clare had to walk around the block.

Rocky watched Blossom through the corner of an eye. They had not spoken since his declaration of affection. Disquietly they had stared forward, seeing the crowds school by. Blossom sat with her arms folded, angry, but also betraying hope at the invitation to sell her *Apologies* in Tijuana. Rocky sat wishing she would speak, presuming she would not, but expecting at least *something* would be said before their parting. He knew his revelation would stagger her. Also, he knew she would reject it, instinctively, and possibly even see it as a betrayal. Moreover, he understood she was too preoccupied right now to engage his romantic avowal. Any obligation outside her mission was simply impossible for her at the moment, let alone the shackles of someone else's love. But Rocky counted on Blossom to understand that he knew these things. Later, upon reflection, this should weigh importantly with her, and might even introduce some latitude into the question. Anyone else courting Blossom Silver courted a concrete wall. With Rocky, however, she would realize that nothing had to change necessarily. They could go on like before just knowing between them how he felt, just knowing that Rocky would accept her heart if ever she grew inclined to bestow it. Rocky did not seek to obligate Blossom. She would comprehend this. Today's protestation was more for his own sake, a burden he just had to lay down.

As they wrapped up, sleeving and packing away all the paraphernalia of their zine displays, still nothing was said. They dallied over the table, briefly, in the scuffy shuffling of the musicless room. Blossom inhaled finally as if to speak; but then, taut in a kind of righteous fury, she said nothing.

For the first time in their friendship, Rocky and Blossom parted without goodbyes.

Viola typed:

"Are our fairies catching fire? Did something finally click? Has that moment come that all of us wait for? I am crossing my fingers, my fays. It is possible. And the timing could not be better, right? Day after day we plod on, adjusting our brand, attempting somehow to be both authentically ourselves but also a product. We arrange all our tools toward that moment that finally we catch on. You got the social networks ready so they can follow you. You got the shop ready so they can buy. You got the email list set up so they can get your spam. All of this for that day that suddenly we blow up, that we wake up to find ourselves spiraling skyward like some kind of weirdo rocket. This has not happened. (Not yet.) But based on the day I had today I know that *something* is happening. I don't know where it came from. I haven't done anything different than usual. But I've never sold so many units of *O, Kindred* as I did today. I am turnt up! Issue six sold out and when people heard that they started buying up issue eight. I netted more coin than at any other single zinefest in my entire life. Where did all that interest come from? I am going to order another run of six for sure. If I was not so confident six is somehow driving this bump, I might save today's windfall for a rainy day. But it's breaking. The wave is breaking. I gotta ride it. This may be the hit we've been waiting for.

"I'm on the Surfliner again, by the way. Heading back south, sliding myself homeward to Daygo. Shout out to Reggie, Paula, Maureen and the rest of ya'll who stopped by to chat. Love it when my peeps crash my table. For now, my fays, Happily Ever After,

V."

Chapter Nine
Monday, August 20

Blossom's phone dinged. Her cheeks crimped with vexation. She ignored the device, left it lying on her desk. Blossom swabbed her flushed face. The wet rag cooled her.

Her original Littlefeather zine filled three sheets of paper, tightly. That meant twelve pages when folded into booklet form. Now that Blossom planned to include a copy of that bullying cease and desist letter, and pictures of that stodgy 'snitch' who surveiled her table at The Feast, she had to add a sheet of paper. This lengthened the folded booklet from twelve pages to sixteen. But she had only fourteen pages of material. She needed, therefore, either two more pages of content or to re-format the zine in some manner that stretched it to sixteen pages.

Blossom hovered over her desk contemplating this riddle. She wore her homey soft brown t-shirt over boxer shorts with her finely curved bare feet crossed beneath her thighs. Down the back of her shirt ran a dark damp stripe, the seeping of sweat off her spine. On the desk next to the zine and a pile of mismatched ear gauges sat a small bowl of ice water with a rag in it. Her tiny attic room was a sauna. The angles of its honeycomb seethed, even pulsed and warped with the heat. The gable window stood open. The door to the stairwell stood wide. And Blossom had positioned fans to suck air from the stairwell through her room and out the window. But still, lacking air-conditioning, her hovel had been barely livable for days.

The discomfort fucking pissed her off.

Gotta get outta this place.

Blossom's phone dinged again. She checked the screen: Rocky, as expected. Again her glistening golden skin drew tight over her cheekbones, irritated. She sighed. She ignored him.

Maybe just widen the margins. She decided to try this trick and see how much length she might cheat without weakening the overall strength of the zine. As she clicked the page setup tab she pondered the last page also. Possibly she could transplant the picture of Littlefeather there to page 15, and leave the back cover blank. That might do it. On the other hand, why not just add more photos inside?

She flipped over the hard copy of the original zine lying before her and studied once again the image of Littlefeather on its back. The printed screenshot showed the moment she raised her hand to indicate to presenter Roger Moore she would not receive the Oscar. Moore stood slightly inclined, holding forward the trophy, offering it. Littlefeather's palm was flat and open -- a gesture of refusal. Blossom asked herself why she had not tried to contact this intrepid woman. She had been so absorbed in exposing the booer that she had failed to interview the woman who provoked him. Feeling so alone now, as Blossom did, and even beset by a system designed to protect Howell for being a jackass and penalize her for seeking justice, she longed to approach Littlefeather for advice. She felt her situation paralleled Littlefeather's. She was being silenced just as Littlefeather had been. And for the same reasons: For refusing to bow her head in submission. For attempting to right a wrong. For refusing to allow the injustices of the past to stay unanswered. For confronting the oppressor squarely. For refusing to remain a docile little fry bread girl.

Detoured by these musings, impulsively Blossom opened a fresh browser tab and goggled Littlefeather. A familiar Wikipedia article, she found, and news items related to the 1973 Oscars. A beat later she was typing into the search bar at Privacy Invader, the same service she employed to locate Brunton Howell. But nothing. Absolutely nothing. Was Littlefeather even her legal name? But then, suddenly, alarms shot through Blossom. Rattled, she sat. For she realized that to contact Littlefeather would be to draw the woman into the complications of her own predicament; and that Howell might even see Littlefeather's aid, however slight, as an opportunity to sue her as well. Blossom thrilled with dread. By no means should she contact Littlefeather! Cringing now, feeling nauseous even at her near misstep, Blossom instantly killed the browser tabs.

And her phone warbled this time, an actual call. And Blossom saw again Rocky's avatar animating her screen. Deeply she sighed, her vexation edging toward frank anger. She leaned back and took up the rag from the bowl of ice water to squeeze away its excess dripping and wipe the cooling cloth over her burning face and shaved crown. *Too fucking hot, Rock. This feels good. The heat's pissing me the fuck off, Rock. Leave me alone.* Blossom wound the cool rag up her left arm, spiraling it with the blue-black vine of thorns to her shoulder. *Ahh.* She knew what Rocky wanted to talk about. At least once per day since The West Coast Zine Feast he had reached out to her. But Blossom was not ready to entertain his issues. She did not want Rocky to apologize. And she knew he would do so even though their friendship had long since transcended such sorries. Blossom would not allow Rockford Williams-Ong to love her right now, not that way. She would not tend to his soul. Rocky's protestations had flabbergasted her. *Did not see that coming.* She loved the man, of course. But she loved Rocky partly because she felt so safe with him. His revelation stripped off that sense of security, their air of mutual ease. The man had pushed his tender heart on her and she would not, could not accept that responsibility right now. Blossom closed her eyes. *Poor Rock. Fucking love you, boy.* She pulled the lukewarm rag around her choker of blue black thorns. She lay it over her navel stud. Blossom dried her left hand on her boxers then and gripped the phone off the desk.

When it stopped ringing she buttoned it off.

Maybe she could fill out the zine with the parallel she kept revisiting in her mind. Maybe she might include herself, how her situation mirrored Littlefeather's, albeit without the spotlights and movie stars. Already she was defiantly publicizing the cease and desist letter in the zine. So why not fully articulate that Howell's letter silenced Blossom Silver much like his booing silenced Sacheen Littlefeather?

Blossom switched browser tabs and scrolled the text of the zine from top to bottom. She had altered the front cover to say specifically "Only for sale in Mexico." Also, she had identified there the sole point of distribution as The Baja Zine Fiesta, along with the exact date of the event, September 29. Based on what she had read during several goggle searches she felt confident her brazen dodge was legally defensible, if not air-tight. These newer details, plus some time-stamped selfie videos on the day of, should render her virtually untouchable to Howell Brunton. In Mexico, Blossom could continue her mission without trepidation, she believed, as long as she documented the fucking shit out of it.

Blossom despised The System. She wanted no truck with courtrooms and attorneys and legal briefs and mahogany walls. She had embraced the punk world, among other reasons, to evade those fucking cannibals. The System was a hang-jawed fiend, she sensed, just drooling to gnaw her bloody. Anyone who observed its functioning, how it manhandled its celebrities and temporarily famous, could recognize this without tutelage. Fuck that noise, Blossom thought. She could not engage with it. But even here, detached from all its open sores, here, unvisibly underground, here, among her enclave of self-imposed internal exiles, The System had tracked her down, had come before her to demonstrate its awesome power over her, had reminded her that, if it really desired, it could eat her a-fucking-live. All Blossom wanted was to be left alone. All Blossom wanted was to speak her truth and share it with folks who would listen honestly. Why must The Man interfere?

Then she decided.

The loosened formatting filled out all but page 15 of the zine. She would put there her story. Quickly Blossom opened a new document and clicked into the text field. Her chin quivered. She typed:

"I am Payómkawichum by birth. Littlefeather is Apache and Yaqui. Littlefeather was 27 when she stood before those thousands of rich white folks in Hollywood and told them they were wrong. I am 22 and I have attempted to do the same with this zine. They tried to boo her into silence. Littlefeather, however, continued her talk and finished what she had to say with dignity. They have tried to intimidate me into silence with a legal threat. But I am re-issuing this zine here in Mexico because I am following Littlefeather's example. I have found a way to finish what I have to say and to finish it with a dignity inspired by hers. Brunton Howell will fail in his attempt to scare me into silence just as he failed when he tried to boo Littlefeather into silence. This is all I have to say."

Blossom felt slightly affected, almost emotional. Indeed this completed what she had to say. She drew from the ice water again the wet rag and squeezed its droplets between her fingers. While cooling her head and neck and face she decided to scan her signature into the document as a final in-your-face flourish. Proud, Blossom felt. She craved to mail the zine to Littlefeather herself, to show the woman how her brave example was still giving people strength.

Blossom printed the page.

Beside her signature, she sketched a raised fist.

Rocky sat facing the air-conditioner jammed into his window. He tapped the keypad icon on his smartphone and brought its numerical grid to life. With his bangles dangling, he held a cut-out of an athletic woman in white tights sprinting along a beach. Rocky flipped over the cut-out. On the back of the sprinting woman's leg he had scrawled a telephone number. Gulping, Rocky tapped the numbers from the woman's leg into his smartphone. *You can do it, son,* he coached himself. And Rocky touched the big green dial key.

A pause.

A warble.

A recorded voice answering.

And Rocky hung up.

"Okay," he said aloud, breathlessly.

Rocky felt relieved by that machine voice but scolded himself for his self-deception. *You knew that recording would answer and that was the only reason you made that call, you big cowardly asshat.* Rocky crumpled the telephone number of Dr. Jennifer Angevino, M.D. and threw it at the floor, miffed. *Honestly, why is everyone using that 'asshat' word suddenly? It's so unladylike.* Then Rocky scolded himself for crumpling up the sprinting woman. She had a Greek goddess quality to which he might have added galoshes. He reconsidered then, too, that crumples might actually add flavor. *Look, maybe crumpling things might be nice sometimes. Texture. And it fits your rule of style. Look, no one does that now do they? Everyone tries so hard to make stuff look perfect that maybe you should intentionally make stuff look hairy. That's it. Making stuff look hairy would suit you just fine, you big cowardly stooge.*

Rocky puffed, exasperated at the evasiveness in his wandering thoughts. Fretting, he touched the back button on his phone and closed his eyes. The thrumming of his air-conditioner droned at him its soothing cool. He swallowed. His Adam's apple slunk up and down.

Look, you have to make that appointment, you. You just have to!

An online comrade had described Dr. Jennifer Angevino M.D. as both exceptionally compassionate and highly adept at handling bombshells like him. She had actually used that flattering noun: Bombshell. She reported also that the nurse replied to voice messages soon-ish, and not to be dissuaded by that hiccup. Besides, all the reading Rocky had done advised him to, first of all, simply identify a doctor he trusted, one with whom he felt safe. And, anywho, no doctor did anything to anyone in the transition process before having examined one's baseline health, and having chatted with one for a companionable spell.

This is serious, now. And they are serious about it. So if you don't feel perfectly comfortable with this gentlelady, you can move on.

197

Right? So what's the worry. Just a first step. No commitment. I'm not even in the swim of things, yet. I'm just testing the current with my little toe tips. Rocky felt ready to meet a doctor now, he thought. *Yes, I am. But wait, OMG. Am I? After all, I just dialed and could not even sneeze into that stupid voice mail stuff. Oh, those recorded operators have such reassuring voices. Smarmy hussies. What do you think that floozy looks like? I'm thinking purple hair, maybe. You think mauve? If Blossom would only talk to me I could do it.*

So Rocky tapped his Twitagram icon and watched his stream glitchily load. There were no recent reactions to his latest post from a week ago: That fancy figure of a teenage starlet modeling a rose gold sequin romper with a scoop neck. Viola popped up. *Sweet ole Vee, talking about her fairy tales like always. But what's this lobster-dragon thing?* Rocky scrolled. Here was *The Anarchist's Jukebox*. This time Koji was storyboarding Roberta Flack's 'Killing Me Softly', but as a foiled suicide attempt. *That boy is always raising awareness in some way that just scrunches people's spines. I guess if I didn't know his philosophy I might just unfollow him. Trying to keep mental health issues on the front burner. Like that time he vandalized a billboard on the 110 near South Central with the words "Exploit the Poor." He was jump-starting a debate about exploitation then. Now he's egging on one about suicide prevention. Regular provocateur. And always hating on The Man. But so so scattered.* Here was *SlapDown. That* boy! Here was some traveler's commentary on living the afro life in Gringoland. *Why that Trinidad lovely moved her jet rump to a small South Dakota farm town is beyond me. WTF?* Here was an advertisement for a *blah, blah, blah* superhero movie sequel. Here was another advertisement for a *blah, blah, blah* vampire drama, part ten. And another.

Rocky gestured to swipe away Twitagram but hesitated. A few tendrils of hair he twirled behind his ears, thoughtfully. He touched his own profile icon then, tapped to his followers screen, and inserted 'A' and 'P' in the search bar. Blossom's determined face appeared -- The icon for *Apologies In Order* . A moment later Rocky was absorbing her latest TG post. *You're making so much of this cease and desist threat, doll. And you should, I suppose.* He scanned the reactions beneath her reproduction of the uber-imperious letterhead. A few supportive comments were there, and red hearts beside them, which indicated Blossom had liked those comments. *So my princess is still alive. Ignore me all you want, sunshine, but I can still lurk.* Rocky jumped to Blossom's profile. His chest began to ache as he stared. *I need you, love. But nothing here except that cease and desist mess.*

He closed Twitagram.

Next, some news reports. Then some sports scores Rocky did not care about. How were the Angels doing? *Only matters when they play the Dodgers. That Freeway Series is funny haha. Chasing balls in this heat? No wonder those buff boys get such big tips. Look, you'll do anything to avoid returning to that dial screen and calling Dr. Angevino, won't you, you big freak? Is that the Ong in you? Or the Williams? Or maybe the Acevedo? Surely not the Adakai.*

He swallowed.

"Okay," he said aloud.

And email:

Baja Zine Fiesta let me in! Look at that!

Rocky lifted his fingers to cover his wide nose. *Gracias,* he pronounced inwardly, and felt a tremor of affirmation and relief, and the faintest breath of courage. He had submitted his application late -- for no other reason than Blossom. Before she trumpeted her intentions to attend The Fiesta he had felt undecided about revisiting BZF. *Those Mexican boys can just smell a gender-nonconforming man a mile away. And a couple of them always have to just whistle. Not to mention the abundance of micro-aggressions over there for non-binaries.* Then the border agents seemed so baffled by the sex on his passport when he crossed back to the US last year. *Actually, you should take that as a compliment, shouldn't you?* But still ... awkward. So Rocky might have skipped Tijuana this year, but now he *knew* Blossom would be there. She would *have* to face him.

He sighed.

Should I do that to her?

But, grinning, he envisioned himself carrying across his zines and his pretty yellow tablecloth in a picnic basket. *A nice white sundress and flats would be stylin'. Red and green ribbons in my hair -- as a reference to the Mexican flag, of course. Like a schoolgirl, see? Why, maybe a red dress with green and white ribbons. No, maybe a green dress with white and red ribbons. Anywho, I suppose I can't count on sharing her table, can I?* Rocky re-read the email from Baja. It made no reference to table assignments or tablemate preferences. And last year's fest was a free-for-all in that regard, one of those first-come-first-served hipster fights. *No, the email just says welcome.*

Congratulations. Pay registration here. You're the best. We love you. Come to México.

Rocky revelled in the email yet a third time. *I'm in! My fam!* The fact sank in and billowed and brightened the kindling embers of his bravery. Always it emboldened him to be welcomed. He tapped away to his calendar and inserted the late September event, ensuring that he would request that day off from The Lido and keep it clear of all appointments. One of his emphatic *I'm not working no matter what* dates. Pretty Mister Jane would do just fine with so much notice. *Look, I have a life, don't I? Of a sort? Sometimes? Besides, I keep ranting at him that we need another floorwalker. Often it's just too too busy for me to help a girl tap her inner power-flouncer. Maybe my determined absence will tickle his reluctance on that ask.*

Rocky stewed before the air-conditioner jammed into his window. He stared at the screen of his phone.

Then he thought of Blossom again.

Then he tapped to his phone's numerical grid again.

"Okay," he said aloud.

Rocky located his recent calls, indicated the most recent, and … touched that big green dial symbol.

A warbling.

A click.

The recorded message:

"You have reached the offices of Dr. Jennifer Angevino M.D. Para Español oprime el 2. If this is an emergency dial 911. If you need to cancel an appointment dial 3. If you would like to leave a message for a nurse dial 4."

Rocky swallowed. His Adam's apple lurched in his throat. He listened through the reassuring spiel three times more, stalling, telling himself he needed just one more familiarization with that machine voice before taking the next step. Then, his eyes darting back and forth, Rocky took the next step. He tapped 4.

Clare's right hand pressed her plastic phone to her temple. Clare's left hand touched a Diet FizzBang against her teeth. Cold bubbles tickled her sinus as she swilled and listened to her broker politely discourage her. Her features had puckered.

"I read all about those rebuttals," she answered Donner, impatiently. "I'm just having this thing. I need to take more control over my life, or something. I'm doing it in other ways too. I haven't even driven a car in four months now. That was hella difficult in the beginning, but now it's easier. I'm learning to be stronger, Don. I'm changing stuff up, taking agency. I just want to have more control."

Donner understood. He even identified. He called Clare's intentions admirable and insisted there were profitable ways to enact such a philosophy in the markets too. Of course, the decision was all hers. This was her capital. But carrying out these trades exactly as described meant significant overexposure for her. In the markets diversification was safety.

"I read about all that," Clare said. "I'm trying to look forward. I'm thinking about the future. I want to do something worthwhile with my money, something other than just make more money with it. These companies making solar roofs for cars are coming up. What about climate change? It's pretty obvvy they're a good bet. They're going to grow and help. I can feel it. Maybe they'll help stop these gnarly heatwaves. Besides, I've learned a lot lately from my trying to be more independent. You might have noticed this. Extreme difficulty teaches you things. I want to apply my new understanding to other parts of my life."

Of course it was all her decision. But Donner would be remiss, it would even be a form of malpractice if he failed to reiterate to her that sinking all of her capital into a single sub-industry engendered extraordinary risk. Industries, even entire sectors, were susceptible to idiosyncratic pressures. Keeping at least some of her capital in the Telecomm or Utilities sectors, which had always meant reliable gains for her, would shield her from possible volatility in Energy. Even caching some in Treasury bonds or bills would be safer, though it might mean underperformance. If, as she was suggesting, she dropped everything into this solar sub-industry, and then the tech went obsolete, or Energy as a whole wobbled, she risked devastating her portfolio. He must insist on the importance of staying diversified. He must remind her once again that this trade would leave her precariously exposed.

Clare puckered her nose. Her left hand dropped to her hip, clenching the Diet FizzBang bottle. "Yeah, I suppose you're right."

She looked down at the bottle, scrunching her brows. She lifted it again before her and shook it, feeling its carbonation sizzle and sigh within the plastic. She said, "But I want to do it anyhow. So sorry. I've decided to put everything in those three solar corps. Thanks for taking care of that for me tomorrow."

Clare touched the red square on the screen of her smartphone. With a grunt, she plopped onto her cute little Venice Beach loveseat. She scrunched her eyebrows again at the Diet FizzBang.

"Why am I always drinking this shit?"

Clare stood again and glided to her recycling barrel. She levered her foot against its pedal to raise its lid and peered into the leavings of the past two days. Frozen cinnamon roll boxes. Soda bottle. Plastic cookie tray. Soda bottle. Soda bottle.

"I think I'm changing myself," she grumbled. "But really I only *think* I'm changing myself. Oh, whatevs."

She ran some tap water into a drinking glass and sipped. The cola residue so slathered her palate that the water tasted like a diluted Diet FizzBang. She sipped again, reflectively. Clare shook her head and plopped anew onto the loveseat.

Everything's still so safe, she thought. Even my bike fight feels safe to me now. Maybe I should do a zine about mansplaining brokers like Donner. Why is finance so dude-heavy? She buttoned on the television for a roundup of the day's stock actions. I guess I'll table The Baja Zine Fiesta after all.

She had applied for the zinefest weeks ago in a fit of frustration and bravado, defying the dire warnings of Steph, reminding herself that to apply was not to commit. But now, here on her loveseat, mixing again a like frustration with a like bravado, she mentally committed herself to actually risking the perils of Mexico. She had applied with only half-interest, that's true, and a noticeable heart-flutter. But now she downright craved the danger; she thirsted for a challenge.

Today she received her acceptance email.

Why not? she thought. Everyone says every little thing is dangerous. Donner says investing in solar is dangerous. Steph says Tia-juana is dangerous. Diet FizzBang says drinking water is dangerous ... basically. Tired of this. Tired of everyone pushing me around. Gotta think for myself. Gotta rely on my own initiative and resourcefulness. Nothing harder than that, I suppose. That's the real hard part of being strong. Not depending on other people so much. Gotta be tough to do that.

Clare killed the TV. She sipped again from the water glass and rested her eyelids. She wiped her damp palms across her pink shorts. Clare felt a sudden and unfamiliar weariness.

The sky was the color of burnt orange as the lights of the patrol car twirled cherry red and cobalt blue behind Easy in the dusk. He tapped again the *go* button on his phone, for the third time, but still his angels did not fly. The musculature through Easy's broad frame had tightened. Beads of a chill sweat seeped under the brow of his hairnet and dripped to his mustache. Easy's wraparounds had been removed and replaced by his prescription frames.

He knew the best fix for this glitch but tapped the *go* icon a fourth time anyway, in futility.

Gotta reboot.

Easy squeezed his phone and touched the restart button. He considered turning about to reset the drones manually but felt unnerved. The top was down on the Impala. Despite the oppressive heat and the fact his air conditioner worked like new, Easy had continued to cruise topless. That meant this cop could see his every move. He did not want to give the officer cause for paranoia.

He told himself: Look straight ahead, Ezekiel. Don't bob the head, Ezekiel. Don't even shrug. No cover tonight. You know what to do. *Hazlo.*

He craved to reach for a menthol. He sat frozen.

Easy wondered if he had lost his edge. Had the cluster mart attack rattled him subconsciously? Did he fear now violence at the hands of these cavemen? Lately, he had indeed reined in his trolling; and he could not recollect ever suffering this weirdly cold sweat. He knew law enforcement protocols. He knew how to avoid getting shot. But flagrantly Donner had been ignoring those protocols. And emphatically, too, his attorney had been counseling Easy to suspend these provocations, lecturing that although the armed robbery charge had been dropped, it compromised his leverage in these encounters. But Easy had not gone fishing for this chump. Officer *8.20 stroke 1* had pounced upon him unbaited.

The squad car lights twirled behind Easy cherry red and cobalt blue and he felt exposed to them like never before. *Like Never.* Maybe my time with this shit show is done, he thought. Maybe Linda and Mario and Becca are right. But this is when it counts, no? Defiance is hollow when risk is low. It's like students insulting teachers when they're out of the classroom. What kind of craven rebellion is that? Was I only proud and cocky because I understood the consequences only through friends? Merely

203

intellectually? And now that I've felt my own life threatened I've gone soft?

Soft? Have I gone soft?

Easy's phone glared to life again. It dinged with an email notification that had been queued by the restart. Easy did not read the notification. Instead, he fingered at icons to awaken his slumbering cameras: dashboard, side view, angels. Easy checked his rearview mirror again. The streaking police beams strobed at his half-squint. The cop had not stood from his car yet. This was not usual.

Easy craved to reach for a menthol. He sat frozen.

Linda called Easy too self-critical. She theorized that the slackening of his prowls was unrelated to fear. He had moved aside what he was pushing against, she insisted, so now there was nothing to push against. That was all. The 'softness' Easy felt was not a lack of strength, she believed, but a lack of resistance to his strength. Besides, she gushed, he could take the images and evidences he had accumulated in the past four years and build a whole lifetime of activism out of them.

It's true I've learned things they don't want us to know, he thought. I know their limitations as well as they do. And how to exploit them. But here I am, sweating ice. But I guess any combatant might feel the same before an armed engagement while holding a broken weapon.

Easy looked to the computer screen mounted below his dash. Only three of the five windows had resolved. A red box in the corner of one window said LIVE, reminding him that presently he was broadcasting on Faustbook. The viewer count there read 598. Also there he saw the subject line of the email notification which had pinged his phone: "We are excited to accept you for The Baja Zine..." The two spaces on the screen customarily dedicated to his angels were blank. Without that manual reset, the drones had failed to integrate.

He thought, There's a lot more I can do with what I've got. I'm just not feeling this anymore. I have learned Authority's limitations. I have demonstrated its limitations. And I know how to dance around its power. Maybe it's time for me to move on.

Sirens suddenly blared from the police cruiser. Easy jolted. The cop car lurched off the curb then, around his lowrider, and into traffic. It wailed away. Easy was left by the roadside, sweating before his dashcam, alone.

A beat passed as he reoriented his perspective. Then Easy leaned into the dashboard camera. He winked to his viewers. In that dusk, they could not see the sweat soaking his mustache. "Cop *8.20 stroke 1* must have gotten a prioritized call, *damas y caballeros,*" he postulated quietly. Then, "Bye, piggy piggy," he mumbled. "Bye, piggy piggy." Easy wiped his mustache on his shirtsleeve. He tapped off his cameras. He reached for a menthol.

Viola ended the call with Tran in Quebec. Her bed lay papered from corner to corner with loose proofs of *O, Kindred*, issue nine. She leaned, peering over the spreads, her closed fists cocked into the niche of the shallow waist above her deep hips. Page by page Viola reviewed this finalized layout. It pleased. And grateful she was to Tran for consenting to darken Maui's skin -- The last big adjustment. But even as satisfied as she felt with this issue, Viola also felt burdened by it, or burdened really by her fear of *losing* it. She did not want to put this work aside for some stupid job.

The window glowed with dusklight.

"My fays," she sat now, typing. "I decided to pursue some kind of work that allows for telecommuting. I've already sent my resume out to a couple of small publishing houses begging editorial gigs. Like remote copy editing or something like that. Telecommuting would solve so many of my problems: No people hounding me and staring, for one. And no performance anxiety since I know I can do that junk. Phone jobs are a possibility too. But I am also following up on Becca's old suggestion about temporary employment agencies. I wouldn't have to be continually quitting and getting re-hired if I worked through them. That would relieve some stress. She says I can just come and go as I want through those outfits. She also suggested I might get some kind of disability payments based on my agoraphobia. I don't know. In a backward way that would be using *It* to achieve my ends. Seems contradictory to depend upon the thing that's killing me to defeat the thing that's killing me. So I'm not trying to go that route though it is definitely on my list of options in the end. All options open, ya'll. In any event, I am just barely going to make rent this month.

"Demetria came home from her vacation with one of her wild boys late last night. I was enjoying that solitude, was I not? She slept past noon today. The internet bill was due and I didn't have to ask -- She just handed me cash. Normally this would be inconvenient since I can't mail it, but today is the due date so I said thanks and walked on over to the company's retail outlet to pay. Made sure I got that receipt. You should have seen me walking, though. I was just mad and crazy. I been letting go of all control the past couple of weeks, as y'all have seen. Today I felt *It* coming over me and I just started grunting and growling and even barking. Mm-mn. I tried not to do this when others were around, but even some people on the sidewalk far away heard my freak. And I saw their postures stiffen. And I felt my fear dissipating. There is something in the surprise of others, I've noticed, that makes me *forget* my fear. *Forgetting instead of fighting.* This is an important discovery! And my realization of it has come rather slowly. People look at me with wide eyes when I scare them, and I feel the opposite of afraid then, I feel *powerful*. I am determined to explore this. I think it may be my way out of *It*."

Viola stood from her keyboard then. Her shoulders squared and she back-stepped for a second look at issue nine. Her fingers fanned over her hipbone, her wrists crooked, and she bent to peruse from the zine's cover to page forty. With her seashell earrings dangling she imagined the reader leafing along, page by page. She marked the zine's rhythm internally, her great brown eyes sparkling. She grinned finally. Nothing to change. Thoroughly finished. Only mechanics left, and Tran's last adjustment. Viola sat again, strengthened.

"The first bill for my urgent care payment plan came in the mail. I should be upbeat, I guess. All that success I had in Long Beach gives me plenty of reason for hope. Maybe this is my bleakest hour, that last desperate hour before everything suddenly turns around. All that busyness that happened at The Feast felt like a signal. But a signal is not an arrival. And I can get signals all day long, ya'll, and that does not keep a roof over my head. What haunts me most is that I might be very close, right at the edge of breaking through into full-fledged success, but end up falling out right before my arrival, like a marathoner who collapses a hundred yards before the finish line. But I can't see my finish line, right?! Might be years away, even a decade.

"Got into Baja Zine Fiesta. That fest would have been the last of the season for me. And it might have been an important one in terms of coin. But I just shudder too intensely when I think of crossing that borderline. Never done it. So I decided not to go. No way. Who was I fooling? Tijuana is in a foreign country! So only The

Van Nuys Zinefest remains this season. Way up in the San Fernando Valley. Usually, I get enough traffic there to cover expenses, plus some. I cannot count on it for a big haul, though.

"There is, as I correctly recalled, a temp agency down the street. Only 15 minutes away by bus. But whatever jobs they are handing out won't necessarily be so conveniently located. I am pursuing the idea anyway. It may be my lifesaver. I can work one or two days in a row, even a week, and then when I start to get jittery back off for a couple of days. Also, I can pick the days I want to work and mold them around the demands of *O, Kindred*. Becca says folks often get into full-time work through those outfits. Who knows, maybe I will find something I can handle for a minute.

"Still stocking up on cheap non-perishable foods since I'm afraid of hitting rock bottom. Macaroni and cheese. Ramen noodles. And I tracked down the address of the food bank. My life's been sketch now and then for sure, but rarely have I had to think this way. And, of course, I'm telling myself I can just not pay the urgent care bill. I will only do that as a last resort because I think it will damage my credit. And there is no way to find a safe place to live in California without decent credit. Landlords in this state do not *play*. This isn't a problem at the moment. But bad credit in the future could be the big ugly ogre that finally crushes ole Viole's skull for good. Trying to prevent that. In the meantime, my first pick is to telecommute, precious. Second pick is to find something I can do by phone, by phone..."

And Viola typed "by phone" a few more times before concluding the blog entry with a deliberate index-fingering of the period key. She clicked *post* then. Viola turned about to view again the zine proofs ordered across her mattress. A solid engaging issue! She perked. The evening sky glowed through her window. Smiling, Viola went to it. She reached for the Bantu knots she had worked into her hair earlier to give her ends a rest. Still so hot outside. She worried for a moment about the cost of running the air conditioner day and night, but then dismissed the worry. Three children were riding scooters in circles. A hummingbird crossed. Then, summoning that indefensible logic so particular to the artist, Viola decided all of her troubles were worth it.

Stanley Donner Jr. hunched before the tightly closed door at the end of the blunt hallway off his kitchenette. He clamped shut his cavernous eyes. He pressed the heel of his hand against his forehead. His skeletal shoulders trembled. Every other room of the condo had been packed away into moving boxes. Their bed remained, and scattered refuse, and some dishes and utensils to last him until he felt ready to notify his landlord and check out of the condominium. A handful of things he had driven to storage. The rest waited beyond this door.

Stanley Donner Jr. went for a long drive.

He talked to a counselor on the telephone.

He held out for a moment like this one.

And now he opened the door.

Nothing had been moved since America's death. Stanley stepped into the room, determinedly. His throat constricted and tears mottled his sight but he kept to the crisis counselor's advice: *Move, son. Just move. Take one step, son, then another. Fill a box, then a second. When you think you're ready, do it -- just go. This is her real funeral. This is the last time you see her. When you think you're ready, put your wife to rest.*

The empty moving boxes stood stacked outside the door.

Stanley found the center of the floor somehow and hunched over a small set of shelves and began transferring their contents to a box. He would save nothing. He could not bear to keep anything. Here a photograph from their simple wedding. Here a jewelry box full of bracelet charms. Here a portrait of a beloved auntie. Here a mounted collection of antique cameos. Here. And here. And here. Quickly the shelves were emptied. Stanley stuffed a pillow in after these effects to fill out the space of the box. He taped the box shut then and lifted it and walked it out of the room with a strength that surprised him. In truth, he felt improved already. A clarity, in fact, flamed at his awareness, burned at his bleary daze. He hefted an armchair out of her room then, carrying it to the oppressive heat of the front landing. He lifted her mirror and make-up stand, full still of her necessaries, and huffed them to the heat of the balcony. A storm now. Two, three, four boxes, Stanley packed, as rapidly as he might, with bedding, with oval wall-hangings, with mementos, with a laptop. And the room was suddenly empty. He secured its boxes tight, tight, tight. He muscled them out the door. He crowded them onto the tiles of the sweltering balcony. They were just boxes now. Anonymous cardboard boxes. They were no longer America.

Only the closet remained.

Stanley knew she waited inside. *Rattle. Rattle.* Numberless times he had sat on a low stool in this walk-in closet and chatted with her and gazed on her as she dressed. Countless times he had watched her ageless physique twisting and bending and stretching as she corralled its womanly curves into panties and brazier and hose and then accented them with skirt or blouse or pantsuit. Stanley Donner Jr. opened the door and there she was. But he did not see America like he expected to, instead he smelled her.

Stanley enclosed an arms breadth worth of her clothing in a great embrace. With a gesture of shoulders, he unhung the hangers from their rod and sank his tormented features into the manifold fabrics. He smelled America's shampoo there and her perfume. He smelled her body odor there and her powder. Her life was here. Still she lived in her fragrance.

And then a smartphone dropped from a pocket. The phone ricocheted off Stanley's foot and skid to a corner of the closet.

He did not recognize the smartphone.

But moved still by her animal presence, Stanley stuffed the whole of America's wardrobe, armful by armful, belts and shoes included, into the packing boxes lined up behind him. He taped the boxes closed, drying his eyes on the sleeves of his shirt. He pushed the boxes across the laminate floor to the front threshold. There he leaned against the stack. For a while he just rested, sweating, feeling largely purged, his cavernous eyes moist with relief.

But the unfamiliar smartphone ...

After charging its battery and gaining access to its data Stanley found long text conversations between his dead wife and a man he did not know. And a list of long calls between them in the phone's log. And many pictures of them together, intimate ones.

Stanley Donner Jr. realized that for the last two years of her life his wife had been unfaithful to him.

Chapter Ten
Sunday, September 2

From the threshold of that small office building I watched plumes of smoke rise off the wildfires in the distance and lie high and flat over the San Fernando Valley. Desert winds stretched those plumes, drawing and thinning them westward toward the sea as if spinning from them a yarn of cinnamon brown. I remember predicting a spectacular sunset that night and looking forward to it. Then I, Stanley Donner Jr., turned from that smoke and swelter to push through the doors and enter The Van Nuys Zinefest.

My first thought was that organizers will seize on any space available to them, and then wrangle it somehow to their ends, sometimes fantastically so. This fest occupied the ground floor of a small office complex. For fun, the organizers had erected temporary walls here and there, customizing the already avant-garde architecture into a veritable maze. I walked one slope and turned a corner. I followed a zigzag and ducked beneath a lattice. I checked one nook and another, and a third. I was looking for Viola. I really wanted to see her now -- Now more than ever.

Since learning of my late wife's betrayal I had grown keen to face Viola again. Something changed in me the moment I discovered those texts in America's smartphone, and saw those photos, and examined her call log. I woke up. Before that discovery, I was Stanley Donner Jr. Since that discovery I have been someone new. The same flesh and blood, yes, the selfsame soul -- but different: Liberated. In that moment I became the person who would eventually compile and write this book, your narrator.

Anyway, I was seeking out Viola but had begun to recognize other zinesters too. For example, I paused before a young man I remembered from Palm Desert and Long Beach -- That Korean guy who was always frowning into an open book. His zine was titled "I Do Not Have A 12-Inch Dick." I turned a few pages of the zine as it lay on the table and saw that the author's self-caricature on the cover repeated itself inside, identically, from page to page. The content of the speech balloons above the self-caricature changed, but never the caricature itself. I understood then that though the zine seemed a comic, really it aimed to convey text. Twice before I had encountered this zine and both times felt curious. Now I could ask.

"Hello, remember me?" I said excitedly.

The young Korean man did not but pretended he might.

"I stopped and talked to your neighbor at The West Coast Zine Feast. I saw you in Palm Desert too."

Politely the young man faulted the vast size of The Feast for his lack of memory, as well as the large number of new faces he had entertained that day. He frowned. Possibly, though, my altered appearance contributed to my unfamiliarity. Clean and pressed, I stood, closely shaven and well-combed. I looked a different man.

I said to him, not-offended, "I got into The Baja Zine Fiesta, you know. In Tijuana. You going to that one?"

My mention of Tijuana did not unsteady me inside as it had in the months since America's death. I stood, in fact, willingly letting the name of that city float among my thoughts, unflinching before it, despite what it had meant to America and me as a couple. For in the previous two weeks I had realized that I had survived my trial, that I had not succumbed, that while I had every excuse to succumb, and while no one ever would have blamed me for succumbing, for surrendering, for allowing my guilt and grief to annihilate me, somehow I had not let that happen.

I had weathered my troubles.

I watched the young Korean man responding to me and felt solid. He reported he would miss BZF and called the fact unfortunate. He frowned. I plucked the zine off his table now and opened it.

"What is this about, anyway? Every time I see it I pause. But it's too long to read just standing here."

The Korean guy answered, "Let's put it this way: I almost gave it the sub-title 'A Conscientious Man's Response to Third Wave Feminism.'" He announced this fact definitively, as if I should intuit the zine's entire thrust from only this hint and its title. I nodded. I said, honestly, "I don't really know what you mean by that."

"You watch porn?"

I paused. "Not in a long time."

"So it goes like this." He brushed from his eyebrows a few tendrils of black bangs and sat up straighter. He frowned. "One of the objectives of 3rd Wave Feminism is that women become cognizant of how the media warps their self-perception, and free themselves of that warped self-perception. Advertising especially creates the expectation of a certain type of body, and perfect hair, and smooth legs, and perfect teeth and shit. So the Third Wavers call bullshit. Cool. So if you read this entire zine here I'm just arguing that that dynamic no longer applies only to women. If you watch porn you will see lots of dudes with 12-inch dicks. So you see enough of those and you look down at your normal-sized dick and you feel inadequate. I'm just saying contemporary guys have to deal with something similar to what 3rd Wave Feminists complain about. I mean, I don't got a 12-inch dick, man. And sometimes I think I'm a loser because of that."

I stood for a beat, silent, processing this concept. Then, "Never thought of that. Interesting. I guess I'm glad I'm out of that habit. Any feminists reacted to your zine?"

"Yeah. Some. They take my point but say it's different because our dicks are hidden from view, unlike their entire bodies. They say to make it equivalent my dick would have to be showing all the time, and everybody would have to be pointing at it and staring and shit. And then they would have to be deciding whether to hire me or not based on my dick."

"Christ," I said.

He said, frowning, "Yeah."

I added, happily, "Well, for what it's worth, I don't have a 12-inch dick either."

"Right on, bro," the Korean guy responded, ironically. He extended his knuckles for a fist bump. "Give it up for the regular dick club."

I obliged his knuckles and bought his zine. Then I dissolved back into the maze.

"Hello there, remember me?" I offered excitedly to a white woman idling by. "We were in the audience together at that history panel during The West Coast Zine Feast. I sat near you. You talked about starting a zine about aquariums. Did you start that zine?"

The white woman's grin exposed bright even teeth. Lightly, she laughed. "Oh, hi! That one, yeah, it's in the works," she said. "It's all planned and I'm assembling it."

"I made my first zine just a couple months ago," I told her. "You know, I'm already going to participate in The Baja Zine Fiesta, in Tijuana. They let me in."

"That's just marvelous, marvelous. What was your name?"

"Stan."

Our eye contact continued.

I asked, "What was your name?"

"Rosalind."

"Okay, nice to see you. See you around, Rosalind," I said. "I'll be watching for your aquarium zine."

I was still alive inside. I had not died. And I had outlasted all those temptations to eat those painkillers. For months I carried them with me, rattling them in my pocket. Security. If the pain grew too punishing I could just swallow them all, I told myself. And a despair would swell up out of my lower depths and overwhelm me into a daze and I would shake the bottle. A reminder. I had control; it was my decision whether to go on. But I had not ended myself, thank God. I kept myself together. America was gone, yes. But I would live on. Strange that learning of her infidelity freed me so, that in discovering her betrayal in life I felt less haunted by her death. I love America still, but no longer feel pursued by her. My all-consuming guilt had evaporated. More than a year had passed at that point since our highway crash. But she was mortal, like everyone. No saint. So her spirit was not waiting for me in traffic somewhere. I would never find her ghost in traffic. I could stop driving around in circles finally. I could stop seeking her forgiveness in a flock of cars.

I walked tall through The Van Nuys Zinefest. My head rode high. My shoulders were set. I felt raw in my guts, sure, but no longer defenseless like before. Sturdy, I felt. I wanted Viola to see me like this. Straight. Tall. Strong. Sure I looked flushed. Sure my emotions coursed just beneath the skin. But I controlled these elements now, completely. I had survived. I had even started to gain weight again.

I found a corner and leaned against a wall to open Twitagram on my phone. Viola had not posted anything in some time; and scrolling back I saw no indication of whether she intended to table at this fest. Did she rely on some other social network more? I realized I knew very little about Viola. That she was unnaturally kind, I knew. That her voice and manner calmed me, I knew. But I didn't even know where she resided around San Diego. El Cajon? Imperial Beach? Mission Hills? I swiped the app off my phone screen and strode contemplatively on. My attention shone like searchlights now, scanning high and low. My carriage held firm.

Here was a Chicana I recognized from the Zine-O-Rama.

"Hello, again," I greeted lightly.

"Hello," she politely reacted, not recognizing me.

People made so much of this young woman's brother, of his bravery and heroism, but her poetry zine about roadside memorials actually touched me more deeply. Besides, I had noticed her chumming it with Viola in Long Beach.

"I've seen you around some," I said. "Love your stuff. Are you two going to The Baja Zine Fiesta?"

"Yes," she answered with a smile. "Well, my brother is going. I won't be there. And you?"

"Yeah, me too. I'm going. Hey, you know Viola? From *O, Kindred?* I've been looking all over for her. And there is no map for this fest. Is she here today?"

The woman's friendly smile held, but the small muscles around her lips tightened. Her eyes glanced left, then right, then left. She looked away. Unconvincingly, she said,

"I don't know."

My eagerness waned at this disappointment. I offered the Chicana a happy 'good luck' and trod on. Later I learned that as soon as I stepped away from her table Linda had lifted her smartphone and tapped its Faustbook icon.

Clare's hands gripped and ungripped the brake levers as she metered her bike's descent, thunk by heavy thunk, two stairways down into the subway station. She rolled the bike then along the boarding platform to the far wall. Clare preferred the less crowded cars because sometimes she could just plop onto an end seat in them and hold her bike by the headset instead of having to stand over the handlebars the whole trip.

She swallowed from a bottle of water.

As the red line honked and hissed, and then hummed and shuttled her northward toward the San Fernando Valley, idly she watched an old brown woman in a pastel pink cloche staring straight ahead, grimly. She wondered, while trundling underground and contemplating the woman, if the sunset this evening would be as breathtaking from the Valley as from Venice. Three nights in a row now the wildfires had washed the heavens with a stunning palette, streaking and wisping mauves and fire-oranges and lavenders from horizon to zenith to horizon. Skyscapes from a psycho galaxy, they were. Might she begin working such backgrounds into *Moon Bloom?*

Probably not.

215

Today she debuted Volume Four. *Holeus Omniverous.*
Quimbus Chicagoas. Coitus Encirculus. These were three of her more
recent creations. C. Encirculus had been inspired by herself and
some unknown body, male or female. A hungry bulbous shape was
joined by a thin layer of tissue to a rocky core holding a sword. This
is how Earthlings might interpret the flower, anyhow. Clare dared
not explain that on its world of origin, Exoplanet 4.5, or Vagintum
as natives called it, the bloom resembled the bell shape inhabitants
coiled into while mating. With its hues of satiny rose cloven by a
blade of throbbing black, the plant embodied, vegetally, Clare's
aching need.

She squinted.

The metro car hushed to a halt as Clare finished her bottled
water. She stood from her end seat and guided her light bike onto
the platform, wheeling it confidently toward the steep flights of
stairs. Two flights here, she analyzed inwardly, just like in
downtown. So the elevation must not have changed in transit to
North Hollywood. Clare had evolved this method for escalators: She
unhitched her saddlebags and handlebar basket, positioned them
at her feet, balanced the top tube of the bicycle over her right
shoulder, and rode up gripping the handrails. A minute or so after
this ascension her saddlebags draped again over the rear tire
mount, the basket hung off the handlebars, and Clare was
straddling again her horse. She bent toward a map now which
illuminated her phone screen. It said she could hop a bus, but ... *Oh,
c'mon* ... The venue in Van Nuys was just another five miles away!
Clare coasted off, pedaling casually, her wayfarers having just been
donned.

The heatwave taxed Clare as much here as when riding to
Union Station earlier from Sheffield's Rare Books. People kept
mentioning that French artist Redon to her so after a thorough
online investigation of him she had stopped at that old bookshop
on Spring Street to buy a thin folio of his paintings. Clare adored
lingering through old art books as she relaxed on her loveseat with
her afternoon lattes. Anyhow, it felt as hot here as downtown, but
not so hot that it immobilized her. Clare wore a bandana tight
against her hairline to wick away her mistiness through the
thirty-five-minute sprint; and she had learned to leave off her
make-up for longer commutes like these, applying it only after
achieving her destination. The sweating actually cleansed her
pores, she found. And the exertion and sunlight had freshened and

216

pinkened her complexion so naturally that sometimes, after cooling down and swabbing dry her face, she declined to add any make-up at all. The first time this occurred she felt a mixture of astonishment and elation.

Why have I been wearing that shit anyway? she had asked herself.

Clare recuperated under a tree now in the green grass edging a neighborhood softball field. She sat just one block from the zinefest venue, letting her mistiness dissipate. Reclining, she pulled forth a second bottle of drinking water and also her compact for a preliminary judging of her appearance. After hooking her sunglasses over the collar of her shirt, Clare squinted, puckering up at her reflection. Probably she could leave off make-up this time, too, but she would feel self-conscious talking to strangers about her space flowers without it. And, of course, there was Easy to consider. Besides his telling her in Long Beach he would be here today, Clare had seen *SlapDown* on the zinefest's list of confirmed exhibitors. Also, he had mentioned online that he would be tabling.

Clare had liked some of Easy's posts on Twitagram over the past few weeks, and he had liked some of hers. But except for an exchange of comments when she uploaded a draft of her strong new flower last weekend, they both had refrained from any other communications or direct messaging. Twitagram did not suit their chemistry, Clare felt, and shifting to a more personal platform at this early stage seemed forced. At least Clare thought so. Still, she was getting precognitions in her thighs, or something. She sensed Easy's simmering interest. And definitely *he* could ease her *ache*. In any event, Clare could not face Easy at this point in their flirtations, or their signaling, or their whatever-you-call-this-shit without looking as good as that bitch goddess Maybelline could make her look.

She had cooled.

A damp towelette brought her skin round and Clare was suddenly padding paste across her cheeks, and feathering pastel orange over her eyelids, and locking her bicycle to a rack in front of the softball field, and swaggering that final block to the zinefest entrance.

"Clare! Oh my god!" cried a familiar soprano as she neared.

"Hey, Steph!"

Clare had slung her saddlebags up over her shoulder. They bulged with *Moon Bloom* and a tablecloth and her ever-present

217

candies. She wore her wayfarers today, but not to hide behind them. Steph was standing beside a light post in a white business shirt buttoned to the neck. No tie. His schoolboy hairdo draped lazily, complimenting his fine features and thick lashes. Steph smiled at Clare's self-assured gait.

"You look *fab*ulous. Oh my god."

Clare lifted her arms theatrically and performed a graceful dancerly turnabout. "That different?" she prompted.

"You were beautiful before, of course, but ... What are you doing? I'd be posting selfies every day if I was changing that fast."

"The bicycle life, bro. Still. Going on five months now. Way hard, you know, but I'm not as soft as I was, huh?"

"Really different."

And then Steph, after some further gushing, described for Clare the venue, prepping her for its maze-like layout and first-come-first-served table mosh. He said that unfortunately (but not really so bad) the other half of his table had been claimed by Absinthe Zine -- that ancient gay dude who did all those fingernail-sized existentialist comics. But a couple of dope corner spots still remained, he believed, though the lighting in them might be poor. The music, he expected, would be jazzy again, and chill. Remember last year how they picked a particular groove and basically worked out a soundtrack for the whole fest? Remember? Clare did remember and offered thanks to Steph for these heads-ups and their cheeks were kissed then and parting compliments were exchanged then and suddenly Clare was claiming a cute little inside corner -- Three feet of table space wedged between two tall planters full of bougainvillea. *Love that!* Clare dropped her saddlebags on it. All the kids coming and going would have to pass this spot, she figured. Not bad. Possibly someone might miss the table due to the distraction of the bougainvillea, and the funhouse quality of the fest's floor plan, but only if she were absent.

Nonchalantly then Clare canvassed the labyrinth of the entire venue, both levels, tracking through every hall and alcove and stairway.

She found no signs of Easy.

The Van Nuys Zinefest was well underway. Two hours along now and Blossom expected this lull she was sensing to last another hour. The last sixty minutes would be as clamorous as the end of any zinefest, she knew, with all the late-comers hurrying a quick browse before the day wrapped; but this hour preceding the finale usually ticked by with light traffic, as it was doing now.

She had entrusted the table to Koji, her tablemate. Only the cease and desist letter occupied her half of their shared space. It was taped to the actual table this time. Koji's side presented *The Anarchist's Jukebox* and *Lollipop Shotgun*. He sat behind his zines pulling at his beard and occasionally texting his girlfriend Linda, who had scored a spot in the maze one left turn, two right turns, and a squiggle-step away. Blossom's brown boots tromped heavily in her attempt to canvass the entire venue before the fest's culminating rush. She would captain her table for that. The spurs on her heels jangled out of time with the cool jazz mooding the scene.

"Hi, Joannie."

"Hey, Boss. What up?"

"Can I leave this flyer with you? In case you didn't see my TG post about this I'm going around to everyone and giving them a flyer. I can't sell my zine because of a cease and desist letter, but I'm going to be at The Baja Zine Fiesta where the letter doesn't apply and I can sell it there. So I'm just reminding everyone. I'm adding some stuff to the zine too."

"Sure, Boss. I didn't apply to Baja but I might go. I'll take this and pass it on. I've actually heard about your debacle. You posted about Baja?"

"Yeah, there's a post."

A few tables down a stout gender-fluid person sporting all black stood chewing gum. Their zines laid old-fashioned typewriter text over risography prints. The zines hybridized illustrations, poetry, and prose into poignant attacks on society at large. They insisted world suffering was caused not by exploitative corporations, nor neglectful governments, nor any of the usually blamed organisms, but instead by the existence of society itself. The zine was titled *Resist Everything*. This zinester washed out their face with white make-up and then accented their features with black rouge, eyeshadow, and lipstick. Blossom tromped up to them purposefully. She was greeted familiarly, though the two had never formally met.

"Seems like I heard something about your latest *Apologies*," the black lipstick said. "But I didn't hear that part. Cease and desist? Seriously?"

"Yeah, the chooch doesn't want to be remembered for his sins, I guess. But if he's not even going to apologize I'm at least going to fucking make sure he is remembered. But it's just as much about Littlefeather, you know. I want to make sure she is remembered for her strength. There's the web address of the video at the bottom of the flyer."

Farther along a white man with hair grown to his waist fussed over some textile art. Red and black polygons of oil paint decorated squares of fabric. Beside the squares of fabric lay a zine that detailed his artistic process. The wall hangings and zines came as a package.

"They can't really do that," he said. "I don't think." Then, doubtfully, "Can they?"

"How am I supposed to know?"

"You gotta fight them."

"That's why I'm here," Blossom replied testily. Her chin quivered. "That's what I'm doing. In TJ they can't touch me cause it's a different country. I'm re-issuing just for Mexico."

Acceding but still doubtful, he said, "You shouldn't have to go that far. What if you lived in like Arkansas instead of near the border?"

"I don't know what else to do. I don't have the money for an attorney."

"I'll pass this on. I won't be there because last time I went to Tia-juana some nightclub employee was flinging glow-in-the-dark liquid all over the crowd and some of it got in my mouth. But I'll circulate this flyer and find your post and re-post it too. What's that guy's name, by the way."

"Last name Howell. Brunton Howell. He lives in LA, by LACMA."

Blossom's voice was growing hoarse. A half-hour now since she started canvassing and she had hit maybe twenty-five of the sixty tables. Deciding to rest her throat and catch a breath, Blossom tromp-jangled out the side door of the venue's maze to feel the dry September heat instantly parch her eyes. The door eased closed behind her, hissing away the Miles Davis vibe. A plume of smoke stained a far-off sky.

Listlessly Blossom moved in the heat, clomping behind a vegan food truck and its droning gas-powered generator. She leaned against a wall finally as stiff and as straight as a box. From there Blossom viewed an artist silk-screening t-shirts. The black man's equipment supported four pallets on a swivel. He would stretch a black t-shirt over a pallet, tightly lever a stencil down over it, then squeegee white colorant through the stencil and onto the black shirt. The white design portrayed an Art Deco-style diner with a blinking marquee. The marquee advertised: "Today's Special: The Van Nuys Zinefest." A white woman waited for the shirt, watching its silk screening live. The white woman was tall, thin, elegant, and reminded Blossom exactly of the type of girl Rocky just gushed over.

The skin across Blossom's face pulled tight. She checked the time. Rocky would be in a boutique about now, she calculated, doting probably on some rich priss resembling this Farrah. In Anaheim. Or maybe West Hollywood. Blossom marveled at his *loving* her. She considered: What is he fucking thinking? Nothing about these women he oohs and ahhs over have anything in fucking common with me at all. I am no girlie girl. I am no supermodel. I never once suspected the man could look at me and feel attraction. When we've talked about his clients always they've been mysteries to both of us. For him, because he's male and they're female. For me, because their girlie girls while I wear spurs and prefer my head hyper butch.

Blossom lifted her hand to examine the blue-black tattoo which began around her ring finger. She rested that hand against her neck then where the vine of thorns ended as a choker. She studied the Farrah anew. The woman watched the freshly silk-screened t-shirt being flash dried now. Long bouncy-blonde hair, she wore. Blossom scratched her shaved scalp. Dainty fripperish earrings that woman wore. Blossom's hand slid to her ceramic brown gauges. Makeup, that woman wore, which painted her face to mainstream perfection. Blossom wore no makeup at all, just her usual grimace of impatience mixed with fury.

How could he do that to me? Fucker. He starts saying that shit to me at The Feast and immediately I think of all those women he dresses and I know I'm not one of them. Not that I want to be! Not that I envy them! Of course not! But you can't help but see they are beautiful in their way. And people compare themselves; that's what people do sometimes. We're programmed for it. I just can't take that comparison. I'm not strong that way. I stay true to myself by not comparing myself to others, by standing alone. Cruel! Forcing me to think like that. Unforgivable. Rocky should have known better! Besides, he could not have been feeling so strongly for me in that way all this time. How could he hide it? Could he? Is he that good of an actor? You know I would not have noticed this woman just now if Rocky had not started all this. I would not have questioned my appearance. She is another species. When I interact with her type at fests we do not even interact like two women, really. No tension. No comparison. No competition. We're too different. Different languages. Different worldviews.

Blossom checked the time again. Finally, Rocky had quit calling her. Finally, he was leaving her alone. She thought: I hope he's fucking okay. His heart's too big, really. I love that man, but I can't just suddenly become his fucking pole dancer.

Her great brown eyes drifted upward, finding the wildfire sky. She had taken enough daylight, she decided. And her golden skin glistened with heat. Remembering to indulge in as much refrigerated air as possible before returning to her sauna of a tiny attic room, she tromped her heavy black boots back around the food truck and re-entered the hall.

Blossom resumed her canvassing at the first table she met. The Zine Cult from Irvine Nazarene High School. A white girl responded: "They're making you stop?"

"With threats."

"So wrong."

"Baja is my big chance to sell a lot of them in a place where the threats can't touch me. I'm handing these out to make sure I get as much traffic as possible there. Because after that I can't distribute it again, maybe ever. I really want this guy to be exposed. If you can't come and buy one there, please at least pass this on and let people know Baja may be my only chance to defy their attempts to silence me."

The girl had pored feverishly over the flyer since receiving it. Her lips pinched. She was incensed. She said, earnestly, "I'm going to tell everyone I know about this. I'm going to help you. What is that asshat's name?"

And the black woman was saying to Ezekiel Castillo, "You take care, now."

222

He answered with a closed-mouth smile, a nod: "You know me, Vee."

"Yes, I do, precious," she replied. "Too well. That's why I told you take care."

A chuckle rose out of Easy's throat. He shifted off his heels, sidling on and away as a tall woman with long purple hair shouldered toward Viola's fairy tales display. A parting grin, he cast back, toothy, winking at Vee through his prescription glasses. Easy wore a tight t-shirt that day, one that flattered his muscular build. It was blood red, the color of his Impala.

He slipped into the lazy current of attendees who threaded the maze of The Van Nuys Zine Fest. He swigged off his bottle of mineral water. Half the labyrinth Easy had strolled already but still he had not located *Apologies In Order* -- That riot girl who was supposedly outing the chump who booed Littlefeather. He envisioned the rad spurs she wore on her boots and the shape of her shaved head. As he ambled along Easy considered Blossom probably the finest-looking bald and angry woman he had ever seen. But, *homes*, that girl was *angry*. Her toughness intrigued him. Easy's great brown eyes crawled the tables he passed, seeking out her usual presence.

Here?

This zine presentation had been pried into a cranny between a pair of large planters. Bougainvillea draped over a chair left empty by the absent zine maker. The material looked familiar. Easy bent to it.

Oh!

That girl with the bike. The sexy voluptuous one. He had given her a ride to Palm Desert. Easy selected one of the zines, recalling its imagery from The Feast. He paged into this issue he had not purchased. Flowers. *Kinda*. He and the girl had talked. Yeah, then afterward on the sidewalk they had talked more. He remembered her being wooable, maybe. And a palpable chemistry crackled between them. Definitely. That day he had lacked the mental agility for a romantic pursuit, however. So much going on then. Too much push and pull. *Locura*. Easy replaced the zine and stepped back, sweeping the environs of this vacant niche one last time for the steamy girl who invented alien sex plants. He had followed her on Twitagram. He remembered her best by her zine title: *Moon Bloom*.

Easy strode along then, canvassing the rest of the perimeter. He mused: *Come on to Easy.* Then he window-shopped the remaining nooks and alleys of the fair's dizzying arrangement. Alert he stayed for both the riot girl and the flower girl but encountered neither. He concluded: *Over and out.* Then he sat down next to his sister.

She said, "What up?"

He shrugged. "Anything happen?"

She said, "Some skinny white guy came by asking about Vee. He seemed sorta *off.* I DM'd her afraid he might be some kind of stalker. See anything new?"

He shrugged. "She's over in the corner. Next to some zinester tabling shrinky-dink earrings. There was a foo over there selling a long beat poem he's bound. Trip on this: Every single copy of that poem has a different cover." Easy reflected on this for a moment, impressed. Then he drained the last swallow of his mineral water and placed the bottle on the table. He combed at his mustache with his hand, thoughtfully. "I wouldn't be surprised if the dude walked right past Vee in this funhouse, without even knowing it. She and I caught up." He combed. "What'd the guy look like?"

"White. They all look the same." She eyed Easy slyly, curiously. She added, "Skin and bones. Hyped energy. Maybe tweaking."

He said, "Vee's putting on a street face. I get the feeling she's struggling. But *O'Kindred* is growing legs she says. Something about *Encre Perdue* in Paris, France, even."

"Yeah, that's what she said when I DM'd her. She's *buena gente.*"

Easy nodded. An attendee landed abruptly before them then to plunder their minds about the Cluster Mart scandal and what Easy intended to do next. Listlessly he reacted to this wide-eyed androgyne. He even looked beleaguered. In short, Easy reported that his follow-up zine was still in progress, but that charges against him had been dropped. Apparently, the cop who assaulted him might face several charges now so Easy still might be involved as a material witness. But his responses rang indifferent, starved of his trademark swag. No *cholo* in Easy that day. Neither strut nor *suavecito.* This uninterested mood continued through several visitors more until a flyer suddenly appeared on his table. Blazing, the flyer exhorted zinesters to patronize The Baja Zine

Fiesta. Easy looked up to find a shaved head and two raging pupils as the riot girl stood rigidly before him explaining that she couldn't fucking table her fucking zine for fucking legal reasons, but that it would be available in fucking Tijuana, for fucking sure. For fucking goddamn sure.

Easy perked. He grinned. Suddenly his shoulders set into their usual firmness. Straightening, he assured the riot girl he would be there, that he would watch for her zine.

Linda noted this instant change in Easy. Her eyebrows lifted.

After quickly arranging her table display Viola hurriedly checked her face in her phone. She primped the soft protective twists she had woven into her hair that morning and fingertipped away a smudge of burgundy lipstick from the joint of her mouth. Then she positioned herself before the tall wide window behind her table. Broadly grinning, Viola giddily now raised the phone screen away from her beaming features. She pivoted, adjusting herself out of a backlight that had turned her to silhouette. Then Viola touched 'go live' and waited a beat as the timer began to climb. She said, "Hey, my fays, look close. Ya'll see that smoke risin' on the horizon behind me through that window? That's me, precious, that's me. I am lit. You ain't gonna believe this but today I am fearless. Somethin' must have happened in Long Beach. Someone noticed us there and put us on some list or somethin' because a bookshop in Toronto and one in Austin and one in Paris frickin' France all contacted me within the last 24 hours about carryin' our frickin' fairy tales journal in their frickin' stores. I am just standin' up right now at The Van Nuys Zinefest and I am just fearless. Ha! Sure enough takin' a big chance and dicing October rent to run some quick back issues and forward them ASAP. I just cannot let this opportunity pass me by. This may be it, I'm thinkin'. Those suspicions I was feelin' before, after all those sales at The Feast, were risin' sure enough from whatever thang is happenin' right now. I done goggled every combination of words imaginable related to me and *O, Kindred* and just can't find anything. Just nothin'. Must be some unlisted forum in some group on some obscure website somewhere talkin' up our zine. Maybe it's best I don't know. Maybe it'd freak me, gimme some new terror. This way I can only respond logically since I got nothin' concrete to shy off from. Toronto and Paris and Austin? No idea what those cities got in common. I'm just gonna leave it there, I guess. Besides the mystery of all this sudden attention, this does mean a brand new stream of revenue for yours truly. IM-POR-TANT. I already priced re-orders at my printer, by the way. Their turnaround is just days, usually. The cost is what I expected it to be and I do have that many pennies at hand. But to make rent next month I'm gonna have to suspend those payments on that urgent care bill sure enough and just put this head down to work, work, and work some more, no matter what kinda jobs those temp pimps give out. Riskin' the street here, precious, but I gotta. I really do think this is it. Gotta keep this plate hot. Knowin' this might actually give me the strength to survive these comin' weeks, maybe months, while I'm waitin' for this whatever-it-is to up and mature. Can't know when it'll come. Uh-unh. But I'm feelin' so strong right now, y'all. So strong. Fearless, even, like I say. I'm on the beam, on the wave. Just gotta be sure to ride the razzle-dazzle true and don't fall down. I need a run of 100 more units if I'm gonna fulfill the orders of those three bookstores and have some left to put in distros throughout SoCal. Issue six is obviously the number catchin' fire since all three of them joants requested that one particularly, along with the most recent issue. Good ole number six. From that printin' there should be plenty left too, for the next big zinefest in Tijuana. I'm even brave enough to cross that border now. Just paid my registration, though I had to keep to the lower end of that slidin' scale. Are all my fays gonna be there? Ya'll gonna come chat up ole Viole in Baja? I'll be waitin', precious. Hopin' to see ya. And there's still a long minute left for ya to swing on by here and visit me in the Valley. We all know I should not be gamblin' like this, I guess. But I also know I'd deserve a right fine whippin' for not takin' this chance. Mmm-Mn. Ya'll seem to like my vlogs even better'n my blogs so I'm aimin' for more of 'em when they fit. For now though, signin' off from fairyland. Wishin' you, my fays, as always, many Happily-Ever-Afters. I'll be hollerin' at ya'll soon. Adieu."

Viola touched stop, chuckling, still giddy. She pressed save and, as the livestream transformed to video, dropped her hand to her side. Viola exhaled a breath of satisfaction and burbling hope and glanced over her shoulder through the window glass. A reddish-brown haze streaked the sky.

She remembered then her phone vibrating as she recorded. She lifted it again to read the text. "Oh, Linda," she mumbled. And suddenly Viola was speedfingering. "Honey, don't you worry about that white boy. I haven't even had to give him a soft no. He's just looking for support. Thank you, though, for your love. You going to Tijuana with Easy? I'm going to be there and scared. S-C-A-R-E-D-! (That's going to be new for me.) But folks in Paris are interested in *O, Kindred* suddenly. Can you believe it?! I might just be breaking free. Sure feels like it. Just vlogged it on FaustBook. BTW your bro just walked away from my table. He looks as healthy and as strong as ever. Thanks and hugs." And Viola slipped her phone back into the rear pocket of her low-rise denims, feeling it find its usual purchase. She turned about then to gaze full on at the enchanted red haze, resting her knuckles on the niche of her hips. Deadly plumes smoked softly upward in the distance. Their color matched exactly the hue of her flesh.

Then Viola was tapping at her laptop and in a few minutes had clicked away hundreds of dollars she could not prudently spend. Just two days ago she had paid September rent; so this impromptu order left her virtually penniless until her next check from the temp agency. She had just enough cash to get herself home, plus whatever she might pocket today in sales.

The young woman entered Rocky's Anaheim boutique furtively. Her look was wondering, cautious -- as if she felt invasive. Rocky occupied a barstool in the cash wrap at the rear of the sales floor, leaning into a *National Geographic* as he scissored from it safari garb. The pith helmet rankled with its colonialist associations, but the wide retro collar on the bush jacket might just amuse on a one-piece swimsuit. Rocky wore tea-length violet under lace today, and pumps, because the morning had felt to him so very Sunday School -- at least until the heat came on. His wrist bangles he had wedged up tightly over his forearms, to keep them at bay.

Hesitantly and roundaboutly the young woman advanced toward Rocky. He realized she only pretended to shop, that the garments surrounding her did not interest her, that she had come for some ulterior reason. As the young woman neared him Rocky anticipated a question. A dress on layaway, perhaps? Obviously she was not one of these Beverly Hills marms who pranced out with armloads of merch they would never wear, never squirming at any

227

expense. The girl struck him as more along his own line: Maybe in retail. Maybe a barista.

Then, to Rocky's astonishment, the young woman held up a copy of *Shake Me The Boom Boom* as she eased in front of the cash wrap. She said, meekly, "Is this you?"

"Ohh! Emm! Gee! Where did you get that?"

"A friend."

It was one of Rocky's earliest issues. The figure on the front wore a black leather pantsuit complemented by some blue-striped tube socks and a red Kung Fu belt. By the condition of the zine, it had either spent a lot of time dredging someone's purse or had been passed through many curious hands to be thumbed over countless times.

"Yes, that's me. Fancy that! My zine." Even in his excitement Rocky spoke breathily, a drawl. "How funny you found me. How did you know where to look?"

Now sincerely: "You dressed a friend of mine a long time ago. I've been following you on Twitagram for a while. If you could, I'd love for you to help me get ready for something."

Rocky blushed, lifting his fingers to cover his wide nose. He flounced from behind the counter, his blue skirts swishing and his bangles clonking back to wrist. Assuming a stance one arms-length from the girl, he leaned, appraising her appearance. She stood about 5 feet tall. Brown. About 130 pounds. She wore a non-descript hairdress over a flowy thrift store ensemble that was not unremarkable. Clearly she shared Rocky's instincts to not conform, along with his body type, and maybe even elements of his tangled heritage. In conclusion, this young woman carried a glittering aura that easily he could bring to the fore with a zestful mélange of cuts and color.

He said: "I would just love to, darling. Look, you are so beautiful. What is your precious name?"

Saida blushed in her turn, brightening. It happened that she felt perplexed, style-wise, about her mother's third wedding. There would be no public ceremony, neither church nor mosque. Her Egyptian mother was to marry an American man, just the two of them alone, at the cliffs in La Jolla cove. A reception would follow then on Palomar mountain in some gardens away from that big round telescope. Everyone planned to receive the new couple after the nuptials, to dance there and party. But Saida expected a young man to be in attendance who she cared about especially. She hoped for this young man to notice her in a way he had not before noticed her. In short, she wanted to attract the boy.

Rocky saw Saida's bewilderment. He detected hurt in her, too, and a disabling shyness. Saida's sensitivity to her predicament impressed him. Such nuances would be easy to overlook.

"And so," Rocky mused. "You're wondering where to even begin, aren't you?"

Saida shook her head.

He said, "You need to be formal and respectful and not upstage the stars of the show, of course. But also you would like to be alluring in some demure way, and draw a little attention to yourself from this wonderful boy for whom I'm guessing you feel quite a lot of affection. Is that right?"

"Yes, yes. Exactly."

Rocky nodded, thoughtfully. He sighed. His thoughts flit to Blossom. If Blossom encountered him at a wedding would she speak to him again? Would that woman *ever* speak to him again? Or might Rocky fancy himself up in some special way that would command Blossom's attention in Tijuana? Like Wonder Woman, say? Okay, a flack jacket to match hers? He recalled then that Blossom would be at The Van Nuys Zinefest at that very moment, and, according to her Twitagram, was probably dispersing flyers exactly now. He remembered the flex of the muscles in her temple when he confessed to her his feelings, and that bolt of betrayal through her wounded expression. Rocky looked on the girl in front of him and wondered how anyone anywhere in any age had ever survived this blah, blah, blah at all. *It's so simple to fall in love. If only the rest of love was so simple.* Quietened by these reflections, he uttered, through a helpless sigh, "Oh my dear Saida, life is just a lost earring, isn't it?"

Her eyebrows arched at the possible meanings of this interjection.

"Honey," said Rocky, still quietly. "Look, it's tricky because *everything* is tricky. But you've come to the right girl for help. You have an adorable smile and we're going to make sure your crush sees it. What happens after that we can't know, now can we? But by the time you leave that reception you will have made your mark, and maybe made a start with that lucky boy. Now, tell me, my dear, what is he like? Is he an astronaut?"

Saida beamed. By the time she stopped describing "Hasan" to Rocky, they sat together on footstools, knees against knees, gazing up through the boutique's bay windows into the otherworldly colors of a sunset born of wildfire.

"He sounds just wonderful," Rocky lilted, energized by her challenge. "And watching you talk about him I know exactly what to do. But I can't do it in this shop, love. We're going to have to have a date of our own. Away from here. How hard is it for you to get to Pasadena?"

Chapter Eleven
Wednesday, September 19

Viola stood in the middle of Demetria's bedroom. She stood there looking around. She held her phone before her brown deadened face. Viola mouthed at the phone, almost voicelessly, vlogging:

"Demetria's gone. I'm scramblin' for a new housemate. Any gal out there lookin' for a place to live in the south bay of San Diego hit me up. You get a smallish room and a shared bath in a two-bedroom apartment in National City. Not gonna lie: This joant more a module or a cubicle than a crib, and the view from your window will be a car dealership -- but you can walk to the trolley from here without havin' to hear the trolley from here. Half rent and bills. DM me for details. Please."

Viola stared into the screen speechlessly for a moment. She nodded thoughtfully, her gaze inward, groping. Then she turned the phone away from her face to pan the room as she swiveled her narrow waist. The room was empty: Scraps of paper on a bare hard floor. Open closet door. Stray hangers. Cobwebbed corners. More or less clean. Missing light bulb. White naked walls. As she broadcast this vacant space to her followers she uttered:

"I've never missed rent so maybe payin' somethin' down and explainin' the situation might buy me a minute to catch up. Don't gotta bad relationship with that landlord. Been here two years now and I've never bothered a soul. Never even call that man with complaints about plugged drains and such. All this might count for somethin' now. And he seems *okay*, though of course lots a times you don't see that prejudice till somethin' like this come along. People be open-minded when errything perfect. Somethin' go wrong though and here comes that sneer. But lookin' like temp work full-time now, no doubt. Worked overnight last three nights in a grocery store helpin' to set up some new shelves they're installin'. My shoulders done wore out but at least I've got somewhere to go tonight. Should help me keep my mind through this emergency. The agency only lets a girl work one shift per 24 hours: but Demetria was sayin' that by workin' for two different temp agencies simultaneously, one doesn't know you just worked all night at the other. Preparin' me, I guess. Issue nine of *O, Kindred* is totally done, but sure enough I don't have the coin to print it."

The panning screen came back round to Viola's look. It showed the numbness in her visage and her great brown eyes looking off, pondering, gently raised, lost. The woman spoke as if to herself, her voice slightly quaking, removed even. She seemed to have forgotten the many people far far away who listened to her, who viewed. She said,

"The shock of all this makes me wanna just bury my head and hide. The Baja Zine Fiesta is coming up. I already got my vendors packet with directions and errything and might make a handful of pennies there in TJ, but I just can't imagine crossin' that border now. Don't got the nerve for that. Don't got any nerve left at all. Just can't."

Viola trod from Demetria's bedroom then. Her footsteps echoed. The phone recorded negligently. The ceiling, it broadcast, the floor. It swung at her side. Dizzying. Twisting. As Viola stepped into the living room again she steadied the phone before her dead face. Silent she stood. Then,

"She only took her own stuff, though," she sighed. "Left mine alone. Ghostin' my texts and calls. Probably she made a last-minute escape with one of those goons of hers and doesn't wanna face me with it. No warnin' is lower than lowdown, for sure. Probably you noticin', like me, how quiet I am about this. *It* done come alive, see, to choke me dead and I just surrender like this? Without a fight? The other week at The Van Nuys Zinefest I stood on top a the world, didn't I? All that sudden attention from errywhere mixed with that new strategy I found for confrontin' *It* and I felt strong. Ya'll shoulda seen me this mornin' facin' down a man who approached me as I slogged home from that grocery store gig. He was comin' toward me and I felt *It* risin' up in me fast and hard and I got this new angry way of dealin' with my fears, right? -- So I just freaked like a madwoman, no restraint. But ya'll know what? I saw somethin' in that man's eyes I had never before seen anywhere else but my own. I saw that I made *It* worse for him. And when I reflected on that situation I realized that that man wasn't necessarily a *bad* man, that he didn't necessarily deserve *that*. Suddenly I just could not accept that to free myself of *It* I had to transfer it to another broken down soul. I felt dern sorry. And then just tired, you know. Tired. Tired. So tired of fightin' it all. Now, wakin' up to Demetria gone, I feel nothin' but empty. Like I don't exist hardly. But I gotta say there is a kinda icy peace in total defeat. Like ice."

Viola sank onto the sofa. She stared steadily into the camera now. Two velvet braids fell across the blankness of her eyes. Viola backhanded away those velvet braids, revealing the blankness of her eyes. She glanced right. She reached. A large seashell was brought suddenly to her ear. Viola sat with that large seashell against her ear. The video ran on.

"I might put up a go fund me campaign for issue 9, I'm thinkin'. After I stabilize, I mean. Not doin' anything but workin' till I stabilize. We funded issues one and two thataway. Many of y'all who been with me since the start will remember those days."

Viola kept the seashell against her ear.

"Sorry to lay all this on ya'll. Thanks to erryone for supportin' me so long. And right when I was breakin' through, right? Looks like this fairy tale's done come to a crashin' and fiery end ... precious."

And without her usual farewell Viola pulled her elbows in tight against her rib cage and dropped the phone upon her lap. She touched stop. The video processed and rendered. In a few seconds the likes started. In a few seconds more the encouraging comments started. But no one offered any money. Few of Viola's friends had any money.

Still Viola sat pressing the seashell against her head.

I stood in the middle of my empty condominium. Straight I stood, closely-shaven and lately-barbered, with my clothing fresh and pressed. In the last month my sun-burnt forelimb had faded to brown and was fading still toward my natural pinkish pale. My eyes blinked clear and alert.

I watched the owner of my condo inspect the property's condition for check-out. Already I had surrendered the door keys to him and just waited now for the man to assure himself of no damage before agreeing to return my deposit, which I did not really need. Through our years in the condo America and I had not developed a personal relationship with this man and he knew nothing of her death.

Presently we toured the master bedroom -- the room in which I wrote my book reviews and essays. The man rubbed the window sill for excess dust and pulled and wound the blinds to determine that their mechanics still functioned. He held a checklist in one hand. Casually he said,

"Big plans? You buy somewhere near?"

A middle-aged white man, comfortably paunched. I watched him open the closet door and tilt up his head, then swivel

234

his head. He moved unhurried, perfunctory, methodical, like a doctor performing a physical exam. For my part, I had gained some ten pounds by now.

"No. Nothing specific."

I spoke steadily, firmly.

With the master bath behind us, we shifted onto the tiles of the kitchenette and the utility room. The owner opened several doors to view the vacated guts of the refrigerator and the dishwasher and the oven and the microwave and the washer and the dryer. Each cabinet door he opened too, paying particular attention to the storage space beneath the sink. With a suddenly-appearing penlight, he checked the particleboard there for signs of leaks. A doctor again, assessing now a throat. I half-expected to hear the command "Say, ahh."

To preempt this I blurted, "We appreciated, by the way, that this place came with a refrigerator. So strange how they make renters in California buy their own fridges. What kind of renters go around with their own refrigerators? I never understood that."

The owner nodded. "An oddity, yes." He returned the penlight to his hip pocket. "The thing is ... if there is a refrigerator on the property, and it breaks, then the landlord has, by law, to replace it."

I shook my head. Then firmly, "Still, our refrigerator went out in a rental place we lived in in Virginia and the landlord replaced it there. I don't see how it's different."

"I agree, yes," he responded. He lay his wrist over his paunch now and leaned back with a contented air. He said, flicking his wrist philosophically, "That's why I provide them. My theory is that tenants are more likely to stay in a property if appliances are included. It's just that it creates one more liability for the owner. And many in my line stick to the legal minimum. Plus, move-outs sometimes leave them very dirty, you know; and, of course, outright thefts are not unknown."

The owner reviewed America's bathroom. I watched him test the faucets. How many times had I splashed my face there? The condo's smallest bedroom he checked afterward, where my wife and I slept. We reached America's private space finally. From floor to ceiling, he glanced, taking in the condition of the laminate tiles and the lusterless white paint. The windowsill and blinds he fingertipped again, like before. He inhaled, seeming to smell something. I inhaled as well.

235

"Looks good," said the owner, folding his checklist and joining it to the penlight. "And your forwarding address for the deposit? Stanley Donner Jr., right? And I'll be sure to include a refund for the next 10 days."

"It's just a PO Box at the moment. I wrote it down for you on this slip. Actually, we've put everything in storage and will have no physical address right away."

"Well."

The owner fingered the square of paper and examined it critically. At last satisfied, he pried it into a front pocket. Now he occupied America's closet. Again he inhaled deeply. The owner furrowed his brow. His head tilted up and then turned, suspiciously, as if questioning. The toe of his leather loafer tapped a baseboard.

"Is that a deodorizer?"

I answered, unfazed, "Yes. I sprayed the place yesterday with one of those canned fragrances and then left the windows open to air. I guess it lingers."

We had completed our canvassing of the condo's interior now and I trailed him, lingeringly, back through the front room. He slid open the glass door of the balcony. There he opened an exterior utility closet to inspect the water heater.

"Any problem with this thing."

"No. None."

"No address, huh? Going overseas? You in the military?"

"Actually we bought an RV. A 30ft Winnebago. Green. We're going to travel for a while, stay disconnected. We're in a period of flux, I guess you'd say. Probably just float around until we figure out what to do next. That's why we're running off before the end of the month. In truth, we're just really ready to move on. Can't wait any longer."

The owner closed the utility closet door and threw a glance over the balcony's stucco walls.

"Sounds like a lot of fun. Where to?"

I raised my eyebrows. "Yosemite, maybe? We're just going to work our way northward until it gets cold. Tonight we'll probably sleep in the Ralph's parking lot."

"Hah! I did some of that kind of traveling in my 20s. Helluva time. Saw a lot but had no money to really do anything. Later you get some money but are too busy and have too many obligations to go off and be free. I envy you. I saw Yosemite about

236

ten years ago with the wife. Had a fine time. That was before all the fires, though. Everything's different now. According to rumors the goddamn bears are ripping through tents and trying to eat people nowadays. Not sure I believe that one; but in any event lucky you got an RV. Don't guess they can rip through aluminum."

We stood in the living room now. The inspection was over. The owner was relieved and voluble.

"Thanks for your punctuality with the rent these past few years. And this mid-month exit of yours is a boon to me. That young professional couple will be moving in day after tomorrow. I always have good luck with that type. If you need a reference for your next place, wherever that ends up being, here's my card."

I accepted the card, politely.

The front door was opening then and the two of us were stepping out onto the front landing. I descended the staircase as the owner secured the door behind us. At the foot of the steps he gripped my firm, steady hand.

He said, "Good luck and good health to you and your wife."

"Thank you," I said. "I'll watch out for those bears."

We laughed and parted.

Due to the parking regulations enforced by the home owner's association that manages my now-former condo complex I had left my new RV three blocks away, parked on a side street. I expected I might sleep there a couple of nights before finally driving off, before departing, at last, the vividness of America's ghost, and that three-bedroom repository for all my pain. After devouring a large pizza in the strip mall, however, and surrendering my mind to a superhero film, I ended up spending the night right there in the parking lot of the movie theater.

I woke the next morning completely severed from any roots, cleansed now and totally free. I had nothing before me but the rest of my life.

B lossom stood in the middle of a copy shop. She stood over a machine that hummed and milled and shushed. Blossom stood in her heavy brown boots and flack jacket, rectangle straight, monitoring the printing of 100 copies of the sheet upon which would appear pages 1 and 2 and 15 and 16 of *The Man Who Booed Littlefeather*. The papers hissed onto the catch tray. Blossom plucked out a single page, double-checking that the print run was good.

The print run was good.

Blossom stood in the middle of a copy shop watching sheets file out of a copy machine.

She calculated the math in her head. Again. Four pages. 100 copies per page. Together these 400 copies would amount to a 100-dollar job, or, one dollar per unit. Usually Blossom priced a zine of this quality and production cost at three dollars. That covered expenses and provided cash forward for later printings. But for this re-run of the Littlefeather zine Blossom had different priorities. She really wanted the zine to be read, but she only had one day to distribute it. Just a single day. So she would charge as little as possible: just one fucking dollar -- enough to cover printing.

The first 100-page run quit. Blossom lifted the stack of warm paper off the catch tray to the counter. She eyeballed the next sheet, lay it in the feeder, indicated one copy, 2-sided, black and white, and tapped print. The machine whirred. Its churning commenced. A single sheet glided forth. Blossom inspected it. Always Blossom printed a single copy before programming a full run. Occasionally copiers printed her more unorthodox layouts sideways. She did not expect such a malfunction with this more straightforward design, but better to make sure -- it prevented wasted paper and money.

Fine.

Blossom returned the original to the feeder and instructed the machine to copy it 99 times more. The rubber wheels rolled. The whirring began anew.

"Assistance needed in the ink department."

The tension over Blossom's cheekbones drew tight. She had heard that announcement so many fucking times in this shop that it must be some kind of fucking code for the fucking staff. Blossom did not know what the code meant, but she knew those words must mean more than they said. Dozens of times she had instinctively reacted to that announcement by glancing toward the copy shop's wall of ink cassettes. And never, not one fucking time, had there ever been someone fucking over there. Like now. Nobody. So assistance was not in fact needed in the fucking ink department. Maybe to spook shoplifters? Who knew? And that shitty pop music they piped through the joint! Shitty music and deceiving announcements are forever emblazoned upon the memories of every zine Blossom ever copied at that place.

The print run finished.

She ran a single reproduction of the next sheet and then programmed the machine for ninety-nine more.

Blossom stood straight, in the middle of the copy shop, suffering music so shitty it flared her chronic anger toward a stomping rage. Hooking her thumbs into the armholes of her flack jacket, she glared at the ceiling, exasperated. Is there anything in the world worth singing about other than bubble-gum love? Anything? Life is a fucking fistfight. Squishy art like that just lies. Sometimes when Blossom faced an extended printing session like this she would arm herself with earphones and bloody the copy shop's lame tunes with an old Riot Grrrl compilation or some cosmic femme punk. But that night the intensity of her focus had distracted her from this habitual defense. Why do I fucking care? she fumed. Who cares if the fucking ink department announcement is a fucking lie? Still, it rankled.

The print run finished.

Blossom ran a single reproduction of the next sheet and then programmed the machine for ninety-nine more.

She wondered about Rocky. The machine hummed and milled and shushed and Blossom wondered if Rocky was okay. She could not text the man. After weeks of ignoring him, it felt somehow inconsiderate to just text. She had begun to worry, though. He had posted nothing on Twitagram since The Feast. Neither had he liked her posts about The Baja Zine Fiesta. Normally when they became estranged, even by mere days, Rocky would like something random in her stream -- like a years-old post, maybe, or some innocuous comment. That was him saying hello. He had not done that in a while, understandably. She wondered how he was.

Blossom stood in the middle of the copy shop listening to Justin Beiber trill over some doomed dalliance, craving to stomp her heavy brown boots, fretting more and more about Rockford Williams-Ong, and grimacing through the tough angles of her face. Wait, that's not even Justin Beiber. That's some phony Justin Beiber. How can you get more fucking phony than Justin Beiber? Well, by fucking pretending to be fucking Justin Beiber. And there it went again. There was not a single fucking person anywhere near the fucking ink department, but for some fucking reason assistance was now fucking needed there.

Tijuana. Two weeks. Enough time to collate these 400 sheets, fold them, staple them, and then spend thirteen days waiting to go Geronimo. One dollar apiece. Her one chance.

Rocky stood in the middle of his living room. He secured his front door and then stretched to crack a window and invite some fresh air. "My, my, what a glorious day!" He unshouldered his purse to his loveseat and let a few wrinkles crowd his brow. *God bless normal weather,* thought he. *Golden days like this sweeten even the sourest moods. Look, not even much smog.* But then this sham distracting of himself ended and Rocky lay his forehead into his open palm and sighed. And sighed again. These sighs served not to catch his breath, but to steady his inner turbulence.

The date was set.

Riding the Surfliner home from Union Station he had received his confirmation. On to a specialist now, a psychologist to be exact. Rocky had *loved* Dr. Jennifer Angevino MD. She had such a sympathetic manner, and the most saintly great brown eyes. But one of her conditions for guiding a client through the transition was that first a gender dysphoria expert be consulted. *Okay, so now your psychologist interview is scheduled, girl. So now you gotta internalize what this means.* Rocky stared now into his wall mirror. *How trying it's been to get this far without you, my dear Blossom. But I suppose I'm managing ... barely. My little clothes shoppe jaunt to Pasadena with that goo-goo-eyed Saida who fears her Mother's third wedding helped. She gave me courage.* Really, that excursion primed Rocky perfectly for the notification of his appointment. Seeing Saida in love and forging futureward with hope, in spite of her trepidation instilled Rocky with a like resolve. Love is everywhere, it reminded him. Always Rocky had believed that, always he had lived by that notion. *Lately I just let myself forget that fact since love has been tormenting me so. But that nice stroll through some boutiques under those rosy San Gabriel mountains there, and a vanilla latte at a sidewalk cafe, and more whispering about her handsome Hasan, and now I think it's possible that stuff might work out for me too.* And Rocky had styled that jewel of the Nile just irresistibly. A tasteful little A-line with pleats and a flower. Saida was a blushing gem in it, indeed. *Her shoulders and chin were just made for that Queen Anne neck.* But then the text dinged, and the automated call with its blah, blah, blah voice message, and the email.

240

"Your interview has been confirmed."

A month from now.

They really tease you along, don't they? They seem to intentionally take as long as possible so that you have plenty of time to change your mind. Look, by the time you get to the table, Rock, you'll be so old it won't be working like it does now, anywho.

Rocky's mind had steadied. Still standing in the middle of his living room he frowned down at the chaos he had left on his floor that morning -- The proofs for his next *Shake Me The Boom Boom*. The figures and attire had been scissored and pasted into position. The pages had been ordered and taped to be scanned and then converted to PDFs. In this issue deliberately he abutted uncomplimentary patterns and hues. *Do you think people will recognize the erections I hid in those designs? And the miniature shaved vaginas? No! Certainly not! Oh, you couldn't help yourself, now could you? A little scandal never scarred anyone, I suppose. Those macho Tijuana whistlers can just take that!* Rocky had assembled this zine quite fast. *When you're agitated you just go crazy with your scissoring, don't you, girl?* A sudden movement drew Rocky's eye. It was his own. Glancing, instinctively he recoiled at the shape of his body reflected in the mirror. *Just look at that apple-shaped Mexican, Dinè, Chinese-Filipino, White dude. Bah! Thank the Lord I don't even try to conform to that gang fight. But my new zine is ready, isn't it? Just need to copy, fold and staple it. And still two weeks before Baja.* He had time even to make some origami Christmas tree ornaments if he pleased. Rocky hmmphed. Really he did not feel industrious enough for that. He was going to Tijuana only for Blossom.

He examined his reflection.

Still Rocky existed inside this man's physique though already he had surrendered his man-ness. He did not feel exactly imprisoned in his body because of its lifelong familiarity, but less and less the masculine form felt his own. Borrowed, the body seemed to him, temporary, like a rental car.

He examined his reflection.

Rocky turned his profile to the mirror, smoothing with his palms the tight yellow mini skirt that cupped his round rump. He pointed a toe, modeling the sheer black of his stockings. He plucked out the calico print of his blouse. With a giggle then Rocky rattled his wooden bracelets with a flourish, cocked his hands on his hip bone, arched his back theatrically, and threw his head askew à la Marylin Monroe. *Oh, Marylin.* He studied the make-up that deaccentuated his wide nose. *I fancy you look just fine from this angle, despite it being the end of the day. Yes, dahling.* He critiqued the lines of his arms, the angularity of his shoulders, and that *stylin'* hollowness behind his clavicles that deepened when he drew his breasts together to create decolletage. *And, OMG, the coif, my sweet. You* are *a woman, you. No wonder those cruising bad boys kept tooting their horns at you on Colorado Boulevard.*

Rocky sighed.

But, look, then you got this, son. Rocky hiked up his skirt to expose his yellow panties. And there protruded his bulge -- That uncomfortable worm twisted into a kind of sink drain shape. He grimaced. *Not so much.* He kicked off his block heels and reached down to scooch off his stockings. A back twist of the arm then and he untied his blouse. It dropped to the floor. *And what about these?* He unhooked his padded brazier and flung it to the couch. *Princess, if it wasn't for your waxing sessions these 'breasts' of yours would be just covered with apish hair.* After a final medley of wiggles and tosses Rocky stood nude in front of the mirror. Before him hung his cock. At him stared his manly nipples, and his perfectly teased do, and his perfectly painted face. He reached down with his right hand and cupped his balls. He squeezed his balls. Then, disrespectfully, Rocky pinched the tip of his member and stretched out its shaft comically.

He said aloud, "I'm gonna be glad to see you go, little one. Aesthetically you are a strange piece of work. No wonder Blossom hates me."

Clare stood in the middle of a jewelry store squinting down at a ring that lay on a square of navy blue felt. A tall and bald Mr. Li examined that ring as well, but through a hand lens, stooping. Clare puckered her features watching Mr. Li. A hopelessness possessed her chest, a hollowness her gut. She knew the retail value of this ring. But also she knew that the price of a thing you have bought rarely equates to the price of the thing when you sell it.

Decidedly Mr. Li said, "We are able to pay six hundred dollars for this ring, ma'am."

Clare sighed, weakly. With a quake in her voice she put, "Oh, c'mon. I paid nineteen for it just three months ago."

"I understand," the tall Mr. Li replied. His tone melded graciousness with apology. A polite pause followed. He affirmed,

"But at this time we are able to pay six hundred dollars for this ring. It certainly is a beautiful one, and you have a cultivated taste, indeed. But for us that is its value at the moment."

After a faraway swallow Clare asked, "Can I bring it back? Will that price stand later or is that price for today and no other time?"

Mr. Li added a note of welcome to his delicate tone: "Any time within the next few weeks and the amount we are able to pay will not change, I expect, unless something quite unexpected happens. I cannot guarantee the price forever, of course. If you brought it back a year from now everything might be completely different. We might even pay more."

Clare understood. Painfully well. Three separate jewelers in this mall had made comparable offers. And shame simply forbade that she revisit the ring's original artisan on boutique row. Too much of a facepalm. She thanked the tall Mr. Li and returned the chic band to her left thumb. She flexed her renewed hand. And flexed it again. Clare mumbled appreciation for the jeweler's time then and shuffled to the door. As she slipped into the airy echo chamber of the mall's concourse she began the math. Six hundred dollars! What else was there? Well, she owned more rings and charms and bracelets, for sure. And those antiques she had in storage certainly would fetch a fair sum in the Fairfax District or on Ventura. And she had her Saab. Her Saab? But not her vintage Saab! No, no, no. She should keep a vehicle no matter what! Unconditionally! But must it be a Saab? Clare considered now the possibility of garaging an automobile less expensive to maintain and insure. Perhaps a Fiat? But this was just too much. This onrush of so many unappealing options and maybes and questions and even necessities just befuddled Clare to tears. Quickly she fitted her sunglasses over her flooding eyelids.

She was walking down The Avenue of the Stars.

The unexpected crunch in the renewable energies industry had flatlined the value of her portfolio. No stock dividends coming, no income. Ever again. Luckily she had cash on hand. Some ten thousand plus in a checking account. But, again doing the math, Clare ballparked that those reserves would only support her for two more months in Venice Beach. After that, she would be bowing to Mr. Li.

Nervously, Clare began now to balance her resources against her exigencies in a more orderly manner. Okay, what do I do? As Clare marched along she puckered up her features behind her wayfarers and aimed her frightened intelligence squarely at the problem. One, get a grip: She had enough funds available to adjust herself to these circumstances; she did not face homelessness October 1. Two, do not call mother and father. Besides the ire and shock and scorn Clare feared, she had left Rochester against their wishes, defying their ultimatum. You're on your own now, she told herself. Time for some adulting. Three, you're not doomed, kid. Stop this wimpy weeping. Try to stay pozzy.

But what next?

Four: Well, she would have to work! Lots of people did that. Working was normal. Clare knew a lot about restaurants. How many convivial evenings had she wiled away in them! And she had heard that often restaurants had openings, and that the positions in them required little experience. Perhaps at *Les Freres*. Frequently she patronized that bistro. What a wonderful Sunday brunch they served with those delectable brie scones. And their happy hour was always a gas. Clare knew the servers very well and always tipped generously. Perhaps they would hire her as manager. Or maybe she could take over a boutique on Rodeo Drive. Celebrities and rich folk did not intimidate her one bit. She knew how to communicate with them. Perhaps she could run one of those shops. She had a degree in cultural anthropology, after all. Clare began to feel better about her situation. This thinking through her next step buttressed her confidence.

Five, but probably she would have to move. Clare frowned. *Definitely gotta get outta my place.* Browsing apartments online had taught her that Venice and Santa Monica demanded much higher rents than other LA neighborhoods. She had not known this. Downtown would apparently exceed her means too. And even West Hollywood. And could she bring herself to reside in central Los Angeles? Maybe in a house out there? Surely not in one of those old tenements around Koreatown. A new depression began to impress itself on Clare. So many possibilities here. And not all of them exactly appetizing. Where else? Anaheim? She had noticed some less costly rents there. Or out east. East LA? Am I about to become a cliche? And what about a roommate? Could she do that? She so valued her private time!

"Thank God you toughened yourself up," Clare coached herself, aloud. Then, internally: It's like your impulses were precognitive, or something. Like you knew this was coming. Like you knew you were going to need this strength and self-confidence and self-sufficiency. It's been hella hard the past few months but where would you be if you hadn't suffered through it? Certainly much less ready psychologically.

By now Clare's pensive toddling from the jeweler's and along The Avenue of the Stars and up Santa Monica Boulevard had delivered her to her coaster. She had chained the bike to a post in front of Macy's. Clare unlocked her ride and at once was rolling very slowly, her rear axle clicking a traceable beat. She considered bearing for Westwood, to hop the Expo line back to the pier, but did not feel spunky enough for the navigating that entailed. And the exertion of this light pedaling on this noisy sidewalk against this upward slope was dampering her alarm. Clare did not want to dismount the bike. She did not want to cease this pedaling. The exercise was gifting her a feeling of control.

Why didn't I listen to Donner, she complained at herself. What kind of idiot puts everything they have into a bunch of little-known corporations schlepping some novel tech? What was wrong with me? Oh, whatevs! Donner should have been more forceful, I think. No! No! It's on me! I have to accept responsibility for this! It's all on me!

Intellectually Clare understood what it meant to risk her money -- But only intellectually. In truth, she had not comprehended the full meaning of actually losing her wealth. Her life experience simply did not admit of her being penniless.

Money isn't real until it's gone, she thought. If I had truly understood what I was doing, I would not have gambled it so casually.

Clare became fatigued finally with this long bout of pedaling and rolled off Santa Monica Boulevard and onto the sidewalk again to step off her coaster and push it to the next bus stop. She had a bus pass. At least she had that. Clare plopped herself onto a steel mesh bench then, leaning back into a billboard seat that hawked a new crime show on Netflix. A white man with a top-heavy shopping cart slouched against a graffitied wall across the street from her, beside a nail salon. His mismatched boots were propped up on the cart's bottom rack. The white man stared at Clare defiantly, aggressively, as traffic swished between them. Clare, hiding behind her wayfarers, studied the shopping cart man uneasily until, at last, the beach bus hissed to a halt before her. She wheeled her coaster around the front of the coach then and lowered the bicycle rack. Puckering up her features, Clare heaved up the coaster with a grunt and skid it into the rack. She raised the spring-loaded safety hook then. The hook thunked over her coaster's front tire.

Ezekiel Castillo was standing before a window in a conference room, looking out. His broad shoulders were squared, his head held high. Opposite him, across an oval table, sat a carefully-groomed gray-haired man in a cheap brown suit and red necktie. The man's overgrown eyebrows visored the face of a person who had seen a lot of bad, but who had somehow not been hobbled by the bad he had seen. This man was a lawyer in the Los Angeles County District Attorney's office: A Mr. Johnathan Vonnelle, esquire. Behind lawyer Vonnelle, on the wall, hung a portrait of Ronald Reagan. A slender window beside that portrait gave onto the mild green leaves of a Eucalyptus tree that towered over Broadway Avenue. Flanking the oval conference table were two large bookcases stretching from floor to ceiling tight with leather-bound tomes. The table itself was built of fine red mahogany. Reynolds, Easy's attorney, was also in the room.

"...continuing," said Johnathan Vonnelle. "I want to reiterate how much we appreciate your cooperation, Mr. Castillo. This preliminary interview should suffice for now, at least until the trial date approaches. If, that is, Donner and his counsel decide to go to trial instead of pleaing out."

Ezekiel turned from his view of the parking lot to place upon Vonnelle his great brown eyes. The lawyer raised his shaggy brows off his audio recorder, meeting Easy's glare through reading specs. Erect Easy stood, his imposing brawn proud, his lush black mustache wrapping the corners of his mouth, his thick eyeglasses riding beneath the hairnet that shrouded his slicked do. Easy had buttoned on a business shirt for this interview. And he had refrained from bobbing his head defiantly today. After some moments Johnathan Vonnelle cleared his throat. He said, "You have not sat this entire time, Mr. Castillo."

Easy replied, pronouncing his newscaster diction with civility, "I prefer being on my feet."

The lawyer nodded. He slumped slightly against his chair back. After a few moments of reflection Johnathan Vonnelle leaned forward again, folding his hands over the closed brief on the table.

He did not shift to rise.

Easy did not move from the window.

"Mr. Castillo, before his regrettable mishap you had never entered this building before, I gather. For no criminal arrest. Not even for a parking ticket. Yet I know your name so well. And here you are, finally in my presence." Vonnelle paused. Then, "How this thug made it to be a police officer in this city is worthy of an investigation in itself, one which we will suggest officially and with vehemence. He does not represent all of us in the justice system, you know. Because of your manner toward me today I am guessing that you already understand this. It seems to me that though you have provoked law enforcement often enough, it is not out of contempt for us as human beings. Please, I do not mean to speak for you. It's just that for a person in my position, with my background, and having wondered about your motivations now and again, I cannot resist the temptation to try to understand those motivations better and this is how I am getting at them. Am I right about how you view us? We are not all villains, are we?"

Easy's proud stance had not relaxed. He blinked behind his glasses, looking down on the man. Noncommittally Easy bobbed his head. But then an answer more appropriate to Vonnelle's naive appeal occurred to him. Wrinkling his mouth, Easy said, "One Three One Two. You ever heard that? You office guys know that code? One Three One Two?"

Vonnelle repeated, "One Three One Two?"

"Yeah, barrio lingo. One stands for A. Three stands for C. One stands for A. Two stands for B. Or, in other words, ACAB, or, 'All Cops Are Bastards.' One Three One Two."

The lawyer's over-hanging brows looked on. Vonnelle kept silent.

After a beat, Easy shrugged. He said to the man, "You're close. All cops may be bastards, yeah. But I've dealt with enough of you guys to know not all cops are monsters. There is a difference." Palpably then Easy felt the push and pull between himself and this official, between his own power as a person supposedly protected by laws and the power of this man's office to enforce those laws. Reynolds, Easy's attorney, hunkered near in a seat behind the mahogany tabletop. So far the interview had transpired exactly as Reynolds had predicted. No worries. But Reynolds had not prepared Easy for this personal turn of discussion.

Johnathan Vonnelle spent some breaths assimilating Easy's unvarnished response. Then he continued, "Thank you for that answer. But, if you don't mind, I would like to go just one step farther."

Easy leaned back against the windowsill. He cocked his elbows into it with a sigh, impatiently gauging Vonnelle's aging aspect. What else was there to say after *that,* Easy thought. But, feeling a mixture of suspicion and curiosity, he allowed the attorney a tolerant nod, inviting he proceed.

"I'll put it bluntly. It is a frank question: Why do you do what you do?"

And Easy startled. For the first time that day Easy stumbled internally. The question stumped him. He had never before considered his cruising in such stark terms. Easy and Vonnelle studied each other for a beat. Then Easy squinted down at the red mahogany conference table. Then he beheld, too, slightly unnerved by them, the many imposing books surrounding him, and the wall's heroic portrait. Through the slender window, Ezekiel saw the sunlit sky under which Opie was buried a few miles east. He shifted forward, finding again a steadiness on his feet -- on these feet which had fled arbitrary police abuses at the age of 14. And then Easy noticed Reynolds near. Reynolds, who few of the folks he cared about could afford like he could. Finally, he returned his gaze to Vonnelle.

He said, shortly, "John, look ... for people like me, in this society, there is only dignity in revolt. It's that simple. This is my form of revolt. It is how I preserve my dignity."

Their eye contact held. The two men judged one another long enough that Ezekiel Castillo became convinced Johnathan Vonnelle had heard his words and had listened, though presumably he had not truly understood them.

Finally, the attorney said, "Thank you for that insight, Ezekiel. I suppose that sums up everything. For what it's worth, I'm sorry that's how it is."

Easy pressed his lips. He sniffed. He could not even respond to such a useless apology.

But he realized then, as the three of them took up their particulars and rounded the table to exit the conference room, that never before had he distilled the motivation for his cruising so concisely. Easy realized that in this one statement he had condensed the essence of *SlapDown.* These words justified his tempting of Authority, and his taunting of Authority, and his denying Authority any meaningful power over him. Here was his own personal manifesto, he realized; and Easy felt with its articulation the tingling of a new direction.

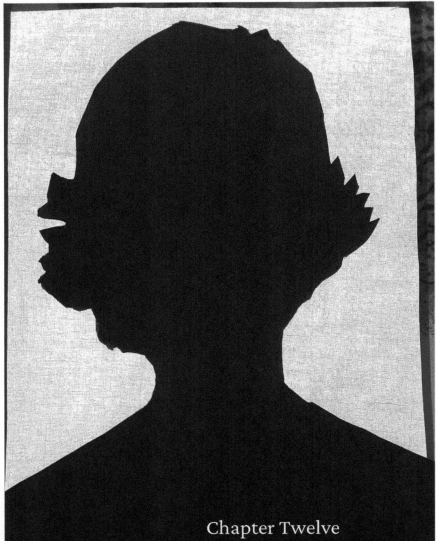

Chapter Twelve
Tijuana

Everything about Tijuana startled. Immediately upon arriving the city purged from each of us all of our mental habits and routines. Perhaps it was this that prevented our sensing the rich potentials crystallizing around us as we arranged our zinefest materials near one another and then sat down behind our tables shoulder to shoulder. We were each so bent upon parrying the novelties of that day for our various reasons, or upon engaging and outmaneuvering them, that we did not notice our being positioned for irrevocable change. Blindly we stumbled into Tijuana's formative midst, unaware that the contours of our individual struggles were about to interlock with the efforts of others, that the meanderings of our separate streams were about to converge and pour finally into a common river of collective onward purpose.

1

Clare had thoroughly studied the entire layout of the border installation online. It encompassed more than seven acres of office space, auto lanes, and pedestrian corrals. But most importantly -- *the turnstiles.*

She had decided to use the foot crossing on the east side of Interstate 5, behind the trolley stop and the Shaft Burger, instead of pedaling over to the west side of the highway, over and beyond the pedestrian bridge. Clare's research had ushered her right up to the perimeter of this terraced plaza. And, just as pictured in her maps app, there rose at the plaza's far edge a high facade proclaiming "Mexico" in tall brushed steel letters. Beneath those letters waited the turnstiles. The ominous turnstiles. Clare had read that those turnstiles rotate only one direction. Once you swing through their chromium bars you cannot turn back. To spill yourself out of them is to arrive on foreign soil.

Clare hid behind her sunglasses.

She had vacationed in Vienna and Paris. Clare had visited London and Frankfurt. So foreign lands, per se, did not intimidate her. But this was different. This was *Mexico.* This was *really* foreign.

251

But what more could happen to her? What more to fear for someone who had just lost everything? In truth, Clare did not feel exactly self-protective right then. Quite the contrary, in fact -- a kind of recklessness possessed her. The dangers that Steph and the other kids had warned Clare against wafted among her thoughts, yes, but her financial traumas had numbed her to their *oh so terrible* implications. What did it matter now?

At least that was what Clare told herself as she hid behind her wayfarers.

She could bring along her rad pink bicycle. Good. She had learned this combing through traveler forums. This meant she could maintain her no-car discipline then for the final two days of her six-month automobile fast. Also it meant she would not have to go walking alone to the zinefest venue. Neither would she require a taxi. Clare preserved a certain self-sufficiency by bringing along her bike -- like somehow she would be sitting on a piece of the United States as she went pedaling. Clare had also investigated cellphone service and had upgraded her plan to run data abroad. This trick she learned by reading through the comments on travel websites. Clare paid particular heed to topic titles that highlighted the perils of Third World journeys and how to inoculate oneself against them.

But Clare did not care about danger anymore. No, not at all. Why care when you're a pauper?! What's to lose? And she owed it to herself, by the way, to finish what she had started. Her life was about to change. And dramatically. So some courage was in order here, and some resourcefulness and ... dignity. This was the last zinefest of the year. In fact, The Baja Zine Fiesta looked to be the final event of her old life. After today everything would be new. After this weekend she would even start driving again.

So there, beyond that uniformed agent gripping the leash of that drug-sniffing German Shepherd, waited the ominous turnstiles. As she ascended the terraces of the plaza Clare knew what to expect just before the turnstiles, and she knew what to expect once returned to daylight on the far side of Mexican customs. Internet photos had taught her all this. To this part between, however, to this actual talking to the Mexican officials and presenting to them her documents for entry Clare went totally blind, and palpitant.

Clare puckered up her features.

She tightened her wayfarers against her brow.

Clare guided her pink bicycle into a turnstile.

I parked my six-week-old RV in a pay lot off Camino de la Plaza in San Ysidro. The banner straddling the entrance advertised "8 dollars," but I knew this price actually meant 8 dollars per hour. I didn't care. A thin man in a reflective vest tore off a ticket stub for me and I strode from the sloping lot, away from the neighboring duty-free shops, over the pedestrian bridge that spans the last few hundred yards of Interstate 5, and toward my preferred border crossing to Tijuana. Beyond the eastern end of the footbridge, I passed a blinking neon sign that read 19.289 and 19.793. These figures were the day's exchange rate of Mexican pesos to US dollars. I stepped to a short line before an oval window and considered how many pesos to buy. Since I intended to stay overnight I lay in the aluminum tray $200. If I needed more than 4,000 pesos I would use my credit card.

The woman gave me a smile of recognition and a friendly nod. As she thumbed out my pesos I noticed she had shortened her hairstyle; also I noticed in the reflection of the bullet-proof glass how much I had changed in the past six weeks. My clean and pressed shirt no longer draped from my shoulders like off a clothes hanger. My formerly gaunt face was fleshing out now and closely shaved. My carriage held firm and erect. And though my attention still slightly quivered, it was quivering now with alertness. I scooped my pesos out of the aluminum tray with a familiar *gracias* and angled around the trolley tracks to mount the terraced plaza which leads to what America liked to call the "point of no returnstile." The ground squirrels on the embankment there still begged like before. And, not unusually, some Chinese tourists were obliging their entreaties with snack crackers. I passed an older woman puffing against the steep steps as I ascended, and then a US Border Patrol agent gripping at the leash of a leaning drug-sniffing German Shepherd.

Beyond the turnstile the line for foreigners was empty and after waiting for only a single person I handed my passport card to a grinning red-headed Mexican man.

"Well, Señor Stanley," the man said to me in Spanish. "I have not seen you in much time. Have we just missed each other or were you not visiting for so long?"

I responded in Spanish. "It is true that I have not come for a while, Señor Diego." Then I said, steadily. "There were troubles with my family that did not allow that I visit your country."

"And the kind señora? She is well, I hope. The two of you were coming predictably for so long. And then a little less. And then suddenly I did not see you."

I nodded without flinching. But my mouth had flattened. A flutter rose in my chest. But I mastered that flutter.

"Thank you for remembering, Diego. In truth, she is with God now. She died in a car accident. I was driving, you see. It cost me much time to mend, as you can imagine. To be honest it was the trial of my life and I have only survived the guilt and the grief with the help of God. But, look, now I am better. I come here to begin again."

"Ay!" Diego had erupted, reflexively. The news stunned him. He had lifted a hand involuntarily. "A shock, indeed!" And then, very earnestly: "Señor, please know that I accompany you in your feelings. Please know that you will be in the prayers of my family."

We remained silent for a moment, maintaining eye contact. Diego looked down finally, pressing his lips unnaturally as he penned data into the blanks of my tourist visa.

"Thank you," I said in English.

"Always Mexico is missing you, señor. You are in your home now. Are you visiting Tijuana only for today or perhaps doing something more adventurous?"

"I will return tomorrow, I think. There is an event near Plaza Cecilia that interests me. I expect the customs inspectors will be encountering many bags full of self-published booklets today. It is for that that I come."

"Seems to me interesting, yes," Diego said, adding his agent number to the tourist card then, and the flourish of his signature. Diego stamped the card.

"Thank you for the kind welcome, Diego. It is refreshing to return to this enchanting land after so long an absence."

Diego replied, feelingly. "God be with you, my friend. Hasta luego."

"Hasta luego."

The guard toting the assault rifle on the other side of customs seemed to recognize me too. We nodded to each other, though of course his ski mask prevented my noting his identity.

254

The registration on her old Honda was expired so Blossom elected to fucking leave her car in a parking lot on the American side of the border instead of risk some fucking problem when crossing back. Eight dollars seemed a fair price for all day anyway, she thought. According to the printed map she held in her left hand there were actually two crossings here. One on the far side of a pedestrian bridge which she saw arching over to the east side of the I-5 freeway. And one on this west side of that bridge, nearer where she parked. Blossom decided to take the crossing on this west side of the footbridge.

Her spurs jangling on the heels of her heavy brown boots, she tromped a crosswalk toward an institutional edifice. A row of taxis, she strode by, and folks standing numbly around a bus kiosk. She tromped about some more, alert for the crossing promised on her map. A portal? A gate? Blossom could not discern where to actually cross. The building here rose several stories huge. People filed out of it, toward her, but no one moved oppositely, toward Mexico. She jangled her spurs still more, circling, marking the width of the facade. Where do you fucking cross?

Finally, Blossom anchored herself before the only aperture she could identify. A breach in the wall of glass through which folks were filing outward from the building. She peered in: Handbags there, rolling along an x-ray conveyor: A German Shepherd there, sniffing at pockets and pantlegs. The skin over her cheekbones tightened. People just entered the United States here, they did not exit. This couldn't be it. Mystified, Blossom floated confusedly toward the bus kiosk. A young Latino man there with a bored stare noticed her. She asked him.

"I … Do you know how to get across into Mexico?" A grandmotherly woman hovered at the young man's elbow. Long ago Blossom had learned never to approach elderly ladies. Her shaved head and choker of blue-black thorns rendered them starkly mute. Her chin quivered: "Where would I cross?"

The Latino guy narrowed his stare. She felt him examine her ears gauges and Medusa stud. She felt him survey the curveless fall of her pants and flack jacket. But only slightly he judged her, Blossom felt. His conclusion said *meh*. He pivoted at the waist to point to a gap in a brown brick wall.

"That little alley," he said.

She looked.

"That? Really?"

She had jangled past that little fucking alley three times. It had seemed to her a service ramp, or at most some restricted access point for authorized personnel. She never would have presumed that little fucking chute to be an international border crossing. She tromped to it, gazing down its length. A turnstile stood at its far end. Above the turnstile was affixed a faint unimpressive sign that read "Mexico."

Alright.

Blossom cinched her backpack of one hundred zines closer to her shoulders. She tromped then her heavy brown boots down the alley. Blossom forced her way through the turnstile.

The last time Easy stood here, when crossing the border some years ago for a cousin's quincañera in Rosarito, that long narrow concrete chute had not even existed. Neither had the large building looming beside it, or, for that matter, the still larger building next to the trolley stop on the other side of Interstate 5.

Easy's first impulse had been to cross where usually he crossed, by the trolley stop. But seeing that on the US side nothing about the border resembled his memory of the border, he just tapped the maps application on his phone and chose the most direct route to the zinefest venue.

At the end of that long narrow chute waited a turnstile. Another bit of walking followed. Then the presenting of his passport, the removing of his wraparound sunglasses so that he could ink in a tourist visa, the conveying of his night bag and box of zines through an x-ray machine, and finally the strutting out onto a large slab of pavement where he paused to light a menthol. Easy idled on that slab for some beats, surveying the scene absorptively, smoking. Stunned, he stood. For he recognized nothing. He replaced his wraparounds over his eyes.

A taxi driver approached on foot, slowly.

Easy said, in Spanish, "Everything is different."

The *taxista* smiled and nodded, continuing in Spanish. "Been much time, *paesano?*"

"Several years."

Easy appraised the man. The taxi driver wore a mustache groomed like his own, but bushier. Over his upper lip, it draped, its side pipes reaching to his jaw.

"To where are you going?"

"Close to Revu," said Easy. "Plaza Santa Cecilia, off Primera. You know it?"

"How not? Mariachi corner, no? Beneath the arch. Five dollars, nothing more. I'll take you there."

Easy bobbed his head. With a comradely amusement he said quietly in Spanish, "Done." Then he trailed the finely pressed *taxista* to a yellow and white Toyota.

"You mind if I smoke?"

The Mexican border agents wear official uniforms, of course, but Easy had not bristled at them like he usually does at uniforms. Differently, they triggered him, by being Mexican -- Like somehow they were as oppressed as he. Even the relatively benign transit cops on the American side who had been policing trolley fares at the E Street station in Chula Vista had twisted Easy's spine up and kindled his disdain. So much so, in fact, that he had laid his head back into a cholo opaqueness when showing them his ticket. *Here you go, piggy piggy.* Not so with the Mexican guard. A routine query about Easy's length of stay had been asked and then a kindly welcome offered. Never had Easy felt contempt.

Then, as the taxi crested a small bridge over the border crossing lanes, Easy glimpsed a panorama of Tijuana. Inspiration flooded him. *México!*

"Señor..." he addressed, politely familiar. Easy stubbed his cigarette into the half-full ashtray which opened off the rear of the armrest.

"Digame."

"You know how the arch is at one end of Revu. I think I would like to be dropped off at the other end of the avenue and walk from there."

"Ah, as you say, señor."

And the driver clutched and geared and checked his blind spot, repositioning himself to hug a leftward curve in the upcoming *glorieta* instead of maintaining his straighter trajectory. He asked, "You spent much time here before?"

"Enough. Until some seven or eight years ago."

"Yes, it is different now. You are going to see. I know this because I am a native here. I will deposit you at the new high-rise condominiums."

"Condos? On *Revolución*?"

"Yes, you are going to see. Would you like maybe a tour of everything that has changed in Tijuana over the last while? Just ten dollars, you know. There are a pair of new housing blocks out by the state art center. And a row of new expensive restaurants in the gastronomical zone. I am a native of this city. I am privy to its secrets."

Easy chuckled. His elation ballooned. Excitedly he brushed over his mustache with his palm. "No, no, I would just like to walk."

"As you wish, señor. But I would do the tour for five dollars, you know, since you speak Spanish."

Easy chuckled again, from the full well of his throat. His great brown eyes rounded. For no longer was he pushing against something, he realized. Suddenly, right here in this cab, Ezekiel had stopped fighting, had stopped reacting, was now just *being*. The unexpected transformation edified him. A lost freedom, it seemed, regained. The sensation mirrored, in its solidity, the drifty waywardness which had dogged him after the Donner affair. Easy felt open now -- buoyed instead of submerged, full of vigor instead of listlessness. This was a readiness, maybe even a purity.

He chuckled. "Well, well. There they are." He pulled away his wraparounds, looking up through the taxi window. "Condominiums on Revolution Avenue. I cannot believe it."

Rocky had crossed his wrists over the lap of his simple yellow cotton sundress and was monitoring the man sitting beside him through the corner of his eye. He said to the man, cooing his question:

"The internet told me that this new shuttle is a convenient way to enter Mexico, and safe. Have you used this shuttle before, sir?"

The man was older, a Mexican tradesman of some sort with a soft carpet of white stubble endearing his jaw. He did not look to Rocky.

The man said, "Yes."

After a wordless pause through which Rocky allowed the white stubble plenty of time to hospitably elaborate, he ventured, breathily, "Well, it drops us off on Revolution Street? Is that correct … sir?"

Again the Mexican man did not look.

He answered, "Yes."

Rocky smoothed the lap of his simple yellow sundress, nervously. *I fancy this brute does not want to chit-chat with me,* Rocky puffed silently. *Look, you haven't been mean to him, now have you? You haven't done anything offensive, now have you? Probably he is sensing that you are a man who is unhappy being a man. A man happy with being a man perhaps cannot identify with such a mental quandary. I can understand this, I guess, since I cannot identify with being happy with being a man. Why, at least he is not being frankly rude, now is he? Or wolf-whistling like they do here. Or calling me names. What small blessings. I suppose my bangles or my hair ribbons tipped him off.* Rocky sighed. *If only Blossom knew what I am suffering for her.*

Rocky lifted his basket of zines off the floor of the shuttle and, dusting off its bottom, situated it on his lap protectively. Through the corner of his eye, still he watched the tradesman. Shortly the van scooted through an auto chute and pulled into a long bay before a guard who wore a tan uniform and an official-looking cap. Rocky's nerves quivered. His prominent Adam's apple pumped in his throat. Another guard then boarded the shuttle wielding some kind of satanic computer orb that scanned laminated cards extended toward it by each of the dutiful passengers. When Rocky held up his passport the guard stopped scanning and murmured a statement in Spanish. Rocky failed to understand the statement and this compelled the guard to gesture declaratively at the guard on the tarmac. Rocky glanced about, wary, realizing no one else had been ordered off the van. Fleetingly he wondered if he should disobey. He had heard *stuff* about Mexican border guards. But the guard with the orb was smiling a highly reassuring smile now and no one nearby showed the faintest alarm at these occurrences. Rocky stood. In a beat, his pretty yellow lace-up flats (which he had dyed in his sink just yesterday) were pitapatting him to an outdoor lectern under an angled steel umbrella. The tarmac guard received him firmly, all business. His document was reviewed and officialized and in moments Rocky had folded into his passport a stamped visa and was climbing again, wonderingly, the steps of the van. He sought a different seat this time, away from that brutish monosyllablite. Here sat a girlish lovely cradling a swaddling of cloth against her shoulder. Rocky

259

supposed the swaddling to be an infant human being. He wondered if it was boy, girl, or intersex. He thought: *Just let the poor creature not grow up to be some horrible conformist, or to be cursed with an apple-shaped body like mine.* This was an inward prayer Rocky said over every child he met.

After the shuttle ran some concrete straits and ducked into a jungle of twisted streets congested with lolling pedestrians and sad-eyed children selling chewing gum, Rocky quizzed the young lady. His sing-songy tones rang rather crisper than usual, befuddled as he was by the particularity of his border treatment.

"Why was I the only person to do that, dear? To have to get off like that?"

The girl twitched an apologetic smile. Her brown cheeks said, "The driver made a mistake. Non-Mexicans are not supposed to be able to board this shuttle without a passport card."

"Oh my, a card? What's the difference?"

"Passport cards don't require permits for entry the way normal passports do. They just scan them and the vans roll through. No wait."

Rocky offered an embarrassed sorry to the young mother and added an emphatic OMG as the beauty widened her smile and insisted no blame was due. Lunchtime had not yet arrived, she reminded. So no one was going to starve. She patted the baby's back.

"They drop us off on that Revolution Street?"

"If you want, there's another stop in front of the mall by the river. Where are you going?"

Rocky unfolded his map.

Slightly the girl tilted over it. She advised: "Get off on Revolution. It's just a short walk from the bus stop to the arch."

"The arch?"

"Is that red circle where you are going?"

"Yes, that's right."

"That red circle is just across from a big silver arch. You'll see it when you get off."

"Why ... thank you so much ... *señorita*." Rocky lifted his fingertips to his wide nose, tittering behind them at his plucky employ of the Spanish word. He thought to inform this sympathetic darling he was part Mexican, among other ancestries, but felt self-conscious about not speaking the tongue. He cooed, instead: "I appreciate your kindness, sweetheart. I really do."

The girl shrugged, smiling.

"My fays! Somehow I did it, as you can see. Ole Viola had no choice. When one fear overwhelms the other you just find the strength to overcome that weaker fear. You just got to *try*, I coached myself. Then, as I stood before the joant itself, I found myself just puttin' down my head and blockin' *It* out as best I might and forgin' onward. Because rent day is two days away, ya'll. And I don't got it. A red-headed man checked my passport and was quite reassurin' and welcomin', almost as if he expected me. Then there was this gang of masked guards with assault rifles who watched me clumsily pass through customs. After that, as I walked out into the Mexican sun, wheelin' my box of zines behind me, I saw that the maps app on my phone had quit. I need to tell ya'll straight up that that moment was nothin' but extreme and blindin' terror! This was panic, ya'll. Paralysis. But when I looked up, see, slightly panting, I caught sight of some brown girls all tatted and pierced, and I recognized among them the unmistakable shaved head of Blossom from *Apologies in Order*. Whew! How my heart thumped! I followed. A-hurryin', a-hurryin', a-hurryin'. When I caught up to them, breaffless, I asked if they were lookin' for the zinefest. Those girls did not look half as terrified as me, but they did look relieved to know my face. This is true. They asked if I knew where was the venue. I was gigglin' maniacally by then, quietly though, and told them not so much as they ascertained that they had been walkin' the exact wrong direction. But suddenly we were all less afraid. Lost together is better than lost alone. That's how it goes with fam. We retraced their steps and then crossed a footbridge soon and here it waited. So here I stand, outside this venue, jacked into the zinefest's wifi already and streamin' at you my video freak-out from a foreign land. I have to say I am still comin' down from too much adrenaline. Sure enough you can tell that. I cheated my trolley fare ridin' south from National City and maybe I should not have risked that. A guy was gettin' ticketed by the transit cops at the H Street station in Chula Vista. If they had not pinned him, they might have pinned me. Last thing I need. It's like I'm so beaten that I'm transcendin' myself somehow. It's like crossin' that border was a step over the edge of some abyss, was me fallin' into my own annihilation. So maybe I have, maybe I am. Wish me luck, my fays. Ya'll know the stakes."

261

"Blogging instead of vlogging, my fays, because I would feel self-conscious talking so personal and loud while in such close confines with so many people. My old boyfriend Ezekiel is sitting right next to me, and who wants to confess things in front of their old old man? I might have sat away from him but I need to tell you that it is quite a fright to be here. I'm only like a mile, maybe not even that far from the actual boundary line, I guess, but it feels like another planet. I mean, even the hand soap in the bathroom smells different. And, see, my old boyfriend speaks good "Mexican," as he likes to proudly joke. Just knowing he's next to me and reliable in that way makes me feel not so vulnerable and estranged from safety. He's something familiar, a known strong. We two have never been angry with each other, by the way. It just didn't work. I'm not the hero he is.

"I have felt sweaty now and again since I arrived but Easy and I have been chatting and he promised to let me walk with him back to the border when the fest closes up. I guess *O, Kindred* isn't quite the right material for this fest because while people stop and look at our stuff, only one person has bought it. Folx seem more interested in my fro than our fairy tales. I did pick it out as proud as possible today, though. If I'm not gonna blend in, might as well blend out. That wounded white boy who dropped into the scene back at the beginning of the season is here, too, sitting right next to me, on the opposite side from Easy. He always seems to just appear. And while I know what that probably means, and while my heart goes out to the man, and I even feel some chemistry with him, there is just too much stress in my life right now for any kind of romance. Did I just say that to the whole wide world? Precious!

"The vibe here is noticeably different from other fests: Like a house party cut with a barbecue. They got a DJ spinning some Motown and EDM behind me, and live punk bands upstairs, they say, though I don't know about those bands first-hand since I can't leave my table to check them out. Don't want to miss a sale. They're cooking up some Mexican soul food behind the bar over there. And tons of folx, both Americans and Mexicans, are walking around with big green bottles of beer. Everyone is very chill and friendly and having a good loose time and a lot of people are feeling the zines in a communal kind of sharing and appreciative way, cheering each other on. And no one is just sitting and waiting for the fest to end, thank God. All of this has calmed me. But I don't see much coin changing hands. And I need coin to change hands. We're approaching halfway and it looks like I won't even make enough to cover the cost of my table registration. Whatever hopes I had of saving myself at this zinefest were way misguided. I'm pretty much doomed, y'all.

"I'd go on and relate how nice it is to talk to Easy again, maybe even detail our chat, but I guess that's not for the public. On the other hand, I tell ya'll everything else in these blogs so why not? You may know him as the man behind that suddenly famous zine called *SlapDown*. You put together what he's about plus my internal problems and you can imagine why we just could not make it work. All I did was worry about the boy. I hoped his sister would be here today. We connect strong. But she's not. Shout out to Linda. Love you, Precious.

"But a Mexican guy just walked up to the wounded white boy's table next to me. And what's that? That *white boy* is speaking *Spanish!*"

Rocky had come to see Blossom and there she sat.

He had arrived before her, and waited and waited and waited, hoping to present himself to her as a dainty lady. Finally though, his nerves just suffocated his fidgety stalling and he selected a vending spot close to the door. Soon after, of course, Blossom entered. She tromped behind a table not exactly near Rocky, but not far off either. So they *were* in the same room. There was that. Yes, two other rooms were available to Blossom and she had not chosen one of those. So there was that.

Rocky lilted at the woman beside him, breathily, "The first person to look at my zines saw all my hidden erections."

"Were you not expecting that?" asked his tablemate. She puckered her nose.

263

Rocky half-smiled over his simple yellow sundress. He smoothed its cotton skirts against his thighs, weighing her question. Shaking the bangles loose on his arm, he frowned, faintly. He pinched a speck of lint off his lap and raised it before his wide nose before dropping it aside.

"Oh, I fancy I wasn't. They weren't blaring obvious, you know. But I wasn't exactly going for subtlety either, I suppose."

"Not like mine? Look at this."

And then Rocky was fingering a zine full of space flowers. He found the page indicated. Blooming up at him was a star-shaped clump of pretend foliage which appeared to him more a throbbing cock penetrating a moist vulva.

"That's quite a stem. You make me look like a nun."

Clare laughed. Then a young Mexican fellow stooped over Clare's presentation.

So there Blossom is. Five chairs down from me. I've glanced a couple of times, discretely. I've looked, too, just plain looked. *Should you look again, you? How many times should you look? She knows I'm here. Okay, but my Blossom is thinking about nothing but that blah, blah, blah* Apologies. *She is not caring about anything right now but disseminating that exposé to the entire world without getting sued for it. I hope a bunch of people buy it, for her sake. But it looks like everyone is just walking on by. More people have hovered over my stuff so far than hers. OMG, and hers is so much more meaningful. How does one justify these predilections not based on quality? It is a mystery how some fluff will be snatched up in a second while a masterpiece sitting next to it will lie languishing, ignored. How is this explained?*

And then, from the corner of his eye, Rocky noticed Easy spying Clare with sly desire. He sat on the other side of Clare. And then Rocky wondered if Easy might help him cross back over the border. Rocky had managed to arrive by that new shuttle, but he had not investigated how to return by it, if that was even possible. Rocky supposed Viola had emplaced herself beside Easy with similar motives. But she and Easy were close too. And would that shuttle even be running when the fest wrapped? *I could horn in, I suppose, and let my Williams-ness show. Vee won't mind. But really it's the afterparty that defines this shindig. Everyone comes here for that, don't they? You go the whole season bumping shoulders with all these beautiful zinesters and then, at the end, in Tijuana, you finally get a fancy dance with them. It's like the afterparty for the entire season.*

Rocky sensed Easy waiting for a chance to address Clare. Rocky watched, witnessing the coiling of Easy's tension. Easy calibrated his moment. He strategized its effect. Then he made his move.

"How was the crossing for you?" Easy said.

Clare nodded. "Loved it. Did it on my bike. Piece of cake."

"Tough," Easy said. But then a sinuous Mexican woman in drapey white hippie garb interrupted him.

Rocky saw Clare's hands trembling when Easy turned back away. The dear reached for a pot of hand lotion to disguise her quiver. Rocky studied these two affectionately for a few beats. He realized they were in love. *Oh, love,* he thought. *You are just everywhere, aren't you?* Rocky beheld Easy and Clare and almost pitied them. *Love, you are so treacherous. These beautiful people just wanting to brew you between them, just hoping to bring you to life; but they are both so afraid of the pain you can cause, and too proud to be vulnerable, and so unsure about how to go about you.* Rocky swallowed. His Adam's apple rose and fell in his throat. *Oh, love. Why do you do this to us?*

Rocky engaged more small talk with Clare, and verbally admired the originality of her mismatched blouse and sneakers; but really he was hoping she would make love to Easy that night. *If I can't be with my Blossom,* he thought, *at least let them be together. Oh, my beautiful souls! Look at you! Why must you wander about so alone and hurting when all you have to do is take each other's hands?*

Rocky glanced down the row to Blossom. Still no one had paused before her zine. He felt his heart breaking for just so many reasons.

An American man glided by Clare's table, bouncing his shoulders to The Supremes. He hardly viewed her zine long enough to identify its particular breed -- be it text-based, an art zine, or something else. The zoo effect had set in, Clare concluded. Psychologically, cruising a large zinefest parallels the cruising of a vast zoological park. The barrage of novelty jades one. By the time you finish bingeing the fest's multi-stimuli, you could pass a pink gas alien from Saturn without noticing. Most attendees were even ignoring Clare's candy dish now.

"Asshat," she muttered.

Rocky sighed. The bouncy American had overlooked Rocky's wares too.

"Can I check out your stuff?" Clare asked after the American Motowned away.

"Of course, my dear," Rocky cooed. "I have so many. Here, this is an earlier one. The one with the penises that I brought for today has too much angst in it for a new friend. This one is more like what I'm usually like."

Ezekial shifted in his chair beside Clare. He had greeted her affably at the beginning, when first she approached and plunked her lilac saddlebags onto the table beside him. He had seemed in fact glad of Clare's arrival, and even ready for a long chat. But then that black beauty Viola claimed the chair to his left and Easy had stiffened toward Clare. She feared now she had misread their chemistry.

"Fashion, oh my," Clare reacted, paging slowly and distractedly through Rocky's zine.

"Yes, a little fashion thing I do. Oh, I love women's clothes on a woman. But when they're off a woman I love more than ever to just plain *disturb* women's clothes."

"Reminds me of paper dolls or something."

"Oh, I know. I call them my figures, though. Do you like the shiny machine gun?"

"Love that! How did you come up with such an idea?"

"I work in a boutique, you know. I'm quite an admirer of a beautifully dressed woman. I try to help women dress beautifully."

Clare turned to Rocky full on then, awakened. The artistry of his cosmetics struck her: That pastel yellow eyeshadow and the matte black which coated his lips. Clare noted how the framing of his hairstyle scumbled his jawline, and how the spaghetti straps feminized his manly shoulders while supporting the bodice of the delicate yellow dress. With aroused interest, she inquired, quickly,

"Which boutique?"

"In Anaheim. Mostly. Not too far from the history museum actually. We're called The Lido. It has a nice gondola on the sign. I don't like that gondola."

A jowly Mexican man swayed up to Rocky, clutching the neck of a green bottle of beer. The man's eyes scanned the *Shake Me the Boom Boom* covers on the table and then rose. They held Rocky for an unsettling beat and finally startled. Recovering from his surprise, the Mexican man offered Rocky a conspiring grin and

266

sidled on to Clare's side of the table, sucking a swig off the bottle mouth. He grazed her zines indifferently. More thoughtfully he eyed her candy dish but took nothing. Then the Mexican man swayed on to Easy's display. There he halted with interest. He bent. Complimentary words followed in Spanish as the Mexican man wavered a hand over a glossy photo of Easy's lowrider. The Mexican man's head was bobbing with camaraderie. And,

"What exactly do you do?" Clare asked Rocky pointedly. She squinted with seriousness. "That sounds neat. Working in a boutique. What's the work like?"

"Oh, wonderful," Rocky began. "Like a bartender, I fancy -- if the myths about bartenders are true." The singsong in Rocky's voice edged toward dreamy. "Lots of heart to hearts with beautiful dears trying to be the best woman they can be. My heart goes out to them sometimes. I help them feel better about themselves by making sure their best qualities are flattered by their attire and accessories. Oh, sometimes I guess someone comes in for a special occasion and wanting to accomplish something very specific, like attracting some acquaintance. These subtleties are very important. A woman trying to network I dress differently than a woman looking for love. But, you know, strangely, the difference between one outfit and the other is oftentimes very subtle. But I know how a straight man looks at a woman, you see. Sometimes it's just as subtle as unbuttoning the top button of a blouse and wearing a different brazier beneath. These little adjustments can make a world of difference. Make a change like that in the ladies' room at an office party and you go in all formality and come out quite the tiger."

"Doesn't sound like a bad job."

"Oh, no. I love it. Every job has its downers but my clientele has much confidence in me. I love the dears."

Clare smiled at Rocky's zine now, as if she saw in it some new possibility. But also she was tilting her head to eavesdrop on Easy and Viola. Their conversing revealed an intimacy, Clare thought. Clearly, those two were more than friendly. And yet she discerned a coolness in Easy also, a deliberate distancing inserted by him. Clare strained but failed to make out every little thing they said. The *ache* just throbbed in her as she strained, as slightly she leaned toward him, as she felt Easy near. Finally, he stopped talking. Clare heard Viola responding then to the white man on the other side of her. Clare untilted her head.

267

"Would you like to trade?" Rocky cooed. "I like your thing too. If you have one which would seem a fair trade, let's do it, yeah?"

"Yes, yes. Your figures are very curious," she agreed. "But I swear, something about the way you pose and position them makes them look lonely."

"Oh, honey," said Rocky. "That loneliness stuff just comes out. We're all lonely. Just look at me. The love of my life is only five seats away from me and we aren't even speaking, you know. And all this without even having a fight. All I did was make clear to her my feelings. I was just too honest, I suppose."

After a silent but feeling nod, Clare looked down the row of tables. She counted Rocky, herself, Easy, Viola, an older white man (that's me), and a punk woman.

"The punk girl?"

"The very one."

"I would never have guessed."

"Neither would she, apparently."

Clare chuckled, but with commiseration. "So sorry," she squinted. And then, tenderly chiding Rocky, even with a flirty croon, she remarked, "I read you as *queer*."

"I confuse *lots* of people. And you? Are you lonely too, my dear?"

Clare tensed, as if stung. "What a question."

"Honey, it was you who brought up my *tendencies*. I believe that gives me license to ask you just about anything."

"Oh, please excuse. I feel unusually comfortable with you, and natural. I was relating to you like a woman, I guess."

"That's my gift."

"I'm lonely too, of course. You're right. We're all lonely. You're lucky to be sitting five chairs away from the love of your life. Mine is right next to me."

Rocky nodded knowingly. "Oh, yes. He's quite a man." Rocky winked.

"I thought we had something. I was going to pursue it; but maybe I was wrong."

"Are you worried about Viola?"

"I'm not sure worry is the right word. I don't think I have the right to worry. We've hardly communicated, really, just casually. But sometimes I can't quit thinking about him."

"Call it what you want, love, but don't worry. That's Viola now. She and Easy were a *thang*, as she puts it, a couple years ago. They're just friends since then. Probably she sat next to him because she's worried about being in Tijuana. She's nervous about a lot of things but quite courageous in her own way. You see that quite clearly in her blog. That boy speaks Spanish, you know."

"Really?"

"Yes, he's second generation and not taking any shit."

"I mean about Viola."

"Oh, honey. If you're into Easy, Viola is not to be worried about."

Rocky pronounced these words at some volume, basically prompting Easy to turn his head, which he did. Easy matched Rocky's friendly grin. Then Easy looked to Clare, who stared down self-consciously at Rocky's lonely figures. She held the *Shake Me the Boom Boom* open with both hands, pinning its edges to the table with her fingertips spread. Rocky made a kissy-kissy sound then at Easy. Easy glanced over the rims of his glasses, chuckling.

"Ezekiel, deary, do you know Miz Clare here sitting next to you? She thinks you're quite a handsome hombre. Don't you think she's beautiful?" Caught off-balance, Easy fixed his attention on the figure between Clare's hands. It was a cut-out incandescent light bulb dressed in a shiny gown of navy blue. Rocky clucked his tongue. "Come now, my hero. You can say it. I've seen you looking at her. Let's get this all out in the open, you two. Easy, don't you think Clare is a beautiful woman, perhaps one of the most beautiful women you have ever seen in your entire life?"

Clare puckered her features at Rocky. Her brows were knit, as if to say: C'mon! What are you doing? Why are you betraying me? If Rocky had not been radiating love and sympathy so frankly in that moment, Clare's confused embarrassment might even have flared into a rebuke. But then, just as she cocked her head to quiet the man, she heard this:

"Yes," Easy answered. "As a matter of fact, I do."

Rocky stood. "Why don't you two have a little chat. I need to go to the men's room." And he pattered off then on his pretty yellow flats.

Easy sat near enough to Clare that he felt her body heat. So he heard, but could not quite distinguish, her quiet responses to

269

Rocky's sing-song way of joshing her. That she had plopped her gear down beside him, and so brazenly, and with such sexy mischief in her eyes, had surprised Easy into an uncharacteristic timidity. He knew Clare had detected this. He liked it. Now he had something to prove to her.

He tipped and swallowed from a bottle of mineral water. He petted his mustache with finger edge and thumb. Easy had been chatting with Viola. He continued, "That old *cabrón* gave me a manifesto without even realizing it."

Viola answered, "I've heard of The Man making that mistake."

Easy was astonished to find Viola in Tijuana. He knew her intimately and could not fathom what provoked her to such boldness. Tijuana was not the monster Viola would fear it to be, he knew. But that was because Easy carried the city in his blood and bones, and spoke its tongue. Inwardly he marveled that Viola had mustered the courage to engage with Tijuana's foreignness, to cross that international boundary, to penetrate this urban labyrinth where she could not even read a road sign. And all this considering he had seen the woman shirk at boarding an Amtrak to Oakland.

Easy warmed for her an affectionate, closed-mouth smile.

"Thanks for the support," Viola said, watching him pour more bubbles past his lips.

"Are you kidding?" he winked. "*Chale*, sister!" Now he bobbed his head. "I can't believe you're here. If all I have to do to help is like sit nearby, I can do that. That's what old friends are for; at least when they used to be *close* and managed somehow to split up without hating each other. Well, well. Whatever would coax you here?"

"It ain't no thang."

"No, not really. But, Vee, we both know you're way outside your comfort zone."

Viola replied that Easy's evolving ideas interested her more than her own personal whims. The comment was blatant evasion, of course, but Easy understood from it to let the topic die. She added, "Maybe later, hon. Last time I saw you I thought you might be winding up your razzmatazz. So how did that old man give you a manifesto?"

Easy shrugged. He swallowed a mouthful of bubbles and his thoughts tripped back over the past ten days -- To his conference with that Johnathan Vonnelle chump, and how it had nudged him out of his limbo and back into his authentic self. *He thought.* For the very next afternoon Easy had cruised his old turf, rumbling off in the low low as cocky and *cholote* as ever, with the top down and his angels booted and chanting *sooie* and *come to Easy* and *here piggy piggy.* But by dark his reborn excitation had fizzled. Something had changed. Ezekiel puttered home realizing he had turned a corner in his life. To troll like he had, for the same reasons he had, was faking it now. Plus, his articulating for Vonnelle and for himself that ultimately he cruised to preserve his dignity had stalled his momentum. For there are many ways to preserve one's dignity. Permutations of these two observations had circulated through Ezekiel during the previous week and a half. Now they flowed out of his mouth and into Viola's sympathetic ear as a tall carefully kempt man sidled up to Blossom's table three seats down from his, browsing *Apologies In Order.*

Easy continued his explanation for Viola. But he fit his glasses on tighter now to more clearly view Blossom's profile. His appreciation lingered along her fine perfect lines. And did he recognize that tall attendee? Wait, he seemed American Indian. Like Morongo, maybe? From Palm Desert, maybe? He wore a red and brown striped hoodie. Easy finished the update on his life's events finally and swallowed the last drops of his mineral water. Then the would-be Morongo stepped in front of him.

"No monitors, huh?"

"Only brought zines today, *'mano.*" Easy addressed the man like an old friend. "Because of the border. It's a hassle to bring all kinds of electronics over the border. I checked the specs on that mess. Didn't even drive."

"Left that ride of yours?"

"In Chula Vista."

The tall man inquired after the latest *SlapDown* and Easy indicated two fresh issues, both produced since the Donner affair. One was the official *SlapDown* version of the Cluster Mart attack, with sketches, screenshots, and commentary. The other was a sort of manifesto. Easy tapped the manifesto zine. Nothing in that one but words. He explained he had never considered his cruising in philosophical terms until pressed by a suit-and-tie-type chump from the DA's office. He described how the attorney had asked why he did what he did, and how the challenge triggered in him an unexpected insight.

"This zine is a verbatim transcript of our exchange. My lawyer was there so everything was recorded. The punch line is my reason for provoking cops the way I did."

"What reason is that," the guy asked.

"It's about dignity. Not very complicated."

Viola interposed, "Wouldn't be much of a manifesto if it was complicated, hon."

"I agree with that," said the maybe-Morongo.

"There is only dignity in revolt, my friend. That's what I believe. My cruising for hits was my form of revolt -- As is this proud mustache I still wear, and my slicked-back do, and my hairnet. All of this is my form of resistance."

The man swayed his head. "Heavy." He savored the zine a few beats more. Then, "But you just said 'was'. You're talking about this like it's over. You done?"

Easy flinched. The look he flashed the man duplicated his initial response to Johnathan Vonnelle's challenge. Blank was Easy's expression, inarticulate. Once again a simple direct question had smarted him. And once again to answer it meant self-definition. An instant later though Ezekiel had the words. He chuckled from the depths of his throat. "Yes," he said. "Done." Then he added, "I don't need it anymore. Over and out."

The man replied, "Right on. Shit evolves. I'll be watching to see what comes next from you. You say fifty pesos? That's all?" He unfolded for Easy a cream-colored one hundred peso bill. Easy returned to him a hot pink fifty. They slapped palms and bumped fists.

About then Easy heard Rocky pronouncing his name. More than once Rocky pronounced it. Swiveling, Easy adjusted to Rocky's croon, curious to see if he was actually being called. The heat of Clare's flesh caressed Easy anew. He sensed her voluptuous form emanating its warmth. Easy screwed down the cap of his empty water bottle.

Here she was, breathing right next to me. Beside Viola I sat now, watching attendees pass or pause or stoop or laugh with her. So far they had purchased only a single fairy tale zine. Me Viola greeted gently and with recognition, even with a smattering of warmth. But mostly since taking my seat I had monitored her banter with the Latino man sitting next to her – the guy from

272

SlapDown. Apparently their history provided enough depth for some meaningfully unfinished sentences and pregnant winks. But I sensed a reserve between them too. Their mutual kidding felt forced, I thought, contrived to soften some awkwardness. I gathered that a barrier divided them which neither wanted removed.

Finally, Viola pressed the Latino man about Tijuana. She darted her eyes about the room, warily, and cleared her throat, and confessed to feeling nervous in the city. Viola admitted that only by summoning all of her courage had she crossed the border. The Latino guy reassured, allaying her several articulate concerns. He even promised to escort her to the border crossing later if she feared a solo return.

I listened carefully.

Their reacquaintance drifted out as the Latino guy turned rightward, toward a white woman. Soon that conversation proceeded through much different tones. I saw my opportunity here and so addressed a passing Mexican man in Spanish, inviting him to my table. Politely the guy gave my two eight-folds a glance and I gestured him on to Viola's *cuentos de hada* zine, describing it as *fantasias muy originales*. The Mexican guy expressed some genuine interest, and actually picked up and squinted at the man-horse issue, but apologized finally for preferring to read in his native tongue. Once he ambled away, with our farewell, Viola said,

"Stanley, you speak some Spanish?"

"Yes," I smiled. My overture had worked. "I studied it in college and have kept it up since, mostly traveling and writing about Mexico, but especially here in Tijuana."

"Oh, you know Tijuana well?"

"Yes, I do. I have come here literally dozens and dozens of times. I know it very well."

Viola turned inward then and I let our brief exchange settle into the background noise of the fest. I did not want to push her. Musingly I sat behind my green tablecloth, watching the zine folk saunter by, hearing the next DJ start her set with some Bachata. I sat straight. I sat firm. I sat unflinching. And I felt alert and clear-eyed and solid. I wondered if Viola had noticed my freshly-pressed attire and shaved cheeks. I wondered if she had remarked how much more readily I spoke now, and how much more steadily I moved. But a boredom finally descended. And at last, it felt safe to rekindle the Tijuana topic between us. So I did. I showed a fondness for the city that still lives in me even today.

"This city would surprise you, probably."

"Yeah?"

"Many non-Hispanic Americans near the border dismiss it. But it is actually an influential Mexican city that contributes a lot to Mexican culture. It's not just some neglected border town."

"You don't say."

And I described for Viola a few locales which, in my opinion, go shamefully overlooked by most white visitors. I talked about some formalized cultural spots, and the anarchic ones, about state-run centers, and the vitality of the underground. I mentioned the professional soccer team, and the large university, and a certain 'gastronomical zone' rarely sampled by gringos.

"These places are totally authentic," I confided like a spy.

I praised then the annual book fair that America and I discovered by accident, and thereafter never missed, and the cafes and live music along the Pacific boardwalk. By the end of my eulogy Viola looked genuinely intrigued.

"I never would have known that."

"Yeah, most don't. The only catch is you need a little Spanish. A lot of this stuff has entered my life simply because I know the language."

Viola watched me speak, nodding. "You really like it here, Stanley. I can tell that."

"Yes I do. In truth, it has been an important part of my life in many ways at different times."

My spiel ended. We sat quietly. Attendees floated by to hover occasionally over my table or hers. I conversed with the woman to my left. I listened to Viola speaking again with the Latino man. Though that man remained hospitable to Viola, he seemed now less amenable to her attentions, even shy of them, as if they created some inconvenient impression. Finally, well past halfway through the zinefest, I made my offer:

"I heard you talking to the *SlapDown* guy earlier, you know. If for some reason he can't accompany you to the border later, just say something, I'd be glad to go with you. It's a simple affair really. Just a cab ride. But it helps if you can tell the *taxista* exactly where you want to be dropped off."

Viola said, "Thank you, Stan." The smile within her black velvet halo broadened. She seemed to relax. "I just might take you up on that."

That Blossom found herself sitting beside a white man mystified her by its irony. Here she was: to prove him evil, to right his misdeeds. But here he sat: Right fucking next to her. The white man was impossible to out-maneuver. No matter your subtle tactics, no matter your nuanced workarounds, always once you turned that strategic corner another one of them stood in your way. Call him what you will. Prove him Lucifer in disguise. But still he owned the fucking planet.

Blossom scowled, refusing to look to her right. The skin over her cheekbones pulled with ire. Her ear gauges hung like sacred shields, deflecting away the ill humors of this chooch. She sensed his energy trained off her anyway. Small blessing. The white man seemed preoccupied with Viola. Blossom placed her left elbow on the tabletop, cupping her chin in her palm, her vine of blue-black thorns snaking down her forearm and back up around her bicep.

A Mexican zinester glided by her table, perusing her single zine. *Apologies in Order: The Man Who Booed Littlefeather.* She mustered the words for her sales pitch but the man kept gliding, to stop then before Viola. A pair of Latinx women commenced their tour of the fest at Blossom's table, too, but only glanced at her in passing. Maybe, Blossom thought, I should not have stationed myself right at the entrance. She originally reasoned that being first would invite more pause, as attendees would not yet be glutted on the blizzard of zine fare. But now she sensed folks were less apt to buy so early. At table one the libertine vibe of the scene had not yet wooed or wowwed them into the plunking down of dollars or pesos.

Blossom felt warm. Her golden skin glistened. She twisted out of her flack jacket and let it drape over her seatback. She leaned forward in her brown t-shirt, her elbows planted again on the tabletop.

Then someone stopped.

An older white woman. She wore a flowery green muumuu and a fuzzy chin. She opened *The Man Who Booed Littlefeather.* Blossom always waited for a prospect to turn a few pages before she commented on the content. This time, just as Blossom's soft-sell rose to her lips, the woman laid down the zine and edged sideways to the white man.

"Hello," Blossom heard the white man offer, gently.

"Hello," said the woman in return. She took up his zine thoughtfully. Blossom identified that zine as a simple eight-fold.

The white man said, "It's just stick figures."

"I see."

The woman laid the eight-fold back down. "It's very sad."

"I'm better now," the white man replied. "I made this one for today. It's like the other side of that coin. They come as a pair. Look at it so you won't feel bad."

The woman lifted the other zine. She paged through it, again thoughtfully. She smiled. "Yes. Oh. I'm glad you're better." She glanced to Viola with a chuckle. The woman took up again the white man's sad eight-fold and bought his pair of zines. After the white lady ambled off Blossom heard Viola say to the white man: "See there?"

"Hard to believe."

"Different people connect with different things," Viola said.

A young Mexican man cruised by Blossom's table. He scanned her tabletop briefly and stepped to his left, away from her. In fact, through the first two hours of the zinefest, not one single person bought one single copy of *The Man Who Booed Littlefeather*. Blossom saw few California zinesters. Most, apparently, did not cross the border that day. Disheartened was not potent enough a word for how Blossom felt about that. She was losing all hope now. With the passage of one uninterested attendee after another, the harshness in Blossom's features drained away to bland. The bottom fell out of her stomach. She hung her shaved head.

Down the row of tables, in the lulls between the beats the DJs bumped behind them, Blossom heard Rocky's voice. Still it had his lilt. Rocky did not sound exactly unhappy to her, but neither did she hear his usual vim. Blossom bent forward to steal a look. He spoke affably with a white girl she recognized from other events. Clare, was it? And there sat Easy, next to the white girl, engaging with Vee. If she remembered correctly those two had been romantic once. Blossom absorbed this tableau, dejectedly, tumbling now completely out of her righteous fury, entertaining even the depressing certainty that she had wasted considerable resources on this one fruitless fest. Then the white man beside her asked to see her zine.

Squirming in her chair Blossom handed him one.

So Rocky is okay, she thought. So Rocky has moved on. He is surviving. So Rocky can live without me, I guess, unlike what he intimated at The Feast. Blossom's rage rekindled, but then, just as suddenly, perforated and collapsed. She felt like she might fucking cry. She knew she would not cry, but she felt like she might. Nothing is right. Everything is wrong. What has fucking happened?

"You have so much passion," the white man said to her quietly. "I love this zine. It's heroic." He handed her a one-dollar bill.

One. Finally someone had bought one. Another zinester, sure, but Blossom considered that meaningful. Every copy mattered. The heartbreak in Blossom lightened, creeping back off its cliff of despair. She would not sell one hundred copies, she knew, but the current of her cause did not have to cease here in Tijuana. Today was not a dam. She would continue. She could find some other outlet.

"I ... What is your zine about?" Blossom asked the white man, revealing her rather flinty version of politeness.

"You can look at them if you want. They are a pair. The blue one I started thinking about after I went to The Palm Desert Zine Fest. Before that, I had no idea what a zine was. It's how I was those months back. I've made several versions of it. This green one I made this week. For today. I'm much better now."

Blossom accepted the zines.

"The blue one comes first."

She gazed on the light blue zine. The cover bore no title. On it instead was a stick man standing to the left, frowning. To the right, waving happily at the frowning stick man, stood a stick woman. Blossom opened to the first page and found this stick man and stick woman now holding hands. They were drawn with a large heart behind them. That heart pulsed and the stick man now smiled. On the next page the stick couple rode in a car, smiling still. Through the windshield you could see that they still held hands. Where their hands touched the white man had drawn a pulsing heart again. Blossom turned the page and saw a car wreck. The car of the stick couple was on its side now. The windshield was broken and the stick woman lay on the ground with a flat mouth. The stick man stood in the foreground with his hands on his head and his mouth open. Traffic waited behind them. The following page was blacked out with ink. On the next page the stick man stood alone, holding a broken heart in his hand. And on the next page was drawn only a large broken heart. Still it pulsed. The last page was blacked out with ink.

Blossom looked to the white man. Her eyes traced the crisp lines of his profile as he peacefully watched the milling zine folk. He had appeared to her a recovering survivor of the opioid crisis when first he sat down today. She realized now his sickness had not been of drug dependency.

Blossom turned then to the green zine, the second of the pair. The cover said, in handwritten script, "Happiness." Blossom opened the zine to see a stick woman with a big afro bending over a drooping flower. Through pages three, four, and five that flower became empowered by beams that radiated off the afro. The flower undrooped. Then on pages six and seven the flower grew taller and taller. Finally, on the last page, the stick woman with the afro picked the flower. Now the flower radiated beams of its own.

Blossom pressed her lips. She glanced again to the white man, then just beyond him to Viola. Viola's features, framed by her impressive fro, looked into her fairy tale zine with a stooping attendee. The white man made eye contact with Blossom now. He stated, matter-of-factly,

"My wife died last year. That's what the first one is about. I didn't think I could go on. There are not words for such a thing. It helped me to draw that zine. When I began working on it I began to heal." He took a breath. "Never take people for granted, you know. They are as temporary as everything else around us. Every minute counts."

Blossom squinted. The sharp angles of her face turned again to his zines. To the blue one. To the green one. She raked her left hand over her shaved scalp. She raked her scalp again.

"Keep them," the white man told her. "A gift. Like good luck, you know. I'm sharing my first zine with my first tablemate." Then he murmured, "The second one is about Viola, but don't tell her I said that."

Blossom met the white man's blue eyes. Steadily his eyes welcomed hers as she discerned his inner sensibilities swimming with love. The man's expression reminded her of Rocky. It recalled to her the sweetness of Rocky's desperation when he unburdened his feelings to her at The Feast. This is what's right, Blossom thought. *This.* Her chin quivered. Breathlessly she answered the white man. "Thank you," she said.

Blossom sold five zines.

In terms of her objective, the zine fiesta was an absolute catastrophe. She bent in smoldering defeat. Her mission lay in ruins.

As the final interactions of the fest ebbed away, Blossom noticed Easy rise and slip out of the venue to soon return and scamper up the stairs with that white girl Clare. Then Viola and the white man rose too. Together, a little awkwardly, they padded out, dragging Vee's wheeled box behind their unsure tread. Rocky sat just five seats from Blossom then. Silently, he sat, his hands clasped in his lap, waiting.

The last prospect to stop at Blossom's display was an olive-complexioned man, an American Indian clothed in a black and red hoodie. He had sauntered through earlier and spent some time in conversation with Easy. The man asked Blossom if she kept her zines only loose like they were on her table, or if perhaps she had brought them in a box or a bag. Confused by this question, Blossom haltingly informed that she transported her zines wrapped in a plastic bag.

"How many are there?"

"Altogether ninety-five left."

The olive-complexioned man withdrew his wallet from his hind pocket, unfolded it, thumbed forth a one hundred dollar bill, and laid the cash on the tabletop. "I was sent here to buy them," he stated.

Wide-eyed, struck even with suspicion, Blossom stared at the man. She doubted. Had she mistaken? Did distributing the zine in Tijuana somehow defy the cease and desist letter? Was this person collecting evidence? But ... too late to turn back. Hesitatingly, glancing again to the man's serious face with uncertainty, Blossom stood and heaved the bag of zines off the floor and onto the table. The man fit the bag into the grasp of his strong arm and pivoted to exit.

Then he paused.

He turned.

He said to Blossom, gravely, "I was also sent here to offer you compliments from my mentor. Littlefeather sends you her gratitude, cousin. We Apaches thank you."

And with that, the man marched away.

Hey, my fays. Viola in the house. This place we're eatin' in is called La Maillol, after some European painter. That's right. You see those jazz boys boppin' that stage behind my fro? Wait a second. Hold on. I'm gonna turn round my phone. Better. You see this white boy's face now? This is that white man I keep bringin' up to ya'll. That Stanley. Me and ole Stan sat beside each other at today's zinefest. That's right. And after he kept tellin' me about this strip -- Revolution Avenue -- I was finally prevailed upon to enjoy a good plate of supper with him before crossin' back to San Diego. Uh huh. Can't believe it. But I have to say I'm already feelin' cool with the scene. This drag reminds me of ole Bourbon Street in New Orleans, but in Español. Watcha think? Check out this fish the waiter just laid down for me. Mmnn-Mnh. Seein' it? Wait, ya'll hear that? That was ole Stan speakin' to the waiter in Spanish. What'd you say to that man, Stanley? 'Muchas gracias?' Hell, I know what that means. Say somethin' more impressive for my vlog followers. Okay. Now that sounded real fine, very distinguished. What'd those Spanish words mean? What? You said: 'Something more impressive?' Ha! I guess you got yourself a sense of humor too. I'll be hollerin' at ya'll soon, my fays. Now I'm gone fishin'."

One by one the obstacles between them disappeared. Rocky felt bodies rising and departing, felt souls reaching into the next phase of their being, whatever that might be. The transformation swirled about him. One by one his friends peeled away and the controlling idea of his mind became only that fewer and fewer people now separated him from Blossom.

Now there were four.

Now three.

Now two.

And now only Rocky and Blossom faced their tabletops.

Blossom sat four empty chairs away from Rocky, her eyes glazed with astonishment. She had not left; and Rocky knew why Blossom had not left. One, because she was trying still to internalize the scope of her triumph. And, two, because she loved him.

There were no other reasons Blossom might delay.

She loved him.

Okay, Rocky thought, *now all we have to do is look at each other. Okay, we'll look at each other and then speak to each other, and then we'll be happy together for the rest of our lives. Why is this so difficult for you, Boss? Why, Rock? Where is your courage? It's all so obvious.*

Rocky swallowed. His Adam's apple pumped in his neck.

Then he scooted his chair counter-clockwise and opened his great brown eyes on his truest love and rested them there and would not detach them from Blossom until she acknowledged him. *You are not so subtle, are you? But this overture is as good an as any, isn't it? We know each other. Pointless to pretend we are not thinking about what we are thinking about. This is not some first date, some nervous doorstep kiss. Yeah, just look at her. Please, Boss, look at me.*

And so Rocky watched Blossom until Blossom returned his gaze. She stood. She thumbed the one hundred dollar bill into her wallet. She sat again. She rotated her chair with a clockwise thunk and matched Rocky's desperate intensity with a commensurate fierceness.

Rocky's heart crowded his throat. Tears swamped up. He knew Blossom Silver and he knew this look she gave him. With it, she had just recognized his wordless entreaty in a way that promised reciprocation. Blossom had just promised him herself. In that one look, their future together became sealed.

"What happened?" he asked, hoarsely.

"I don't know," she said. "It's just time, I guess." And, after a pause: "You know."

Together then, in a kind of fogged slow-motion, Rocky and Blossom moved to pack away the remnants of their zinefest materiel, folding off their tablecloths, buckling and cinching up their bags. They were standing. They were thinking of each other.

I can't believe this is happening. Am I so lucky? Really? Finally will I have a person to love truly? As my own? Someone to give everything to, to share everything with?

281

Rocky felt a craving to hold Blossom, to embrace her. He did not want to make love to Blossom, or to explain to her everything, or to promise her forever, or to please her. He just wanted to hold her, to pull her to him as if she were a part of him.

The music boomed and thumped upstairs but Blossom did not go to it. The people from whom the tables and chairs had been rented had arrived and were folding up the zinefest and loading it onto a truck. The music boomed and thumped above her but Blossom gravitated instead to an old brown couch behind the abandoned DJ stand.

Here, to the first floor, folks descended from dancing, to cool, to chat and flirt by the window, to smoke or have a rest.

Blossom sank onto the sofa, tired and spent. She sloughed off her brown backpack, which rode her left shoulder much more lightly now than upon arrival. After an interval Rocky followed, asking to join. Stiffly they sat at first, catching up on the previous eight weeks, their mutual defenses dissolving little by little into their rekindling intimacy.

Blossom had chosen one end of the sofa and Rocky the opposite. The music boomed and thumped upstairs and dancers descended and ascended for hours. Blossom watched them, listening to Rocky comment on their dress, feeling Rocky's energy focused totally on her.

There was nothing for Blossom to say to Rocky, nor for Rocky to say to Blossom. Everything had already been said. Blossom rose and tromp-jangled to a window like she had seen so many others do. Rocky met her there. They stood breathing the crisp night air, gazing outward, silently. Eventually Rocky returned to the brown couch, claiming now Blossom's corner. When Blossom fatigued and went to him she sat down just beside Rocky and leaned back against his chest. For a long while they reclined together like that, listening to the booming above, watching the people come and go. Blossom felt Rocky's tender hands caressing her shaved head, stroking it, caressing it over and over again. Then, even through the music, the two of them slept.

No one bothered them. The music stopped about dawn.

When the music ceased Blossom awoke. For a few beats, she lay unaware of where she was. But then she remembered her location. Blossom felt the even rhythm of Rocky's chest rising and falling beneath her cheek. Then, for the third of only three times in this entire book, she smiled.

Hey, my fays. This is Viola comin' at ya'll from some chill little joant called what? "Pah-sah-hey Rodriguez?" Yeah, that. Ole Stanley walked me on over here from La Maillol, he says, because it's a hangout for Tijuana artists. He explained how actually this is an alleyway between two rows of buildings. They just covered it over with a roof -- made it into a *galeria* as he calls it. Wouldn't know that by looking. Not at all. Tile floors. Storefronts. Lots of handcrafts on the walk: Incense, hand-painted t-shirts, totems, leather goods, stickers. I even saw some seashell earrings, mind you. I'm jacked into a cafe's wifi with my feet up on my box of zines as Stan and I rest over an after-dinner coffee. That fish was somethin', let me say! We're fittin' to head back to San Diego now. Stan seems to know this turf just inside out. And I'm havin' me a fine time not cogitating on no day after tomorrow. And honestly, I have to confess that green bottle of beer I sipped over my fish has done sent *It* right away. Sure enough you'll understand that better'n ole Stan here who's just a-squintin' his blue eyes like he wants to know all about us. Well, friend, you just keep on a-squintin'. A little wonder and confusion never hurt anyone. Like me. Right now I feel like I've found myself on some neon planet; or like I've tripped down some rabbit hole and into one of my own fairy tales, or into *O, Kindred* itself. You know that I mean all this friendly, Stan. But he does know that, my fays. He just smilin' as he looks at us. I'll holler at y'all soon enough.

The zinefest did not so much end as blend into music and dancing. Little by little as evening drew on more of the zinesters were lingering for longer periods in front of the DJ on the third floor, abandoning their zines and displays with less and less concern. After a spell they would return to the first or second floor woozy with the infectious rhythms and quickly pack away their wares to ascend anew. Little by little this continued until Easy realized attendees, too, were now scuffling through the zine presentations without giving them any heed. The lower levels emptied. The ground floor became a place to catch your breath, to converse by a breezy window and drag from a smoke. The zinefest in earnest had ended. The celebration of whatever had begun.

Easy arranged his zines into his light duffle bag, and, without a farewell to anyone, tripped his brawn down the wooden steps of the venue and into the pedestrian alley. He had reserved a room two blocks away in a cheap hotel on third avenue. Soon he returned from stashing his belongings to find Clare standing over her table, squinting at him, stunned. She was waiting for him, Easy read, and she had feared he had left for the night. Clare's attention held Easy until finally he approached her.

In minutes they were dancing on the third floor and Clare had taken Ezekiel's hand.

Easy knew what Clare desired but he sensed too that she prefer it outlast one night. The woman had chosen him and he would not deny her. En route to Palm Desert that day she had attracted him. But this was different! Tonight she held him spellbound! *This girl could move!* Easy watched Clare writhing in the melody and the smoke and the strobes of cherry red and she was a conquering being begging him to conquer her; and he was both conquered by her and ready to possess. They danced and he clasped her pulsing fingers and he knew somehow that this enchantress would not fight him, but neither would she succumb, that always between them would be a vigorous push and pull. He felt that she would play fair, that very soon she would locate his affections and his dignity, and that certainly she would hold them in her spell, take complete control over them, insistently, but never would she betray them. Here was a woman to submit to because the only way to submit was to vanquish. Clare twisted delectably, sinuously, and he felt her strength, her sorceress powers. Easy pushed and Clare reacted to his resistance. Simultaneously he revolted against her charisma but sought its dominance.

The rest was darkness shrouding his thoughts, and the cobalt blue strobes of the dance floor piercing that darkness, and his realizing that no longer was he a man of war.

Then it ended.

The DJs finished and Easy and Clare walked down a shallow slope hand-in-hand, soaked with sweat and stumbling with fatigue. Her bicycle had been stolen. They fell asleep together in his room, still fully clothed, but made love twice before breakfast.

Clare felt disconnected from her body. The pulsing rhythms and the lights strobing the smoky darkness had unhooked her from the worldly part of her being, freed her from the heaviness of her daily mind. The orientations that usually kept Clare trapped inside her circular thinking had simply vanished; and Easy's acceptance of her had released a tension that she had not previously recognized, and a doubt about herself, and a questioning. In this seething half-light, unable to sense anything but their sweat and the boom and their moving and Easy's strength, Clare found herself welcoming a fate she had neither sought after nor foreseen. She comprehended suddenly a virgin direction, a reborn chance, and it would be totally and completely hers. In the same moments her old world had crumbled at her feet she had discovered something new toward which to rebuild its debris. And she had the power to rebuild it! She knew this now! With the cherry lights blinking, with the swirling spiraling meandering pinpoints of cobalt blue streaking them, and with their being for these few hours creatures of freedom, and somehow other than themselves, and still together, Clare was lifting her arms above her head and touching with Easy a future they did not yet have to articulate. She was liberated from her past for this short while and still unburdened by what trials might come; and yet she could feel it all, both the yesterdays and the tomorrows, in their soaring ranging splendor. Clare felt what had been and what would be meeting there and depending upon one another in those moments, feeding each other, germinating. She was ready. And Easy danced around her. And the DJs played till dawn.

Freshening themselves in the cool morning air then, stumbling together happily, her lilac saddlebags over Easy's shoulder, they found the lock broken where Clare had secured her bicycle to a signpost near *Avenida Revolución*.

The bike was gone.

"Oh, c'mon!" she blurted.

"*Pinche cabrones.*"

After squinting at the naked pole for a few beats, stupefied, Clare gazed up through the wraparound sunglasses she wore and asked, "What does *pinche cabrones* mean, anyhow?"

Easy said, looking back at Clare through the wayfarers he wore, "Lousy bastards ... more or less."

"And that was my good bike."

285

"Probably why they took it."

Clare ought not walk back to the border crossing alone, but she did not have to. Easy had a hotel room. Too tired to make love, they spooned through a few hours of oblivion, sleeping the sleep of total depletion. Then, upon waking, and upon sharing a piece of spearmint chewing gum, they made love. After showering together they walked, hand-in-hand, to a Sunday buffet Easy knew in a cafeteria with large windows.

"Love this place."

He smiled. "We can come back whenever."

They taxied then to the border crossing.

Last shot, precious. I am losing my dern battery and, if you don't mind my sayin' so, downright tired of talkin' to this smartphone. Stanley proposed we catch the nightlife before headin' back to San Diego. Said somethin' about a row of *discotecas* on Revolution Avenue and claimed we could even *bailar* the whole night through if the spirit so moved. But, as y'all fays know so well, I am not a loud joant type of gal. And what were we gonna do with this box full of zines I been wheelin' errywhere, and my laptop? I brought all this to ole Stan's mind and he just laughed agreeably and signaled a taxi which brought us to this outdoor mall. I didn't have any problem with that at all. The best thing about this mall is the clown walkin' around givin' people a hoot. Look, there he go. See that? You ever seen a pair of shoes like that in an American mall? People be gettin' sued! We followed this brother round and watched him jugglin' ninepins for a minute, and then he was inflatin' little toy balloons for all the arm-stretchin' children. Stanley appeared with some soft-serve ice cream after that, vanilla. Then some stranger appeared and handed me a rose, a white rose. Hey, Stan! You paid for that? Lawd! Ole Stanley here says the movie theater is amid some sorta festival of old American romantic comedies. He promises they screen 'em in English, just with Spanish subtitles. I suppose I could do that. He keeps sayin' it might be fun to see both Annie Hall and some Cary Grant somethin' they're playin' afterward, with maybe a little meal between. Don't know. Guess I might. Anyways, Happily Ever After, my fays. This has been one long day and it doesn't look like it's ended. Signin' off. Hasta la next time.

The cab buzzed down Paseo Fundadores as I leaned forward to point at the *Chamaco Real* statue. Already the *taxista* was nodding. The statue rises two stories off the street corner, a pudgy brown boy with a red apron and golden crown, skipping along, childlike. He holds a hamburger on a plate above his head. Never had I ridden a cab to this all-night diner. Always before I had walked from my preferred hotel room in the La Cacho neighborhood just behind it and down the hill.

"What a bizarre figure," Viola said, squinting up from the curb.

"Weird, yeah. A Mexicanization, I think, of 1950s American diner kitsch. Surreal, for sure. But the fare they serve here will look very familiar."

The *Chamaco Real* statue grins with an eerie lifelessness. We passed under his rusted-out armpit, skirted some dead landscaping, crossed the restaurant's threshold, and forthwith occupied a vinyl booth that looked on the intermittent night traffic of Fundadores. The clock said 1 a.m. I recognized the cook through the kitchen window, but the waiter seemed new.

"No menu in English here," I apologized. "But everything's got a picture. Just point."

Viola chuckled.

We shared a hearty feast then and, with the plates being quickly removed, I introduced Viola to the Latin custom of the *sobremesa*, or, that long conversation over coffee that oftentimes follows a sociable meal. We talked about the romantic comedies we had just seen. We talked about Viola's origins and mine. We talked about regional cuisines and lost relatives and the curious dreamlike quality of being about in a foreign city in the middle of the night. And then I mentioned that recently I had moved out of my condo and into a camper.

Viola responded, "Sounds like you're about as down and out as I am, Stan. No wonder you been flashin' that credit card all night."

I answered, "In my own way, I am definitely down and out."

About 3:30 a.m. a crush of nightclubbers roared through the door, livening up the restaurant considerably. Viola began to fret over the harried server so I promised to tip him well and drew her attention to the coolness of his composure. We laughed easily together now as slyly I watched the turn of Viola's plush lips, and studied that burnished cinnamon color in the flesh of her lithe arms, and that lustrous velvet halo encircling her oval face. Finally Viola commented on how different I seemed. She recollected the first time she had seen me, six months previous, but also how I had appeared at The Feast just weeks ago.

"Different but the same," she said. "A similar aura, just more steady, more controlled. You standin' up all straight and strong now. That's what's different, I guess. What happened since then? You seemed so beat down."

I told her about America and my troubles. I told her everything. I told her about driving around in slow traffic, about feeling ravaged and suicidal and dazed, about losing fifty pounds while combating my self-destruction, about being forced from my condo by my memories, about hanging around beach campgrounds for the past two weeks while waiting for The Baja Zine Fiesta, about hoping she would be at The Fiesta since I wanted to get to know her.

She moved her head knowingly. My attraction was no secret to her.

"What about me you like?" she put bluntly. Late night conversations often arrive at such a bald frankness, even for mere acquaintances.

I tilted my chin.

"Somehow you make me want to go on."

Viola nodded. She looked down at her decaf.

Then I asked, "What do you think of me?"

She let that query sit and we talked for a long time about Viola's fears. I saw her unconsciously squeeze her arms in tight against her ribs as she detailed for me her concept of *It*, as she described her agoraphobia and performance anxiety, as she outlined her life strategies and how they worked, usually. I beheld her great brown eyes plunging inward, churning these several gears and paddles and wheels, profoundly introspective.

"I finally just accepted it," Viola finished. "My fear's not goin' anywhere. If I've learnt anything it's this: That to go forward I gotta go *with* my fear, not *against* it. I'm never gonna defeat it. I know that now. It's always gonna be there. But there is a kind of coexistence with it. And if I can handle that, if I'm strong enough to let that fear live in me *without immobilizin' me*, then I am workin' round it, see? Because then it's not keepin' me from livin'. I'm

288

afraid all the damn time still. It's just that now I go on doin' errything anyways. It's possible to be afraid and keep your dignity. In the last couple weeks I've come to understand this better. And, believe it or not, bein' here in TJ has shown me this too."

I let Viola sit quietly then, solid. I did not press her with questions. I thought instead about how my struggle will never cease either; that, just like her, regardless how long I fight to quash my guilt those demons will always maintain a foothold within my depths and occasionally bubble up to consume me. And now, writing this down so much later, I can add that regardless how hard Easy works to check authority, authority will always spring back to test its limits anew; and that regardless how thoroughly Rocky might buck conformity, conformity and its reassuring seductions will never fade away; and that regardless how vigorously Clare fights to be strong, she cannot keep up her strength without a constant diligence; and that regardless how justly and successfully Blossom might right a wrong, always there will be another wrong to right. So, just as Viola suggested to me that night, it cannot be the victory that matters in our struggles, really. In truth, such victories never come. What matters is the fight to not succumb. In *that* we find our dignity. Only there. In our resistance.

But I did not think the question through to these conclusions in those moments. Instead, we restarted and expanded a subject we had earlier explored concerning my preoccupation with literature and her preoccupation with fairy tales, and what these parallel forms of expression have meant to the evolution and preservation of cultures.

By then we felt hungry again so I initiated Viola into my favorite part of the *sobremesa*, or, the eating again. We swamped our tabletop with another smorgasbord of platters about 5:30 and lingered over them, conversing still, delving deeper into each other's aspirations, comparing our value systems. We finished about 7:00 and ordered ice cream for dessert and more coffee.

About 8:00, well after daybreak, we finally stood to leave. West of Tijuana's downtown, among some quiet residential lanes there, sits a picturesque plaza where I like to take a morning stroll on occasion. I suggested this to Viola, asked if it might interest her -- just to wake up our senses, to breathe some fresh air.

As we strode beneath the trees there, over the crisscrossing walks of that classic Mexican park, Viola said, "Stanley, that was one of the most original nights of my life, I think. A long night but I do not feel tired at all."

"Me either," I responded.

She asked, "You really don't have a place to live?"

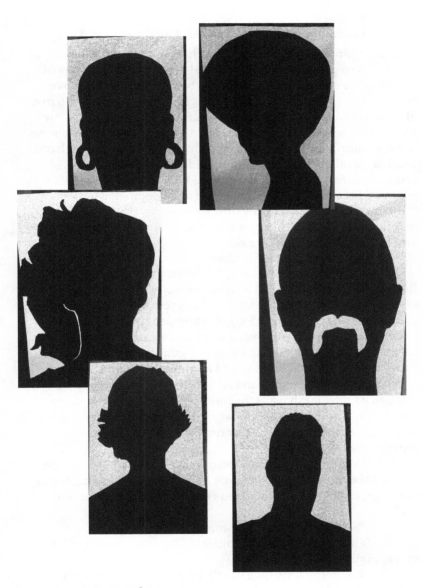

A New Chapter

That night in Tijuana each of us found and forged a new intimacy that cannot be undone. But the following morning an event of even greater moment occurred -- our intimacies merged. At last, as we stood in line to cross the border back into our own country, we, as six separate tributaries, flowed into a common river of understanding and direction and purpose. We each had vague ideas about what, personally, we might do next. But in the hour we passed waiting, and conversing, and sharing possibilities with one another, we all realized that our individual aims were complimentary, and that they could be blended, and that the potentials of each would be quickened and heightened by support from the others. In fact, by the time the six of us stood again on American soil the basic form of what we have since become known for had already begun to take shape.

Our crossing went like this:

Rocky and Blossom forded an open gate on the Mexican side, passed through a small abandoned but official-looking vestibule there, climbed the zigzag of an ascending ramp, and then found themselves striding a long elevated pedestrian bridge. This bridge shuttles foot traffic over a warren of Mexican customs control. At the end of it waits a turnstile guarded by US Border Patrol agents. There all of us would re-enter the United States. As Rocky and Blossom jangled and strode the long bridge they viewed through its steel mesh walls the profile of downtown Tijuana and the distinct international boundary where the concrete bed of the Tijuana river spills its seasonal waters over the untended vegetation of US territory.

"Well," said Rocky to Blossom as they strode. "I fancy that was just the most disturbed night's sleep I've ever enjoyed. Or was it just me, doll? Loud as firecrackers but it didn't bother me one bit."

The two of them were holding hands.

"First time we've slept together," Blossom murmured, her spurs jangling.

"Yes, my beauty. On a couch. In our clothes. And with an audience. LOL, I never even let down my hose."

Rocky looked on Blossom. Her face was as fierce and as tight as ever. But a golden softness had come to cushion her great brown eyes. He could see it. Rocky craved to smother her bald head with kisses, but she would never tolerate such gushing, so, he said:

292

"This unnerves me -- having to navigate this mouse maze to get home. Feels so vulnerable. Last year I caught the girl double-checking the gender on my passport and drilling her professionally trained identification gaze right through my brazier. I suppose they're about to do that stuff to this yellow dress. And it's so rumpled."

They had traversed half the length of the footbridge and Blossom saw Easy and Clare turning the corner at its terminus, still far ahead.

She said, "Look! I ... Are *they* holding hands?"

"Who is that? Clare and Easy?"

"What a match!"

"Not so odd. Not if you know their story. I sat next to her yesterday and she was just talkative talkative, in a girlfriends kind of whispery way, you know. It's been brewing. And can't you just see the toughness in her even from here? Stylin'. The dear's been bicycling everywhere, she told me. She feels strong, she said. Maybe even strong enough to handle that firebrand."

"Fucking fearless."

"That boy knows his stuff. Never seen any person in my life who so thoroughly proves that knowledge is power."

Blossom agreed.

Some minutes after this they turned that same final corner and began spiraling down off the elevated pedestrian bridge toward the guarded turnstile at ground level. As they descended, Clare and Easy, already in line at the bottom of the spiral, looked up and saw them. They all acknowledged each other. About the time Rocky and Blossom arrived at the rear of the line the border agent at the turnstile gestured and the looseness of the line tightened. People were pressing forward to pass. Clare and Easy flashed their passports for preliminary review. Less than a minute later Rocky and Blossom did the same. And then, as Rocky and Blossom sidled through the turnstile, they discovered Clare and Easy had held back for them, waiting to proceed with them to official passport inspection and customs.

Easy smiled beneath his mustache. "Which line?" he asked.

"Which line?" Rocky joshed in his sing-song way. "You mean you're not going to taunt and tempt these bluffing badges?"

Easy chuckled now, from the back of his throat. "General public, it says. I don't know what 'Sentri Lane' means so I guess that isn't us."

293

Clare said, "General public must be it."

The four of them shuffled up to the end of the general public line then -- together -- and heard:

"Hey, y'all."

They turned.

Viola was wheeling her box of zines behind her, and guiding along, by the hand, a smiling white man, or rather, me.

"Hey, Vee," they answered severally.

But Viola discerned that her friends were politely checking their curiosity about this beaming white man, and about how her fingers were so familiarly interlaced with his. As she trundled up to them, therefore, and stopped, she responded frankly to their quiet wondering.

"This here is Stanley Donner Jr.," she told them. "Now don't no one give me no shade about my holding this white boy's hand. Since this morning, y'all, me and ole Stanley here -- Well, we're a *thang*."

Easy and Clare laughed.

Then Rocky laughed.

Then, for the first and only time in this entire book, Blossom laughed.

We were on our way.

THE END

About the Author

John Dishwasher made his first zine in 2017. Since then he has tabled his zines at more than 20 Southern California zinefests. His "Zine from the Future Describing the End of Civilization" was a finalist for Best Political Zine of 2021 at *Broken Pencil Magazine*'s International Zine Awards. His plays, stories, poems, and essays have appeared in scores of independent literary journals and zines around the world, touching virtually all genres. He lives in the San Jacinto Valley with his wife Jody and their three rescued cats Tinsel, Possum, and Houdini.